WHERE LOVE GOES

WHERE LOVE GOES
JOYCE MAYNARD

Crown Publishers, Inc.
New York

Grateful acknowledgment is given to the following: "Passionate Kisses," Lucinda Williams. 1988 WARNER-TAMERLANE PUBLISHING CORP., NOMAD-NOMAN MUSIC, LUCY JONES MUSIC. All rights administered by WARNER-TAMERLANE PUBLISHING CORP. All Rights Reserved. Used By Permission. "If I Needed You," Townes Van Zandt. COLUMBINE MUSIC, INC.

Published by Crown Publishers, Inc., 201 East 50th Street, New York, New York 10022. Member of the Crown Publishing Group.

Random House, Inc. New York, Toronto, London, Sydney, Auckland

CROWN is a trademark of Crown Publishers, Inc.

Manufactured in U.S.A.

Design by Cynthia Dunne

Library of Congress Cataloging-in-Publication Data
Maynard, Joyce
Where love goes / by Joyce Maynard. — 1st ed.
p.   cm.
I. Title.
PS3563.A9638W48   1995
813'.54—dc20   95-7337
CIP
ISBN 0-517-70177-4

10 9 8 7 6 5 4 3 2 1

First Edition

For S., B. and C. With a white flag.

ACKNOWLEDGMENTS

A number of early readers contributed significantly to this novel—in particular, my dear friend Gerry Scott-Moore and the most insightful reader I've ever met, my sister Rona Maynard. I also want to thank my editors Karen Rinaldi and Ann Patty, as well as Penny Simon at Crown, and my agent and friend Gail Hochman, whose support and encouragement is unfailing. My thanks also to Albert Weeks and to Charlie Donohue, for advice on personal injury law, and to Dean Haskell, my baseball consultant.

My friend David Gray is centrally responsible for helping me to produce the soundtrack CD to this novel—a notion we came up with, driving home from a Mary Chapin Carpenter concert one night with the radio on full blast, thinking about how music has enriched our lives and our work. I owe a large debt to the artists, musicians and songwriters who contributed their work to the *Where Love Goes* CD, and to the record company and publishing executives and music producers who helped make this project possible. Two artists in particular deserve mention: Lucinda Williams, for granting me the use of her song "Passionate Kisses"—my main character's anthem—and Townes Van Zandt, for the use of his beautiful love song "If I Needed You," and for recording that song, with Jonell Mosser specially for the soundtrack to this novel.

My gratitude and love always to Alan Temkin and his open-hearted family, for giving me a safe harbor to work in, and to my children, Audrey, Charlie, and Willy Bethel, who gave me their blessing when I left home to write this book, and their love and support when I came back—and every day of my life.

Finally, I want to thank the men and women who have written to me over the years in response to my work, entrusting me with tales of their lives. Some of you I've met or talked with. Many I know only from your letters. You gave me so many of your stories. I give this one back.

Is it too much to ask
I want a comfortable bed
That won't hurt my back
Food to fill me up
And warm clothes
And all that stuff

Shouldn't I have this
Shouldn't I have all of this and
Passionate kisses, passionate kisses
Passionate kisses from you

Is it too much to demand
I want a full house
And a rock and roll band
Pens that won't run out of ink
And cool quiet
And time to think

Do I want too much
Am I going overboard
To want that much
I'll shout it out to the night
Give me what I deserve
Cause it's my right

Shouldn't I have this, shouldn't I have this
Shouldn't I have all of this and
Passionate kisses, passionate kisses
Passionate kisses from you

—LUCINDA WILLIAMS, "Passionate Kisses"

— SPRING

There's this game Claire plays now and then when she goes to the supermarket. Wheeling her cart through the aisles, lifting the one-percent milk down off the shelf in the dairy case, she entertains herself with the idea that one of these days a man might wheel his cart up alongside hers and kiss her so passionately she would toss her coupons into the middle of the frozen foods. "Come away with me," he says, snatching her up like the most wonderful delicacy in the gourmet section.

Her too-full cart could be discouraging to these men, so when she plays the game, Claire takes care to include among her family-size packages of English muffins and ground beef a few items that say other things about her besides that she's a mother. Things that are also true: That she is a lover of garlic and goat cheese for instance. That while she doesn't need expensive wine, she doesn't get the cheapest stuff either. That the color she favors is red.

She always checks their ring finger first. And she is always careful to keep her own ringless fingers plainly visible. If there's a man who really interests her at the seafood counter she may buy calamari. She always buys herself flowers and kiwi fruit, or a mango. Smoked trout. Jalapeños. Never Little Debbie cakes. Never Vaseline or toilet bowl cleaner. If an old Beatles or Dylan song comes on the Muzak, as they do so often these days, she sometimes finds herself singing a few bars under her breath. She might stand there picking through the strawber-

ries while he chooses a melon. She may hold a bunch of rosemary to her face and breathe deep. Nothing more than that.

Only three times in all the years since her divorce has Claire actually struck up a conversation with one of these bachelor shoppers. Of those three, one invited her to share the steak he was buying at his backyard hibachi later that evening. She could tell the minute he opened his mouth that it wasn't a good idea. One man asked her what you did with Jerusalem artichokes, then explained that his mother had asked him to pick some up. One of these men pointed to the mussels and said, "I hear they're an aphrodisiac."

Still, Claire plays the game. It's just one of the ways she gets through her days, allowing herself the hope that a man who would love her wildly might be just one more aisle away.

The funny thing is that today just such a person has come to this same supermarket with a shopping list of his own. His list does, in fact, include Little Debbie cakes, because he has an eight-year-old daughter who likes them in her school lunches. A daughter but no wife. And sometimes, as he picks out the groceries for another long week of caring for her alone, he plays the same game Claire does. Only in his game the person who comes along somewhere between Produce and Frozen Foods is a woman. A woman who looks, in his fantasies, like Claire.

He walks in the electric-eye doors at just the moment she is pushing her cart out to the parking lot, in fact. Maybe he sees her in passing, but her cart is full of bags, so even if he does, he'd probably assume she's married. They just miss each other.

Arms full of groceries, Claire kicks open the back door of her house to find her ex-husband, Sam, in his painter's pants and sleeveless T-shirt sitting at the kitchen counter sucking a Popsicle. Their daughter Sally has her leg up against the sink doing one of her ballet stretches. Travis, Sally's boyfriend, is braiding her hair. There's an unfamiliar-looking girl perched on the counter—also eating a Popsicle. The Beastie Boys are turned up loud. Somebody must have said something funny right before Claire came in; they are all laughing. Nobody makes a move to take one of the grocery bags, although when a container of yogurt falls out the bottom of the bag that has been giving way, Sally picks it up, opens it, and reaches for a spoon. "Thank God you finally got a little decent stuff to eat, Mom," she says. "I was starting to think we were living in Rwanda or someplace."

Claire drops the bags on the floor, unable to make it one more step to the pantry. She wishes she'd taken the time to put on her eyeliner before she left for the store this afternoon. Claire has been working at the children's museum even longer hours than usual this week, in the final stages of getting the Pioneer Room ready for next Saturday's opening. Her hair's a mess.

Even now—five years since she and Sam parted—she still likes to look her best when he sees her. He had predicted when she left that she'd eventually realize how lucky she had been to have him, and come back on her knees. "I mean, no offense, but you're not exactly Cindy Crawford," he told her.

"*I know that,*" she said. *Hadn't he commented once that her breasts had started to look like udders?*

"*That's what breast-feeding does to a person,*" she told him. *Breast-feeding and gravity.*

Why should it be that having children should cause such wreckage to a woman's body while a man can father those same children and still possess the body of a twenty-year-old? Still, it didn't seem like too much to ask that the man with whom you shared your bed might look up now and then when you pulled your dress over your head. Even if you had been married twelve years.

"*One of these days after you've finally left you're going to wake up and realize you had a good thing going,*" he used to tell her. "*Nice house. Great kids. A husband who doesn't drink or smoke or hang around in bars. . . .*"

"*I need to feel there's somebody on the face of this earth who just plain adores me,*" she told him.

"*You know your problem, babe?*" he said. "*You listen to too many songs on the radio. You still believe every single thing you heard the Beatles sing on the 'Ed Sullivan Show' when you were ten.*"

Now here he is, five years later, sitting in the kitchen of the house she bought when she moved out, come to collect their children for the weekend. The last time Claire came home from work to find him sitting in her kitchen this way, she asked him to please wait outside while the kids gathered up their stuff.

"Why do you have to be so unfriendly to Dad?" Sally said to her. "You think it feels good to him, standing out on the steps like that?"

"I never go inside our old house when I pick you up at your dad's," Claire wanted to say. *"You think it's pleasant for me, parked in the driveway, studying my old perennial beds where his girlfriend has planted all those dumb chrysanthemums?"* She doesn't say these things because, among other reasons, as far as Sally's concerned, Melanie's just the cool college girl who used to babysit for them and still comes by to say hi when she's home from college for vacations. From what they say, it appears that Pete and Sally believe their father hasn't had a girlfriend in five years.

Sally returns to the kitchen carrying her overnight bag and her Walkman. Sam crumples up his Popsicle wrapper and pitches it at the trash can.

"Good shot, man," says Travis.

"You play hoops?" Sam asks him. Travis says he used to be on the high-school team but he quit on account of his skateboarding.

"Maybe we could go one on one sometime," says Sam. "Of course, you'd probably whip my butt. I'm out of shape at the moment." He bounds out the door carrying Sally's bag.

"Can you believe my dad?" says Sally to her friend, who Claire suddenly realizes is a girl she's seen dozens of times. Valerie. Only the last time Claire laid eyes on Valerie she didn't have blue hair and a nose ring.

"You should see his stomach. It's like a washboard," Sally tells Valerie. Claire is a slim person herself, but her own stomach is mottled with stretch marks.

"Your dad's hot, all right," says Valerie. "Cuter than any of the guys in our class, that's for sure. Present company excluded, of course, Travis."

"Sam was telling me about this book he read that has these hallucinogenic mushrooms and this shaman-type guy called Don Juan," says Travis. "I can't believe you've got a dad that actually reads books about tripping on mushrooms. All mine ever does is check the stock reports."

"Not only that," says Sally. "You should see him on a skateboard."

Claire is still unpacking groceries through all this. Broccoli, pears, grapes. Spaghetti sauce, frozen pizza, Honey Nut Cheerios. Two gallons of milk. More Popsicles. Sally lives on those. Moving back and forth between the cupboards and the refrigerator and the pantry, she feels practically invisible, except for the one time when Valerie's leg is blocking the door to their cereal cupboard and she moves it.

"Eat some real food over at your dad's, okay?" Claire says to Sally. *"Protein."*

"Jeez, Mom," Sally says. "Can't you ever let up on being such a *mother* all the time?"

"Mine is the same way," Valerie says. "I ate a slice of turkey this morning and I thought she was going to have an orgasm, she was so happy."

Sam comes back into the kitchen and drapes his arm around his daughter. He evidently knows the words to this particular Beastie Boys song. He always plays the hippest radio stations when he goes out on framing jobs.

"Before you go, Sam," says Claire, "I need to talk with you a second."

"So," Sam says to Sally, ignoring Claire, "you got your stuff all packed? What do you say we hit the road?" He punches Travis on the upper arm and gives one of Valerie's dreadlocks a gentle tug. "Catch you later, huh guys?" he says.

Pete re-enters the kitchen. "You coming, Dad?" he says.

"Just a second, Pete," says Claire. One of the eggs she was putting in the egg tray of their refrigerator has just broken in her hand. She wipes a bit of yolk off on a towel. "I needed to remind your dad about the money for your cleats."

"Coming, Pete," says Sam.

"Wait," says Claire. "The cleats cost fifty-eight dollars. I need to know if you're going to come through with your half. Not like Sally's trip to Quebec City last month and the ski boots you told the kids you'd help pay for." Claire always manages to provide these things for her kids, but it's a stretch on her museum director's salary.

"This isn't the time or the place for that kind of talk, Claire," Sam tells her. "You know we both agreed we wouldn't have money discussions in front of the children."

"Believe me, I wish we didn't have to do this," says Claire. "But every time I call you up to talk about it, you're busy. When I send you bills, you don't respond."

"Really now, Claire," he says. His voice is a whisper almost, a hiss. "You should be ashamed of yourself, doing this to our children."

Claire breathes deep, the way she has learned in yoga class. "What am I supposed to do, then?" she says quietly. "What do I tell Pete about the shoes?"

Sam bends so he's eye-level with his son and puts a hand on each of his shoulders, the way a dad would in a TV show. A dad like Bill Cosby maybe, or Robert Young on "Father Knows Best." "You shouldn't have to worry about this money nonsense, son," Sam tells Pete. "I'm sorry you had to hear this crap. Of course you can have the cleats."

"You always tell them that," says Claire. She still has an egg in her hand. She wants to throw it at him. "But you never end up paying."

"You and I both know I give you money every month, Claire," he says. He speaks slowly, with exaggerated enunciation, as if he were talking to a very young child, or a person who is slightly retarded. And what is Claire supposed to do, stand there on their back porch explaining to their children that Sam's two hundred and thirty dollars a month hardly covers Popsicles and cereal these days, much less cleats? Ask him how much that motorcycle helmet cost that he bought last month, or the new mountain bike that Pete was bragging about the other day?

"My dad's bike has twenty-one speeds," Pete told Jared. "But he can ride up Mount Lowell and he doesn't even have to use the highest gear."

"Do you think I'm magic?" says Claire. "And whatever our children need that you can't see your way to providing, you figure I'll always come up with it, anyway?"

"What I think is, you need to get a grip, Claire," says Sam. "I hope you're still talking with that therapist."

"Give me a break," Claire says. "Maybe I wouldn't get this way if you didn't leave it to me to take care of everything. Sally's friends might think I was pretty cool too, if I could just breeze in off the basketball court and sit around with them listening to tapes." She got up at five-thirty this morning to go over to the museum and whitewash the walls of the one-room schoolhouse so she could be back home in time to wake the kids and get them off to school.

"Why do you have to bring my friends into this, Mother?" Sally says. "Why do you always have to make a scene? Just once can't you lighten up?"

"Come on, kids," says Sam. "Let's get into the car. Your mother's just a little hysterical right now, but she'll calm down. What do you say we pick up some Chinese food?"

They hurry into his pickup, with its Grateful Dead sticker on the back window—a row of rainbow-colored dancing bears. As he opens the door on his side, Sam looks back at Claire one last time as she stands on the sidewalk. He shakes his head with a look of pity. He gets into the driver's seat and turns the key.

"Hold on a second, Pete," Claire says, through the open truck window. "I wanted to remind you about your President report. It's due Monday, right?"

"Just the oral part," he says. He starts to tell her something else, about the diorama of Teddy Roosevelt hunting in South America, but the truck is pulling away while he's still talking. Pete calls out something to Claire. She can't hear what.

"Love you," Claire calls out. Not that they'll hear her. As the truck disappears down the street, she can see her son stick his baseball cap on his father's head. She sees her daughter's long, slim leg outstretched on the dashboard, and Travis, hoisting his skateboard under his arm and loping down the sidewalk with Valerie. Her blue dreadlocks blow in the wind.

Claire goes inside.

Sam told Claire the night they met that he couldn't wait to have kids. He asked her to marry him within a couple of days. She said yes. Years later, when it had long since become plain to her how little real enthusiasm or interest he felt for her, she would sometimes ask him, "Why did you marry me, anyway?"

You had to hand it to Sam; he was never one to dish out the kind of easy compliments that might have bought her off. "You wanted to have a kid," he told her. Not many young women just graduating from art school did, back in the late seventies. And though Claire would have wanted to have children eventually, regardless, it's also plain to her what fueled the particular urgency to have one back in 1976. That was the year her father's liver finally gave out from years of living on straight vodka and not a whole lot else. Her brother joined a religious cult in Washington State and hasn't been heard from since. Her mother sold their old house outside Portland, had their black lab put to sleep, and went off to San Miguel de Allende to study painting. More than anything, what Claire wanted was to be part of a happy, normal-seeming family. So did Sam evidently.

They met in Michigan, but that spring they made a road trip to see the old house in Vermont Sam's grandfather had left him, and they ended up staying. Three months later Claire got pregnant and they were married by a justice of the peace.

She gained fifty pounds with Sally but she didn't care. She thrilled to the sight of her huge belly. She read every book on pregnancy and childbirth and checked her reflection in every store window she passed. She gloried in her swollen breasts. Nothing in her whole life had ever felt as real to her as the feeling of her baby's kick from deep in her own body.

She loved childbirth. Finally her body was overtaken by sensations so intense and enormous, as the sex in her marriage never was, they obliterated all other feeling. To her, giving birth was like surfing this enormous and terrifying wave. It could have knocked her down and pulled her under, but she rode it right in to shore.

From the moment Sally's head emerged—ripping the skin

around her perineum as it did, landing in Sam's outstretched hands on their bed—Claire knew she was free of her parents' family. Now Sally was her family—and Sam, of course. And eventually Pete, when he came along three years later.

Claire loved nursing her babies. She loved how full her breasts became and how ripe and bountiful it made her feel having milk in them, and how sweet the milk was. She loved her amazing, cartoonlike profile, in the size-forty brassiere she briefly wore, and the way she practically burst out of her bathing suit the summer after Sally's birth. She had never felt so womanly. Nothing she had ever done in her life had been so real.

Sometimes simply hearing her baby cry would be enough to make milk squirt from her nipple. Sometimes, as she settled in to feed one of her babies and pulled down her bra to expose a breast, her baby would forage against her skin looking for the nipple, and her milk would begin to shoot out on his head or his cheek, and he would get this look on his face that Claire believed could only be amusement, followed by this other look: total contentment. Taking him off her nipple to put him on the other side, she would see him become, very briefly, frantic. The suction his lips would make, small as they were, was so great she'd have to slide her little finger underneath his mouth just to detach him, and for the split second that separated the moment she took him off one breast and the moment she put him on the other one, he would sputter and pant, flailing his arms, moving his little fish's mouth, searching.

She had friends nursing babies at the same time she was who kept their infants on schedules. Every four hours and never in between. "Their stomachs adjust," one woman told her. "You wouldn't believe how quickly they learn."

Who needs to learn such a lesson? she wanted to ask. Your child will learn soon enough about doing without. What she wanted her babies to learn was what it felt like to have everything, absolutely everything, a child could need or want. Hers did.

Sally nursed for thirteen months and then weaned herself. Pete lived on her breast for a year and kept nursing another year after that, until Sam said it seemed to him that once a child was undoing the buttons of his mother's shirt, it was probably time for her to stop breast-feeding. Regretfully she agreed he was probably right.

For Sam, after that, Claire's breasts might as well have been radioactive for all he touched them. Breast-feeding had wrecked them, but it went beyond that. He practically recoiled when his hand touched her body now. It was as if once she became a mother there was something forbidden about wanting her.

Sam had been a runner when she met him, and in the later years he trained for marathons. He was out of bed before dawn, earlier even than a person has to get up for a baby, and he was in bed again by eight-thirty or nine most nights. Where Claire's body softened gradually over the years of their marriage, Sam's became like chiseled stone. He slept flat on his back—no pillow, far away from Claire. When they had sex it was rough, athletic and cursory. Feeling the hardness of him, she felt shame at her own soft over-ripeness. She knows he must have kissed her sometimes, but she has no memory of his lips, only the part where he thrust himself into her, and afterward, when he would roll over to his side of the bed and fall asleep.

She seldom asks herself anymore, as she used to, did he ever love her? All those years of his unremitting coolness have turned her own feelings for him into a frozen lake, with only the smallest patch of water left at one end that she wouldn't safely skate on. At one time long ago she remembers loving him.

Mostly she remembers other things. At first she had been happy to give up her artwork to care for the children while Sam worked as a carpenter, but when the building boom slowed and they needed a second income, there were endless battles between them over money and child care. Especially after she got her job at the ad agency and it became clear that Claire was going to be the major breadwinner, she would tell him she needed more help from him with the children and the house. She was tired all the time. "Maybe I'd help you more if you didn't nag so much," he said. One time he picked up their video camera and pointed it at her face while she was weeping. "If you could see yourself," he said. He shook his head and went to the TV room to sleep on the couch. When she followed him and tried to talk some more, he turned on the set.

After she got her job she started getting up earlier and earlier to draw, and by the time the children woke there would be the cheerful sound of laundry tumbling in the dryer and the smell of blueberry muffins about to come out of the oven, fresh-squeezed juice, flowers on the table, a "Sesame Street" record playing, a second pot of coffee on the stove. Then she'd pour the cereal into the bowls. Take off the nighttime diaper, powder the bottom, pull the T-shirt over the head. In the car on the way to day care and preschool they'd sing all the verses to *The Fox Went Out on a Chilly Night* and play Grandmother's Trunk. Pete liked her to recite the words to *Goodnight Moon* in the car. Sometimes they stopped at Woolworth's on the way and had a cup of hot chocolate with whipped cream or a bowl of oatmeal with brown sugar and raisins, even though they'd had breakfast at home already.

They seem so distant now: all those years when her children were little and she was always scrambling to get to work, get to day care, get home, with never enough time—as she used to complain to Sam—to go to the bathroom. Whatever she did, it never felt like enough. It's as if I'm pouring water in a sieve, she used to think. No matter how much I pour, it never stays filled.

Above all, what Claire wanted was to spare her children pain and disappointment—even small pain and minor disappointment. Especially those, in fact. The large pain—her bitter arguments with Sam and her tears in the night—felt out of her control.

She always baked the children's birthday cakes from scratch, with elaborate frosting designs in whatever theme occupied their fantasies that year: maybe He-Man, maybe Ninja Turtles, maybe trolls, or—Sally's passion briefly—duckbill platypuses. For Christmas she always baked a gingerbread house and let Pete and Sally stick on the Halloween candy they'd collected a couple of months before that she didn't like them to eat. She sewed clothes for Sally's Barbie and flannel pajamas for Pete's bear just like the ones she made Pete. One time Claire crocheted a hat for Sally that fitted over her head like a helmet, in black and yellow striped yarn, with stiff black antennae that stuck straight up. It was Sally's favorite, but one day when Sally was mad she threw it out the car window and then didn't tell Claire until they'd driven a few miles down the road. Claire drove back and forth over the same stretch of highway for half an hour until they found it.

Even now, from a distance of all those years, Claire can remember in the pit of her stomach the feeling she had then, of grief and loss and dread over the lost hat, the same way she felt when they visited the National Zoo in Washington and Pete dropped his special blue ribbon that he liked to wrap around his index finger and twirl inside his ear while he sucked his thumb. Sam told her she was crazy, they could get another, but Claire ran through six different pavilions at the zoo, trying to find that ribbon before closing time. When she finally spotted it in the monkey house and came panting back to the bench where Sam was waiting with Pete and Sally, Pete had simply reached out his hand for it. He wasn't surprised his mother had found the ribbon. She always did.

One year there was a blizzard on the day of Sally's birthday party. All the mothers called to say their children couldn't make it, and Claire went to pick them all up in the four-wheel drive. There was that time Pete got a coffee bean stuck up his nostril. The time Sally lost the shoe to her Crystal Barbie and Claire tore apart the whole house before finding it lodged in a heating grate. She remembers waiting with the kids for Sam to cross the finish line of the Boston Marathon, and Pete breaking out of her arms when he saw his dad, and the feeling Claire had at that moment, that whatever was missing between her husband and herself didn't matter so long as her son had a father who would be there with open arms when he came running.

Claire can still see the photograph on their annual photo Christmas card: the four of them posed under the tree and smiling a little tensely, Sam with his arm resting on the shoulder of the holly shirt he'd given Claire one Christmas that she wore every year, but only for this picture. He always set their camera on the tripod with the shutter on the self-timer before leaping over the coffee table to get into the picture on time. Pete would be clutching that blue ribbon he never wanted to relinquish long enough for Claire to wash it. Sally would have this smile on her face, as if someone was awarding prizes for the most exposed teeth. If they weren't really such a happy family, they looked like one anyway.

She remembers a morning—early spring, the brook still high from melted snow—when she snapped at Sam as he was getting ready to take off for some 5K race up a mountain. "Don't I ever get a Saturday morning off?" she asked him. She had been putting in extra hours every night that week on a presentation for a radio station and making favors for Pete's birthday party: pirate hats. For this particular party she had also made treasure maps and individual treasure chests filled with chocolate coins that she had hidden around the house.

Sam looked her up and down, not unpleasantly. "You know, Claire," he said. "You wouldn't know what to do with a morning to yourself if you had one."

She opened her mouth to answer but stopped. What he said was true. She'd been listening so intently to the sounds of small voices calling out their needs for so long by then, she no longer heard her own.

It had been catching up with her, though. More and more, in those last few years, Claire would watch herself lose control of her temper as if she were observing some other woman in a movie, not her self. Mostly she was keeping up her Perfect Mom routine, but there was an infrequent visitor at their house now, a woman who looked like Claire but acted like nobody she'd ever known, except maybe her father, only when he acted that way he was drunk, and Claire was stone sober. Just tired.

"Nobody takes me seriously," she would cry, coming into the kitchen to find Sam reading the sports page while Pete sat fingerpainting with instant chocolate pudding and Sally drew unicorns on the back of her advertising presentation for a new condominium complex. "All I am around here is a servant." Then she would get down on her knees and begin to scrub the floor, still weeping.

"I'm jumping out of this car," she said to Sam one time as they were driving home from a party. He had just finished telling her that she had monopolized the conversation at dinner. She actually opened the car door that time, and he grabbed her arm to pull her back in. She hit her chin on the edge of the door. She still has the scar.

Christmas morning, the year Pete turned two: They had just opened their presents. This was the year Sam had given Claire an electric knife sharpener and the holly berry shirt. Wrapping paper and pamphlets printed with the directions for putting toys together were scattered everywhere. Claire was trying to get the turkey in the oven and construct the Bûche de Noël with butter-cream frosting and meringue mushrooms. Sam and his brother had turned on the set to watch the

football game. "Later, babe," he told her when she said she needed
help.

"That's it. Christmas is over!" she yelled. She stood over the garbage
disposal, smashing their Yule log down the hole. Like a drunk. Now
she was stuffing the holly berry shirt into a trash bag while the children
clutched her legs and begged her to stop.

"What is this, PMS again?" Sam said.

Claire read a novel once whose author had dedicated her book to
her husband. "Essential as air," the woman had written about
him. Claire has forgotten the name of the novel; it was that dedica-
tion that stayed with her. She was thirty-five when she realized
she'd rather be alone with at least the possibility that someday she
might feel that way about some man who might feel that way
about her, than stay one more winter in that chilly bed. So she
moved out.

Ursula was four and a half when
her mother left. Her name is Joan, and she liked Ursula to call her
that, although sometimes Ursula forgot and called her Mommy.

She remembers the day because Halloween was coming and she
was trying on her fairy costume when they came in her room and
said they had something to tell her. She knew what it was going
to be. She had been casting spells that whole day while they yelled
at each other. Her magic wasn't working.

"Come sit on my lap, Urs," her dad said. His name is Tim, but
Ursula calls him Dad. "Come sit on my lap." Her mother was
standing in the doorway wearing that velvet dress she had that
had to be dry-cleaned, so you couldn't touch it. She was very
beautiful.

"I'm busy," she said. "I'm making potions." She knew how bad
things must be since her mother wasn't saying anything about the
smell in her room. Ursula had taken a bottle of her perfume and
poured the whole thing into an old aspirin bottle and mixed it
with some baking soda and toothpaste.

Her dad picked her up. She wasn't fat then. Her fairy costume was pink, see-through, with layers of lace billowing like wings. She and her dad got it at the Salvation Army.

"You know Mommy and I aren't getting along with each other, don't you Ursi?" he said. "I know you hear us yelling a lot, and I bet it worries you, doesn't it?"

"No," she said. "It's fine." She was polishing her glasses on his shirt.

"Well, it worries us," he said. "It isn't good for kids to grow up with their parents yelling all the time."

Ursula knew she had to do something. She wished she was bigger so she would have a good idea. She was trying so hard to think she thought her head might pop. "A–B–C–D–E–F–G," she sang.

"Urs," he said. "Listen to me." He put his hands on her cheeks and turned her face around. She closed her eyes.

"Ursi. Ursi."

Why wasn't her mother doing anything? All she ever did was stand there rubbing her hands on her forehead. She had the thinnest fingers. Ursula's are like her dad's: chubby sausages.

"But we both love you so much," he was saying.

"Q–R–S–T–U–V–W," she sang. "N–J–R–T–C–X–W." She thought maybe if she pulled on his earlobes that would make him laugh. If she put her hands over his mouth he would stop talking. His cheeks were wet.

"Sunny day!" she yelled. "Chasing the clouds away." She didn't even like "Sesame Street."

"Ursula!" her mother yelled. "Stop it! Stop it! Stop it. Just shut up for once, okay?"

"What are you doing, Joan?" he said to her. "Can't you let up on her, even now?"

"It's always my fault, isn't it, Tim?" her mother shouted. "You always side with her. You have no idea in the world what it's like to be me!"

"Please, Joan," he said.

"Always Mr. Reasonable. Always Mr. Parent. Always Mr. Fuckhead," she screamed.

Ursula knew it was impossible then. There was nothing she was going to be able to do. "Okay," she said. "I get it." She climbed down off his lap and picked up Jenny's chew bone. "Here, Jenny," she called to her. "Here girl."

"That was just great," her father was saying to her mother. "You must feel really proud of yourself."

"She's fine," her mother said, quiet again. "She'll be better."

"Listen," he said. "You can do what you want to do. Just don't kid yourself."

Ursula's mother moved away the next day. She went to New Zealand with a man named Elliot. She sent Ursula a postcard. "You wouldn't believe how beautiful it is here," she said. "I'm thinking a lot about art." Ursula couldn't read back then, of course. Her dad read it to her. There was another part in there about how much she missed Ursula. Her dad was probably making that part up. Or her mother was.

Ursula decided to be a ghost that Halloween. She and her dad trick-or-treated at every house on their street, all the way past the gas station to the bridge. She never saw so much candy.

Her mother would have told her she could only have one piece a day. Her dad just dumped it in a big bowl in her room where she could have some any time she wanted.

It's been just the two of them living here in Blue Hills for a long time now—Ursula and her dad. They're doing fine too.

School days she wakes him up and he makes her eggs. She puts out the silverware and pours him his juice. Sometimes she pretends she's a waitress and he's the customer. "What can I get for you, sir?" she asks him in this voice she has that sounds like a grown-up.

"Cup of coffee would be just dandy, little missy," he says. He has made it, but he lets her pour his cup now, and she has never spilled, not even once. He takes milk and sugar.

"Your paper, sir," she says.

"Much obliged, ma'am," he says. He talks in a cowboy accent.

"Why don't you just set down a spell and join me? Give them dogs a rest."

Then the two of them have their eggs, and maybe a bowl of cereal and a doughnut or a muffin. Saturdays he makes French toast. Sundays, waffles. They watch cartoons together. She may color. He reads the sports page.

On school days he walks her to the bus before heading out for his job, teaching biology at the community college. Ever since her dad heard about the big kid that used to tease her at the bus stop, he waits until Mrs. Kolivas pulls up. "You're my little treasure," he whispers in her ear as he hands her her lunchbox. They bought it before she found out that all the popular kids just carry paper bags. She still carries the lunchbox so she won't hurt his feelings.

Jake—the big kid—never messes with Ursula anymore. Not since her dad went up to him and told him, "I understand you've been making some comments to my daughter. Mind repeating them to me?"

All the kids at the bus stop looked at them then. Jake is a very big kid—fifth grade—but Ursula's dad is much bigger. He used to be on the wrestling team. Also football. He could squish Jake with his little finger.

"It was nothing," Jake told him finally, after a minute or so passed and Ursula's dad was still holding on to the back of his jacket. "I didn't mean nothing."

"You think calling a six-year-old kid Miss Piggy is nothing, huh?" he said. "You planning on holding on to your nuts a few more years?"

Ursula knows some kids would be embarrassed if their dad did something like this. But she was just proud. Nobody in the whole world has a dad like hers.

"What was that?" he said. "I didn't hear an answer."

"Yes," said Jake. "Yes I do."

"You plan on giving my daughter any more trouble, son?" her dad asked him. He was still holding on to Jake's jacket. None of the other kids at the bus stop was saying anything, not even Wayne, the patrol. Ursula knew patrols were supposed to report it if grown-ups gave anybody trouble at the bus stop. She also knew

Wayne never would on account of he also planned on holding on
to his nuts.

"No way," he said.

"That's what I thought," said her dad. "Just checking."

After school the bus lets her off
at the bottom of the hill and she walks the rest of the way to their
apartment by herself. Her father doesn't get home from his job at
the college until four-thirty, but they have a plan for that. She
keeps their key on a little chain around her neck and lets herself
in. Jenny is always lying right there on her special blanket in the
front hall waiting for her. Jenny is almost like a sister.

They go up the stairs together. If something bad happened at
school she tells Jenny, and Jenny licks her face. "They're just dumb
kids anyways," she says. "Who needs some dumb Brownie troop?"

Her dad always leaves an after-school treat out for her, and one
of their NFL collectibles glasses all set out for her milk. Before she
could read he'd leave her a note all in pictures, but now he prints
words for her and he doesn't even have to make the letters very
big anymore. Sometimes the note tells her to preheat the oven to
350 or put the laundry in the dryer. She knows how to do many
things now. Why would he need a girlfriend when he has her?

Then she watches "Live and Let Live." She wishes somebody
would tell Pamela her husband is having an affair. That woman is
such an idiot. She likes Andrea the best. Andrea would be a nice
mom, she bets. She wonders if Andrea has any kids in real life. Of
course, if she does, they are probably home alone right now eating
a bowl of Cheerios just like her, watching their mom on TV. TV
moms are the only kind that act so nice all the time.

After "Live and Let Live" comes "Wheel of Fortune." Vanna
White, that turns the wheel, is going to have a baby, but Ursula
doesn't think she will be a very great mom. Too skinny. She's the
kind that would buy skim milk and give her kids celery sticks for
an after-school snack. Plus she'd always be worried about messing
up her outfits.

So far on "Wheel of Fortune" Ursula has won fifteen trips for two to Disney World and one trip to Bermuda and a complete kitchen of General Electric appliances and a bedroom set from Broyhill and a ton of other stuff she doesn't even remember. She wishes she could've won the first-class trip for two to the Super Bowl for her dad and her. He would have loved that. Some woman got it that didn't even look like she knew who Troy Aikman was.

Her dad usually doesn't get home till a little after "Wheel of Fortune" ends, but she still turns the TV off as soon as the show's over. Any more television than that and her dad says she could turn into a potato. One time for a joke she left the TV on and set a big old sprouted potato right on the spot in their TV chair where she always sits for him to find when he got home from work. Then she hid behind the couch until he came home.

"Oh my God!" he said when he came in and found it there. "It's finally happened. Just what I was afraid of. I can't say I didn't warn her."

She was giggling so hard by this point she thought she might wet her pants.

"Little girl," he said, "can you help me? I think my daughter has turned into a vegetable."

"It's me, Daddy," she said. "I'm here."

"I'm not your daddy," he said. "I'm Ursula's daddy. And now she's lost to me. I guess from now on I'll have to call her Spud." He was sitting on the couch with his head in his hands and the potato in his lap, making crying noises.

"Daddy!" she yelled into his ear. "It's okay! I'm Ursula!"

"Don't tease me," he said. "Can't you see I'm a broken man? I've just lost the light of my life."

"It's okay," she said, patting his shoulders. "I'm back. I never left."

He looked up then. "You're here?" he said. "Is it really you? No; I must be dreaming."

"It's me! It's really me!" she cried. She jumped into his lap. He threw his arms around her.

"Whew!" he said. "Boy, was that a close one."

"I would never leave you, Daddy," she said. "You know that."

"What would I do without you?" he told her.

Years before Joan and Tim started living together back in graduate school she had gone through a severe case of endometriosis which was supposed to have left her sterile.

Tim was working on his dissertation at the time—a paper about the propagation of mushroom species. Joan was a performance artist, at work on a piece about the subjugation of women in Third World cultures. "Womb-an Weep" never had much of an effect on Tim, but the climactic scene—of an African tribal clitorectomy ritual—attracted the attention of an alternative theater in Knoxville, Tennessee. They invited her to come and do a residency there. Her bags were packed when she and Tim found out she was pregnant.

It was Tim who persuaded her to have the baby. Her gynecologist agreed it was amazing that she'd gotten pregnant at all, and said it was highly unlikely that she'd ever conceive again, especially after an abortion. So Tim made her the deal: If she'd have the baby, he'd take care of it. He'd come up with the money, too. All she had to do was carry it nine months. For some reason that still surprises him she agreed.

Ursula was breech. In the end they performed an emergency cesarean, with Joan heavily sedated. She hemorrhaged so badly she didn't see Ursula for a whole day. Tim has always wondered if that was the beginning of Joan's problems as a mother. She had insisted on giving the baby her own surname, but in every other way Ursula was Tim's from the beginning.

Joan hated nursing, said it made her feel like a cow. Tim held Ursula against his bare chest while he bottle-fed her and carried her in a Snugli while he worked on his dissertation. When she cried at night, he was the one who got up.

It probably didn't help Joan's feeling about motherhood any that Ursula was, from the first, a dead ringer for her father. Where Joan was fine-boned and white-skinned, with black hair and a birdlike body, Ursula was large, pink, and solid, with big hands and thighs like a Sumo wrestler. When she was three and a half and a girl she admired in preschool started taking ballet classes, she said she wanted to take ballet, too.

"That's ridiculous," Joan had said. "She'll just make a fool of herself if she puts on a leotard and tights."

At the time, Joan was having an affair with a poet she'd met at a workshop that winter, but he was married and a lot older. She didn't go to any great lengths to conceal what she was doing from Tim. He hoped it would blow over and they could work things out for Ursula's sake, but after Frederick came Elliot, who asked her to come with him to New Zealand. Joan left when Ursula was four. Tim and Ursula have seen her twice since then. "My mommy doesn't want me does she?" Ursula asks him.

Tim is never sure how to answer this question. Sometimes he thinks it's better for her to get used to the idea and let go of false hope. Other times all he knows is that her sadness is unbearable to him and he has to protect her from the truth at all costs.

"Of course she does," he tells her. "Mommy misses you so badly she can hardly stand it. She just can't take care of you right now. But I can."

"When I'm ten I'm going to go live with Mommy," she tells him.

"If that's what you want, then you will," he said.

"If I could, I'd go live with Mommy now. You just don't let me," she told him. "You're mean."

"If you think so," he says.

For the first year after Joan left it was all Tim could handle, just getting Ursula off to preschool in the mornings and getting out of work early enough to pick her up, maybe buy a few groceries, and get home in time to make the macaroni and cheese. After dinner they might do karate or cut out paper dolls before her bath. "I'm going to wrap myself up in paper, tie myself with string, stick some stamps on top of my head and mail myself to you," they would sing while he scrubbed her. Running the washcloth over her tender pink skin—her tinkler, Ursula called it—Tim could hardly remember how long it had been since he'd touched the body of a woman. He felt like a eunuch.

Then one day when he was grading papers in his office at the college, this very beautiful graduate student had come in and shut the door behind her. Almost spilling out of her halter top, she had bent over his desk, with its framed Sears portrait of Ursula and the drawing she'd made him for Father's Day. "Listen, Professor Shepherd," she said. "I want to fuck you." How could he say no?

Galen was twenty-four years old. She wasn't anyone he'd bring home and introduce to Ursula, but after five years of politically correct and highly infrequent lovemaking with Joan, with her hard little breasts and the clenched, angry, joyless way she'd lie there, with her vibrator and her tube of K-Y jelly, and another year and a half of spending his evenings playing Candyland and reading *Angelina Ballerina,* Tim saw Galen as an angel of mercy.

She had large, wonderful breasts and a round, wide ass she liked to get down on her knees and show him. "I'm your puppy," she would say, and then she'd nuzzle against his cock and lick him. She even wore a collar one time. Or she might come to his door dressed as a nurse, late into the night when he was grading papers. She had amazing things in her doctor bag: Chinese balls she rolled over his body, feathers, massage oil. She was playful and shameless, with her Girl Scout leader's uniform and her press-on tattoos and her tasseled pasties and G-string. One night she filled her mouth with ice cubes, to chill her tongue she said, then spit them out and took in his cock. One night she brought real police-issue handcuffs and asked him to clamp her to his bed. Tim had to work hard that time to get Joan's voice out of his head, lecturing about the subjugation of women. "It's okay," Galen whispered. "We're just playing. Nobody's getting hurt. I want it, remember?"

All that semester and part of the next they fucked like that, usually between one and four A.M. She only stayed overnight that one time, when Tim got his neighbor Paula to invite Ursula for a sleepover with her daughter, who didn't really get along with Ursula very well. There was never any question of Tim and Galen spending family time with Ursula. He had no doubt she could think up great things to do in a bowling alley, but bumper bowl with a five-year-old was probably not it.

Tim never felt he was using Galen. There wasn't any question of love between them. He knew she was getting as much pleasure out of him as he got out of her. But there came a point when keeping up with his disconnected life began to wear Tim down. Rising from his bed after nights of burn-it-up fucking with Galen after maybe two hours of sleep, he'd stand there at the stove cooking Ursula's eggs with his cock sore and his butt aching, and instead of feeling replenished, he felt spent. When he was with his daughter, the nights didn't seem real. When he was with Galen, it was as if Ursula didn't exist. Licking a piece of jam off his hand as he was buttering her toast, he suddenly got a wave of Galen's scent from his fingers and felt like a thief.

Ursula was usually a heavy sleeper, but there was this one night. Galen was tied, spread-eagled, against the washer/dryer in the laundry room, and he was fucking her from behind with the dryer set to tumble, hot, so it vibrated her breasts in a way she loved. "I promise I'll do a better job on your shirts next time, Mr. Woody," she was pleading. "I'll never leave that ring around the collar again." All of a sudden there was Ursula standing there, holding her blanket, looking at them.

"I wanted juice," she said, in that husky, nighttime voice of hers. "I kept calling. You didn't hear me."

Tim covered Galen with a couple of towels that were folded on top of the dryer and wrapped another one around his own waist. He was untying Galen's wrists while he talked to Ursula.

"This is a friend of mine," he told her. "We were doing laundry."

Ursula drifted into the kitchen. In the glow of the refrigerator he reached for a Dallas Cowboys cup and poured her Hi-C. Neither one of them said anything more about Galen. When he tucked her back into bed, he said, "Sometimes kids see stuff that might seem scary. That just means things happen sometimes that you're too young to understand."

"I understand, Daddy," she said. She patted his head. "It's okay. You do a good job."

Galen left quickly. Tim called her the next morning to say he couldn't see her anymore. "I have to just be a dad right now," he said.

"It's been fun," she said. She said she'd like it if they could still be friends though, which surprised him, considering that they'd hardly ever done anything besides screw.

It turned out that Galen loved nineteenth-century English novels, Jane Austen in particular, and that she had a fascination with moss, which was the subject of her master's thesis. (She liked to fuck on it, that much he knew. But she also knew a good deal about moss propagation and little-known species, it turned out.) He ended up advising her on the thesis, and sometimes, late at night, she'd call him and tell him about how things were going with her current boyfriend. The guy liked to spank her with a leather strap, and she wasn't always sure, this time, if he had a good attitude. She told him to stop one time and he just kept hitting her harder. Tim knew the strap she was talking about, of course. The thought of somebody doing that to Galen sickened him. He was ashamed that he'd ever spanked her himself.

The memory of their nights together is not much different than a movie he watched a long time ago. Since Galen he has lived like a monk. Or like Mr. Rogers, he used to tell her, although he knew, if he and Galen were still seeing each other, she would probably want to have him put on a cardigan sweater and let her suck his cock while he sang "It's a Beautiful Day in the Neighborhood."

Blue Hills isn't much of a town for nightlife, especially if you aren't part of a married couple, because most people in this town are. Weekends when her children go with their father Claire rents movies from the thirties and forties—romantic comedies mostly—and watches them in bed with her long underwear on and a big bowl of popcorn. She puts on the country albums her kids hate—Patsy Cline, Vern Gosdin, Randy Travis, Patty Loveless, Emmylou Harris, Vince Gill. One time she played George Jones singing "He Stopped Loving Her Today" twelve times in a row. There's a love story for you: a song about a man whose heart stays true to the woman he adores, decades after she's left him. The day he stops loving her is the day the undertaker hauls his body away.

Sometimes Claire barely hears another human voice from Friday evening until Sunday dinnertime, when she picks the children up. She may take a walk or go to the gym with her friend Nancy, who is also divorced, but without kids, and sometimes she'll tackle a big job like putting up or taking down the storm windows or preparing her taxes. She may put in some time over at the children's museum preparing grant proposals or sending out letters to potential donors. She is usually in bed by nine on weekends.

Tonight, though, Claire is going out on a blind date. She hasn't done this in almost a year. It scares her to realize how excited she is at the prospect. And for so little reason.

A woman she knows from the gym set this up. The woman mentioned that she had a friend who had recently broken up with the woman he'd been seeing. Forty-three years old, two kids, working in something to do with real estate. Bob's been divorced eight years, she told Claire. This is a good sign, Claire knows. The ones freshly out of the stable are still obsessed with their wives. "He's got that cute, teddy bear look, sort of your basic Tony Danza type," Pauline told her. Claire figured she was supposed to know who Tony Danza was, so she didn't ask.

It's not a lot to go on, but the simple fact of knowing that her doorbell will ring tonight, and there will be a man on the other side ready to take her somewhere, anywhere but her own kitchen, somebody to do the driving for once, is enough for Claire at the moment. When she gets home from the supermarket she will take a long bath and give herself a facial. She'll put on her good underwear and shave her legs. She will pour herself a glass of wine and put on an album of Stan Getz and Joao Gilberto, timed so it will still be playing when he arrives.

Claire knows that the moment she's enjoying now as she blow-dries her hair and pulls up her stockings may well be the most exciting point in the evening. Now, before she meets him, anything is possible. She can hold on to the hope that she is about to meet a man who will sweep her off her feet. She can still consider the possibility that this may be the very last blind date she will ever have to go on, and that tonight might in fact be the very last Friday night she carries out the trash for the early Saturday-morning pickup alone. She has entertained this possibility twenty times over the course of the last five years' worth of blind dates: a dozen or so, in those first few wildly hopeful, energetic months after leaving her marriage, before she met Mickey. None at all for a solid year after Mickey left, followed by a second flurry, during a period in which she figured that since she'd never find anyone like Mickey again, there was no longer any need to seek out the love of her life. Forget about getting swept off your feet, she told herself. Go for the nice guy who'll take out the trash.

Claire opens the door to find that the man on the other side is a couple of inches shorter than she is. He also wears his hair long on one side and combed over the top of his head in a way that he must suppose will conceal a sizable bald spot.

"Let me guess," he says. "Clara?" He makes the fingers of his right hand into the shape of a gun and points it at her. "You can call me Kreskin," he tells her.

"Actually, my name is Claire," she tells him.

"Right, right," he says. "Bob Getchell." He extends a hand as if he were launching into a sales pitch.

"Nice place," he says. "You rent or own?"

"Own," she tells him. "Me and the bank."

He shakes his head. "Place like this has probably dropped ten, maybe twelve percent in value in the last two years alone," he says. "People just don't want the upkeep, you know. I only mention it on account of I've got a party I'm working with currently that's in the market for a place like this."

"I'm not selling," she says. How has she got to such a ridiculous point so fast? she wonders.

"You got a couple of rug rats, I understand?" he says. Bob has picked up Pete's signed Mo Vaughn baseball that he doesn't like anybody to touch. "I got two of them myself."

"I'll just get my jacket and we can go," says Claire. She feels a hundred years old suddenly. She thinks longingly of her bathtub and her solitary bed. The sooner they get going, the sooner she can be home.

He opens the car door for her—a small, unexpected courtesy. Settling into his own seat, he clicks a tape of Michael Bolton into the cassette player. "This guy sure can sing a song, huh?" he says.

"I guess so," Claire says. "He's never been a favorite of mine."

"You're kidding," says Bob. "I thought all you girls creamed in your pants over him."

Let me out here, she's thinking. She could tell him she suddenly remembered she'd left the iron on, run into the house, lock the door and turn out the lights. After a while he'd give up and go away.

"I gotta tell you," he says, "Pauline has hooked me up with some real bowwows. I was actually gonna blow this one off, figuring you'd be another one, only she said, 'Trust me, Bob, I've seen her in the steam room.' Boy, was she right this time." He is looking straight at her breasts as he says this. Claire imagines herself staring back at his crotch in a similar fashion, but she's afraid what she might see if she did.

"So how old are your children?" she asks.

"Girl thirteen, boy fifteen," he says. "Seems like every time I turn around, their mother's asking me for more cash. Know what I mean?"

"Kids that age need a lot of things that cost money," Claire says. "I bought my son a pair of sixty-dollar cleats just last fall, and he already needs a new pair." She talks to fill the air, and to keep him from saying something worse. Keep the conversation on shoes, she figures. And real-estate values.

"Oh, sure, you got your necessary expenses," he says. "But some of these individuals out there just gouge you for all you're worth. Take my wife. She says the boy needs therapy at eighty bucks a pop. Now our daughter's supposed to see this dermatologist in Boston. Prescriptions alone run twenty, twenty-five bucks. You think the kid ever heard of Clearasil? That was good enough for us, huh?"

Claire says nothing. Michael Bolton is singing his rendition of "Since I Fell for You." Bob has pulled into the parking lot of a not very good Italian restaurant. He reaches across Claire's chest to undo her seat belt.

"I can handle it myself," she says.

"Yeah, there's some other things I'd like to see you handle," he tells her.

"You know," she says, "I think I have to go home now."

"Listen," he says. "It was just a joke. I wouldn't want you to get the wrong idea. I know you gals are a little sensitive these days."

"Fine," she says. "I'm just not feeling very well."

"So let me give you a Tums," he tells her. "I keep them handy all the time, on account of my ulcer. I was going to warn you, in fact. If you hear gurgling, not to worry, it's only my gut kicking up."

"I have to be honest with you, Bob," she says. "This isn't going to work. So I think the best thing would be for you to take me home. Save your money."

"I don't know what's the matter with women these days," he says. "Nobody's got a sense of humor anymore. One false move and a guy's dead meat. Look at a person sideways and she's slapping you with a sexual harassment suit or some shit."

Claire is getting out of the car now. "Actually, I think I'll call a friend to take me home," she says.

"Fucking cunt," he calls out after her. "I give you three years, four tops, before your estrogen supply gives out, and you can't give a guy a hard-on to save your life."

Nancy isn't home. She's away at a yoga retreat, Claire remembers afterward. In the end, Claire walks home in the dark, tripping a couple of times. Her good shoes will be ruined. The first thing she does when she walks in the door is reach for the phone.

She calls Mickey. It's the number she keeps on the emergency card in her wallet to call in case of an accident. Mickey's is the number she would remember if she forgot every single other thing, even her name. When he picks up the phone and she hears that familiar voice, dear as her own children's, all she can do is cry.

He knows it's her. "Baby," he says. "Come on now, baby. Tell me what happened."

For a few more moments all she can do is cry. But just hearing his voice murmuring to her from a hundred twenty miles away, that it's all right, he's here, she can feel her breathing become more regular until finally she's able to speak.

"Oh, Mickey," she says.

"Bad night, huh, Slim?" he answers. He knows her so well she doesn't even really need to tell him the particulars. He can guess.

"I'm so tired, Mickey," she tells him.

"I know, baby. I know you are."

"First it was Sam," she begins. He knows what it's like for her when Sam comes to take the children. Even though he has never met Sam, Mickey has heard enough stories about Sam's Friday-night pickups to hate him.

"Then I had this date," she says.

"Let me guess," he says. "It wasn't Sean Connery or Dwight Yoakam."

She was going to tell him the whole story, but what's the point? All she really wants to say—all she ever wants to say—is that the guy wasn't Mickey. Once again.

"You know you're my true love, don't you, Slim?" he says. "You know I'll love you forever. Nobody else will ever love you like I do."

She's crying again, but not the great gasping sobs anymore. "I miss you, Mickey," she tells him.

"You don't have to miss me," he says. "I'm right here."

"Weren't you supposed to have a date yourself tonight?" she asks him. It has come back to her that when they last spoke, yesterday afternoon, he was planning to take somebody named Angela to a concert of Bulgarian women singers.

"She told me during intermission her favorite jazz musician was Kenny G," he says. "I took her right home. We didn't even stay for the second half."

"Oh, Mickey," she sighs. "What am I going to do?"

"Same thing you've been doing, Slim," he tells her. "Raise those chilluns of yours. Keep baking the chocolate-chip cookies. When we're eighty-five and the last one's out of the house, maybe we'll get together in Miami Beach and play shuffleboard."

She's heard this line before. She knows them all by heart, but there's a comfort in hearing him tell her again.

"You all right now, Slim?" he asks her. He's telling her, actually, that she is.

"I'm all right, Mickey," she says. "I'm going to bed now."

"Red Sox have a new relief pitcher that looks promising," he says. "Throws sidearm."

"Good night, Mickey," she says.

"Night, Slim."

Now she can sleep.

She met Mickey through an ad in the personals of a Boston newspaper she'd been reading one night almost a year after she left Sam. It was close to midnight—also a weekend when the kids were with their father—and she'd been listening to Lucinda Williams and finishing off a bottle of wine. So she called the 900 number and spent an hour just listening to people's voices telling who they were, what they wanted in a relationship. Or what they said they wanted, anyway. Mickey's was the twenty-third message she listened to. She liked his Southern accent. Most of all she liked his voice.

In the voice-mail message she left after listening to his recording, Claire didn't mention her two children or the more than a hundred miles separating the town where she lived in Vermont from the one outside Boston he had chosen largely for its proximity to Fenway Park and lots of good jazz. The end of his own marriage had coincided—maybe not by chance—with the birth of his one and only child.

He had noted Claire's area code when he called her back, naturally. He said he wasn't into long-distance relationships.

"I don't know about you," she said, "but I'd rather drive two hours to have dinner with somebody who really interested me than walk down the block to have dinner with somebody I don't care about." She told him she'd drive in to the city to meet him. He said okay. She hadn't even mentioned her own two children at this point.

She arranged for Pete and Sally to have sleepovers with friends that night. She bought a new dress, red, with a pleat up the back. Claire had gone out on plenty of blind dates by this time, but none whose prospect left her feeling so excited. All week long she'd thought about his voice on the other end of the phone.

He had chosen a little Brazilian restaurant in a part of town she'd never been. Always before this when Claire went into Boston it was to take her kids to the science museum or bring Sally to the ballet. The restaurants she knew were all the kind you'd bring children to. Here the menu was printed in Portuguese and there was percussion music playing and oilcloth on the tables and the smell of spices Claire had never cooked with. She had arrived early, regretting her choice of dress once she saw what the rest of the mostly foreign-looking clientele were wearing. She went to the ladies room and washed off her makeup, put her pearl earrings back in her purse, mussed up her hair.

When she came out again she saw him. She knew from his freckles he couldn't be Brazilian even before she heard his soft Alabama accent asking the waitress if she had a quieter table. He wasn't a handsome man exactly, by conventional standards, but she maintains that she fell in love with him the moment she saw him. Later he admitted to Claire that he felt that way himself. "It was so plain, you were so ready to be loved," he said. "You looked like an orphan. I just wanted to put my arms around you and take you away."

Not that he did. He was very formal with her that night. He got up from the table when she approached him. He shook her hand. Before they sat down she asked him whether he thought her car was all right parked where it was. Her station wagon looked as if it had pulled up at the end of a long and hair-raising car chase, with the front end up over the curb and the rear pointed out into traffic. She had been so distracted when she got to the restaurant she hadn't even noticed.

"So," he said with a regretful smile, looking out onto the street in the direction of her messy station wagon, with its ɪ ♡ soccer bumper sticker and the tumble of empty juice boxes and school papers in the back. "How old are your kids?"

For twelve years Claire's children had been the central focus of her life. She could talk for twenty minutes about the pros and cons of circumcision or the desirable number of years between children before it would suddenly occur to her—hearing the sound of her own voice—that the woman she used to be before children had virtually disappeared. To Mickey she was that woman again. Or a new one she barely recognized.

Mickey told her that first night that he didn't get involved with women who had children; it violated his sense of romance. "The worst thing that could happen would be for you and me to fall in love," he said. "Because we couldn't be together"—not together the way Mickey liked anyway—"and it would break both our hearts." By the time he said this it was also plain that there was some powerful pull between the two of them. When they danced she didn't have to keep her eyes open or think about how to move. She didn't even notice when the music stopped.

"Now that's one heck of an interesting place for a person to have a birthmark," he said. He had noticed a tiny mole between the third and fourth fingers of her left hand. No doubt he had also noticed that her eyes were moist.

"Back then you were like someone dying of thirst after days of traveling across a desert in a hundred-and-ten-degree heat, and I was just the first person who offered you a cup of cool water, that's all," he told her later. "It was like your skin had been turned inside out. You were so ready to be touched."

They stayed at the restaurant four hours. He took her back to his house, he said, just because he could tell looking at her that she would fall asleep on the road if she tried to make the long drive home so late at night.

He led her to the room his son slept in, weekends he was there, with its baseball-print sheets and framed photograph of Nolan Ryan. He gave her towels and a toothbrush even. He keeps a supply on hand. He was going to simply tuck her in with a kiss on her cheek, fix her coffee in the morning, and send her on her way, he told her later. He was planning on never seeing her again.

She was the one who reached up and took his face in both her hands as he leaned over the bed, kissed him on the lips and wouldn't let go. She was the one who said, "Don't you believe in stealing bases ever?" And when he said no, actually—not if the odds were heavily against him; he knows his limitations—and he pushed her away, she was the one who wouldn't leave it there. She got up out of his son's bed and walked down the hallway to his bedroom, where the light was still on and a record was playing that she still can't bear to listen to—Johnny Hartman and John Coltrane.

This time when she kissed him he didn't push her away. He just sighed more deeply than she has ever heard anybody sigh, before or since. "You win," he said. But really, it was always Mickey who won. On the baseball diamond or off it.

Mickey operates a recording studio where he composes music and records the mostly unexceptional work of would-be musicians in need of demo recordings. He pitches on a fairly competitive weekend baseball team, and during baseball season he attends Red Sox games when the team's in town. He is also a devoted father to his son, Gabe, though he's a very different kind of parent from the kind Claire is. "It's crazy what happens to people when they have kids, and they give up everything else they ever cared about," says Mickey. Mickey would never have bought a Raffi album for Gabe. Gabe has been raised since infancy on the Beatles and jazz. For Christmas Mickey hangs lights on his cactus plant and sticks baseball cards in a stocking, period. For Gabe's birthday Mickey gave him a saxophone.

Mickey loves his baseball and his music and his boy. He's also practically made a career of loving women. Not necessarily sticking it out over the long haul. But adoring them, anyway, and lavishing on them a certain kind of undistracted fascination and attention to the most minute of details. He keeps the photographs of women he's loved hanging on the walls all over his house, the same way his son has mounted the cards of all his favorite ballplayers on the walls of his room. Explaining Mickey to Nancy, Claire told her about the time, fairly early in her relationship with him, when he had been describing to her his first serious love, the girl to whom he'd lost his virginity at sixteen. "She had," he said, his eyes practically misting over at the memory, "the most beautiful nookie. . . ."

"Imagine," Claire told Nancy, "a man who not only remembers that information from a distance of twenty-five years. But imagine a sixteen-year-old boy who would have paid attention to that kind of thing in the first place."

Mickey is still friendly toward his former wife, Betsy, Gabe's mother. Her picture hangs on a particularly prominent spot on the wall in his recording studio and he will still reminisce fondly about a trip they took one time to New Orleans, or her exquisitely shaped fingernails, the shape of her rear end. They parted amicably shortly after Gabe's birth, and since then Mickey has held to his view that parenthood spells the death of romantic and passionate feeling between men and women. He wants no more of it. No more children of his own. None of anybody else's children either.

For years since his divorce Mickey has filled his dance card, as he likes to put it, with women he meets through the personals, the same way he met Claire. Eventually he mailed Claire a copy of the letter he typically sent out to the women whose ads he answered, which he kept on his computer. By the time Claire read Mickey's personals response letter, she was already in love with him, but if she hadn't been, she figured the letter would have done it.

Dear Stranger,

I liked your ad—ethereal yet pithy. Joni Mitchell crossed with Tina Turner maybe? I dunno. Whatever it was I read between the lines you wrote, it got to me.

As for whether the feeling might be mutual, I'll give you the basic data. I'm poking forty with a short stick, brown hair, brown eyes, no broken bones, don't smoke or dope, six feet tall on a good day, with one hundred seventy-six pounds of ballast and a boyish plethora of freckles. My friends tell me I'm reasonably attractive, but then who's going to tell you to your face that you're reasonably ugly?

I grew up in Alabama, the only state in the union where you can be your own uncle. My sport is baseball, and I guess I'd better tell you right off that I'll be unavailable during World Series week. I spent my formative years pitching dirt balls against a barn door pretending to be Don Drysdale, but I didn't fool anybody.

My life's other consuming passion is music. I appreciate everything from Laurie Anderson to Frank Zappa, but what I love best is jazz: Miles, Monk, Mulligan, and Ella Fitzgerald, my favorite woman of all time.

Given a choice, I would've been a pitcher, but the fact is I was a high-school band nerd. Round about age fifteen I started playing in rock 'n' roll bands—strictly opening act material, mind you, but it kept five guys in motel rooms and pot for a lot of years and more miles.

Round about the time I hit thirty it came to me that I'd rather never see forty at all than find myself, at forty, still playing "Proud Mary" to a roomful of drunks half my age. So I went home to Birmingham, got married, and had a kid. The marriage proved to be a mistake early on but it did produce the one pure joy of my existence, my eight-year-old son, Gabe. Trumpet player, get it? I would've named him Louis, but he was a little too pale for that.

Back when my marriage was in its last throes, the little woman and I left Alabama for Massachusetts and I found this great old cape on the North Shore that we could almost afford, with a barn out back that I've turned into a sixteen-track recording studio. You wonder how it is an Alabama boy like me would move fifteen hundred miles to a place he didn't know a soul, I'll tell you. I love Fenway Park, and I refuse to watch another game of baseball played on AstroTurf. Turns out around these parts there's enough would-be musicians— and believe me, I use the term loosely—that I can make something that resembles a living recording their demos. Not a single John Lennon in the bunch.

*I get Gabe every other weekend, during which time I at-
tempt to educate the boy in the finer things of life, meaning
jazz and baseball. I bring him to a lot of Red Sox games on
the theory that now is as good a time as any for a kid to learn
about disappointment. We buy a ridiculous number of baseball
cards.*

*Weekends I pitch for the Salem Hornets. The Sox haven't
drafted me yet, but we are the number-three team in the North
Shore league. As far as music goes, my band these days comes
to me by way of a synthesizer. Let me tell you, I get a lot less
grief out of my Kurtzweil than I used to from my old drum-
mer. I think maybe I've finally found the perfect musical
relationship. Give me my mixing board and my baseball glove,
my boy and a good margarita now and then, and I'm a happy
man.*

*Or would be, if it wasn't for this damned need I feel for my
one true love. I admit it. I'm a hopeless romantic, a guy that
still believes every lyric Cole Porter ever wrote. What I'm
trying to say is, I want to feel my pulse racing. I want to feel
that old Van Gogh kind of love that makes a guy want to cut
off his ear and gift wrap it. Come to think of it, I'm not
growing enough hair anymore to cut off my ear for you, so
maybe you'd settle for a dozen roses. Come to think of it, a
dozen roses might be a little much for my budget. Maybe you'd
settle for a card.*

*So here I am sitting on my back porch with an ice pack on
my rotator cuff (I pitched last night), sipping a beer and
listening to Ella. Now I'm going to toss this message in a
bottle out to sea. Who knows? Maybe it'll wash up on your
shore.*

The year she spent with Mickey,
this is how Claire lived her life:

Back home in Blue Hills during the week, she tried guiltily to
be a perfect mother. That was her way of earning the right to be

with Mickey. Even more diligently than before, she made sure she was home every night to read to Pete and Sally and tuck them into bed, sometimes getting back to work on ad layouts or account proposals once they were asleep. She hardly ever lost her temper with her children anymore, she was so happy and well cared for. She joined the playground committee at Pete's school and volunteered to be a chaperone on Sally's class trip to Washington, D.C. She typed her kids' book reports without giving them her usual lecture about how she wasn't anybody's secretary. She got up before her children every morning to pack their lunches and get breakfast on the table and she made sure they had a good meal every night at six, even if it was just spaghetti. Before they ate she always made her children hold hands and sing grace. They say this is the dorkiest thing they've ever heard of, but she also suspects that if she ever stopped insisting that they do it, they'd feel vaguely disappointed.

Late at night she'd call Mickey, or he'd call her just to say good night, except for Wednesdays, when he played basketball. She counted the days until the weekend, when she'd see him again.

Claire went to divorce mediation with Sam that year, and to therapy with Pete and Sally. Eventually, when the therapist himself said he thought they'd done as much work as they could, for now, she let it go. "Your children still have some unresolved anger to work out," said Dan, the therapist, "but evidently they're not ready to deal with it yet, and we have to respect that."

Weekends Claire had her other life. As soon as Pete and Sally left for their father's house Friday afternoons, Claire threw her own overnight bag in the back of her station wagon and drove to Mickey's. She wore her new silk underwear and played the jazz tapes Mickey had made for her, timed to last exactly as long as the drive took her: two hours and fifteen minutes. Mickey would have dinner waiting, and he'd make her eat, even if she wanted to make love first. "Somebody's got to look after you for a change, Slim," he'd tell Claire.

From Friday night to Sunday afternoon, when she'd make the drive north again, she was nothing but his lover. She didn't talk about the children with Mickey—not hers, and seldom his. He didn't want her to do his laundry. If they went grocery shopping, they never needed a cart, just one of those plastic baskets you take if you're going through the express line, because all you have is wine and jalapeños and fresh mussels and coriander.

Sometimes Mickey's son, Gabe, would be with them for a night or two, but having Gabe around was nothing like having her children around. "You don't even talk in the same voice when your kids are in a one-mile radius," he'd say to her. "We can be having a conversation, then Pete asks you to make him a sandwich and you stop everything and do it."

Mickey's voice seemed to call to her through the brambles of her life, *"Come out, come out. This way."* She wanted to disentangle herself; she just didn't know if she could.

As much as Mickey disliked the person Claire became around her children, Claire's children disliked even more who she became around Mickey. "My mom gets this weird, whispery way of talking when she's around him," Sally said once during therapy. "The two of them are always touching each other and whispering stuff. Sometimes they even sing these old Beatles songs together in the car. It's really dumb."

They were accustomed to Sam's way of treating Claire. To them, Mickey's brand of tenderness and concern was evidence of what Pete called his wimpishness. "He's always doing stuff like putting pillows under her feet and giving her neck massages," he told the therapist. My dad would never do something like that, is what he was probably thinking, Claire knew.

Claire remembers a visit their family had taken to Disney World, back when she and Sam were still together. There was this couple at Epcot Center kissing under the fake Eiffel Tower—a kiss that lasted for the entire five minutes they were standing in line for whatever movie it was they were showing there. Watching them kissing like that, in a way she and Sam never did, Claire had felt her legs go weak.

"Can you believe it? They've got their tongues in each other's mouths," Sally had said. Then she and Pete laughed. That night in their hotel room, alone with Sam after the children were asleep, Claire wept to him about that kiss. "We're raising children who think expres-

*sions of affection are comical," she said. "You only kiss me when you
want to have sex."*

"Give it a rest, Claire," said Sam.

With Mickey there was never a shortage of kissing. He touched
her constantly.

"How'd you get this?" Mickey asked Claire one time, a few
minutes after she arrived on Friday. There was a deep cut on her
thumb. He noticed every little thing about her. Claire just
shrugged. When her children were around, she didn't pay attention to what happened to her.

With his son, Mickey played catch and attended jazz concerts
Sunday afternoons. Gabe had long since learned to entertain himself at events like this. Pete and Sally would have been asking
when they were leaving or requesting money for the arcade next
door, not that she would have taken them to a jazz club in the
first place. But Gabe, who was almost the same age as Pete, always
sat there patiently looking through his baseball cards, and when
Mickey would ask him a question like "Who wrote that song?"
he could tell you it was Thelonius Monk. At bedtime, Mickey read
him the box scores for the American League or a book on baseball
tips for Little Leaguers, with chapters like "How to Bunt" and
"Theories of Base Stealing."

For Claire he would stop at three different stores until he found
the kind of coffee beans she liked, which he'd grind fresh for every
pot he made her. He'd warm her bathrobe in front of the fire
when she was having a bath, and then he'd put the towel on her
hair and dry it. Before it got to be time for her to leave, Sundays,
he warmed up her car for her, checked her oil and her tires. He
made her call him when she got in the door of her house after she
got back home, so he knew she was okay. "No offense, Slim," he
said. "But you drive worse than you sing."

Claire and Mickey used to talk about how they might work
things out so they could live together. Secretly Claire believed that
once he got to know Pete and Sally better, Mickey would realize
what wonderful children they were and his view of blending families would change. Sometimes when they were making love she
even allowed herself to imagine that they could have a baby. The

one time she brought it up, he actually shivered. "Horrifying idea," he said. Shortly afterward Mickey had his vasectomy.

As anxious and uncertain as it made Claire feel, knowing the intensity of Mickey's resistance to spending time with her children, it was also part of what she loved about him. He loved her too much to share her. Nobody had ever loved her that much before, or stood up for her in the face of the constant demands of her children the way Mickey did.

He would say he wanted to take her to see the Red Sox play Oakland, and she'd say, "Can we get another ticket and take Pete?" Mickey would say no, I want it to be just you and me. Imagine Sam saying that.

Hearing that Mickey took his mom to a ball game—without including him, Pete was not so much resentful as puzzled. He had never thought about his mom having a life apart from him, or desires beyond his and his sister's happiness.

Observing the arrival one day of a Victoria's Secret shipment Claire had ordered, Sally commented a little sharply, "How much does all this underwear cost, anyway?" Always before, if a mail-order shipment came, it would have been for Sally.

"You know how long it's been since I bought anything for myself?" Claire told her. "You know how many years I've been wearing maternity underpants?"

On the phone with Mickey, she would say to Pete, "Don't interrupt," and keep talking. She was practically sweating, this was such an unfamiliar thing to do. When she brought the children down to Mickey's house with her, she and Mickey would leave them at the house Saturday night with a babysitter and go out to some club.

"I can't believe it," Sally would mutter. "You drag us all the way to Boston, where all this cool stuff's going on, and then you leave us at some guy's house we don't even like while you're off having a great time." Worst of all were the occasions when Gabe would be there too, and Claire and Mickey would leave the three of them sitting glumly on the couch (not Gabe, of course; Gabe never complained), watching a video.

"I get to have a life," she told them. Mickey had told her that, and she wanted to believe it.

Eight or nine months into their relationship Claire had actually begun to consider whether it was possible that after the end of the school year her children might just move in with their father while she moved in with Mickey. That was how much she wanted to be with him.

"You leave your kids?" he said. "You could never do it. I'd never let you either."

"Maybe I could," she told him. "As long as they're happy, I'm fine. They don't have to be happy with me. Just happy."

"But they wouldn't be. And neither would you. You're a *mom*." It was almost an obscenity the way he said it, but Claire knew he was right.

Mickey was getting worn down, she could see it. "I feel like I'm trying to live my whole life in two days a week," he said.

"Even when you're here, you're not always here," Mickey told her. He was right too. They'd be eating their dinner by the fire, listening to Chet Baker, Mickey rubbing her back. Suddenly he'd feel a tightness in her neck.

"What it is it, Slim?" he'd ask. "Oh, nothing," she'd say. Then she'd start talking about this crazy grapefruit diet Sally'd been on, and her worry that her daughter might be borderline anorexic. Just when she'd let it go and he'd be kissing her again, he'd lose her again like a radio station whose signal is weak.

"Pete's so hostile and disrespectful to me these days," she'd say. "It's as if Sam's in our house in Pete's body. I talk to him and he doesn't even answer. I'll hear him on the phone to his dad, whispering about me, and I know that instead of backing me up when I enforce some kind of boundaries, Sam just commiserates with him about how unreasonable I am." And then she'd tell Mickey about how she'd confiscated Pete's boom box last week when he had neglected his chores again. And Pete's response: "You just want me to be perfect, like your stupid boyfriend's kid."

"Where have you gone, Claire?" Mickey whispered to her. "Come back to me."

By July Claire couldn't make love with him without crying. She could see their time together closing in as clearly as if they were staying in an apartment whose lease would soon be up. From the moment she arrived on Friday nights all she could think of was how much time was left before she'd have to go.

Remember this, she'd think as they would sit on his porch swing having a beer and listening to Ella, or on his couch some evening, listening to a particular recording of Bud Powell he loved, her head in his lap while he read the sports page. She knew now this was a country she was visiting and her visitor's permit was about to expire.

She started asking him for the names of certain jazz albums he played a lot, asking him to tape them for her. She went out and bought a couple hundred dollars' worth of perennials and planted them in Mickey's garden. Sometimes she'd wake in the middle of the night and just lie there watching him sleep.

At the end of July Mickey saw his son off to camp in preparation for the month he and Claire were going to spend together. The day she was supposed to go to Mickey's, with her bags packed in the backseat of her station wagon, she got a call from her lawyer telling her Sam had decided to file for custody of the children on the grounds that she was an emotionally unstable parent. Claire called Mickey and told him she couldn't come and be with him in August. Or ever again.

"You do what you have to, Slim," he told her. "I always knew this couldn't last forever. I was just going to enjoy every second for as long as I could, and I did too. You ride the ride until it's over. Then you get off. Simple as that."

On the other end of the phone Claire was weeping too hard to speak.

"Hey, baby," he said. "None of that. You know you're my true love and you always will be. It's just one of those things."

After she put down the phone she walked over to the stove, where she had been making her leek and potato soup to bring to Mickey's house. She picked up the pot, and threw it with all the strength she had against the black and white tiles of her kitchen floor. There are three chips still missing from the place it landed. She stood there for a long time after that, her whole body shaking, calling out his name.

Then she took out the mop and cleaned up the mess. Over the course of the next four weeks, while her kids were off with their father, Claire met with her lawyer and defrosted the freezer and canned thirty-two quarts of tomato sauce. She sewed a patchwork quilt for Pete's bed, using fabric from all his outgrown flannel shirts, and stenciled a row of flamingos along the ceiling of Sally's room. She organized their photograph albums and ordered enlargements of all her favorite pictures of her children, which she framed and hung in her bedroom. She cut off her braids—not in some desperate, middle-of-the-night rampage, but calmly, with nail scissors, at her bathroom sink. Later she went to a Newbury Street salon that charged her a hundred dollars to shape what was left of her hair into a chic, French-looking style that everyone says suits her well.

The day before her children were due to come back home from their father's house, Claire spent an afternoon listening to every one of the tapes Mickey had made for her. She left till last the tape of herself and Mickey singing together, taped in Mickey's studio. Then she put the tapes away.

When her marriage had ended, Claire experienced a heady, exhilarated feeling of release, as if a great weight had been lifted from her. But with Mickey gone she felt like a widow. Every time a Beatles song came on the radio, she imagined Mickey's hand tapping out Ringo's drumbeat on her thigh. A wave of feeling washed over her and made her knees buckle and her stomach turn over, sometimes took her breath away even. And it could hit her at any moment: from the news that a particular Red Sox pitcher had blown out his arm or a weather report mentioning storm warnings for the North Shore, from the taste of jalapeño in somebody's guacamole, the sound of some kid practicing the trumpet, drifting out a window when she was out on her bike. She'd hear it, see it, taste it, feel it, and there he was again. There he wasn't, actually.

Once her kids came back from Sam's house and school started, she was occupied, and that was good. She attended Pete's soccer games and Sally's dance recitals. The director of the children's museum, whose brochures Claire had always designed for free, moved to New Mexico, and when her job was offered to Claire, she took it even though the salary was a little less than what she'd been earning at the ad agency. She had always dreamed of making a place like this—rooms full of treasures where children can touch anything they want, and instead of adapting to the rules of the adult world, it's what they care about that matters.

The custody hearing in her divorce from Sam was scheduled to go to court right before Christmas that year. She sold the Thomas Hart Benton drawing her father had left her to pay the rest of her lawyer's retainer. "You keep your nose clean and we'll win this thing," he told her, "but it's going to cost you twenty, thirty thousand dollars."

A guardian ad litem was appointed to evaluate Claire and Sam as parents and make a recommendation to the court concerning custody. The day before the guardian was scheduled to pay his home visit Claire spent the entire afternoon cleaning their house. An hour before he was due to arrive she put bread in the oven and set her baseball glove out on the counter. Past the point where pride remains a consideration, she put the Mother's Day card Pete had made, "For the #1 Mom in the Universe," up on the refrigerator. Maybe she should set out a pair of Sally's jeans to mend?

How do you begin showing a total stranger, in a matter of an hour or two, what kind of a parent you are? What is there a person can say that gets the point across about how she loves her children? Where does she begin?

Craig, the man the court had appointed to evaluate Claire's fitness as a mother and make a recommendation that would determine the next half dozen years of all their lives, turned out to be very young: twenty-eight, thirty tops, father of an infant daughter. "So," he said, "what sort of father is Sam, in your opinion?"

"He loves the children, naturally," Claire said. "He's just never been all that involved in a lot of their lives. I don't think he ever took one of the kids to a doctor's appointment or stayed home when one of them was sick." When she told him how Sam would speak of "babysitting" their children, on the occasions when he'd take them for a morning, Claire observed a flicker of discomfort

on the guardian ad litem's face and realized that this man probably used this same term concerning his own participation in child
care, which was probably equally spotty. Her palms were sweating now.

"I don't know how you gals do it," he said. "Jobs, kids, aerobics
classes, doctor's appointments, the whole shooting match. Me, I'm
still trying to figure out how to fasten the tabs on a Pamper."

This guardian work was a sideline for Craig. He was actually a
paralegal, but he'd taken many courses in child psychology. He
was only a few credits away from getting his master's, in fact.
"You know, Claire," he said earnestly as she told him about Pete's
migraine headaches, and how they often coincided with his return
from his father's house after the weekend, "there's more to kids
than meets the eye."

In December she went to court, where Sam testified that Claire
was prone to hysterical fits and uncontrolled rage, like her father.
He told about the time she had thrown the dessert for their Christmas dinner down the garbage disposal, and how she threatened to
jump out of the car that time, and dumped a bag of trash on the
floor when all he'd said was that he hoped she'd get around to
taking it to the dump soon.

*"I was worried about her mental state," Sam said. "Knowing the
history of psychological instability in her family. My own parents have
a very happy marriage, with no history of substance abuse. That's
probably why I have an easier time keeping my emotions in check."*

Claire wanted to reach into her purse and take out the lucky
baseball Mickey had sent to her for her day in court, that he used
the day he pitched the one-hitter back in Birmingham. She wanted
to hurl it at Sam, but of course that only would have proved him
right. "Just don't get hysterical on me," her lawyer hissed at her.
So she was stone.

In court Craig, the guardian ad litem, testified that he had some
concern about Claire's status as an Adult Child of an Alcoholic
and her tendency to be overemotional. "Knowing Mrs. Temple's
family background, and her apparent history of occasional out-
bursts in front of the children, it would probably be a good idea
for her to get some therapy," he said. "But since at this point in

time she doesn't appear to present a threat to herself or the children, I'm recommending that the children continue to maintain primary residence with their mother, and that the court mandate liberal weekly visitation with their father." The judge concurred.

Claire and Sam have been apart now over five years, divorced for three. In the yoga class she signed up for in an effort to get Mickey out of her brain and find some respite from the bitterness of the custody battle, Claire met Nancy, who was still married at the time, but not for long. They took to going for walks in the early-morning hours before her kids got up. Because of the walking and the low-fat diet Nancy has put her on, Claire is very lean now, and Nancy has become Claire's best friend in Blue Hills. They have taken country line dancing class together and gone camping on Lake Champlain while Claire's kids were off with their father. One Christmas they bought themselves matching gold lamé dresses and performed a karaoke number together at the Ramada Inn that won first prize. Claire always laughs at Nancy's dirty jokes as if she's never heard them before. Nancy doesn't mind it when Claire calls her up at night and she's feeling lonely, no matter how late it is.

For months after Claire and Mickey parted, while she was fighting to hold on to custody of her children, just the sound of Mickey's voice brought tears to her eyes, so she didn't talk to him. Sometimes he would send her tapes—Timbuk 3, Miles Davis, Milton Nascimento, Peter Gabriel—in which every song, every wailing trumpet, every chanting Bulgarian seemed to be speaking directly to her. She knew he still loved her, same as she still loved him. There was simply nothing to be done about it.

After almost a year of taking out the thought of Mickey and turning it around in her brain almost hourly, the sensation of missing him was no longer so much a shooting pain as it was a dull, bearable ache. She hadn't forgotten the look of his body, naked, or his particular, distinctive windup when he threw a curveball out on the pitcher's mound for the Hornets. But now she could consider these things without an accompanying stab.

Claire had been dating a divorced lawyer in town for a few months at this point, and she was having occasional, companionable sex with him, without any illusions on anybody's part concerning love. One day without any deliberation at all she picked up the phone and dialed Mickey's number. When he answered, she said, "It's Claire, Mickey. I just finished listening to the new Joni Mitchell album and I was wondering if you'd heard it yet." Then she realized he was playing the same album, right then.

"Some good songs on this one, all right, Slim," he said, as if it had been yesterday when they'd spoken last, instead of almost a year ago. "But Joni's got to give up cigarettes. Her voice is shot."

He was back in her life. But it was different this time.

Before long it got to be her habit to call him up every day. First thing she'd do as soon as the children went off to school was pour herself a cup of coffee and dial Mickey's number. "You know what, Slim?" Mickey told her during one of their morning conversations over coffee, "I think this might just be the perfect relationship."

Nancy, who has never met Mickey, considers it bizarre that in the two years they've been doing this, Claire and Mickey haven't seen each other once. He sends her his baseball team portrait every year, though, along with an annual report on the state of his hairline. Now and then he sends a photo of Gabe, and one time she sent him a picture of Pete and Sally dressed as John Lennon and Paul McCartney for Halloween. When Claire won a big grant to mount a multicultural exhibit at the children's museum and a professional photographer took a portrait of Claire for their new brochure, she sent Mickey the contact sheets. He wrote funny captions under every shot except for one he circled with a china marker.

"Get me a print of that and send it to me, huh, Slim?" he asked her.

Talking on the phone as they do now, they seldom refer to their old history together. They tell each other about blind dates they go on, music they're listening to, lovers they have—Mickey's many, Claire's few. Mickey tells Claire his theories about what the Red Sox are doing wrong. Claire tells Mickey about the petty politics at the museum, her battles with the board and its director, Vivian, who wants her to put more emphasis on computers and video technology and makes barbed remarks about Claire's failure to drum up more big corporate contributions. Though they seldom discussed their children when they were lovers, now, surprisingly enough, Mickey often tells Claire something Gabe's been up to and asks about her kids. She tells him about little things Sam does like forgetting to bring Pete and Sally's bikes back from his house or sending them home, Sunday nights, full of sugar and video games, with none of their homework done, or the time Claire came home to find Sam upstairs taking a shower.

"You need to tell that guy if he keeps leaning over the plate, he's going to get hit with the pitch," Mickey tells her. The next time Claire sees Sam—and he makes one of his little digs at her —that is precisely what she says. There is a trace of Mickey's Alabama accent in her voice as well as his strength as she delivers the line. Sam looks at her strangely. But he backs off, too.

Often in her confrontations with Sam Claire will pretend that Mickey's standing there in his Hornets uniform, telling her what to say. He may be talking baseball, or whispering in her ear in his scratchy-voiced Miles Davis imitation. *"Smooth and slow,"* Miles *will tell her. "You don't have to blow hard. Just blow."* Or he may just be Mickey, reminding her that she is good and strong, and not the dysfunctional hysteric her ex-husband likes to make her out to be.

"I'm sorry, Sam," she tells him, "but it won't be possible for you to take Pete out to the comic store again tonight after his game. Until he gets his act together about the chores I ask him to do, he's got to get to bed by eight-thirty."

Sam will shoot Claire an angry look then most likely, followed by a gesture to his son that says, *"Women.* What can you do?" But for once he doesn't take it further.

"You have to draw a line in the dirt and tell him he can't cross it," Mickey says. "Your problem is you spent way too many years with that guy and those kids of yours drawing new lines every time they stepped over. And now you wonder why they don't respect you."

Mickey had told Claire when they were still together that no-body would ever love her the way he does. It's not something they speak of anymore, but this knowledge allows her to hear about his other lovers with a feeling that approaches pleasure. She loves him so much she wants him to be happy and cared for, she explains to Nancy. He loves her so much he wants the same for her. The only lover who could ever threaten her would be one he didn't tell her about. Same thing for her. She pays more for long distance every month than she pays for food.

"So tell me what she looks like," Claire will say, having heard from Mickey that he's taken some new girlfriend to a Texas Rangers game, and knowing that means it's serious. Serious for him, anyway.

And he will describe her extraordinary skin or the elegance of her calf muscle. She has no children, of course.

"Have you told her about the vasectomy yet?" Claire will ask, once the relationship has progressed to a certain point. Knowing what it's like to love him and lose him, she maintains a sisterly protectiveness for these women. But she also knows that Mickey doesn't reveal to these women the most precious and irreplaceable parts of him, which makes it easier for them when they discover they aren't going to get to keep him forever.

"Has he met the children?" he'll ask her on the infrequent occasions when the tables are turned, and she's the one with a prospective partner. He can barely conceal his surprise if she says, with some defensiveness, "Yes, and he thinks they're great."

"We went to Martha's Vineyard with them for the weekend," she tells him. She no longer expects this sort of thing to get any kind of a rise out of him. The fact that a relationship allows for this kind of family-ish togetherness only confirms for them both that it must lack the passionate intensity of their love affair. They all do.

On rare moments she gets a little shaky during these phone calls. "Come on now, Slim," he'll say. She imagines his hand stroking her neck. "Stop that now. We've been through this. You know the rules."

And she'll snap out of it.

Sometimes Pete hears his mother crying on the phone. He will be lying in the dark, at an hour so late she supposes he's asleep, and he will hear that record of organ-violin music she sometimes puts on that's like what they'd play on a soap opera night after they found out someone had a brain tumor. The saddest piece of music in the world. Other than that, she mostly listens to country now. All these songs about relationships that didn't work out.

"Sometimes I just don't know how I'm going to keep taking care of everything," she's saying into the phone. "I feel so alone."

Sometimes he hears her talking about her job, and what will happen to them if they don't renew her contract at the children's museum. They didn't reach their fund-raising goal this year and his mother has had to cut her own salary back by three thousand dollars. Sally needs car insurance once she gets her license this fall. His mom still owes her lawyer so much money he's going to attach their property, whatever that means.

"All day long I'm taking care, taking care," she sighs. "There's never anybody taking care of me."

She thinks Pete hasn't noticed, but he has. He has seen her, mornings after a blizzard, out in the driveway shoveling out their car. He has watched her struggling to get their basketball hoop up. "Three-quarter-inch socket wrench!" she says. "Who would think you'd need four different-sized wrenches to put up one lousy hoop?" Finally she got it up, but it has never been quite right. It wobbles. Every time he plays basketball, it's a reminder that other people have their dads to put up their basketball hoops. He has his mom.

She can't get the lawn mower started. Nobody told her you had to mix in a special kind of oil with every two gallons of gasoline, and now the motor's clogged. They have maggots breeding in their trash bin, and although it is his sister's job to carry out the trash, Sally refuses to go anyplace near it. His mother tries pouring bleach in the bin, tries boiling water, but nothing kills them. Finally, with rubber gloves on, she scrapes them out and flushes them down the toilet. This is a day when the toilet flushes. Sometimes it doesn't. Then his mother tries to work the plunger, but sometimes it's no good.

In spring their basement floods, and his mom has to run out and rent a sump pump. Pete stands at the top of the steps watching her in hip boots sloshing around in the dark, cold water, with boxes of Christmas ornaments and old school projects floating around her like little rafts.

Moments like this Pete wishes he was a man. He would do something. He is ashamed and disgusted with himself to see his mom down in the basement like this, or up on the roof, or out in the freezing cold running jumper cables from her battery to their neighbor's when their car won't start. He hates it that she's the one who has to bury their cat when he gets hit by a car, and catch the bat that gets into Sally's room in the middle of a slumber party of screaming girls. In April, a few weeks before baseball sign-up, when she hears him talking about all the competition in senior league for pitching positions, she offers to catch for him. She means well, but there's no way she could catch his pitches. Your dad does that, not your mom.

She tries hard. Every spring she buys tickets to Fenway Park just for the two of them. Sitting in the bleachers beside her, Pete looks around. Every other kid he sees has come with a dad. Either that or both parents.

She doesn't understand the game. When one of the Red Sox hits a pop-up, she cheers, evidently thinking—because it goes so high—it must be a really great hit. She's always surprised when the outfielder catches one of these type of hits, which he always does, of course. "Gee," she says, "I thought that was a homer for sure, didn't you? It looked like that one was headed straight over the green monster."

A couple months back—Sally's prom night—the two of them sat on the porch after she drove off with Travis, Claire sipping her coffee, Pete with a mug of hot chocolate. "I know I should be past all this," his mom said, snuggling up to him on the porch swing, "but just once I'd like some handsome prince to come along and whisk me away to the ball. Pretty silly, huh?"

He can't do anything about that. In fact, on the rare occasions when somebody has shown up to whisk his mother off (usually just to the movies, or some restaurant in town), the guy was nothing like a prince. Pete knows he is never very polite to these men. He knows his mother wishes he would be more pleasant. But they're just such geeks. Why does she need to go out on dates, anyway?

But it's no good when she stays home all the time either. She gets grouchy and mad. She's always yelling at him to pick up his room and mop the kitchen floor, but really, he figures, she's just sad about other stuff. Money for instance.

When Pete hears his mother cry, he would do anything to make her stop. He has been listening to these ads they have on the radio about the Mega Bucks lottery. Every week the jackpot keeps getting bigger. Somebody's got to win soon.

"Imagine the feeling," the song goes, on the radio. *"Imagine it was you."*

So he does. He imagines it was his mom, because he would give all the money to her. All except a couple hundred dollars for a dirt bike, or maybe a Jet Ski.

They would go to Club Med, the one his friend Jared has told him about where you get to ride go-karts and learn to fly on the trapeze. There would be yoga classes for his mom, and drinks with parasols in them, and scuba diving.

They would buy a Range Rover and a jukebox and a CD-ROM. His mom would hire a cleaning person to wash all the dishes and do the vacuuming. She would never have to look at another maggot again. Anytime something broke she wouldn't even think about trying to fix it. She'd just call a handyman. Maybe she'd even keep one on staff, full time.

Once they won the lottery she wouldn't be so mad at his dad anymore for not giving her enough money. His dad could come into the house without her getting mad, and Pete could show his dad his room that he's fixed up with this Nike poster of Michael Jordan's arms stretched out from one end of the room to the other. He could go to that baseball camp where they make videos of you and analyze your motion and get all the practice with his pitching he needs. They would teach him a slider, and when the Cubs announced that they were making Pete their starting pitcher, Bobby Arnold could just eat his heart out.

"Listen to the latest," he hears his mom saying into the late-night

phone—*to Nancy, most likely.* "*Sally gets this eye infection, so I send her back to the eye doctor. Eye doctor sends her to a specialist. Specialist says she's developed an allergy to her contact lenses and she needs this special gas-permeable kind that cost four hundred and twenty-five dollars. Naturally my insurance doesn't cover it. And of course you know Sam will be no help. He just tells me he thinks she looks fine in her glasses.*"

"Stop it, stop it, stop it!" Pete wants to scream.

"*Sometimes,*" *his mother says into the telephone,* "*I just want to fold up my tent and give up.*"

Pete can't bear listening to this anymore. So he goes back to his dream, where the announcer on Megabucks Minute is calling out the winning numbers for this week's six-million-dollar jackpot.

Pete is holding his ticket and checking the numbers off as the announcer calls them out, and amazingly enough every one has matched so far. It's down to the last number. His.

"*I got it, Mom,*" *he tells her.* "*I won the six million dollars.*"

"*Oh, son,*" *she says, crying again, but happy tears this time.* "*Everything's going to be all right now.*"

Claire and Nancy walk together almost every day before Claire's kids get up. They have covered a lot of ground on this road. Each of them knows the awkward, agonizing circumstances under which the other relinquished her virginity. Nancy knows the story of how Sam asked Claire to marry him a few days after they met. Claire knows about the years Nancy spent trying to have a baby with her husband, and her current position, which is "Thank God I didn't." Claire doesn't push this any further, and Nancy doesn't pursue her belief that Claire should give up talking on the phone with Mickey and use all the money she saves to buy herself a ticket to Hawaii next winter. "When will you get it about him?" she says. "He hardly ever even pays for the calls. *Let it go.*"

Claire no longer tries to explain, because Nancy doesn't understand. In all other areas, though, she's such a good friend. They can tell each other anything.

It's on this road that the two of them analyzed the data concerning whether or not Nancy's husband was having an affair with his paralegal. This goes back three years now, and he was. Their divorce became final shortly after Claire's, but without the long and costly legal battle. "There's a lot less blood if no children are involved," says Nancy. "As in all areas of life."

Historically, Nancy has been the more adventurous of the two of them, romantically or at least sexually speaking—although Nancy would say that nothing she's ever done is as brave as having kids. This hill is where Nancy described to Claire how she made love on horseback that time with Billy, the deaf horseshoer she met pumping gas at a self-serve. Here's where Claire told Nancy about her uncharacteristic decision to go to bed with a man she met at a museum design conference, and her shock when he took out a reusable goatskin condom. "Better for the environment," he said. "I don't want to go littering these things all over the place, right?"

"My date told me he couldn't bear to wear one, because it created a wall between us," Nancy told Claire about Victor, the investment banker. "I told him, 'You want to talk about walls, I'll talk about the door. It's over there.' "

"He showed me a photograph of his mother," Claire told Nancy the morning after a blind date with a never-married bassoon player named Lionel. No second date necessary.

"Not a good sign," Nancy told Claire when Claire described the way Arthur, the urban planner, had asked her for a copy of that snapshot he had taken with her camera of Sally's friend Kim in her shorts and halter top, with her legs stretched out in the back of the station wagon. Kim was fourteen at the time.

"He only likes oral sex if he's smoked marijuana first," Nancy told Claire about Richard, the anesthesiologist.

"Not exactly unconditional love," Claire says.

"He's the best man I ever met," Nancy told Claire about Frank, an accountant who sent her flowers every Friday and cooked wonderful Italian meals for her. Frank wanted to marry Nancy, and was planning to go on Weight Watchers just as soon as he got through tax season. "He would do anything, absolutely anything, for me," she told Claire. "I'd be crazy to leave him." Claire could tell from the sound of Nancy's voice that Frank was history. She had said the same thing about Boyd, the single father she met at Pete's soccer tournament that time, who changed her oil on their second date. He was too nice.

"I didn't like his smell," Claire said. "Not that he's dirty, you know. It's just the wrong body chemistry, you know?" No arguing with that one.

Claire and Nancy know that some women they're acquainted with—married ones—regard certain aspects of their way of life as romantic and exciting. It has probably been quite a while since the husband of Jared's mother, Cassie Walters, made love to his wife on a sailboat in the middle of Buzzard's Bay or spent a weekend with her at a twenty-dollar-a-night motel in Maine. It's doubtful that many of these women keep massage oil in the back of their medicine chests. They have not felt the need to take an AIDS test on the way to the soccer game.

There was this one time when Claire was taking a whole car-load of Pete's friends to Taco Bell after baseball, and when she reached into her purse for a handful of loose dollars and coins, what scattered out onto the counter along with the money was a Trojan-enz packet. The boys didn't seem to notice, but the girl behind the counter did all right.

Even Sally, who is pretty preoccupied with her own life these days, notices the difference between the mothers who are married and the ones who aren't. "Divorced mom, definitely," she said one time, nodding in the direction of a woman eating dinner with a girl about her own age at the next booth at the diner where they'd stopped for dinner on the way home from shopping.

"How do you know?" Claire asked her. "Maybe her husband's just home with the other kids tonight." The truth was, she was pretty sure Sally was right, and interested in how her daughter had arrived at the same conclusion she had.

"Check out her outfit," Sally said. "Also the hair."

Divorced women are more likely to wear theirs long, probably layered, and permed. Their skirts are shorter, if they can get away with it, and sometimes even if they can't. They belong to a gym. They hardly ever leave the house without their makeup on. The ones who haven't thrown in the towel utterly, that is. The others may put on a lot of weight and join some choir.

. . .

"Your life is so incredibly exciting," Cassie said to Claire one time when she stopped over to pick up her son on an afternoon when Claire's kids were going to spend the weekend with Sam and Claire was packing to go away for a couple of days with Mark, the lawyer she had gone out with for a few months, a couple of years after Mickey.

"I love Tom to pieces, of course," she told Claire. "But sometimes you wish you could just take a vacation from your marriage for a month or two."

It hasn't been just a month or two for Claire, though. In Cassie's fantasy version of Claire's life the part of the blind date is played by Harrison Ford or Mel Gibson, conversation scripted by Woody Allen. In real life, it is likely to revolve more on the unfair child-support settlement the guy ended up with from his divorce or the particulars of his sex life with his ex-wife. He may talk about other women he has dated in recent months and his sex life with them. He is probably carrying around an extra twenty pounds, although she knows that if she were equally overweight, he would probably not have asked her out, and it is unlikely that he still has more than half of his hair. He may drink too much. When he puts a tape into the cassette player of his car, it may turn out to be Barry Manilow. He may mention that he'll be getting a bite to eat on his way over to pick her up, thereby avoiding the issue of whether or not they split the tab at dinner. There was one man who shared with her, on their first date, the details of his recent bout with kidney stones, and what he went through before passing them. A guy Nancy went out with once spent an entire dinner describing in detail the dental work he was having done. Every year since her divorce—every year since ending things with Mickey, that is— she has gone out less, and with fewer men, than she did the year before. So has Nancy, who has had sex only seven times, as she pointed out to Claire recently, for the entire duration of the Clinton administration. "I guess I used it all up during Bush," she said, shaking her head. "But then, so did Bill Clinton, evidently."

Sometimes, when Claire is talking with one of the married mothers of her children's friends, one of them will complain that her husband has been out of town on a business trip for five days and she's going crazy. Not for sex. What's pushing her over the edge has to do with the responsibilities of driving kids and dealing with car repairs, normally shared, that suddenly fall to the wife alone.

"He's been away six nights now," this woman may say. Or maybe he was away when the hose on their washing machine broke, or when her son fell off a slide and had to be rushed to the emergency room with bruised ribs. He was away during the chicken pox. She had to prepare their tax return alone, because he was preparing a big annual report. She had to get their boat in for the winter while he was at a convention. She reports these facts as if they were on a par with living through Hurricane Andrew.

"If Rich doesn't make it home by the weekend, I'm filing divorce papers," Beth Donnelly told Claire the other day when they ran into each other at the food co-op. Claire could've pointed out, of course, that filing for divorce was one way Beth could ensure a great many more weeks and weekends of partnerless homemaking, but she didn't. She knew the next thing Beth would say was that they should have dinner together while Rich was out of town. Most of her dinner invitations come this way. It must've been three years since anybody invited her to a dinner party of couples, but she is regularly invited to join female acquaintances whose husbands are away.

"Thanks but I'm busy that night," she says. It's her yoga night with Nancy. It's not that she dislikes these women. They just inhabit different continents, is all. And the handful of times Claire has had the experience of being kissed in the front seat of a car as few husbands she's observed kiss their wives, are nothing compared to the miles she's navigated behind the wheel, driving home from someplace late at night with her children asleep in the backseat, and nobody next to her checking the road map.

The morning after Tim and Ursula finished reading *Little House in the Big Woods,* Tim sees in the paper that the children's museum has opened a new exhibit with a Pioneer Room. He really should spend his day off working on his research paper about the effects of fluctuating saline levels in estuaries on inland ecosystems, but he can't bear watching his daughter spend another Saturday glued to the shopping channel.

He turns off his computer and goes downstairs to their TV room, where, sure enough, Ursula is curled up with her blanket, listening to a couple of women demonstrating the Thighmaster.

"You should get me that," Ursula says. "My thighs are lots chubbier than hers."

"Your thighs are just perfect," Tim says. "I should get you a Brainmaster, is all. To put some sense into your silly head."

"Guess where we're going today, Urs?" he says.

"The Laundromat?" she says. This is their usual Saturday excursion. That or B.J.'s Bargain Warehouse, where the cereal comes in plain boxes with no pictures on the back, but it's lots cheaper. Now that Ursula's learning to read, Tim pushes the cart and she carries the coupons, watching for the special bargains. At the Laundromat, she's in charge of sorting. He could never handle all the jobs without her.

"Nope," he says. "We're going to the Ingalls' house."

"Who?" she says. She and her dad don't get invited to people's houses much.

"*Little House in the Big Woods,* remember?" he says. "The Ingalls family? It says in the paper the children's museum's got a special room now where it's all set up like in pioneer times."

"I wish I had a olden-days dress to wear," Ursula says. "And those lace-up boots like in the American Girl catalog."

"Never mind," he says. "We can pretend."

"I bet there's going to be lots of kids there," she says. "Not like the kids in my class. Nice ones."

He says they'll put in a load of wash at the Laundromat on the way. Maybe he'll take her out to McDonald's after. Either that or he might just bring along his twenty-two and rustle up a wild turkey or two for their vittles.

In the one-room schoolhouse, a little girl asks her mother if this was the kind of classroom she attended in the olden days. At the front of the room, an older child —eight years old, maybe nine—holds a pointer in the direction of a map of the United States as it would have looked in the year 1843, when Laura Ingalls Wilder attended a school like this. Then he waves it at his friend. Watching him, Claire makes a note to herself to replace the pointer with a less sharp implement. How could she have forgotten what happens when you give a little boy a long pointed stick?

They've got a good turnout at the museum today, and they needed it, too. The United Way decided to take the children's museum off its list this year, which has left Claire thirty-eight thousand dollars short in meeting her budget. Already she has had to let her part-time secretary go, and her only full-time staffer. These days she has to rely on volunteers and Veronica, her half-time clerical person, to help her run the place. For the construction of the pioneer exhibit that has been unveiled today she hired a couple of carpenters and a designer, but that still left a lot of loose ends Claire had to handle herself. Last night, for instance, she was up until three preparing the materials for one of the activities in the Try It Room: simplified samplers for kids to stitch and bring home. Now she leans against the rough-hewn boards forming the walls of the Pioneer Room, wearing her long calico skirt and a high-collared blouse and a gingham mop cap. It is one of those rare moments when she gets to stand back for a moment and simply survey what she does here, and she's feeling good about it. All around her are happy-looking children and parents.

A boy she knows well, Roland, is rubbing his face in the sampler supplies at the moment. Claire has never asked Roland's mother what his problem is, but she assumes he's autistic. Sometimes when he comes here he is animated and friendly, other times he may not respond at all when Claire speaks to him. He may even bite. His mother is a taut, frantic-looking woman who brings him here almost every day. She always comes in carrying a *People* magazine and a thermos of Dunkin' Donuts coffee and sits in the Parent

Resource corner, reading, while Roland careens around the museum. At various times Claire's volunteers will comment to her that somebody really should say something to Roland's mother about this. "We're just not set up to provide babysitting services for kids like him," one of them said to her just the other day, on an occasion when Roland had been emitting a strange, high wail for a good hour.

"She looks exhausted," Claire said. "Let's leave her alone."

Today when Claire sits down beside Roland he is evidently in one of his affectionate moods. He climbs into her lap and begins to nuzzle against her breasts as if he wanted to nurse. Roland is probably ten years old, although it's hard to tell. One thing's for sure: He's not stitching any sampler.

"Tell you what, Roland," she says to him. "Let's go churn some butter." She takes his hand and leads him into the pioneer kitchen, where there's a butter churn set up, and a pitcher of cream. She pours some in.

Often the museum is practically empty when he comes here, but there are many other children in the Pioneer Room today, on account of the unveiling. Roland looks anxious. He can't see his mother.

"It's all right," Claire tells him. "She's just in the other room. But you know me. I'm Claire."

It occurs to her that he may not recognize her with this hat on. She takes it off, and a look of recognition comes over him.

Claire sits Roland in front of the churn and places his hands on the paddle. She puts her own hands over his and moves them back and forth. "Churn, churn," she says. She has learned from other times with Roland that repetition is always comforting to him.

"What's the matter with that kid?" a boy is asking his mother. "The one with the thick glasses?"

"Churn, churn," says Claire. "We're making butter, Roland. When we're done, we'll put some on a piece of bread and give it to your mother. One for your mother, one for you."

Up in the loft bed, a bunch of little girls are playing with rag dolls. "My baby's prettier than your baby," one of them says. "Nu-uh," her friend tells her. Now they are debating the question.

"He's a re-tard," another girl says to her mother. "I saw him here one other time. He bites."

Roland appears to be totally absorbed now in his butter churning. Claire takes the girl who has called Roland a retard aside. "I know you didn't mean to hurt his feelings," she says. "But if you call him that, you will."

The girl's mother shakes her head. "If you don't mind my saying so," she tells Claire, "I don't think it's right to let kids like him in here with normal kids. He could hurt someone."

"This room is supervised at all times," Claire says. "Many children act inappropriately now and then. We're here to make sure that everybody treats each other with respect and consideration."

"Well, I'm just saying you'd probably do a lot better with this place if you didn't let the retards in," the mother says. "Next time maybe we'll go bowling."

"I'm sorry you feel that way," says Claire. Right now she wishes she could just go sit in the Parent Resource corner herself for an hour or two. Make that a month.

Roland has begun to emit his high-pitched wail again. Only this time it sounds joyful. When Claire goes over to him, she sees his churn is filled with butter.

"Look what you made, Roland," she says, putting her arms around him. Roland is practically singing now, he's so excited. "Butter," she tells him. "You made butter. And all by yourself, too."

She breaks a piece of bread off the loaf that is sitting on the trestle table and spreads Roland's butter on it with a round, dull knife. Roland puts his face down on the bread and begins to chew. Now he has buried his face in her skirt.

She wraps her arms around his head and holds him like that for a couple of minutes, thinking how long it has been since anybody kissed her. Even her own children.

Over in another corner of the Pioneer Room, Tim and Ursula have been pretending that Ursula is Laura Ingalls, heading out to get a doctor for her mother, who is about to have a baby. Tim is Charles Ingalls, her father, racked by grief and fear for what will become of them all if his wife dies and leaves him with four motherless children, not to mention the new baby and their horse, Star, who is also about to give birth. Outside, a blizzard has left snow so deep it comes almost to Laura's waist. But what can Charles do? Somebody has to get the doctor or his wife will die.

"Don't worry, Pa," Ursula/Laura tells him. "I can make it to Doctor Baker's. I won't let Ma die."

"Be sure to carry your lantern, Laura," Tim/Charles tells her. But the truth is, his attention has wandered from their game. He has been watching this woman in a long pioneer outfit, sitting at the butter churn with a boy who appears to have some kind of mental problem. There's something about her that makes it difficult for him to concentrate on what his daughter is saying.

"But, Pa," Ursula/Laura says. "We have no wood left for the stove. How can we keep Ma and Baby Brother warm while I'm gone searching for Doctor Baker? We may have to burn my doll."

"Okay," he says. The woman is holding the boy and rocking him very gently now. She is whispering something in the boy's ear. Tim wishes he could hear what she says. Her long skirt covers her hips and legs, but he can tell she's got a long, lean body, although her breasts are surprisingly round and full, in that bodice-fitting white blouse she's wearing.

"No, Dad," says Ursula, impatient. "That's not what you're supposed to say. You're supposed to say you'll burn your favorite rocking chair, that your father gave you right before the ox stepped on him. Then you're supposed to wrap me in these furs and send me out in the night to get the doctor. And you don't know there's a raccoon right outside the door that has rabies."

Tim has long since stopped trying to follow this. He is mesmerized by the woman. There is a way she tilts her head as the boy nuzzles up against her that seems so wonderfully tender. She is spreading butter on a piece of bread for him now. She gets a little on her fingers and licks it off.

Over by the butter churn, the woman in the pioneer outfit is stroking the head of the boy, who seems to be singing. Tim has to find out who she is.

Ursula/Laura has found a baby doll someplace, which she has wrapped in a pillowcase and brought to him. "Here you are, Pa. My new baby brother. But I have very sad news to tell you. Ma died."

"Good," says Tim/Charles.

Ursula moans. "That's not what you'd say, Dad. Don't you get it? You'd be sad. Your heart would be broken."

The boy is kissing her wildly on the mouth. Watching him, with his thick glasses and his funny black work boots, Tim feels this crazy jealousy. I want her, he thinks. He imagines what it might be like to kiss her himself. To touch that neck.

"I give up," Ursula tells him. "You're no fun to play with. I'm going to check out the rooms downstairs." She sets down the baby doll and heads down the stairs.

So Tim is alone now. Amazingly enough, so is the woman. The strange boy in the thick glasses has also disappeared, carrying his butter-slathered piece of bread. This is Tim's chance.

"You dress like this all the time, or do you work here?" Tim asks her.

"Oh," she says, putting an odd-looking cap back on her short, boyishly cut head of thick brown hair. "I'm the director here. Big deal, right? Staff of one and a half."

"You've done a great job," he says. "My daughter loves it here. We just finished reading *Little House in the Big Woods*. I'm divorced."

She laughs.

"You think that's funny?" he says. "I'd say you've got a weird sense of humor."

"Not a bit," she says. "Believe me, I know firsthand. My name's Claire."

She's divorced too. He feels his heart lift. "Tim," he says, offering his large hand. With no further deliberation he asks her if she'd like to have dinner with him. Tonight for instance.

For a moment she just looks at him with a puzzled expression.

"Believe me, I'm not some nut who goes around picking up women in children's museums," he says. "I'm not some butter churn fetishist or anything."

"I have kids—" she says.

"Me too," he says. "Kid, I mean. One. Seven. I mean one kid, seven years old. She's in your Mineral Room at the moment most likely. She has this thing about pyrite."

"It's not like mine need sitters anymore," she says. "I just don't go out that much."

"Me, I'm out playing pool and carousing with loose women every night," he says.

She finally smiles. She has a gap between her front teeth. He imagines what it would feel like to place his hand at the back of that long neck of hers.

"I won't be finished here till six or six-thirty," she says. "I guess I could call my children and tell them to order a pizza for themselves tonight."

"I'll get a sitter for mine," he says. "Pick you up here?"

Pete is on the phone with Jared when his mother calls to say she won't be home for dinner. "Hold on a sec, will you, Mom?" he says. "I've got someone on the other line." It's Jared, recounting the plot of the new Christopher Pike novel, *Bury Me Deep*.

"Guess what?" he tells Jared. "My mom's not coming home for a while. Why don't you bring over your dad's *Playboy Playmates* video and that pack of Red Man?" The two of them have taken up chewing tobacco in secret lately.

"So I was thinking you and your sister could send out for a pizza," his mother tells him. "Unless you need me, of course."

"I'll be fine," he says. Sally isn't home. Since Travis got his license, the two of them are off driving all the time.

"You can rent a video if you want," she says. "There's money on my dresser." This must mean she's going out on a date. Otherwise she wouldn't feel so guilty.

"You haven't seen *Free Willy* yet, have you?" she says. "That's supposed to be terrific." His mom is always trying to get him to watch these wholesome, family-type movies.

"Good idea, Mom," he says. He and Jared have watched the Playmate video three or four times already, but they're usually so worried about one of their parents walking in on them they just fast-forward to Miss September. They haven't ever had a chance to see the whole thing straight through.

"Can I talk to Sally?" his mother asks.

He tells her she's out. She and Travis probably drove over to the post office to buy a stamp. They won't be heard from for hours.

"Well, at least I've still got my boy," she says. "For a few more years anyway, right, honey? I'll be home before bedtime," she tells him.

Over Spanish omelettes at the Two Brothers Diner, Tim tells Claire he's a biologist, teaching at the college and working on a book about the effect of fluctuating saline levels in estuaries on the mussel population. He has full custody of his daughter; she's with him nearly all the time, except on the rare occasions when his parents take her, but they live in Ohio and they don't have a lot of patience with kids anymore. Claire tells him her kids go to their father's almost every weekend, but that isn't always easy, either.

"The pickup times are hard," she says, "but going to get them Sundays at our old house is the worst. They're always in a weird mood when I pick them up—grouchy and hypercritical. On the drive home they always seem to need to find fault with me for a million little things. It's as if they've swallowed some kind of toxic substance and they have to vomit up all this bile before they can be okay again."

Tim tells Claire about what it was like with Joan, and over the year since he's been on his own with Ursula. "I can handle the laundry and the cooking and my job at the college and all that," he says. "The part that gets to me is no matter what I do, I can't be a mother for my little girl. And she never stops wanting one."

A couple months back, he says, Joan called Ursula at seven o'clock on a Sunday night—the first time they'd heard from her in half a year. Since then, Ursula won't go anyplace on a Sunday night, even though that's when they show free movies at the library. She and Tim used to go every week and walk over to Friendly's for ice creams afterward.

"Now they could be giving away Barbies down at Wal-Mart and it wouldn't matter, if it was a Sunday night," he tells Claire. "Ursula would have to stay in that chair of hers next to the phone. 'I think this is the night, for sure, Dad,' she says. 'Any minute now she's going to call.' Only she doesn't. Usually I just let Ursula stay there in the chair until she falls asleep. Then I carry her up to bed and she doesn't talk about Joan again until the next Sunday."

Long after Claire and Tim have finished their omelettes they're still sitting in the restaurant. She's surprised to hear herself telling him about that last terrible winter of her marriage, when she seemed to have lost the ability to sleep. She might lie down for a couple of hours in the bed she shared with Sam, listening to him snoring at the far end, and sometimes she'd cry in this soundless way she had. Sometimes he'd wake up complaining that her crying was making the mattress shake. "Take the boohooing someplace else would you babe?" he'd tell her. "If I don't get some sleep, I'll be no good on the job tomorrow."

So she'd get up. She might do a load of laundry or bake bread. She alphabetized the spices and polished the silverware. Sometimes she'd creep into her children's rooms and sit there on the floor sorting Legos into bins according to colors or lining up Pete's Matchbox cars on the shelf.

Three o'clock, maybe four, she'd feel bone-weary, but she knew if she went back to bed with Sam, it would start all over again: She'd reach for him. He'd push her away. She'd cry. The bed would shake. He'd tell her to take it someplace else. So this time she'd go lie down in one of her children's narrow single beds, under Pete's He-Man quilt or Sally's with the ballerinas. Then finally she could sleep.

Years later, when Sam decided to fight for custody, this was one of the things he told in court as evidence that she's an unfit mother. "I never had any evidence that she, you know, touched them inappropriately," he told the Marital Master. "But you have to wonder. The state she was in, there was no telling."

There on the stand, in the same blue blazer he wore on their wedding day, Sam recounted the story of the time she had stood in the bathroom holding a pair of scissors to one of her braids. "What can I say?" he told the judge, shaking his head regretfully. "She was hysterical."

"And what did she do then, Sam?" his lawyer had asked him. A woman.

"She said she was going to cut off her hair if I didn't talk to her," he answered. "It was very frightening to the children, but I tried to put their minds at ease. I told them, 'Mommy was just having one of those days.'"

"I have primary custody of the children now," Claire tells Tim. She also explains that she has never got over the feeling that was left with her from the experience of going to court, that she is always being watched and judged as a mother. She can't ever afford to let her guard down. She has to be perfect or it could all happen again.

Claire doesn't weep, telling Tim about her marriage and divorce, but Tim's eyes become moist as he listens. Though she knows there are people—Sam for instance—who would look with disdain at a grown man sitting across from her in the diner brushing the tears from his eyes with his napkin, for Claire there's something wonderfully comforting and tender about him.

"He's very big," she will tell *Mickey tomorrow when she calls him. "He looks like he just came in off the football field."* But there is also something almost feminine about him. Once she had supposed there was safety in attaching herself to a strong, tough-seeming man. Now she knows there's more safety in softness.

. . .

"Partly I hate your husband for doing these things," Tim says. "But I also feel sorry for him, that he has to live the rest of his life knowing he's lost you."

"If he had ever treasured me that way he wouldn't have lost me in the first place," she tells him. "That was the point."

"How could he let you go?" Tim says. "If it was me that had had you and lost you, I don't think I'd ever get over it."

Up until this moment Tim hasn't touched her. Mostly because if he started he could never stop. He hasn't taken his eyes off her though. He has missed nothing. Not the way she runs her hand over her eyebrows sometimes as if she were smoothing a sheet, or the way she runs her fingers down her neck as she talks about this man, Mickey, she tells him about—as if she's feeling his touch at that moment in just that spot. He loves her Hopalong Cassidy watch and the surprising heartiness of her laughter. He notices a small scar under her chin and knows he will ask her about it later. He sees that she has a few gray hairs, and when she looks up to see the Special Coffee of the Day he can tell from the very slight narrowing of her eyes that she must be nearsighted. Some dentists would probably tell her to fix that gap between her front teeth, but he would like to put his tongue there. There, and on her neck, and in her ear, and all over her.

Partly he knows it's the way she looks that has such an effect on him, but it's something else, too. Although she has told him she'll be forty on her next birthday, there is this startlingly playful, girlish quality about her. But there is this other thing about Claire: It's so clear to Tim what a good mother she is, and he loves that. Same thing Mickey hated about her.

She's stroking the handle on her mug and looking into the bottom of it as if there were tea leaves with a message there. "I can't believe we've been here three and a half hours," she says. "My children will think I've been murdered and thrown in the basement of some madman. Either that or they will have rented a video."

Mine will be in bed, he knows. It's been over a year since he's hired a sitter for his daughter, and until now the thought of her hasn't crossed his mind all evening. Ursula. For a moment there it was as if he'd forgotten her name.

He reaches his hand across the table and touches her palm. Just that.

"I could look at you for a long time," he says.

O n the steps to the museum where he drops her off, because this is where her car is parked, he tells Claire he wants her to write a letter. It turns out they both have fax machines. Claire's is in the little attic office she's set up at home for her fund-raising work and grant proposals.

"Sometimes it's easier for me to say what I'm really thinking on paper," he says. "Talk is cheap."

To Claire—who has been spending at least an hour a day on the telephone with a man she's still in love with, who lives a hundred and twenty miles away, that she hasn't seen in over three years—this is not necessarily so. Although it occurs to her that in all the years she has been talking with Mickey, missing Mickey, aching over losing Mickey, the only piece of mail she's ever gotten from him was the form letter he keeps on his computer to send to the women who answer his ad in the personals.

So the idea of a man who lives only a few blocks from her but wishes to have a correspondence with her has a nice old-fashioned feeling to it. She gives him her fax number. For a second there, she's sure he's going to kiss her, but he just takes her hand and holds it for a moment. Then he leaves.

W here were you?" her son asks her when she comes in, a little after ten. Pete's sitting at the computer playing Flight Simulator with Jared, who is evidently sleeping over. They're piloting an F-15 over Paris. The Eiffel Tower whizzes below in a blur.

"I had dinner with a friend," she tells him.

"Nancy called," he says. "Also, Dad wants to know if he can take us out Thursday night instead of Wednesday."

"Fine," she says. She's thinking about that moment in the restaurant as she was telling Tim something Sam had said to her once, when it looked as if Tim had tears in his eyes.

"Of course I'm not 'in love' with you," Sam told her one time. "Being in love is for teenagers and country music. We're married, for Christ's sake. We have kids."

Claire is thinking about those big hands of Tim's, and what they would feel like in her hair. She has never made love with such a big man. She wonders if he would crush her, knock the wind out of her, rip her skin.

"The garage door opener's jammed again," Pete's telling her. "I had to bring my bike in the back door. Plus there's something funny with the toilet. It keeps making this gurgling noise."

He has a little girl. A motherless child. And who is Claire if not a mother? She is other things besides that, too, she knows now—better than she used to. But there is also this place in her that will always want to bend over other women's carriages and pick their babies up, take other women's troubled sons on her lap and help them churn butter. She thinks about the story Tim told her tonight, of how Ursula sits by the phone Sunday nights, and of the question Tim says she keeps asking him: What did I do bad to make my mother stop loving me?

Claire hasn't laid eyes on this child, and already she wants to wrap her arms around her. Her and her father, both.

Early the next morning Tim faxes Claire a poem about estuaries. Estuaries and her neck. "I didn't want to say good-bye to you last night," he writes. "After you left I just sat there in the parking lot of the children's museum, thanking God that I met you."

Imagine Mickey saying something like that, Mickey thanking God. Mickey, who won't even let Gabe sign up for Cub Scouts because of that line in the pledge about doing your duty to God and your country. Mickey, whose religion is Miles Davis and the American League. Usually when she compares some man she's met with Mickey, the new man looks like a pale, flat stranger. This time, imagining the two of them side by side, Claire actually smiles.

She faxes Tim a drawing of herself fixing pancakes for Pete and Jared, who have taken off on their bikes now, happy that the snow has finally melted enough that they can get out exploring again. Sally won't be up for hours. *"Thank God I've still got one child who leads a wholesome, active life,"* Claire writes. *"All my daughter does these days is sleep, watch snowboarding videos with her boyfriend, and ask me to take her for driving practice."*

"I can't imagine what it must be like to see your daughter driving a car," he writes back. *"Mine's just learning to ride a bike."* At the bottom of the page he has made a drawing of a man standing next to a bicycle. There is a little girl wearing a helmet on the bicycle, and a balloon coming out of her mouth with the words "There's nothing to riding a two-wheeler, Dad." The man is doubled over as he holds the bicycle, pushing her along. Buckets of sweat pour off him.

"After I take Ursula out on her bike this afternoon, I'm dropping her off at T-ball practice," he writes. *"So how about coffee?"*

Claire could just pick up the phone to answer him, but she doesn't. She faxes back a picture of herself—same bathrobe—tossing the pancakes into the air as she answers, *"Yes. Yes. Yes. Yes."*

Tim stands over his machine watching as her fax scrolls out. His daughter is calling to him for another bowl of cereal but he doesn't go right away as he usually would. He can't leave his desk until he's seen her fax.

There's nothing glamorous about the cartoony way Claire has drawn herself in this picture. She's wearing a ratty-looking bathrobe and her breasts seem to droop exaggeratedly underneath it. Tim remembers these breasts well from yesterday and they looked beautiful to him.

In the picture Claire's short mop of hair is sticking up in tufts around her small thin face. There are bags under her eyes and though when he saw her he guesses she must have been wearing contact lenses, in her drawing she's wearing glasses. In one hand she holds a spatula and in the other a bowl of pancake batter. All around her are broken egg shells, sticks of butter, maple syrup tipped over sideways and dripping on the floor. Even the flowers in the vase she has drawn, sitting on the counter, are drooping. Her kitchen is a mess.

But she's wearing earrings. She has also given herself a heart-shaped locket in this cartoon. Her eyes, in the picture, are looking skyward, as if she's just caught sight of a bird out the window.

He thinks about all the song lyrics he's ever heard and how inadequate they are. He sits at his computer wishing he could play it for her like the most beautiful guitar she's ever heard. *Mark Knopfler. Ray Phiri. Gerry Scott-Moore. Chet Atkins. Django Reinhardt.*

In the same way that he would love to touch her all over, he would love to pour all sorts of words over her. He would like to tell her that he wants to touch her like the map of a place he's never been. He wants to say that from the moment he laid eyes on her, he knew as he has never known about any other woman that he would never run out of things he wanted to tell her or questions he wanted to ask. That he suspects the day isn't long enough to finish loving her. He would like to tell her that he knows, looking at her thirty-nine-year-old face and her thirty-nine-year-old body, that he would still love her seventy-five-year-old face and whatever body it is that will come with it—and given the chance, and God help him, the strength, he would still want to be making love to her then too, the way he does right now.

In the next room, Ursula is calling to him, more insistently this time. *"Daddy,"* she says. "I told you, *cereal.*"

"Coming, Urs," he says, but he doesn't move.

What is there to say to her that's substantial enough for how he feels without scaring her away?

"I have no destination in my mind but loving you."

"I want to be the end of your search."

"Let me be the next exit you've been looking for, the crack in old plaster that comes from nowhere and goes all the way across the room,

the sound the constellations make wheeling across the sky unseen in the middle of the day, a phone call you've been waiting for, a song you like and haven't heard in a while, coming on the radio. Let me love you like the weight of a lawn upon the ground beneath it, the movement of water down a slick rock in some quiet place you've always wanted to be."

Maybe I'm getting in over my head, he thinks. Very likely so. *But I would rather drown in your pool than swim in anybody else's. My skin is turned inside out, and if you send me away and I never see you again, I know it will burn like acid through me, and still I have no regrets, because I could not feel as full of possibilities of extraordinary things as I do right now if I didn't also know I have never been in more danger of more pain.*

"You are the best woman I've come across," he writes. *"You make me want to be a better man than I have ever been."*

"I want to be a bench for you to rest on. I want to be your air."

Pete has headed out early this morning to get to the ball field, where a couple of kids he knows—Ben and Will—have got together for some batting practice. He needs someone to catch him while he works on his pitching. Baseball tryouts are this week, and Pete is hoping for the starting pitcher position on his favorite team, the Cubs. Last winter he leaned an old mattress against a wall in their basement so he could practice his aim. He got to the point where he could hit the strike zone eight out of ten pitches, and most of those were right on the **X**.

Lately, though, he'll get into his motion and he'll be just at the point of releasing the ball when this little picture zaps into his head. Sometimes it's a picture of himself doing something really dumb like peeing the bed. Sometimes he sees his father standing on the steps of their house telling his mom, "There you go again, Claire, making a mountain out of a molehill." Sometimes it's his mother's voice on the phone late at night whispering things he can't hear, or things he can hear that he wishes he couldn't, or his sister and Travis, up in her room when nobody else is home and he isn't supposed to know, breathing heavily. It's not even pictures exactly that flash across his brain. It's more like the split second that sometimes occurs on the computer, when it's booting up and the screen goes dark for a moment, or what happens when you're switching gears on your ten-speed and for just an instant there the chain isn't engaged yet. The picture that zaps into his brain only stays there for a hundredth of a second most likely. Just long enough to screw up his pitch.

"Don't sweat it, Temple," Ben tells him. "You're lots better than old Bobby Arnold or any of those others. You're sure to get the top pitching slot."

Pete doesn't say anything. He doesn't dare tell them how much he wants it.

Vivian, the chairperson of the children's museum board, has stopped by Claire's house this morning with a plate of extra appetizers from yesterday's opening. "We had a lot of these left over," she says, handing Claire a tray of biscuits. "My kids are so particular they won't eat anything that isn't fresh that day, but I thought you could use them."

Claire and Vivian are not exactly friends, although they talk almost every day. Claire's original proposal for the new exhibit was a room dedicated to Tibet, actually, but the board shot her down on the grounds that nobody in Blue Hills really cared about Tibet. "They have one of the oldest and richest cultures on the globe," Claire had said. "And it's being wiped out. They have this very beautiful religion, all built around the yak. You should see the craftsmanship of some of these Tibetans." At the time, Claire had just seen a documentary about Tibet that had moved her to tears. Shortly after that she traveled to New York City to hear the Dalai Lama. Even though she was way at the back of the crowd, there was this amazing feeling of peace in the place. She didn't manage to get any of this across to the board when she had presented the idea. They voted in favor of the pioneer idea instead. Even with the more crowd-pleasing theme for this year's new exhibit, however, they're way behind in meeting their fund-raising goal.

Now Claire figures Vivian must have some other reason for stopping by besides delivering a few day-old biscuits. "So," Claire asks Vivian, "how did you think the opening went?"

"That sampler activity was cute," says Vivian. Some people are concerned, though, she tells Claire, that they aren't doing more with computers at the museum. "At this party Joe and I went to the other night, Harry Simons from the bank was saying the first question they always ask whenever he's approached about corporate contributions is whether the organization's online, technologically speaking."

"I don't know, Vivian," says Claire. "It seems the whole point of the pioneer exhibit is to give children a taste of a simpler life. If you ask me, they've already got way too much technology in their lives."

"I'm just telling you what I heard, Claire," says Vivian. "It's your job, not mine."

Claire turns her wrist slightly so she can catch sight of her watch. She's meeting Tim at two, and she wants to take Sally driving and change first.

"So who was the man you were talking with yesterday?" Vivian asks her. Nothing gets past this woman. "Veronica said it seemed like he couldn't seem to keep his eyes off you all afternoon."

"It was the hat, probably," says Claire. "His name is Tim. He's just a friend."

"The friends we need to concentrate on right now are the ones with deep pockets," says Vivian. "Times like these, in the world of nonprofit fund-raising, a person in your position needs to spend all her professional time drumming up the big bucks. Or you may not have a position. I don't mean that as a threat or anything. It's just how things are. A friendly word of warning, you might say."

"Did you get a chance to try the butter churn?" Claire says to her. "You should, one of these days. I was a little worried about whether kids could stick with it long enough to get results. But it worked like a dream."

"That's great, Claire. Really," says Vivian. "Just don't lose sight of the big picture here. Bottom line: no money, no museum, no job."

Next time my mother calls me up, I'm going to tell her I can ride a bike now," says Ursula, sitting upright on the seat of her new two-wheeler with her helmet on while her father runs behind her, pushing. Tim has taken her to a parking lot out behind the elementary school so she can practice her riding. He hasn't removed the training wheels yet, but he's lifted them up a ways. He bends over low to steady her as she pedals—hands gripped tight to the back of her bicycle frame. Tim is a very large and strong man, but still, this is hard work. His back will be sore tonight.

"I'll give you one of my special back rubs when we get home," Ursula tells him. It's not uncommon for her to read his mind this way. "I know how hard it is for you to push me."

In fact, Tim has been pushing Ursula for a long time now. Not just on her bicycle and her tricycle, but on her *Little Mermaid* scoot-along before that, and before that, on her *Ride 'Em My Little Pony*. For eight years Tim has been pushing his daughter on swings, pushing her in the cart at the supermarket, pulling her on her wagon, guiding her along on her double-runner skates and her roller skates (also *Little Mermaid*) and her Tiny-Tot skis. Even when she was in a stroller it was always Tim who pushed Ursula along.

One time Joan had come upon him taking an infant Ursula out for a walk. She burst out laughing. She was on the way home from the art studio she had rented after Ursula was born, so she could concentrate someplace quiet. Tim didn't know it at the time, but she had already embarked on her affair with Frederick, the chain-smoking poet.

"I can't help it, you just look so silly," she said. "A big old jock like you with a Snugli fastened on your chest. I should get you a piece of ribbon so you could wear a pacifier around your neck at all times. To complete the look."

Ursula's a lot bigger now, of course. Big enough that Tim has to ask her to stop pedaling for a second so he can catch his breath.

"You silly old daddy," she says. "You can't keep up with me anymore, I ride so fast."

Tim is thinking about Claire, and how he will see her again in just two hours. Today he will kiss her.

"I'm going to get some streamers for my bike, okay, Dad?" says Ursula. "And those little beads the big girls have on their bikes that you put on the metal wires around the tires. And a bell so I can warn people to get out of the way when I'm coming, because I go so fast."

"We'll do that," he tells her. *We'll go someplace dark and cool, in the woods, and I'll spread out a blanket and lean over her and she'll press her body against my chest and wrap her legs around me and we'll lie there for a very long time like that, with our tongues exploring each other's skin.*

"Okay, Dad," she says now. "You've rested long enough. I want to ride some more."

He takes his position again, bent almost double, like an old man. Ursula doesn't pedal fast enough yet to keep the bike up by herself, but Tim would never let her fall.

"Now when my mom comes to see me, we can go bike riding together," she says. "Just us girls."

"I bet you will," he says.

"And she'll be able to keep up with me, too," says Ursula. "Not like my silly old daddy."

"I hope so," he says, panting. "You're fast as the wind."

"I'm like Elliot in *E.T.*," she says. "If I wanted to, I could just fly up into the sky and ride away over the tops of the houses and you'd never see me again. And you'd miss me so badly you'd never get over it. Because I'm your favorite girl in the world."

Travis and Sally are driving. There is no place in particular they're driving to, they are just driving. Travis doesn't have a cassette player in his 1982 Chevrolet Impala, but they have put batteries in Sally's cassette player so they can listen to music while they drive. At the moment it's Nine Inch Nails.

The cassette player is on Sally's lap. Travis's hand is in the same vicinity, only instead of resting on top of her skirt, it's underneath.

He fingers the lace on her bikini panties. He has not yet attempted to place his hand inside them, but he has been thinking about it a lot. This could be the day.

"I saw Edie at Taco Bell last night," he tells her. Edie is this girl in their history class that likes him.

"She is such a slut," says Sally. "She'd screw a tree."

"Yeah, well, she has her good points," he tells her. He is talking about sex, as they both understand. Edie started going all the way in fifth grade.

"Sounds like you'd like to go out with her," says Sally coolly.

"I didn't mean that," he says. They are on a dirt road, and he has pulled the car over now.

"All in all," says Sally, "I can't imagine why you'd be with me, considering how many good points Edie has. Although let me tell you from personal experience, since I was in gym class with her, she stuffs toilet paper in her bra."

"I'm with you because I think you're cool, and I like talking with you and stuff, and we have fun driving around," he says. "Only you don't know what it's like for a guy. It gets hard."

She laughs. "I noticed," she says.

He doesn't laugh back. "It's a real problem," he says. "Sometimes when I leave your house I think my balls are going to explode, I'm so hot for you."

He is still driving, keeping his eyes on the road. They pass an old Subaru wagon pulled over under a clump of pine trees, the silhouette of two people necking in the front seat. "Way to go, buddy," Travis mutters. "Those people have the right idea," he says to Sally.

She ejects Nine Inch Nails and puts in Tori Amos—a cassette Travis calls her Sensitive Female Music.

"You know how I feel about you Sally," he says. He slides a single finger under the elastic of her panties. She doesn't stop him, though he can feel her drawing in her breath.

"It's a big deal to me, Trav," she tells him. "I'm not sure I'm ready."

"It's a big deal to me, too," he says. "I think about it all the time. Every single minute."

"I don't like to feel pressured," she tells him.

"I don't want to pressure you, either," he says. Two fingers. One stroking her soft blond hair. One inside her.

"I love you," he says. "I love you so much. To me you're the most beautiful girl in the world."

She is no longer saying anything, but she doesn't stop him, either. If you asked her right now whether she felt good or not, she couldn't tell you.

Claire sits in a late-model Subaru station wagon with a My Little Pony hanging from the rearview mirror and a bunch of old Happy Meal boxes on the floor. Also a placemat from Friendly's that someone—Tim's daughter, Ursula, no doubt—has colored in, careful to stay in the lines. But Ursula isn't here; she's at her T-ball practice. The two of them are driving nowhere in particular, but in the general direction of a pond he sometimes takes his students to do fieldwork, where he knows of a wonderful bed of moss.

He has put a Van Morrison cassette that Claire also owns in the machine. In a moment, she knows, they will get to the part where Van starts moaning as if he were making love.

"I can't believe I feel so nervous and shy," he says. "At my age. I feel like a kid."

She doesn't laugh. "It never gets easy," she says. "I know that."

"Sometimes it's easier than this," he says. "It's easier when you care less. But with you, I just want to do everything right."

"Don't worry so much," she says. "We could be friends, okay?"

"I would like that," he says. "But I have to be honest. I would also like more than that. I couldn't stop thinking about you last night."

"You probably just had some questions about pioneers, right?" she says.

"Making my daughter's lunch today, I couldn't even focus on what she was saying," he tells her. "I was reading her *Beezus and Ramona* last night and I couldn't even follow the story. Which wasn't that complicated, believe me."

"I know," she says. "I practically have that one memorized."

"I'm not usually like this," he tells her. "I actually made a decision after the last relationship I was in that I was just going to focus on my daughter until it felt like she didn't need me so much."

"I've had the same general idea," Claire says. "It doesn't always work so well, does it?"

"I thought I was doing all right," he says. "I wasn't even thinking about finding a woman. I just saw you and it was like somebody shot a thousand volts of current through me."

"I don't know if I have anything to offer you, Tim," she says. "It feels like every ounce of me is spoken for. With my job and my kids and everything. Even though mine are older than yours, it's still just about all I can manage sometimes, giving them what they need."

He pulls the car over and turns it off. He takes her hand. "Maybe if you didn't have to do it all by yourself it would be easier," he says. "Did that ever occur to you?"

"Sure," she says. "In my fantasies. It's just the logistics that are hard to figure."

"Could be you figure too hard," he says. "You might just have to let go and let your life happen." He bends over her and kisses her very hard on the lips.

She kisses him back. She also puts her arms around him tightly and presses her chest against his. Her body is shaking.

"I can't," she tells him. "I have to be a mother."

"Of course you do," he says. "What else should you be?" It is at just this point, as he is pressing his tongue into her mouth, that a car goes by she thinks she recognizes. A fragment of very loud music drifts in the window like the smell from a neighbor's barbecue caught on the wind. Then it fades away and they're alone again on the dirt road, so still and quiet this could be the day after a nuclear holocaust, and they could be the last two inhabitants on the planet.

Tonight Tim has cooked eggplant parmigiana for himself and his daughter, with Caesar salad, garlic bread, and asparagus tips in lemon butter. For dessert he's baked double fudge brownies, which they will have with whipped cream and chocolate sauce while he and Ursula watch "Rescue 911." He can't make a meal like this every night, but he tries to as often as he can. If he could just make enough good food, maybe his daughter might be satisfied and content in ways he knows she is not. He understands it doesn't really work that way, but he puts so much love into his cooking, he has to believe some of it makes its way to her.

In the next room he can hear Ursula watching "The Price Is Right." "Take the dining-room set, you dummies!" she is calling out to the television screen. Jenny, their dog, barks.

"Too bad, folks," Bob Barker is saying. "Looks like you went over on this one. Tell us what we have for the Fergusons to take home with them, Johnny."

"I told you so," Ursula is saying. "I knew you were going too high."

"I knew they should've stuck with the dining-room set, Dad," she is calling out to him. "Now alls they got is a dumb exercise bike."

Tim is thinking about kissing Claire. He imagines how it would be if she was here right now, tossing the salad next to him maybe, while he lifts the asparagus from the steamer. He thinks about setting another place at their little card table. He imagines her next to him on one side, and his daughter on the other. Claire would slip her foot out of its shoe under the table and lay it in his lap as they ate. He would place his hand there and rub her toes, one at a time. Ursula would be telling them something about a show she'd watched that day or something her teacher said, but instead of the old lonely weariness, he would have Claire's foot to hold as he sat there listening. The two of them would exchange glances over the funny things his daughter says.

Later, clearing away the dishes while Ursula splashes in the tub, he would bend over her and kiss the back of her neck. She would be covering the eggplant parmigiana with aluminum foil while he sponged off the counter, and he would whisper in her ear, "Ten minutes till her bedtime."

He reads his daughter a bedtime story—a chapter of Greek mythology, tonight. He turns on her Raffi tape and switches on her nightlight.

"Don't forget to kiss Phillip too," she murmurs. He kisses her doll—an anatomically correct boy baby her mother sent her last Christmas. He sings Ursula her special song: "Hush, little baby, don't say a word."

"I love you, Daddy," she says, half asleep already as he tiptoes out of the room. Upstairs, he knows, Claire is already waiting for him, propped on pillows, reading a magazine with her glasses on. She's wearing a pair of his pajamas. She smells of bath oil and baby powder. The dishwasher hums, at the end of its cycle. His dog snores. He turns out the last of the downstairs lights. Claire has set down her magazine now, hearing his foot on the step.

He mounts the stairs with the anticipation of a weary traveler at the end of a long day's journey, pulling up to the watering hole at last—a Muslim arriving at long last at Mecca, a pioneer catching his first glimpse of the turquoise Pacific, Admiral Byrd planting his stake at the North Pole. He is exhausted, but still he burns for her. This is the way a person is supposed to end his day.

Claire is lying in bed when the fax line rings—five A.M. five-thirty maybe. She leaps out of bed and runs upstairs to her office. She would like to read his fax right away, but she doesn't. She rips it off the machine and stuffs it in her bathrobe pocket instead. Then she goes downstairs and makes her coffee. Only when all the water has dripped through does she let herself pour her mug and settle in to read what he has written. Nobody else is up at her house.

She reads his letter slowly to savor it. She pretends she is having her coffee with him, the way she has been having her coffee with Mickey these last three years. Only with Mickey there was no hopefulness and prospect; with Mickey, she could only look backward, never forward.

It's different with Tim: Tim is like an unopened present.

She supposes her children must have noticed that something's up. Sally has asked her why it is the fax line keeps ringing at such odd hours now. "Can't you tell them to send their grant information at a more reasonable time?" she tells her mother. "I'm trying to sleep." Upstairs in her office, Claire rips his letter off her machine. Three pages—the longest yet. She sighs as she settles into her chair to read it.

"I want to give you all sorts of good things," he writes. *"The first ladyslipper of spring. The arrowhead I found when I was eleven. I wish I could write you poems and paint you pictures. I wish I could stitch you a velvet cape. I want to grow you grapes and feed them to you. I am drunk with love of you."*

Ursula and her dad are snuggled up on her bed reading after her bath when he tells her about the woman. He has put mini marshmallows in their hot chocolate.

"So, I have some news," he says.

Her mother is coming from New Zealand—not to visit this time. To stay. She has dumped Elliot after he shaved off his beard and she discovered he didn't have any chin underneath. Her parents have realized they're still in love. They're going to move to Orlando, Florida, and get a kitten. She's going to have a baby sister.

"I've met somebody," he says. "A woman."

"So?" she says. She has to be careful here. She can tell.

"Her name is Claire," he says. "She's really nice. I think you'll like her."

Ursula feels like she's just got sucked inside their TV set. She's Crystal on "Live and Let Live" and he's Tucker, who has fallen in love with Natalie, the cocaine dealer. After they get married, and Natalie becomes Crystal's stepmother, the police arrest her, but her dad takes the rap for her and goes to prison. Then Natalie sends Crystal/ Ursula to boarding school and gives all her toys to her own kid, Brittany, who takes horseback-riding lessons.

"What's this got to do with me?" she says. She is looking at a mini marshmallow melting in her mug.

"We've been getting to know each other," he says. "We haven't spent a lot of time together yet because she's got kids too, and we're both so busy, but I think we're going to be seeing more of each other. I like her a whole lot."

"So now you want to ditch me?" says Ursula.

"You nut," he says. "You know I'd never leave you. I'm just going away for the weekend."

"What are you talking about?" she says. The room has begun to spin and she has this sick taste in her mouth like when you start to throw up but it doesn't come out all the way. Her father has gone out on a couple of dates before this, but that was just for a few hours. She was usually still awake when he got home. Her babysitter doesn't know how to sing their special song. Nobody else does.

"Claire invited me to come for a sleepover at her house," he says. "Sandy and Jeff said they'll take care of you." His downstairs neighbors. He has given them a big box of Ursula's old toys and clothes for their baby, Keith, and her car seat in return.

"You already had this all figured out!" she yells. "You didn't even ask me."

"I'm asking you now," he says. "I'm asking you how you feel about it."

"Bad," she says.

"I'm sorry to hear that," he says. "I thought you might want me to be happy."

"Why can't you be happy with me?" she says. "I thought we were going to work on my bike riding this weekend. I thought we were going to rent *House of Blood*."

"You can do that with Sandy and Jeff," he says. "You can do it with me, next weekend."

"Sure," she says. "Next weekend you'll probably go off and marry her."

Tim arrives at Claire's house at
eight o'clock on a Friday night with his old high-school gym bag
in his hands, along with a bouquet of supermarket daffodils. He
knows her children have gone to their father's for the weekend.

The fact that Claire evidently keeps her Christmas lights up
year round—and lit—seems appropriate.

"I haven't been able to think about anything else but you all
day," he tells her. "When Ursula woke up she said she felt hot. I
felt like a jerk, but all I could think of was, what if she came down
with something, and I couldn't be with you tonight?"

"She's all right?" Claire asks. She is wearing a long lacy dress
with some kind of leotard underneath and an apron one of her
children must have made for her, with a crayon picture of a
woman and a couple of kids on the front and the words "World's
Greatest Mom" in rainbow letters.

"She's fine," he tells her. "I'm the one that's burning up."

She brings him into her kitchen, where she has a soup on the
stove, and salad and French bread. She sets the daffodils in a vase.
Sting is singing "Fields of Gold." She pours him a beer and sets
their soup on the table. They sit and look at the food. Neither one
of them makes a move to eat.

"It looks great," he says, still not touching a thing.

"Vichyssoise," she says. Also motionless.

"So what's been happening at the museum?" he asks her.

"We just got a bequest of this old Lionel train setup," she says.
"Buildings, tunnels, bridges, a whole little world in miniature.
Now if I can just raise the money to build the addition we need to
house it."

"I always loved trains," he says. Silence again.

He has got up from his seat and come over behind her. He
kneels beside her chair and puts his arms around her, burying his
face in her lap. "I never wanted anybody the way I want you
now," he says.

"Well, then," she says. She takes his hand and leads him up the
stairs to her bedroom. He is dimly aware that she is lighting

candles, and that the room smells of something wonderful, jasmine maybe, but he can't take his eyes off Claire.

She sits on the edge of her bed. He undresses her very slowly. She can hear him draw in his breath as her blouse falls away. He touches one finger to the hollow at the base of her neck and traces it down the space between her breasts to her belly. She tightens her muscles slightly; even lean as she is now, she feels self-conscious about her stretch marks.

He shakes his head. "I love everything about you," he says. After that there are no words anymore, just his big arms, his broad back, his chest pressing against her, his cock, his tongue. His hands are trembling. His mouth is everywhere. He's like a child seeing snow for the first time, like an old prospector reaching into some stream for the ten millionth time to find a nugget the size of his fist. He's like a drowning man who has caught hold of a life rope at the last possible second. He will never have enough of her.

Tim and Claire don't get out of bed until Saturday afternoon, except to eat a couple of times and go to the bathroom. When the phone rings Claire lets the machine pick it up.

"I should call Ursula," he says. Then they start kissing again and he lets it go.

"I should call Ursula," he says a few hours later.

"Right," she tells him. Every part of her is sore.

"But I don't want to. I don't want to think about her now. Just you." Then they start in again, and the next time he thinks about his daughter it's ten o'clock. Way past her bedtime.

Sunday morning Claire finally plays her messages back. The first one is from Nancy. Something about a yoga class. Then a child's voice—deeper and more insistent than Claire had imagined, but of course she knows right away who it must be.

"Where are you?" the voice says. No hello. "Why haven't you called me?"

The next message is from Pete at his dad's, reminding her to feed his iguana. Then Ursula again.

"You poop face. You dope. Call me *now*."

Tim is standing next to her as she plays these back. "God," he says. "I've been terrible. I've got to call her right away."

"I hate you," the next message begins. "Don't bother calling. I never want to talk to you anymore anyways. You're the worst daddy in the world."

There are more, but he isn't waiting to listen to them. He's dialing.

Claire stands there a few inches away from him. Before this he had been kissing the back of her neck. Now he has stepped away like a dog who's been discovered peeing on the rug.

"Ursula?" he's saying. "It's Daddy, honey. I'm so sorry I didn't call you back sooner. I was out."

Claire shakes her head. She knows she should leave the room, but she's frozen to the spot. She has to hear this.

"That's not true," he's saying. "You know I do. I'm so sorry, sweetheart. I'll never let it happen again."

Claire has her head in her hands by this point. Tim doesn't seem to notice.

"No," he says. "I will, really. I'm bringing you a treat when I come home. Maybe we'll do something fun after school Monday, what do you think? Go out for a milkshake maybe, huh?"

Even with the receiver pressed against Tim's ear, Claire can make out the sound of Ursula's voice berating him. *"Never again,"* he's saying. *"I swear."*

Claire doesn't know what he says next. She has left the room.

When it's finally over and he hangs up the phone, he finds Claire in the kitchen washing dishes noisily.

"I can't believe you," she says. "One minute you're a big, strong, sane grown-up man, and the next thing I know your eight-year-old child has brought you to your knees. How could you let that happen?"

"You don't understand," he tells her. "All these years I've been the only person she's had. I never left her like this before. She didn't know how to handle it."

"That's no excuse for letting her treat you like that," Claire says. "Anyone would think she was the parent and you were the child. You're supposed to be the one in charge, remember?"

"She's just a kid, Claire," he says. He reaches out to touch her neck, but there's something almost guilty to his touch now.

"Exactly my point," she says.

"She told me she didn't think I loved her anymore. She said you were my favorite."

"Oh, great," says Claire. "So I'm in competition with an eight-year-old."

"There's no competition," he tells her.

"You get to have a life," she says, hearing Mickey's voice.

"I know," he says. "You've given it to me."

Because Sandy and Jeff kept Ursula overnight on Sunday and brought her to school straight from their apartment, Ursula doesn't see her dad again until she gets off the bus Monday afternoon. He's there waiting for her. This is the first unusual thing.

He has bought her a bag of Gummi worms. Another dead giveaway, in Ursula's opinion. What kind of an idiot does he think she is, anyway?

He gets down on his knees to hug her. He used to pick her up and whirl her over his head, but he doesn't do that anymore and Ursula knows why. She weighs seventy-nine pounds.

"I missed you so much," he says. *Liar.*

"Let's see your picture."

"It sucks."

"Hey, does not. This is a beauty, Urs. I love the way you made the clouds."

"You smell funny," she says.

"Here," he says to her. "Let me carry your backpack. Tell me about your day."

"So," she says. "Did you kiss her?"

"Yes I did," he tells her. "I care about Claire a lot. When people feel that way about each other, that's what they sometimes do."

"Like you used to kiss me?"

"I still kiss you," he says. "But different. One kind of kisses are the kind a dad gives his little girl, and you will always be my little girl. The other kind are the kisses a man gives a woman, and that's the kind of kisses I give Claire."

Blahblahblahblah. She puts her hands over her ears, but she can still hear him. She starts singing the Barney theme song. This used to be their personal joke, hers and her dad's. Because they both think Barney is such a jerk. Now he's probably told her all about it of course. The woman he kissed.

"Listen, Urs," he says. "You'll like her. If you give her a chance." He has a begging sound to his voice. She feels bigger than him. At that moment she knows she could squish him if she wanted to. He's the one who taught her, in karate, the most vulnerable part on a man. The balls.

"Do you like her as much as you used to like my mom?" she asks him.

"Yes," he tells her. "Yes I do. And she likes me a whole lot too. And she's very anxious to meet you. She asked me to give you this letter, in fact."

He takes a piece of paper out of his pocket. She can see a cartoony type drawing on it of a woman and a couple of kids. The thought of her having kids hadn't even occurred to Ursula until this moment. They will hate her. They'll think she's fat and they'll be right.

" 'Dear Ursula,' " he starts to read.

"Shutupshutupshutupshutup!" she yells, covering her ears again. She's singing the Barney song again, very loud this time.

"Ursula," he yells, grabbing her by the shoulders to keep her from spinning out into the road. "You've got to listen to me. I'm the parent here. I'm the one in charge."

The woman must have told him to say that. Either that or he read it in some book about how to raise kids.

"You'll like her, you'll see," he says. "Do you think I'd ever pick someone to be with that wasn't nice to little girls?"

"I'll hate her," she says. "And she'll hate me. And we'll all be miserable. Just wait and see."

Claire has never had a lover like Tim, who wanted even more than she did. It almost scared her about him when she discovered it, but it also thrills her. For as long as she can remember, she hasn't been able to get Mickey out of her bed. It's been close to three years since she laid eyes on the man and still, somebody else would touch her in a place that reminded her of a moment he touched her there, and she would see his face over her, plain as a hologram. "Baby," the lover would whisper as he collapsed onto the pillow beside her, and she turned her face and wept quietly. Her lover would think this was just the aftereffects of an orgasm, but it was always Mickey.

With Tim it's different. His hunger for her is so vast, his energy so explosive, he seems to drown out the old waves of sadness that have become as much a part of having sex for her as kissing. Thinking about Mickey while Tim is making love to her would be like trying to keep some gentle Irish tune in your head at a Rolling Stones concert. She loves the wildness of him, and the bigness: It takes her breath away.

The other thing about Tim is the bigness of his love for her, which might alarm someone who hadn't experienced big love herself. Last weekend, their second together, she woke up in the middle of the night and found him just lying there studying her the way she used to study Mickey as he slept. "I can't believe I have you," he said. "I don't want to miss a moment of you."

Just watching her undress—or watching her dress again, which is harder for him—Tim looked as if he might cry. "What's the matter?" she asked him.

"I can't help it," he said. "I just love you so much."

"Nobody will ever love you the way I did," Mickey had said to her.

"You're wrong," she tells Mickey now, in her head, as Tim lowers himself over her, stroking her leg as if he'd never felt skin before.

 SUMMER

Tim doesn't know what to do. He has to be with her. Once he's known the feel of kissing her, of being inside her and having her legs wrapped around his back, he can't bear to be away from her anymore. He has to be, of course. He has used up nearly all the money from his grant, and he's only teaching one class this summer, which cuts his income down by two-thirds. If he can't get his new grant proposal finished and approved, he'll run out of money by the end of the summer. As it is, he's had to take out a loan to send Ursula to day camp once school gets out. She doesn't want to go, but he knows if she stays home he won't get any work done. Tim's having a hard enough time keeping his concentration.

He would want to spend every minute of his day with Claire if there weren't kids involved. He would build a post and beam house for her, for the two of them, somewhere in the mountains, near the sound of running water. He would want to make them a home. Because he knows he would never get tired of looking at her. Or touching her. *"You are the only woman I have ever known who just flat-out deserves to be loved round the clock," he says.* Just making his bed, all he can think of is this: her in it.

Mickey was every inch the bachelor lover, a man with four kinds of jalapeño peppers in his refrigerator and not much else, and ticket stubs from six different jazz clubs in his pockets, a man whose address book is filled with almost nothing but women's names, jazz clubs and take-out food places, a man with stereo speakers in every room of his house, including the shower.

It's different with Tim. Tim seduces Claire with his tender domesticity. There's something almost unbearably touching to her in the picture of him struggling with French braids and the microscopic hooks and eyes on a Barbie flight attendant's uniform. He clips coupons and shops for tofu and makes his chicken stock from scratch. He watches Monday-night football and keeps a basketball in his car at all times, along with the needle to inflate it in case the air is getting low. He also wonders why his daughter's T-shirts emerge from the dryer a dingy shade of gray.

"Call me a madman," he writes to her, "but I'm simply the kind of guy who actually loves kids' Christmas concerts and putting on storm windows. I enjoyed changing Ursula's diapers—sick, huh? I want to go with you to get the car inspected. I want to grind the beans for your coffee and bring it to you in bed." What he is, at his core, is a family man.

An envelope arrives from him. By regular mail this time. Inside is a colored museum postcard of a Chagall painting called *L'Anniversaire*. It's a painting of a man and a woman in a room. The woman is holding flowers. There's a meal on the table, and a sort of flowered spread on the bed. The man is kissing the woman. As is so often the case in a Chagall, his feet are not touching the ground. He is flying, in fact. His head is bent as if he were a dolphin, so his lips can touch the woman's. She is leaning forward to meet these lips of his, so her body is at an angle that no body could maintain in real life, no body could maintain without toppling over. Her skirt swirls around her dainty ankles. It is an image of love and ecstasy.

This is not a new postcard. Claire can see several places where tacks have been stuck around the edges, as well as a place on the back where a piece of tape used to be. There is also a note in the envelope.

"Years ago when I was in graduate school I bought a couple of shoe boxes of postcards for a few bucks," he writes. "Joan used to cut them up and use them for collages at one point. But when I moved out of our bedroom, I took several of my favorites from her studio and put them above my computer. Of all of them, this one was my most favorite. No big mystery why: It depicts what I was missing in my life. Nothing for me captures better than this painting the spirit of what I hoped to know of love—the bed, the food, the flowers, the wholesome, uplifting feel of it all. All I ever wanted in life is in this picture. All I ever wanted I have found with you."

Tim and Claire have arranged for Claire and Ursula to meet at the Two Brothers Diner on a Thursday afternoon when Pete's playing baseball and Sally's at ballet. Claire has seen pictures of Tim's daughter but she wasn't prepared for the sight of her. Ursula's glasses are so thick they actually magnify her eyes, which are a pale, red-rimmed, watery gray. She is also bigger-boned than Claire imagined. Like her father, but it's a less successful look on a little girl. There is nothing little about her as she sits hunched over the table, playing with sugar packets.

Ursula's hair is a pale strawberry blond, and thin. Her skin is also very pale and pink, almost transparent. "No fun at the beach," Mickey would say. Which also applies to Tim, of course, although, knowing how Claire loves the ocean, he has gone there with her, slathered himself with number 45 sunblock and kept his legs covered. Tim would go anywhere with Claire. He is crazy in love with her, and she can tell that Ursula knows this, too. Ursula seems to know everything.

"I'm fat," Ursula says as Claire settles herself at their booth. "Is that all you're eating?" she has asked, looking at Ursula's bagel, which she has hardly touched. Claire reaches out her hand to shake Ursula's, having decided on the drive over not to hug her right off.

"I'm Claire," she says. She knows better than to tell Ursula, "I've heard so much about you."

What she tells Ursula is, "I always wanted red hair." That part is true. Just a different shade. She tells Ursula she loves her dress, which is the loose, Empire style parents buy when they're worried about their daughter's weight. There was a brief period shortly after her separation from Sam when Sally appeared to find her comfort in peanut butter sandwiches, and she put on weight for a while. But that was a long time ago. Sally is tall and slim now, and beautiful. After seeing a recent photograph of Sally, and knowing she had a brief chunky phase, Tim told Claire she made him feel hopeful for Ursula. Claire did not say—though it was what she was thinking at this point—that her own daughter was never like Ursula. Even when she had that belly on her, there was always a lightness to Sally.

Ursula, on the other hand, seems not simply heavy but heavy-hearted, too. Claire sees it in the way Ursula sits in her chair—slumped over and defeated-looking. It's in those sad, watery eyes behind her unflattering glasses frames. It's her fingernails, which are bitten below the quick, and the baby-talk voice she uses as she tells Claire, "I bet my dad likes you better than me." The truth is, Claire has never seen a sadder-looking child.

She kisses Tim. Not their usual kiss—which would have been the long kind, mouths open, pressed up against each other hard. This one is a peck on the cheek, like something June Lockhart would deliver to her husband on "Lassie."

"You're so pretty," Ursula tells her, still in that baby-talk voice. "I wish I was pretty."

Claire knows she's being baited and takes it. "Of course you're pretty," she says. "And pretty silly, too." Claire has always believed in talking to children basically the same way you'd talk to anybody else. She says something about how women are never happy with the way they look. "Me, I've got straight hair and I always wanted it to be curly. And you probably want yours to be straight, right?"

"Just look at my thighs," Ursula says. "They're disgusting."

"Everybody's legs look bigger when they're pressed down against a chair," says Claire. She's familiar with these kinds of conversations. She used to have them with Sally.

"Kids call me fat at school," she says.

"And what do you say?" Claire asks her.

"I tell them they're idiots," she says. "I tell them they're poop heads. Or else I give them a karate kick. Everybody hates me at school. I used to have a friend, but she's got cerebral palsy and now she goes to a special class."

Claire is trying to think of a great-looking tall, big-boned woman to use as an example for Ursula. She knows there are many, but at the moment the only one she can think of is Anna Nicole Smith, who recently posed for *Playboy*. She figures this is not a very great example.

So they discuss Barbies—a mutual interest. "What's the next one you want?" she asks Ursula. It has been five or six years since Sally put hers away. At Wal-Mart Claire still likes to wheel her cart down the Barbie aisle.

Listening to Ursula tell her about Bend 'N Stretch Barbie, Claire can just glimpse the child Tim has told her about, who plays a perfect Natasha while Tim does Boris, and practices karate with her dad. Her voice is very deep and low for a child. Describing the Rollerblades that come with California Stacey—purple wheels and real laces—she has an intensity about her that reminds Claire of Tim. I could love this child, she thinks. And for a moment this wave of feeling so strong it almost makes her dizzy comes over her as she pictures all of them together: her and Tim, Pete and Sally, and Ursula.

Claire knows Tim is thinking that, too, and that he's watching the two of them: his two favorite women in the world, heads bent toward each other as they discuss Ken. They don't include him in this conversation and she knows he doesn't mind.

"You should see Claire's dollhouse, Urs," he says. "It has lights that work and everything."

"You have your own dollhouse?" she says. "Isn't it your kids'?"

She explains to Ursula that the dollhouse she gave Sally, many years ago, is still at Sally's dad's house, where they used to live. Sally kept saying it was too big to move, and finally Claire gave up asking. "So I said to myself, 'If you want a dollhouse so much, get your own,' and I did," she tells Ursula. She keeps it in the bay window in her living room, and when people ask her why she'd have a dollhouse here—knowing Sally's almost sixteen now, and Pete certainly isn't into it—she always explains, "It's for when little girls come to visit."

She tells this to Ursula now. She tells Ursula that she has missed having a little girl around the house. It has been years since she spent an afternoon making play food out of Fimo. Making doll-sized magazines out of those little stamps of magazine covers that come from Publisher's Clearinghouse every January. French-braiding Ursula's hair. It's still too short. But maybe by winter.

"I want to come over to your house," Ursula says. Tim has paid their check by this time. They are leaving the diner. Ursula has taken Claire's hand. She's skipping, a little tentatively.

"That would be great," Claire says. "Have you ever made doll rugs with a Knitting Nancy?"

"My mom doesn't do things like that," Ursula tells her. Which Claire knows already.

"I don't see my mom very much," Ursula says. "She's busy with her boyfriend and her artwork. She lives far away."

"She must miss you a lot," Claire says. She's feeling generous.

"Doubtful," says Ursula. "I get on her nerves."

"Oh, all kids get on their parents' nerves sometimes," says Claire. "Just like parents get on kids' nerves. It doesn't mean they don't love each other a ton."

"Can we come live at her house, Dad?" Ursula asks Tim in her baby voice, and then she pulls on his arm. *"Canwecanwecanwe?"* It is as if Ursula has watched some TV show where a child talked like that and it was cute, only she doesn't quite know how to do it.

"Hold your horses, Urs," he says. "Maybe we should start out with a visit." They have reached his car by now.

Claire hugs Ursula. Ursula is a little stiff, but that's okay. Claire feels very sure of herself now. She feels like Annie Sullivan. Like

Maria von Trapp as portrayed by Julie Andrews. *Climb every mountain, ford every stream* . . . She is overflowing with hopefulness and love. She can do anything, is what she feels. She can make this sad child happy. She can be a mother to her. They will be a happy family.

She sees all of this as the two of them, Tim and Ursula, drive away. As she pulls out of the parking lot, she can see Tim's car stopped at a red light down the block. Ursula's face is staring out the back window like a deer in the headlights.

Tim calls Claire very early the next morning. "She loved you," he tells her. "I knew she would."

"She's a very dear little girl," Claire says. "I just wanted to scoop her up and take her home with me."

"How about me?" he says. "You want to take me home with you?"

"You know what I want to do with you," she says.

The next call is Mickey. It's almost always Claire who calls him, but he hasn't heard from her in a few days and he wonders what's up. "So, Slim, what have you got?" he says, same as he always does.

"This one might be a keeper," she tells him. She reaches for her coffee cup and settles into her chair.

"No kidding," he says. "That's great, Slim." He has a recording of Timbuk 3 playing, one she has heard often. Like so many bands, this one has become inextricably linked with thoughts of Mickey. She can't even listen to the Beatles anymore, clean.

"He's crazy about me," she says.

"Well, why wouldn't he be?" Mickey says. "And how about you?"

"I think I might love him," she tells him. She doesn't say she's "in love." That one's harder to figure.

"Sex good?" he asked her. This is all familiar stuff for them.

He always wants to know if she's had an orgasm. He always inquires about a new lover's attitudes concerning oral sex.

"If you don't mind," she says, "I think I'll keep that private."

"Oh," he says, with a sudden faint coolness in his tone only Claire would recognize. *"I see."*

She asks him something about the Red Sox. He mentions a new player the Sox have brought up from Pawtucket and a Pat Metheny recording he's just heard. She mentions that Pete wants to go to baseball camp this summer, but Sam won't contribute any money, although she and Mickey both know Claire will find a way to send him, anyway. Sally's taking driver's ed this summer. If she does well she'll get her license in the fall, when she turns sixteen.

"What does he look like anyway?" Mickey asks her. He's talking about Tim.

"Big. Football player build. Friendly kind of face. Red haired," she says.

"No fun at the beach," Mickey tells her. She knew he was going to say that.

Mickey took Claire into the recording studio in his barn this one time. "We're going to record your single," he said. "What's it going to be?"

She knew right off. It was a Townes Van Zandt song called "If I Needed You." She has a recording of Emmylou Harris singing it as a duet with Don Williams. She wanted to sing the song with Mickey.

This was not really Mickey's kind of song, but Mickey can sing anything. She wrote down the words for him. She hummed the tune. "You were almost on key that time, Slim," he said.

First he laid down the lead guitar track for her. Then the bass. He set up his drum machine and laid down a rhythm track at this one place near the end. Then he picked up his banjo and threw a little of that in as if it were jalapeño. Mickey has all sorts of odd, gourdlike Brazilian instruments whose names Claire didn't know. He ran through the song using a couple of those.

"Okay, Slim," he said. "You're on."

He put the headphones on her. He adjusted the microphone.

"Give me something to test your sound levels," he said.

"I adore you, Mickey," she said. She couldn't think of anything funny or silly at the moment. Just that.

"Slim singing 'If I Needed You,' " said Mickey into the machine. "Take one. Rolling." She leaned into the microphone.

"If I needed you," she sang. "Would you come to me? Would you come to me and ease my pain?" Singing these words, she looked into his broad freckled face that she knew so well and at his hands on the guitar strings, hands that had touched every inch of her skin. Could a person ever feel more love?

"If you needed me I would come to you," Mickey sang back to her. "I would swim the seas to ease your pain." And he would, too. She never questioned that for a moment. He looked into her face, too, as he sang.

"In the nights forlorn, the morning's born," Claire sang. "And the morning's born with the lights of love." Claire was almost beyond singing, she was so overcome with love. For all the times in her life she has wished she could sing like Emmylou Harris, she never wished it more than she did right then. She wished there were more notes, more words, more places to put all the things she wanted to give him, all the things she had to say.

"If you close your eyes, you miss the sunrise," he sang, reading off the paper. "And that would break my heart in two." Then they sang it one time through together and she felt as if they were making love.

They did it in two takes. Mickey recorded a harmony part after that and another track with a wailing harmonica coming in at one point. Claire said she couldn't do good enough harmony, but Mickey said no, it'll sound good if it's a little off-key. "Just hum."

Remember this, she thought as she hummed her part on that last track. Remember this room and this man singing into the microphone and that fiddle line.

Remember the plucking of the mandolin, and the way it feels right now, at this precise instant, which will never come again.

How it felt was as if this wasn't a mandolin at all he was plucking

*but her heartstrings—as if his hand had reached deep into her chest
and plucked them.*

*It felt as if no moment she would experience would ever be so
perfectly happy as this one. She was right too.*

Because she didn't want to make
too big a deal of this, Claire decided on hamburgers for dinner,
although she has also made potato salad and grilled vegetables and
strawberry shortcake with homemade biscuits. It's the first time
all year that she's barbecuing, and she has asked Pete to set out
plates on their patio. "Two extra," she told him. "Tim and Ursula
are coming."

So far her children have never laid eyes on Ursula, and they
have only met Tim in passing. The first time their dad was picking
them up for the weekend. Sam was just loading their bikes in the
back of his truck and Tim was getting out of his car, carrying his
overnight bag. "This is my friend Tim," she told them. *What is she
supposed to say, "This is my lover"? "This is the man who makes love
to me virtually without interruption from ten minutes after you leave
Fridays till ten minutes before I head out to pick you up on Sundays"?
"This man treats me well, unlike your father"?*

A few of the men she has gone out with over the years shook
hands with Sam when they met him. One or two actually struck
up a conversation. "How do you like those Celtics?" That sort of
thing. Claire loves it about Tim that he didn't do that. He has
heard what Sam said about her on the witness stand during their
custody hearing. *"Her father was an alcoholic, you know. Perhaps
you're familiar with the ACOA personality type . . . ?"* Tim knows
about Sam's affair with Melanie, the babysitter, and his attempts
during their divorce negotiations to get a half-interest in the
money her father left her in his will, and the accusation he made,
after she slapped Pete one time, that she was a child abuser. *"Of
course my former wife loves the children,"* he told the judge. *"She just
doesn't have the emotional stability to care for them."*

Claire knows Tim would like to pin Sam against the door of

his truck and choke him for those things. She knows he would like to kick him in the balls for that remark he made, make him get down on his knees and apologize to her, but he doesn't. For the children's sake and nothing more, he nodded in Sam's direction when they met, but they didn't speak.

Pete and Sally have seen her talking on the phone with Tim. They've seen the flowers and the windchimes he brought her that hang on their front porch now. One time when Pete was home on a Saturday he had suggested that they shoot some hoops at the school down the street. "I guess not," Pete said. "My dad's coming by soon." Tim told Sally, who has her learner's permit now, he'd be available to take her driving sometime.

She looked at him blankly, almost witheringly. "My parents do that stuff," she said.

"Don't worry," Tim told Claire. "I can take it. They don't know me yet. They'll come round."

Y̲ou weren't thinking we were going to hang around all night entertaining his kid, were you, Mom?" Sally asks her now as Claire's chopping the onions. "I mean, playing Candyland with some eight-year-old is not exactly my idea of a fun time."

"I was thinking you'd stick around awhile and get to know her, if that's what you mean," Claire says. "She's a shy, insecure little girl who has had a lot of hard things to deal with in her life. This is your territory she's coming into. You have your brother and all your friends around. She's all by herself. I'd like you to show a little interest and compassion, yes."

"Sounds like fun," says Sally grimly. Over by the sink, Pete has begun to sing the theme song from "The Brady Bunch" in a high, awful voice.

"You're also almost ten years older than she is," says Claire. "You're supposed to be the mature ones. If you don't want to do it for Ursula, you could do it for me." She hopes there isn't a note of desperation in her voice.

"Listen, Mom," says Sally. "Whatever you want to do with your life, that's fine with me. You can pick your friends. I would just prefer if you wouldn't drag me into it. I have my own life now."

"Yeah, well, I had this crazy idea that I might be part of your life," says Claire.

There was a time—and it lasted for years—when Sally used to beg her parents to provide her with a little sister. Even after they split up, she and Pete would see news reports from Romania and suggest that they adopt a toddler. Sally even had her name picked out: Rose.

"And just where would we put her, this sister of yours?" Claire asked her. It scared her how excited the idea made her. She acted like it was the craziest thing in the world, but the truth was she thought about those Romanian orphans, too.

"She could share my room," Sally said. Pete said he'd teach her how to ride a tricycle. Sally would give her all her old Barbies.

"And I'd read to her every night," she said. "*Madeline* and stuff."

They'd be in a store and see these little sneakers or patent-leather party shoes. Pete and Sally would make this moaning sound and call her to come see. "Don't you just want to die, Mom?" Sally would say. "Have you ever seen anything so cute in your entire life?"

"Yes, actually," Claire would say. "You used to have shoes like that. You also had chicken pox and food allergies and tantrums in supermarkets. You liked me to read you *Strawberry Shortcake at the Perfume Factory* twenty million times a day. There's more to having a little kid around than buying cute shoes, you know."

"We could handle it, Mom," they said. "You'd see."

Maybe it was a way for them to deal with the divorce, she figured. If they adopted a little girl, there would still be four places set at the table. There would be a bigger pile of presents at Christmas. They might feel more like a whole family again.

Whatever the reason for all their talk about adopting a baby, it passed. The kids never mentioned their little sister anymore. Their new phone book didn't have Rose's name scribbled all over the cover the way their old one had. And it certainly didn't have Ursula's.

They arrive on the dot of six. Tim has brought deviled eggs—something Claire's children would never touch—and marinated asparagus. He's wearing a shirt Sally will think is dorky, the kind golfers wear. "I brought this for Pete," he says. It's a baseball signed by Whitey Ford. "My dad caught this for me at Yankee Stadium back in 1964. I was probably just the age he is now."

"I'm so glad we could finally get everybody together," Claire says to Ursula. Claire bends to give her a hug. "Just look at your dress."

Ursula is wearing the jumper Claire helped Tim pick out at The Gap the other day, but not with the turtleneck she chose. Why did I let him buy a size ten? she thinks. He should have got a twelve.

She has put a striped rugby shirt on over the jumper, and a lot of those necklaces they throw out onto the streets during Mardi Gras in New Orleans. Although it's a warm evening, she's wearing cable-knit tights and sneakers.

"I made these for your kids," says Ursula. She holds out a couple of friendship bracelets made of thick yarn.

"This is for you," she says. She is speaking almost in a whisper as she hands the box to Claire. Inside is a blown-glass bunny and a broken robin's egg and something else Claire can't identify.

"One time when I was little, a hummingbird flew into our kitchen when the door was open," she says. "My dad and me tried to catch it but it moved too fast. It just kept bumping into the windows. We tried every day to catch it, but we never could, so we just had to sit there and watch it trying to get out. Finally we got up one morning and it was lying on the floor. Dead.

"So we put it in the box," she's saying. "It was so little it didn't smell. My dad said all the skin part just dried up and turned into dust."

"It's beautiful," says Claire, brushing one finger very softly over the little pile of feathers and dust that used to be the hummingbird. "I never had anything like this before."

"It's a treasure box," she says. "You keep it in your room. If you feel sad you can look in it."

"You shouldn't give me this," says Claire. "It's too special."

"No, that's okay," says Ursula. "I was finished with it anyways."

"I understand you like to pitch," Tim says to Pete as Claire sets out the ketchup. "Football was my sport in college, but I was a pitcher myself, back in high school."

"Great," says Pete in a flat voice.

"So what kind of a season did you have last year?" Tim asks. He knows from Claire that Pete struck out ten players in his last four innings on the mound in last summer's championship game.

"It was okay," he says.

"Maybe sometime I could show you my slider," he says. "My dad used to play triple A ball. He pitched to Jimmy Piersall one time."

"I like your necklaces," Sally tells Ursula, after a long silence.

Ursula keeps chewing.

"So," Sally says to her, "what grade are you in anyway Ursula?"

Ursula whispers something to Tim. "She's in second," says Tim. "Of course, she'll graduate in just a few weeks, won't you, Urs?" Ursula is silent.

"Remember your second-grade teacher, Sal?" says Claire. "Mrs. Foskett? Only you called her Faucet for the longest time."

"I already know how to throw a slider," says Pete. "My dad taught me."

"Why don't you take Ursula up to your room and show her your trolls while I whip the cream for the strawberry shortcake?" Claire asks Pete when dinner's over. She's afraid he might roll his eyes, but he actually puts a hand on her shoulder to show her the way.

She shakes her head and whispers something to her father again.

"Come on, Urs," he says to her. "You'll have fun. He's got this one troll that's dressed like a wizard and one that's a karate guy." Pete looks at Tim suspiciously when he says this. Tim has been in Pete's room before evidently. When Pete wasn't there.

"That's right," says Claire. "Pete even made them their own little house. It's really neat."

"I'll show you," Pete says. Claire wants to kiss him.

Ursula says nothing.

"I guess she's staying down here with us, Pete," Tim says. "But thanks for asking."

Pete shrugs and heads out of the kitchen.

Alone in the kitchen with just the two of them, her father and Claire, Ursula is a different person. Chatty and funny. She is telling a story about a goody-goody in her class who always tells when this boy that sits next to her picks his nose. "The only thing is, she picks her nose too," says Ursula. "I saw her. She even eats it. She just does it in the cubby room, when she doesn't know anybody sees her.

"Your daughter is so pretty," she tells Claire.

"She used to think she was fat for a while there," says Claire. "You'd be surprised."

"Did kids ever have a club about her at school?" Ursula asks her. "Where they sit around and tell how they're never going to invite her to their birthday party? And every time she tried to sit down in the lunchroom the kids at that table would say, 'Sorry. That seat's taken'?"

"Do they have a club like that about you?" says Claire. She doesn't have to look at Tim's face to know what it must look like.

"Not only that," says Ursula. "They make fart noises when I go up to the board."

"What do you do about that?" says Claire.

"I tell the teacher and get them in trouble," says Ursula.

Claire doesn't groan but she feels like it.

"It doesn't matter anyways," says Ursula. "I hate all those kids. I don't even want to go to their parties and play Pickle with them. I'm lucky, because I get to have lunch with the teacher."

They are clearing away the dishes. Claire has told Sally she can go out with Travis now. Pete is up in his room listening to his Counting Crows album. After finishing off her second dish of strawberry shortcake and licking the plate, Ursula is in the living room rearranging Claire's dollhouse. They can hear her making voices for the dolls.

"I think it went fine, considering," Tim says to her. He runs his hand down Claire's back as he says this, very lightly, as if he isn't completely sure it's okay.

Claire doesn't say anything. She reaches to open the dishwasher.

"What is it?" he says. "Tell me."

She stands at the sink scrubbing the same dish for a long time. She doesn't say anything.

"What did I do?" he says. "Whatever it is, I'm sorry."

"There's just so much that has to be fixed," Claire tells him. "I didn't expect it to be this hard, I guess. The kids barely spoke with each other."

"This was just the first time. The first time was bound to be a little uncomfortable," he says.

"I just wanted so badly for them to get along with each other," she says. "I didn't feel there was one single moment of connection between them."

"You expect too much," he says. "They're just being normal kids."

"Mine are normal kids!" she wants to scream. *"Yours is a mess."* A person could spend her whole life making Ursula okay.

If Ursula were her little girl, Claire would bake with her and teach her how to make origami paper cranes. She would teach her jump rope rhymes and all the verses to "The Fox Went Out on a Chilly Night" and they would have a birthday party where all the girls brought their Barbies and they sewed outfits for them and then Claire took out the little tool she got when Sally was this age, that attaches rhinestone studs to fabric anyplace you want them, and all the girls would go home with rhinestones on their shirts.

Claire knows how to do all these things. Has done them. She just doesn't know if she's up for doing them again, with this particular child.

Sally doesn't pay all that much attention to her mother's boyfriends. Not since Mickey, and that was way back. She can remember how it used to bother her seeing them together, and how much in love they were, how yucky she used to think it was when she kissed him. Now that Sally has a boyfriend of her own, she is just as glad when her mother is going out with somebody. It keeps her occupied and out of Sally's hair.

Only this one, Tim, is just such a loser. He just seems so *gaga* all the time. He thinks everything her mom does is great. It's sickening.

He talks in this very serious voice, like everything's such a big deal. He's tried to have some of these serious-type conversations with Sally, but she always manages to get out of them. Like when he wanted to hear her opinion of Nirvana, and he didn't seem to get it that just because she's a teenager doesn't necessarily mean she's some Kurt Cobain maniac.

The worst part is that daughter of his. Sally likes little kids, but this one is just so weird. Sally's mom can't say she didn't try to make conversation with Ursula, but the kid wouldn't even talk. And the father acts like she's made out of glass, always hovering over her. Kids at school must eat her alive.

With the other guys her mother has dated over the years, you knew they were going to leave you alone. They might come over, but mostly they wanted to stay away from Sally and Pete as much as Sally and Pete wanted to stay away from them. Whatever her mother did—and Sally is old enough now to understand that included screwing now and then—she didn't rub their noses in it. At home she was still their mom. They had their way of doing things, and nobody messed it up.

This Tim character is moving in on their world. *Deviled eggs, for God's sake.* The guy has planted squash in their garden and hung up a windchime. One day Sally came home from her dad's and found him in the kitchen making stew.

"Here," he said. "Try this."

"We don't eat stew," she said. She'd heard from her mother about what an incredible cook he was. Like that was going to make a difference to her.

"Just taste," he said.

"I'm a vegetarian," she told him. Well, she is now.

They hated her. Ursula knew they would. Kids always do.

The girl, Sally, probably thought she was stuck up when she didn't answer that question about her teacher.

There were so many things she wanted to say to Sally. *You are even prettier than Vanna White. Did it hurt when you got your ears pierced? Could I touch those fishnet stockings? Can I see your room?*

She said none of those things. She just sat there like she was retarded.

She already knows her dad likes Claire better than her now. Soon he will like the daughter better, too. He has already offered to take her driving. He wants to play catch with the boy. What about the treehouse he was going to build with her, Ursula wants to know.

For just a moment there, Ursula imagines that it could be all of them in that sparkly house of theirs, with the Christmas lights and the dollhouse and the trolls and the cookie jar shaped like a kangaroo. For a moment she imagines them all snuggled up under one of their soft fuzzy blankets with a big bowl of buttered popcorn, watching a movie together. *Killer Clowns from Outer Space,* her and her dad's favorite.

• • •

"Wait till you see this part," Ursula tells Pete. "This part is my favorite." And Claire will pass her the popcorn and squeeze her and she will say, "Come over here and snuggle with me."

"This movie is awesome," Pete will say. "I thought little girls only liked to watch dumb movies like Care Bears and Barney."

"My dad and me hate Barney," she says proudly.

"Cool," says Pete.

She knows better than this. Her dad will leave Ursula with a babysitter some night when he brings *Killer Clowns* over to Claire's house and they will have popcorn and snuggle up and they will all watch it together, all right—him and Claire and her kids— and when the girl and her mother get scared, Ursula's dad will put his arms around them and say, "It's okay to look again. It's over."

He will teach the boy karate, and once he learns it, the first person the boy will beat up will be Ursula.

Then will come the worst. There will be a baby. She will be little and so cute you'll want to die. Ursula will love her so much she will be willing to do anything for her, but when she tries, Claire just tells her not to get so close, she has germs. So she stays in the doorway looking in at them, watching her dad leaning over the bassinet, singing the baby the very same song he used to sing to her.

Ursula knows what she has to do then. One day she will walk out the door and get on her bike and ride away. Just like that song Dolly Parton sings, where she knows she's in the way, and she's leaving forever, and still she's singing "I will always love you."

Or like that famous singer's kid her dad told her about that was playing he was Superman one time and he ran right out a window in their apartment building that was so high up on account of his dad was a famous singer, and he got smashed on the sidewalk. He's dead now. The singer wrote a song about him and one time when it came on the radio her dad cried. "Will you know my name, when I see you in heaven?" the song went.

They will know her name, all right. But they will never see her again. Then they'll be sorry.

All day long Pete has been thinking about baseball tryouts tonight. This morning, very early, he went out in the yard and leaned his mom's mini-exercise trampoline against the back fence the way he likes and pitched to it. When he throws right, the ball bounces back to him. This morning he was throwing practically all strikes.

All day at school he has been picturing how it will be when they call his name and he walks up to the mound. He mentally goes through his windup. He sees the pitches leave his glove, one after another. First a curveball. Then a slider. Then another curve. Then his famous fastball that nobody can believe a twelve-year-old kid could throw.

Finally Pete pictures himself in a Cubs uniform. He pictures Mr. Voorhees, the coach of the Cubs, putting an arm on his shoulder and leaning over to speak to him. "I'm making you my starting pitcher, Pete," he says. "I've had my eye on you a long time now. I think we've got an incredible season ahead of us, and you're the linchpin."

He will call his dad up to tell him. His dad will say he knew Pete had it in him. "Did you remember what I told you about not kicking your leg quite so high?" his dad says.

"I did it just like you told me," Pete tells him. "I carried your lucky penny."

His mom will be happy too. At his games, the two of them, his mom and his dad, will both be sitting on the bleachers, watching. It is the one place he ever gets to see the two of them together now, the one place where you could almost think they were a regular family, if they would just sit closer. This season, though, his parents will be so proud of him, and so happy, they'll forget everything else.

Bottom of the seventh inning—all they play in his league—Pete will be sitting on the bench in the dugout, sipping his Powerade. Normally he's a starter, but he has been sitting out this game to rest his arm. Only the game is tied and the Tigers have last ups, with two outs and a man on third. The batter coming up is Dayton Fusco, a lefty whose uncle once had a tryout with St. Louis. The best hitter in the entire league.

Mr. Voorhees comes over and sits down next to Pete. "I know I said we weren't going to play you today," he says. "But you're the only one who can do the job for us here. I'm putting you in."

Pete adjusts his cap and pulls up his socks.

"Think you can handle it, son?" Mr. Voorhees asks him.

"I'll do my best," he tells his coach.

As he walks out to the mound he can hear the cheering, and from the Tigers' bench, a murmuring hush. He takes the mound. Throws his practice pitches to Dougie Evert, the catcher. Strike. Strike. Strike. Dougie's mitt is practically smoking.

Pete scuffs his toe in the dirt. He looks out to the bleachers for a second until he spots his mom. That's when he sees this amazing sight.

She's sitting next to his dad. She's leaning close in to him, whispering something in his ear. He's smiling and nodding. He reaches over and takes her hand. She rests hers on his knee.

He throws his pitch. Dayton swings but doesn't even get a piece of it.

He throws another. Strike two. The runner on third is making moves like he might steal home. Pete sets him straight.

Pete winds up for the third pitch. By the time Dayton swings, the ball's already resting in Dougie's mitt. He's out of there. Game.

Over in the bleachers, everybody is standing up, cheering for him. His father has thrown his arms around his mother. His mother kisses his dad. The two of them come running out to the field to see him, together.

It's just after three when Pete gets home from school. He told his mother this morning he needed a ride to tryouts by four today, and he can't be late. He doesn't understand why she's not there. The house is empty.

He reaches in the cookie jar, then realizes he's too nervous to eat. He goes out to the yard to throw a couple of practice pitches. She'll be here any minute. She has to.

"Nice arm you got there," a voice says. Pete looks up. It's Tim, the boyfriend. He's standing on the porch. He's eating one of their cookies. He's got a glove under his arm.

"Your mother called me from work," he says. "She got held up in a meeting so she asked if I'd drive you to your tryouts. I thought I'd come over a little early, see if you wanted to throw a few."

"No thanks," says Pete. "I have a system all set up here." He throws one at the trampoline. It's a totally wild pitch.

"If you wouldn't mind a suggestion," Tim says to him, "it might help if you didn't lift your leg up quite so high when you're in your windup. Otherwise, you've got a nice fluid motion."

He throws three more pitches, all terrible. "I guess we better go," he says. He follows Tim out to his car, walking as far behind him as he can. He climbs in the backseat. He's sitting on something. Wouldn't you know—a Barbie.

When they get to the field he bolts out of the car as fast as he can, but Tim has followed him. He has walked up behind Pete as he's filling out his registration form. As he hands over the twenty dollars Pete's mother must have given him, he speaks to one of the coaches, who is collecting the checks.

"Keep a close eye on this one here," he's saying. "He's got some kind of arm on him. Looks like starting pitcher material to me."

"I don't suppose you could be just a little prejudiced now, could you?" the coach says to Tim, with this sickening grin. "I've heard some dads are."

"He's not my dad," Pete explodes. "My dad couldn't be here today."

"That's right," says Tim. "I'm just a friend."

Pete wants to say Tim isn't a friend either, but he leaves it. He takes a number and walks over to the bench where kids are waiting for their turn to try out, first batting, then fielding. He goes to the special area for the boys who want to pitch and sits on the bench.

He has to clear his brain. He tries to tune back in to the channel he was watching today, the one where he was throwing strikes and wearing the Cubs uniform, but now all he can see is Tim, with that dumb grin of his, telling him not to lift his leg so high.

He sees that wild pitch he threw, hitting the rim of the trampoline, and the three that followed, bouncing into his mother's flower garden. They call his name.

He adjusts his cap, feels in his pocket for the lucky penny his dad gave him. He scrapes the dirt with his toe. He goes into the windup.

It's the dumbest pitch he ever threw. The kid, Ursula, could probably throw better.

"Don't worry," Mr. Voorhees calls out to him from where he's positioned, with his catcher's mitt. "A lot of people start out wild. Just take a second and refocus."

Pete winds up again. Just as he's about to release the ball, one of those terrible little pictures comes zapping across his brain. Ursula and Tim sitting at the kitchen counter at his house eating his mom's chocolate chip cookies out of their jar.

A total ball. So is the next pitch. After that Pete isn't even trying anymore. There's nothing left to do but play it for laughs. He turns his cap around backward and makes a face at the guys still on the bench. "Fart up a tree," he calls out. Who cares anymore if Mr. Voorhees hears him?

He makes his Gomer Pyle face, scratches his crotch exaggeratedly. As he steps down off the mound, he looks back over his shoulder and says in his "Beverly Hillbillies" accent, "Holy cow, isn't this the bowling tryouts?" The other kids laugh nervously. They still have their chance. His is over.

He and Tim drive home in silence. That night he gets the call. They have put him on the Angels. Worst team in the league. He's not pitching of course.

Tim is in the middle of writing a grant application to study the environmental impact of acid rain on southern Vermont's wetlands when Claire stops by. She spots the candy bar wrapper on the floor right away.

"You buy Snickers?" she says.

"It's Ursula's favorite," he says.

"You think that's a good idea, Tim?" she asks him. Like a drunk reaching for the first swig from a bottle, she knows this isn't going to lead them anyplace good, but she can't stop herself.

"I've just been so busy with my application," he says. "I gave her a dollar and told her she could run over to the market and pick out a treat." The truth is, ever since school got out last week, Tim has been desperate for ways to keep Ursula occupied. She's already quit T-ball, and she'll only go to swimming lessons Saturdays if he stays to watch. Every morning when he drives her to day camp she tells him she's got a headache and she begs to go home. The first two days of this week he let her, and naturally he couldn't get a thing done. This morning she finally agreed to give camp another try, and he has been desperately trying to finish this part of the proposal.

"Couldn't you give her fruit instead?" she says. "This is a child with a weight problem."

"She's not that heavy," he says. "She's just big-boned. She's never going to be slim like you."

"It's not the point whether she's that overweight or not," says Claire. "The point is, she feels she is. She's uncomfortable with her body. The loving thing to do is to help her get herself into the kind of shape where she can feel better about herself."

"I know, sweetheart," he says. He pulls her toward him and looks at his watch. "I don't pick Ursula up at camp for another forty-five minutes," he says. "Think we'd have time?" He should work. But he longs for her.

She moves into the bedroom. There are Barbies all over the floor and a coloring book on the bed. Also a cereal bowl and another Snickers wrapper.

"Doesn't she ever pick up her stuff?" Claire says.

"I know I need to do better," he tells her. "I've just been under so much pressure with work."

Claire pulls her shirt off. She unfastens her bra and steps out of her jeans. Tim has stripped down already. She has never encountered a man like this. He's never more than ten seconds away from an erection when he's with her.

"Sweetheart," he says, climbing on top of her. He lays his head on her breasts and moans. She kisses the top of his head.

"I had this dream about you," he says. "When I woke up, I was holding on to the pillow and the bed was drenched in sweat."

She wraps her legs around him. He strokes her stomach. "You're so beautiful," he says. "I never get used to the feeling of your skin."

"You think you'd feel the same about me if I had a fat belly?" she asks. She knows this is a very mean question. She asks it anyway.

"I will always love you. It's just hard to imagine you fat," he says.

"Well I can't imagine it either," she says. "I'd be miserable. And so would Ursula be miserable, if she got that way."

He is silent.

"It's no kindness to a child to buy her candy bars," she says. "It may make your life easier at that particular moment when you give it to her, but it's going to make her life harder later."

"I won't do it again," he says. His cock pushes up against her. She's dry and tight. It hurts.

"I'm not ready yet," she says. He kisses her breast again.

"Baby," he says. "Baby, baby."

"I guess I just can't get into the mood right now," she says. "I'm sorry. You mind?"

He would never say he did. What he says is that he is happy just to hold her, just to touch her, just to listen to her breathe.

Saturday morning Claire calls Mickey. "So where did you take your date last night?" she asks him. She knows from the *Globe* that Youssou N'Dour was playing in Boston last night and figures Mickey was probably there. She herself hasn't been going out anywhere besides the Two Brothers Diner for coffee with Tim.

"No date," Mickey tells her. "I rented a video."

"What's the story?" she says. Mickey always goes out Friday nights. Saturdays, too. And often on weeknights besides.

"I don't know what's happening, Slim," he tells her. "The response letter I send when I answer the personals doesn't seem to be reeling them in the way it used to. Last month I mailed out twenty-five and I only got four responses back. Not a live one in the bunch. You think I'm losing my touch?"

"Maybe the word is out about you, Mickey," Claire says. " 'Ethereal yet pithy' and all that. 'Plethora of freckles.' That letter's been in circulation an awfully long time. It might be time for a new approach."

She writes the new letter herself:

Dear Friend,

Your ad in the Phoenix *has caught the eye of my friend Mickey. This letter comes to you by way of introduction from a highly discriminating woman of roughly your age and stage in life who answered an ad of his long ago and has loved him ever since.*

I'll get to the part about how it is that I could hold Mickey in such high esteem as a former boyfriend, lover of women, and all-around wonderful man and still not be with him myself in a minute. (No, he did not suffer a horrible disfiguring accident, and no, I didn't get sent to North Dakota in some top-secret government witness relocation program.)

It doesn't matter how many attractive eligible bachelors you have kept company with. You have never met a man like Mickey. This is a man who gives the kind of priority to love that most of the people who answer your ad have probably been giving to things like getting to be partner in their law firm or reaching the million-dollar sales mark.

Mickey is a true lover of women, is all. And when the woman comes along who is a good candidate for being loved by him and knows how to love him back with equivalent imagination, passion, and single-mindedness, he will be a true and irresistible lover of her.

Mickey's a Southerner who developed early a passion for music and baseball. He's also a devoted father to his son, Gabe, the product of a marriage that ended long ago.

Mickey's approach to child raising is a lot like his approach to romance: one-on-one. Observing Mickey and Gabe together is like watching a pair of bachelor roommates. They go listen to jazz, hang out at Fenway. For Christmas last year, Mickey spent the better part of a weekend making a tape in his recording studio using actual crowd noises, commercials, and hokey organ music and featuring the voice of a baseball announcer friend of his narrating a duel between Mickey (as aging relief pitcher for the Red Sox) and Gabe (as rookie phenom for the Texas Rangers). Needless to say, the duel ended with Gabe hitting the pennant-winning home run and the crowd going wild. I tell you this as evidence of the kind of painstaking care this man gives to those he loves. The list is short, for good reason. A man can't give this kind of attention to more than a few people in his life. And there is basically one slot vacant in Mickey's: for a rare and wonderful woman.

Mickey has set things up for himself in a way that allows him to spend virtually all of his time doing what he likes and almost none of it doing what he doesn't like. As a result, he is not one of your more conspicuously affluent types, but his quality of life exceeds that of any BMW-driving fast-track slave to the time clock I've encountered. Spending time with Mickey is—in addition to other things—wonderful fun.

He will always notice what perfume you're wearing, and if you have a birthmark between two of your fingers, he will find that out. He will open the car door for you. He will make you tapes of wonderful music you have never heard before, and he will listen to every story you tell him and want to see what you looked like when you were a little girl.

When you walk down the street with him, he will occasionally point out the beautiful hair of one woman you pass and the elegant bearing of another, but what I always felt when he did this was that his level of connoisseurship and deep appreciation only made his love and unequivocal loyalty to me all the more precious.

He would name the day John Lennon was shot as one of the saddest in his life, and the day Ella Fitzgerald dies will doubtless be another. He told me the night I met him that he never gives or receives presents—which first left me feeling a little regretful that there would be no bouquets and packages from Victoria's Secret in my future with this man. But the fact is, his love is the gift. And true love in return is the only one he cares about.

Without boring you (this letter is about your romantic quest, after all, not mine), I will explain briefly how it came to be that I am attempting to assist in the romantic search of a man I love so well myself, who I believe loved me in equally large measure.

I had children (still do) and a life he felt would never allow the kind of intense, passionate intimacy he lives for. He said it was better for him to bid me good-bye than to stand around trying to fit in some watered-down version of his brand of loving in between the demands of my kids' games and fixing dinner. And because I love him as I do (which is to say, with a selflessness I once thought could only exist between a parent and a child), if he could find a woman who had freedom and space enough to make loving and being loved by him the central focus of her life, it would make me happy.

You shouldn't contact Mickey if you don't feel up for a major and possibly life-altering experience. Truthfully, I should add, it wouldn't hurt if you are in possession of a good combination of the physical attributes that particularly appeal to this man. Although, being the lover of women he is, they run the gamut from very long legs to adorable petiteness, with a decided preference for dark hair, blue eyes, great skin, a good figure, a beautiful face.

You shouldn't respond if you want babies or have any your-self. You shouldn't respond if you need to get taken to expensive restaurants, or any restaurants, in fact, where entrées go into the double-digit category. But if what truly matters most to you is finding a man of rare intelligence and humor with a large and loving heart, who would look up and take notice every time you walk in the room, and then think about you after you've left it, you will not find a better one. I wish you well.

Claire shows Mickey's letter of recommendation to Tim. He is very quiet as he studies it. Finally he looks up.

"I never opened the car door for you," he says. "I'm sorry. But I did know about the birthmark."

• • •

She shows it to Nancy, who makes a snorting noise when she finishes.

"I like men to give me presents," she says. "I think they should. You're the only person I know who could make a virtue out of a person being cheap. So long as that person's Mickey."

"I was just trying to make a point," Claire tells her.

"Tight with money, tight with love, that's what I always say," says Nancy.

"You don't understand Mickey," says Claire.

"When are you ever going to get over this guy?" Nancy says, shaking her head.

It's such a nice evening Claire has decided to ride her bike over to Pete's game down at Haskell Field. Tim said he and Ursula might meet her over there; these days Ursula likes to ride her two-wheeler everywhere, and now that it's summer and the days are longer, she can ride after dinner, even. One of these days, Claire likes to think, they might all ride together the way some families do that she watches at the park, pedaling in a row like ducks. Father, mother, kids.

Pedaling down Grove Street, she notices two figures up ahead on skateboards. Even before she recognizes them they catch her attention; there is so clearly an energy and excitement between them. They look so happy and playful—like children, but also like lovers. Only when she gets up closer—though not so close that they see her—does she realize the two figures are her daughter and her daughter's boyfriend, Travis. Sally wears her short shorts as usual, cut off half an inch below the start of her firm, tight buttocks. Travis wears those crazy fat pants of his that he had to go to five different stores to find. Size forty-six Wranglers from the Big Men's section, dragging so low only the toes of his AirWalks show. He ties them with a piece of rope, and still it's a mystery what keeps them up over those nonexistent hips of his. He's shirtless as usual, every rib showing on his smooth, flat, hairless chest, and a full inch of cotton boxer shorts revealed above the drooping waistband of his pants.

Travis has given Sally his old skateboard, but she's still just a beginner. She stands on the skateboard a little unsteadily. After a second she hops off and tumbles onto the grass along the edge of the sidewalk, laughing. Travis tumbles down beside her. He places a hand on her belly with a degree of assurance that startles Claire. He has touched her there before, a lot. He nuzzles his head against her neck and whispers something to her. She laughs again.

Claire has gotten off her bike. She's walking it up the hill, partly because the pedaling is hard at this point but also, she knows, because she can't take her eyes off the two of them.

Travis gets up. Sally is still sitting on the grass with her skateboard beside her, but he has set his almost delicately down on the tar. Now he places one foot on the board and kicks off with the other. He glides out into the road.

Here is this boy who has practically been living at her house for half a year, whose lanky frame sprawled on her living-room floor Claire steps over nearly every day as he lies there on that nearly concave belly of his, watching skateboarding or snowboarding videos, depending on the season. She feeds him peanut butter cookies and he drinks their milk a quart at a time, straight from the jug, often with his Walkman playing and the faint sound of rap music leaking out the sides of his earphones under his goofy blond dreadlocks. Now and then, on the rare occasions when he isn't over at their house, and he calls for Sally, and Claire answers, she may ask him, "How's it going, Travis?" But mostly she knows him as a monosyllabic stranger who follows her daughter around like an Irish setter puppy.

She's accustomed to seeing him carrying his skateboard, of course. He's never without it. Sometimes she will see him glide up to their door on it, hopping off at the precise spot where the sidewalk opens out onto their front walk, and parking it on the front porch.

But until this moment, Claire has never really seen Travis ride. Now she watches nearly transfixed by the totally unexpected beauty of him.

He must be as tall as Tim—well over six feet—but where Tim is built like a linebacker, Travis is a dancer, a stalk of bamboo. His face, which she always recognized as handsome—especially if he'd do something about his hair—has a look of total concentration as he zigzags wildly down the sidewalk, then fishtails back. Now he makes a circle directly in front of Sally, seeming to guide his board with nothing but the movement of those narrow hips of his.

Now he's jumping for her. His whole body rises in midair, and somehow he has taken the skateboard with him—his arms outstretched as if he were balancing on a tightrope, and a quarter-inch motion in the wrong direction would send him plummeting. Claire has always thought of Travis as skinny, but now she sees that his body is just perfectly lean. The muscles on his arms are those of a man, not a boy.

He lands on a curb, but instead of toppling over, he jumps again. Now he's twirling. Now he bends low, kicks off with one foot to build up more speed. He careens past Sally in a way that seems to be heading him directly into the path of an oncoming car. Claire is raising her hands to her face too terrified to scream, but just at the moment when it seems certain he's about to end up underneath its tires, he cuts a sharp, impossible-seeming left and stops on a dime. Sally, who must have seen him do this before, only laughs.

Still frozen on the sidewalk, her hands clutching the handlebars of her bike, Claire breathes for the first time in what seems like ages. They are so absorbed in each other, these two, they haven't noticed her, and they won't. She lifts herself back up on the seat and pedals off to her son's game.

I know what that was, she thinks to herself. That was a mating dance.

It's the bottom of the second inning when Claire arrives at Pete's game. Tonight the Angels are playing the White Sox, the only team in the league that's lost more games than they have. White Sox lead three to one.

Other years, even back when his T-ball team lost every game but one, Pete was always the one calling out to his teammates from the field that they could come back and win the game. Last year, when his team, the Tigers, were behind, Pete would turn his baseball hat inside out and start the rally cap cheer. Other mothers would actually lean over to Claire on the bench and say to her, "That's some boy you've got. He does more to encourage the team than the coach. You must be very proud of him."

Yes, she said. She is. The only person she's ever seen to love baseball the way Pete did was Mickey. Whom Pete couldn't stand —although they were a lot alike. Same tenacious aggressiveness up on the mound. Same dry wit in the dugout. These days, though, Pete sits slumped and silent on the bench, silent even when the rest of his team is cheering. He has been placed in right field most of the time and he's low on the batting order. Often he sits out an inning or two. He has been striking out a lot.

At the other end of the bench Claire spots Sam, lithe as a teenager in his ripped jeans and T-shirt, eyes fixed on his son as he comes up to bat. Claire and Sam sit as far apart as they can at games, unless one of them has some piece of information to convey to the other—a pickup time to check on, a piece of business to discuss about Sally's car insurance of Pete's summer camp. This evening, though, Claire has this crazy longing to set aside all the old battles for the duration of the game anyway and slide over onto the seat next to him. She wishes they could just talk about baseball. About their son, actually.

She has already consulted Mickey about Pete's baseball slump this season, as much as a person can by long distance. She has even attempted to describe to Mickey, over the phone, the way Pete has been swinging the bat lately, the way he seems to step away from the ball as it whizzes toward him, as if he was afraid of being hit. He was never afraid of the ball before.

"Can't Tim work with him?" Mickey asked her. But Pete dislikes Tim even more than he disliked Mickey.

Now, as her son ambles up to the plate with that bored, impassive look on his face that breaks Claire's heart, she shoots a look at his father on the chance that he might be looking her way, too. If he did she might actually say something to him about Pete for once, not money or scheduling.

"Can you help him?" she would say. "He's so unhappy." Sam is a natural athlete, good at any sport he tries. No doubt he knows how Pete needs to adjust his swing.

But Sam stares straight ahead grimly as Pete adjusts his cap.

"Easy out," someone calls from the White Sox bench. Claire wants to yell "Hush!"

"Give us a single, Temple," one of Pete's teammates calls out to him in the voice they all seem to adopt during games, a full octave lower than their normal range. Like a twelve-year-old boy's idea of how a man talks.

"He throws junk, Temple," someone else calls to Pete. "You can hit him."

It is a junk pitch, too, high over Pete's head. Only he swings at it, more like someone swatting at a fly than somebody playing baseball. Strike one.

"Choose your pitch, Pete," his coach calls to him.

The pitcher throws another ball. This time Pete's not buying it. Claire says one of her baseball prayers. Three more. All she's asking for tonight is a walk. A walk or a single.

Next pitch is a strike. There's a groan from the Angels bench. "Come on Temple. Not again."

From his end of the bench, Sam calls out, "Be a hitter, son." After all these years of sitting on the bench at her son's games —and Mickey's and Sam's before that—Claire has never really understood the language of cheering from the sidelines the way so many of the other parents do, even a lot of the mothers. She asked Mickey one time what he calls out to Gabe at his Little League games.

"It depends on what he's doing, Slim," he told her. But what he tells his son most often is, "See the ball."

Claire liked that. "See the ball, Pete," she calls out to Pete now.

He swings and misses. Strike three. Pete throws the batting helmet in the dirt and scuffs back to the bench. He has that tough look on his face that Claire knows means he needs all his concentration to keep from crying. Claire shoots a look in Sam's direction again. *What does he think? What should they do?* For a second there it looks as though Sam wants to talk to her too.

Just then Tim and Ursula arrive on their bikes. "Look, Daddy, there's Pete," Ursula calls out. She's using her baby voice tonight. "Yea for Pete!" she yells. "Yea for Pete!"

Tim scrambles up the steps of the bleachers to join Claire and kisses her cheek. Ursula snuggles up beside her. This evening she has evidently decided she likes Claire.

"Sorry we're late," Tim says, a little breathless. "Ursula had a little trouble on the hill. How are we doing?"

"We're losing," Claire tells him. "The coach put Pete in right field again, too."

"My daddy could punch him if you want," Ursula says. "My daddy's the strongest."

"Never mind, Ursula," Claire tells her. "Some problems a person has to work out for themselves."

Ursula has made a deal with her dad. He let her quit day camp on condition that she will play quietly until three o'clock, when day camp would have let out, and not bother him. Last time she asked him what time it was he said ten-thirty. That means she's only got four and a half hours more to wait. But pretty soon she can ask him for lunch anyway.

She's playing Barbies. The girls are going to a party today. Jessica is wearing the blue glitter evening gown. Samantha is wearing a pink mini dress and a fur stole Ursula has made out of a piece of cotton she got out of an aspirin bottle. Because she doesn't have a party dress for Tracy, Ursula has draped a hankie around her waist with a purple hair ribbon to keep it in place.

"Do you think Ken is going to be there, Jessica?" Ursula/Samantha says. She talks in a high, whispery voice like on makeup commercials on TV.

"Maybe yes, maybe no," says Ursula/Jessica. "I heard he was going out with Tammy."

"But he said he was in love with me," says Ursula/Samantha. "We were going to get married Tuesday."

"You never know with Ken," says Ursula/Tracy. "He asked me to marry him one time, too."

Ursula is fastening the buttons on Tracy's cape as she polishes off the last of her M&M's. She wishes they weren't all gone. She wishes her dad would take a break from his writing so he could be Ken. She wishes Jenny could talk.

"Men are shits," says Ursula/Tracy. She heard her mother say this one time and it made a big impression. Mostly because she hasn't heard her mother say all that much. Last time she saw her was the week after her sixth birthday, and in three weeks she turns eight.

Ursula's getting a Bend 'N Stretch Barbie for her birthday. She knows because she's seen it in her dad's closet.

Her dad has asked her what she wants to do for her party. "We could take a bunch of your friends bowling," he said. "Or we could go to Chuck E Cheese." He said maybe they could even rent Rollerblades, if the weather's nice. "We should get the invitations out soon," he told her. "You need to make a list of who to invite." He says this almost every day. "Have you made your list yet, Ursula?" he says. "We don't want to leave it to the last minute, otherwise the kids might have plans."

Her dad is such an idiot. He doesn't get it. The reason Ursula hasn't made up her list is there's nobody to put on it. Tammy maybe, if she knew her phone number, but Ursula doesn't see how Tammy could go Rollerblading or roll a bowling ball, on account of the cerebral palsy. She'd probably drop a bowling ball on somebody's foot. Also, she needs someone to help her swallow her food.

Maybe Ursula's mom will come from New Zealand for her birthday. Maybe the reason Ursula hasn't heard from her for a while is she's planning a surprise. Ursula will wake up on her birthday morning and her mom will be standing there in a flowered bathrobe with a tray. On this tray there will be one of those little cereal boxes her father never buys because they're expensive and they just use up trees in the rainforest. Froot Loops. Also that little kitten pitcher they used to have back when her mom still lived with them, where the milk comes out its paw. There will be an orange cut up in slices arranged like a flower the way her mom always did. And many presents, of course, not just Bend 'N Stretch Barbie, but the Town House and a Lite Brite and something else, her magic present, a heart locket that opens up with a picture of Ursula and her mom in it. Her mom has also bought her a party dress with puff sleeves and little jewels like Ashley Carson had on at the

*spring concert at school. It will not be a Chubbies size, and still it will
fit just right. There are patent-leather party shoes to go with it and
ruffled socks and even jeweled barrettes that match the jewels on the
collar of the dress. Accessories are the kind of thing her dad doesn't
understand. If he was buying socks for a party dress, he'd probably get
her crew socks like he wears, with an orange stripe around the top.
"Just fold it over so the stripe doesn't show, Urs," he'd say. "You look
fine."*

He will get up to make some more coffee soon. She could go ask
him again how many more minutes till three o'clock, but she
knows he will tell her to clean up her room and she's not in the
mood. He never used to be very picky in this department, but ever
since he met Claire, he has been after Ursula all the time to clean
up her room and put her toys away. He used to say they were just
like a couple of hoboes. "A bachelor and a bachelorette," he said.
"That's us, Urs." They used to eat their dinner on a TV tray
watching "Rocky and Bullwinkle," and she could leave her M&M
wrappers on the floor, and when one of them farted, the other one
would fart back. Now he says they should have regular meals at
the kitchen table and they have to clean up right away afterward.
He told Ursula they need to clean up their act. Last night when
they were at the video store and she wanted to rent *Dr. Giggles,* he
said, "You know I've been thinking, Urs. I don't think these are
such great movies for a girl your age to be watching." He made
them get this movie called *Pollyanna* instead, with this idiot kid
that keeps telling everybody how much she loves them and doing
nice things for everyone.

"She makes me want to puke," Ursula said after they'd been
watching the movie about ten minutes. "I bet her farts smell like
perfume." Normally this would have made her dad laugh, but all
he said was, "Come on, Urs. Give it a chance. Seven-year-old girls
are supposed to love this stuff."

You don't have to be a genius to figure out that it was her that
gave him that idea. Her and her perfect daughter that probably
has every movie Hayley Mills ever made memorized. If she came
in here now Ursula would give her a karate kick straight to her

stomach like her dad taught her. One more thing he hardly ever does with her anymore.

"Men are shits," says Ursula/Tracy. *"They always leave you in the end. You can never count on them when you need them."*

"But you don't understand," says Ursula/Samantha. *"I love him. I can't live without him. He's all I've got."*

"Then I hate to break it to you," says Ursula/Tracy. *"But you've got nothing. Nada. Zip."*

This is when Ursula's dad walks in. He used to hang around the house in just his boxers. Now he's got sweatpants on.

"Turkey or tuna fish for lunch, Urs?" he asks her. He hardly ever offers peanut butter and jelly anymore, and Ursula knows why. Too fattening.

"Tuna," she says. She doesn't look up. Just see if she kisses him. Ha.

"And listen, Urs," he says. "After lunch I want you to do something about this room."

They have come to Twinkle-town—one of Pete's favorite places in the universe, he says—for an evening of miniature golf: Tim, Claire, Pete, Ursula, Sally, and even Travis. Claire was very surprised that the two teenagers would have agreed to join this gathering, but amazingly enough, Sally evidently decided there was something cute about it. *"The dysfunctional family goes golfing,"* she says. "Should be wild."

They are at the sixth hole now: a windmill whose blades turn slowly in such a way that they block the opening for a person's golf ball every time they reach a certain point in their rotation. The object is timing your shot just right to get your ball through the hole at a moment when it isn't blocked.

Tim has made the hole in three strokes, which is par. Travis got the same score. Claire took four. Sally, who has the disconcerting trait of giggling and utterly falling apart in all even vaguely athletic endeavors whenever her boyfriend is around, has taken six shots without success or apparent concern.

The surprise of the night is Ursula, who turns out to have an almost uncanny talent for miniature golf. So far she has shot par or less on every hole, with a hole in one at one of the toughest spots on the course. She is practically dancing, she's so excited. "I never even did this before," she says again. "This is just my first time. And I'm the youngest one, too."

Sally isn't bothered by this sort of thing but Pete is going nuts. The first time Ursula made a great shot he just shrugged, but when she got the hole in one Claire thought he might actually throw his ball at her. On the fourth hole, when her club tapped her ball as she was setting up her shot—something Ursula does with enormous care—Pete protested that the tap should count as her first shot.

"Oh, come on, ease up," Claire said, rubbing his shoulders. "It's just a game."

"I just don't like to see people not taking the rules seriously," he said.

"Pete's got a point there," said Tim. "What do you say, Urs? I think we'd better count that as a shot. You've still got most of us beat."

But Pete's not the only one who's playing for blood tonight. Ursula has spotted an enormous stuffed gorilla at the refreshment stand, for the player with the best score of the evening. She wants it.

"The ball didn't even move, Daddy," she says. "He's just mad because I'm better than him." Claire has talked to Tim about Ursula's habit of addressing all her remarks to her father, rather than speaking directly to the other people around her. Also the way she seldom speaks about any of these people by name.

"Well, okay," Tim says. "But then I'm going to take one stroke off Pete's score too." Claire knows Pete will hate this even more. The last thing he wants is to be babied.

They have reached a little suspension bridge Ursula thinks is the cutest hole yet. "I could bring my Barbies here," she says, her voice a low hush. "I can't believe I never knew there were places like this."

"We can come here lots," Claire tells her. Just never again with Pete is all.

Over at the schoolhouse hole, Travis has his hand up the back of Sally's shirt.

"It's her turn," Ursula says, pointing to Sally. "Doesn't she want to hit her ball?"

"I don't think she'd mind if you went ahead and took your turn," Claire tells her. You couldn't exactly describe Sally as being into the game. Travis either.

Ursula lines up her shot again—careful not to hold her club anywhere near the ball as she studies it from ground level, like a professional golfer.

"Jeez-um," Pete groans. "We're going to be here all night."

She gets another hole in one. "Did you see that one, Dad?" she says. "Aren't I good?"

"You're something else all right, honey," Tim tells her.

"We just won't say what," Pete mumbles under his breath.

"Stop that," Claire snaps. She looks at the scorecard. Ten holes to go. The tinny sound system is playing a Garth Brooks tape. Every few seconds there's the sizzling sound of another insect hitting the blue bulbs of the bug zappers.

"He's mean," Ursula says to Tim. Tim looks at Claire helplessly. Pete throws his ball into a miniature pond. Water splashes all over Ursula.

"Go sit in the car," Claire tells Pete. "You're done."

Pete strides off the artificial turf swinging his club like a walking stick, without a word. No batting cages tonight.

"I don't want to do this anymore, either," Sally says. "Travis and I can walk home."

So it's just Tim and Claire and Ursula on the last stretch of the course. Ursula wins. She takes their hands triumphantly as they head back to the refreshment stand to turn in their clubs. "I love this place," she whispers, even though she doesn't get the gorilla. "Can we come here again tomorrow?" She says she's going to keep her scorecard forever.

Claire buys her a push-up pop. She gets one for Pete, too—it's their tradition. Only when they get back to the car he's gone, and he's not over at the batting cages, either. Eventually, when they give up looking for him and head toward home, they spot him on the highway. He's scuffing his feet in the dirt and digging his hands deep in his pockets. When Tim pulls the car over and Claire gets out to talk to her son, he won't even look at her. She can see he's been crying.

"That was always our place," he says. "Why'd you have to go and bring *her?*"

Claire goes to New York for her first conference on fund-raising for small local nonprofits, leaving Nancy in charge back at her house. Vivian has told Claire that unless she can start generating some more substantial corporate donations for the museum she may have to recommend terminating her position and using the money allocated for her salary to hire a professional fund-raiser instead. "Not that I want you to feel pressure or anything," she tells Claire. "Just a word to the wise."

Claire is gone a total of thirty-six hours on this trip. This period of time knowing he is not simply apart from Claire, but that she is also across state lines, is nearly unbearable to Tim. Partly to get himself through it, he writes her one of his letters, and though their usual arrangement is that Tim should fax these letters to Claire only when she's around to take them off the machine right away, he sends it anyway. Just having his words scrolling through the machine will make him feel more connected to her, he believes. So he writes:

> *"I know it's a good thing for you to be developing your professional skills and all that.*
>
> *"But every time I think how important it is for you to do something like this trip, my cock moves in direct defiance to what I think. It makes me uncomfortable wherever I am. Making breakfast. In my office. In my car. Driving Ursula to the library and picking up groceries. My cock insists I listen to its nonstop throbs.*
>
> *"It's not easy being a guy. Your own son is destined for it, so you might as well know. The thing that bothers me the most is that I don't think you can register a cock to vote,*

considering that I can't imagine one pulling the curtain shut at a voting booth. So why does this blood-filled appendage have so much to say about how I feel toward you? It has no respect for authority. No idea of how important this trip is for you. It can't be reasoned with. It doesn't even speak English. It just argues with me all the time in this kind of tom-tom— like manner. You know, Robert Bly bullshit. From my own cock, as if his book weren't bad enough. And I know my own cock hasn't read his book, because I suspect my cock is a terribly stupid thing. Lovable perhaps, but not respectable.

"Nonetheless, I don't want to get rid of it. I've lived with it all my life, it's just never been as obnoxious as it has been in these last few months. It even looks more stupid when I think of you, rather than being this polite little trouser mouse it should be. You should see it at this very moment, for instance, standing at attention as if this was West Point and some four-star general was performing inspection.

"God, it's lucky your children never read your faxes."

They never have before, actually, since the fax machine is up in Claire's third-floor office, where they never go because you might run into bats. Only as it turns out, Sally has been trying to reach Travis on the phone, and Pete has been tying up their regular line forever, in some assinine conversation with Jared about the new Christopher Pike book, *Cheerleaders: The First Evil.* So for the first time in at least a year Sally has just stepped into her mother's office, where the fax is located, with the plan of switching it off for a moment and using the fax phone to make her call. At just this moment Tim's fax scrolls through the machine, and even then she wouldn't have given it a second look except there is this drawing on the bottom of the page which is, unmistakably, a picture of a penis. She knows this from recent dealings with Travis. With whom she is not having sex. Just everything but.

So she reads it, not every disgusting word, of course. But enough to leave Sally with the feeling that everything is going crazy, and everything she used to think was real isn't. Her own mother is acting like a teenager. Her mother's boyfriend is acting like one of Pete's friends. Next thing you know, one of them will announce they have AIDS. They will go on "Oprah." They will French-kiss at her graduation.

A blood-filled appendage. Polite little trouser mouse. Sally feels she has been sexually violated, even though nobody has laid a hand on her. Who would have guessed a bunch of words on a piece of fax paper could do that to a person? Her mother has some nerve telling Sally to take it slow with Travis, considering what she's up to herself.

Once baseball season's over, Pete and Sally go to their father's house for two weeks. Tim and Claire and Ursula drive to Maine. They check into a motel, the cheapest they can find—a little cabin with beds so soft they sag in the middle. Ursula has never stayed in a motel before. She's very excited.

"Look at the little shampoo bottle!" she calls to Tim from the bathroom. "There's even a shower cap."

"The sleeping arrangements here could get frustrating," Tim whispers to Claire, setting his overnight bag on the bed. "I don't know how I'm going to get through a night in the bed next to you this way without screwing you."

"You'll live," she says. "I'm not all that irresistible."

Ursula comes out of the bathroom. She bounces on the bed. "This is the best place," she says. "I want to stay here forever."

"Wait till you see the ocean," says Claire. "You can jump in the waves and slide on the sand dunes. There's sure to be tons of kids making castles." Claire's children have always loved this beach, and one of the things Claire has always liked best about it is the way they find other children to entertain themselves with so she can just stretch out on the sand and read.

Ursula's still bouncing. "I want to do whatever you guys do," she says.

• • •

They have slathered her with number 45 sunblock, the highest number. Tim is also wearing it. Even now, with all the talk of UV rays, Claire doesn't worry much about her own dark skin, but because of Ursula's and Tim's coloring, they have bought an umbrella.

They find a good spot a little way down the beach, close to several families with children the right age for Ursula. Tim spreads out their blanket. Claire sets out the pail and digging implements she has picked up, and the kite. She sets them next to Ursula.

Claire takes out her book and a stack of exhibit proposals for the museum. She mounds up a pile of sand the way she likes, to support her neck. She places herself so her foot touches Tim's. It's a perfect day.

Tim has also brought a book, but he has not opened his. He is looking at Ursula, who sits on her towel with her sweatshirt still on. "Aren't you going to play with me, Daddy?" she says.

Claire watches his face. They are both watching his face, actually. "A little later I will," he says carefully. "Right now I think I'll just stretch out here and relax." Claire has won the point, and they all know it.

Ursula is silent for about a minute. Claire rereads her paragraph. Her hand strokes Tim's thigh. She can feel his tension.

"I'm bored," says Ursula.

"Oh, come on now," he says. "There's a million things to do here."

"There would be. If you'd play with me."

"I will," he says. "Later." There is that supplicating tone to his voice again that always makes this tight place in Claire's throat when she hears it. "Stop it!" she wants to say.

"I'm hot," Ursula says. "I want a drink."

"We'll get some Cokes at the snack bar a little later," he tells her. "If you're thirsty now, you can have a nectarine."

Claire turns her page. Tim picks up his book too. She squeezes his hand.

"I hate this bathing suit," she says. She is examining the folds of skin around her belly. "It makes me look fat."

"That happens to everybody when they sit down in a bathing suit," Tim says. "Even Claire probably has a fold or two, right, Claire?"

"Right," she says.

"Not to mention your old dad."

"You have tons of fat, Daddy," she says. "You should see my dad's love handles," she tells Claire, almost proudly. Then she realizes that Claire has seen them, of course. Ursula is no longer the sole possessor of his secrets.

Another minute passes. "This place sucks," she says.

"Oh, come on, sweetheart," he says. The pleading tone is worse now. "Go play."

"You hate me," she says.

"You know that's not true," he says, desperate now.

This is so ridiculous, Claire wants to scream. Now you are arguing with your daughter about whether or not you hate her.

"See those kids over there?" she says. "There's a little girl just your age working on a sand castle. I bet she'd love some help."

"I don't know her," Ursula says.

"Here's what you do," Claire says. She has gone through this fifty times with her own children, though by the time they were Ursula's age they had long since figured out how to do it for themselves.

"You bring your pail and shovel over and say, 'Hi. What's your name?' She says, 'My name is such and such'—"

"Poop head," says Ursula.

"Right. She says, 'My name is Poop head.' You say, 'Pleased to meet you, Poop head. My name is Ursula, although you are welcome to call me Silly Goose if you want. Can we work on your sand castle together?'"

"She called me a silly goose, Daddy," says Ursula. That whining tone. The worst.

"You listen to Claire," Tim says, sounding like a doomed man. "She's trying to help you make friends."

"You want me to come with you?" says Claire. When Ursula gives no answer she puts her book down and rises from the towel. She brushes herself off and takes Ursula's hand firmly. She hopes she is managing to conceal her irritation as she says, "I sometimes feel shy too. But you'll see. This will be easy. You'll have fun."

"Hi," says Claire. "What's your name?"

The little girl looks up from her digging. "Meredith," she says. "What's you two's?"

"I'm Claire. This is Ursula. We wondered if you wanted help with your castle."

"Sure," says Meredith. She points to a pile of stones. "We got to build the wall before the waves come up," she says to Ursula. "You can help."

Ursula just sits there. Claire reaches for a handful of stones.

"Maybe we could make a moat," she says. "What do you think, Ursula?"

"The waves are just going to wash it away anyways," Ursula says. "This is a dumb castle." After a minute she gets up and wanders back to the towel.

"Lucky I got you to help," Meredith tells Claire. "Or we'd never get this wall made in time."

They leave the beach a little after lunch. Ursula says she's getting sun poisoning. When she says this, Tim looks like a cornered animal.

"It's okay," Claire says. "I think it's going to cloud over soon, anyway."

They go for ice creams. Ursula says she doesn't want any. Then she says she does. Then she says she doesn't. Claire and Tim are licking their cones out on the patio of Barnacle Billy's when Ursula decides she does want an ice cream after all. A sundae.

Walking through Ogunquit looking in shops, Ursula is briefly cheerful, holding each of their hands and skipping. "This is fun isn't it Daddy?" she says in the TV commercial kid voice Claire heard the night she met Ursula.

"I bet her kids are jealous they didn't get to come, aren't they?" Ursula says to Tim.

"If you have something to say to me, say it to me," Claire tells Ursula, as she has many times.

"If you have something to say to Claire, say it to Claire," Tim tells her.

"Can we go bowling?" she says. *"Canwecanwecanwe? Please-pleasepleaseplease?"*

It is as if a cold wind has blown across Claire's heart, so bitter and sudden it has not simply frozen, it has cracked. Ursula lets go of Claire's hand and stands there on the sidewalk, looking her dead straight in the eye.

"I know just what you're thinking," she says, not in the baby voice or anything close. *"And I like you anyways."*

While they were away on their vacation and Tim's downstairs neighbors were taking care of Jenny, she got into the garbage at their apartment house. Now the landlord says the dog has to go.

Tim tries reasoning with the guy. "You don't understand," he says. "Ursula's had Jenny her whole life."

"Tough luck," the guy tells him. "You weren't supposed to have a dog here in the first place. Tenants before you had their mutt put to sleep when they moved in. It's the rule."

Ursula is inside setting up her collection of motel shampoos when Tim gets the word about Jenny. "What am I supposed to tell my daughter?" he says. "You don't understand what this dog means to her."

"Yeah," says the landlord. "And I guess you don't understand what my trash bin means to me. No pooch. No budge."

"She doesn't have any brothers and sisters," Tim is saying. "And her mother's sort of abandoned her. She counts on the dog. This is going to sound crazy, but she talks to it. It's like therapy for her."

"Sad story, bub," says the landlord. "But I ain't letting you keep no canine."

Hearing this, Claire tells Tim she and her kids will take Jenny at their house. "Pete's been begging for a dog, anyway," she tells him.

"Sweetheart," Tim says. "Are you sure you can handle it?"

"She was going to end up in our house soon enough, right?" says Claire. They have talked about Tim's moving in with Claire and her kids a little further down the line. "Your dog is just getting to move in with us a little sooner than you."

Ursula comes back outside. "Come see my potion laboratory," she's saying. Then she sees them. Her dad is kissing Claire with one of those tongue kisses. His hand is under her sweater. Ursula might as well be invisible.

So now he's given Jenny away. "Why don't you just send me out in the forest like Hansel and Gretel?" Ursula weeps. "Don't worry. I won't bring any bread crumbs. I wouldn't want to find my way back to this place."

"Listen to me, Ursula," he pleads. "It was either let Claire and her kids take care of Jenny or have her put to sleep. Would you have preferred that?"

"She'll probably sleep on the boy's bed," says Ursula. "But I'll never show him our special newspaper trick."

"Urs," her father says to her. He has that begging voice again. Ursula feels powerful and big.

"I hate him," she says. "Maybe I'll teach Jenny to bite him."

"Pete's doing us a huge favor," Tim tells her. "You know how much work it is taking care of a dog."

"He'll neglect her. He'll be one of those people that just takes her out the door to pee and brings her right back in. He won't run with her. He won't scratch her spot."

"Maybe you'll help him," Tim says. "You can go over there all the time and help out." This is a new idea. It could be a trick her father's using to make her go along with the idea, knowing how much she likes going over to Claire's house. Ursula needs to think about this.

"Sure," he says. "And in the fall, you could stop by Claire's house on your way home from school. You could get off the bus at Claire's stop and take her out for walks every day. You can even bring her over to our yard and sit on the front steps with her. Just not inside. You can talk to her like you always did."

That was her secret thing. He wasn't supposed to know about that.

"I don't really talk to Jenny," she says. "I'm just singing."

"You can do anything you want with her," he says. "She's still your dog. She always will be."

"You love Claire best now, don't you?" she says. And she could be right.

Ursula's dad has gone to the supermarket—that's what he said—and she is home alone. She goes into his room. Her birthday is in five days and she's looking to see if he's got more presents.

She has already found the Barbie in his closet. Also a box of smell markers and a puzzle and a set of panties with the names of the days of the week on them, but that doesn't really count, since a person needs panties anyways. Ursula is sure there must be something else for her though. Her magical present.

She looks in his underwear drawer first. Nothing. Then she checks the drawer where he keeps his T-shirts and sweats. Also nothing. Nothing in his night table and nothing on the top shelf of his closet. She is just about to give up. (Who knows, maybe that's where he is right now? Getting her special present.) Then she thinks to check his desk.

Papers are everywhere. There's a picture of Ursula here. Also a picture she drew for him a few years ago on his birthday of the two of them fishing. Her dad is reeling in this tiny little sardine. Ursula's got a giant fish on her pole. She wrote X's and O's all across the bottom. She was just in kindergarten then. She didn't know how to write *Love*.

In the middle drawer she finds something. In among the paper clips and unsharpened pencils, there's a little velvet box with a ribbon around it. Ursula draws in her breath. She opens it.

It's a ring, with the most beautiful purple jewel in the middle, and pearls—Ursula's favorite—all around. Her magical present. Better than a toy. Better than a Barbie Town House even. She puts in on.

"Oh, Ken," she says, holding the ring out the way she saw Pamela do on "Live and Let Live" last week, when Todd proposed. "You shouldn't have."

She studies the ring for a few moments, then places it very carefully back in the box and ties the ribbon. She shuts the drawer.

For the first few days Pete stays at his dad's house it feels good sleeping late and playing lots of Super Nintendo, which Pete's mom won't let him have at their house. Pete's dad buys any kind of cereal Pete wants and never makes him pick up and do chores the way his mom does. He cooks chili and they can eat in the living room with the TV on. They watch ball games and compare notes on whose sneakers smell worse. When Pete farts he doesn't have to say, "Excuse me."

But his dad goes to work most days, and then Pete and his sister are stuck at the house. He could ride his bike but there isn't anyplace to go now that all his friends are back in Blue Hills. Plus he has to listen to his sister complaining about how bored she is. Sometimes when they stay at their dad's their old babysitter Melanie drops by and takes them places, but she's been away at summer school.

For the first week they were with their dad, Travis was calling Sally every day and driving over to see her every time he got the chance, at which point the two of them would disappear for hours in his Impala. It didn't take a brain surgeon to figure out why. By the first weekend, Sally told their dad it was nothing personal, but she really couldn't stick around any longer. A part-time job had opened up bussing tables at Friendly's. She was out of there.

Pete's dad was going to take him camping then but it rained, and then his dad got called on a job. So for the last week Pete's been alone in the house most days. He never thought he could get sick of video games, but he is.

Pete's dad is the coolest person he knows. But Pete's glad when the two weeks are up and it's time to go back to his mom's. Baseball season's over, and he didn't make the All Stars, but there's still baseball camp to look forward to, and hanging out with Jared and Ben.

The other thing is, Pete misses his mom. He remembers last summer, how the two of them would ride their bikes into town and get a frozen yogurt. Saturday mornings they like to drive around and check out yard sales. Sometimes they take their canoe down to the river and paddle upstream to this place where they tie up the canoe and have a picnic, and there's this one particular rock you can climb on and jump into the water. Paddling home, they sing all these corny songs Pete learned at baseball camp last summer, like the theme song from "Rawhide," "Hello Mudda, Hello Fadda." They might talk or they might just paddle quietly, which is also good. The nice thing is for once the phone isn't ringing and his mom isn't worrying about bills or trying to do ten things at once or getting after him to pick stuff up. It's his favorite time with her.

This is what Pete's thinking about as his dad pulls his car up in front of their house after his two weeks away. When his mom comes out of the house to greet him, and she's holding a leash, he actually thinks she's gotten a puppy to surprise him, and for a second there he's so excited he wants to jump out right there, before his dad has even turned off the engine. Then this old, ratty-looking mutt comes loping out of their house with a bare patch in its fur, and lies down next to his mother while she clips on the leash. Not that there's much danger of a dog like this one running away. It looks a hundred years old.

"Where'd the dog come from?" Pete says.

"I'll tell you the whole story in a minute," says his mom. "But first you have to give me a hug."

He is just about to do that, too, when he sees her. Ursula. Coming out of his house like she owned it, eating a Popsicle.

Claire can't understand how it can be that Tim doesn't know the phone number of a single child from Ursula's second-grade class. Or their last names even. "Didn't you ever have anybody over?" she says. "Didn't she ever go over to anybody's house to play? Somebody must have invited her to their birthday party sometime."

There was one girl, he says. Her family lived way out of town and they'd gotten lost driving over. Ursula was so nervous that by the time they got there she was crying that all the games would be over, but it turned out there weren't really any games, anyway. The girl had invited everybody in their whole class and they were all running around the yard throwing chips at each other. One girl was screaming because some boy had squirted ketchup on her party dress. The birthday girl was also crying, he remembers. "Nobody gave me anything good," she said.

There was another time when Ursula had come home very excited, saying that this popular girl named Jackie was going to invite her to her party. She'd told her that on the playground.

"We got to get Jackie a very special present," Ursula said. "She's my best friend."

She made him take her to Toys "R" Us that afternoon. She picked out a Roller Baby doll that cost $19.95. "That's way too much for a birthday party present," Tim told her. He may not have known much about birthday parties, but he knew that much, anyway.

Finally they settled on a Pretty Perm Stacie for $12.95. Still a little high in Tim's opinion, but Ursula was so insistent.

A couple days later Tim asked her where the party invitation was. He wanted to be sure he wasn't teaching a class that afternoon, or to make arrangements if he was.

"She's giving it to me tomorrow," Ursula said. But the next day there was still no invitation from Jackie.

By Saturday, when she had still not brought home the invitation, Tim said maybe they should call Jackie. "I don't know her number," she said. "I left the invitation at school. I'll bring it home Monday."

Thursday he called her teacher during lunch. "I hate to bother you with this," he said. "But Ursula keeps forgetting to bring home the invitation to Jackie's party. I wanted to make sure we didn't miss it."

"Oh goodness," she said. "Jackie's party was last weekend. She brought her presents in Monday for show-and-tell. I keep telling the children not to do that because it makes the ones that didn't get invited feel bad. Just try getting eight-year-olds to cooperate though."

In the end they invited Sandy and Jeff and their baby, Keith, from downstairs. Claire asks Pete and Sally if they'd come over, just for the cake part maybe, but when they tell her they're busy she doesn't push it. So it's just the six of them—four adults plus Ursula, and the baby.

Claire takes Ursula swimming while Tim makes dinner and decorates. At one point, when they're lying on their towels, Ursula suddenly sits bolt upright and looks out across Burr Pond. "My mom is thinking about me right now," she says. "I can feel it."

"I bet you're right," Claire says. "Birthdays are important for parents, too. No matter how old your child gets to be, when it's their birthday you always remember how it was the first second you saw them, when they were newborn. A baby is like the most special present anybody could ever get."

Back at Tim and Ursula's apartment, Tim has hung up streamers and a cardboard sign that says "Happy Birthday." He has set the table with a paper cloth covered with pictures of Barbie in all sorts of outfits. He has made Ursula's favorite dinner, macaroni and cheese, with chocolate cake for dessert and mint chocolate chip ice cream. At every place there's a noisemaker and a paper hat that says "Let's Party."

This is the first time Tim has had Jeff and Sandy over for a meal. They're very young—twenty maybe, twenty-one tops. Jeff works as a delivery man for Snapple. Sandy stays home with the baby.

"That Snapple is really something," says Tim.

Sandy asks if he's tasted the Mountain Berry. It's the best, she thinks. Maybe Jeff can get him some free.

The phone rings. Ursula runs to pick it up. A student is calling to ask Tim about the bog trip on Saturday.

"They shouldn't call you all the time like that," Ursula says. "Somebody could be trying to get us and the line would be busy."

"They'd call back," says Tim. He's clearing away the dishes. Sandy and Jeff look uncomfortable. In his infant seat, Keith is beginning to fuss. He pulls off the hat Ursula had put on him and begins to chew it.

"When can I open my presents?" Ursula asks again.

"After cake time," Tim reminds her.

"I can't help it," she says. "I'm just so excited." She looks at the phone again.

"Why don't we go ahead and give her the presents now?" Claire says. "Sandy and Jeff probably need to get home soon."

Ursula opens one of the smaller packages first—the day-of-the-week panties. Then the smell markers. Then the puzzle. Then she opens Sandy and Jeff's gift, a coloring book based on the TV series "Full House."

She opens Claire's presents next—a dress she has ordered from the Hannah Anderson catalog with matching purple tights. Claire has also made Ursula a sewing kit with five different colors of rickrack and sequins and tiny snaps the size for making doll clothes and a little china thimble with pansies painted on it. Also a pattern for Barbie clothes, and some fabric.

"I love this," Ursula says. "I wish I knew how to sew."

"I'll teach you," says Claire.

There's one package left, the Bend 'N Stretch Barbie. Ursula runs to her father when she gets it and hugs him. "This was just what I wanted," she says. "And blond is my favorite."

"So," he says, clearing away the wrapping paper. "Who wants cake?" Sandy and Jeff say they'd better be going. They need to put Keith to bed.

Ursula looks around the room. He is probably saving the black velvet box for the very end, she figures.

He carries in the cake with its eight candles. She makes a wish.

It's many hours earlier in New Zealand probably. Maybe that's the problem.

When they're all done with their cake, Tim tells Ursula it's time to get ready for bed. "Even eight-year-olds have bedtimes," he says. "I'll be up in a minute to read you a story."

She lies in bed waiting for him. This will be the moment he gives her the ring.

He comes in and snuggles up next to her. "I hope you had a good day," he says. She tells him she did. She loves the Barbie.

"I know I didn't give you as much as usual this year," he says. "Money's been so tight."

"That's okay," she says. She closes her eyes. When she opens them, the black box will be lying there on her bed.

"I do have one more thing for you, actually," he says. And then he reaches into his pocket.

It's a night-light.

S ally goes on break at three o'clock, and unless he's working himself, Travis skateboards over to Friendly's most days to join her. She only gets fifteen minutes, but to Travis every second he gets to spend with her is precious. He's usually there by quarter till, waiting. Not just sitting around, naturally; Travis never sits when he's got his board, particularly not when there's a parking lot with good curbs. He has waxed the curb in front of Friendly's, actually—a section of it—so he goes extra fast. If Sally happens to have a second there where she can look up to glance out the window, she will catch sight of him, in midair most likely. He's an acrobat, a landlocked surfer. Better than a surfer, actually. Who couldn't ride a wave, when you think about it? Travis rides concrete, propelled by nothing but the shifting of his own lanky body and the explosive strength in his legs and arms and his concave abdomen. He knows every nick in Friendly's curb, also every line of his board, which he shaves down and alters almost weekly. Put Travis in a physics class and he's brain-dead. But here in Friendly's parking lot, he's a skateboard scientist. A magician.

He does it for Sally. The way some people write poems and songs or paint pictures for a person, Travis dedicates his skateboarding to her. Everything he does now he does with her in his mind.

He wants to get laid, of course. That part is driving him crazy. But how he feels about Sally isn't just about that anymore. He also wants to hold her hand and ride around in his car with her. He wants to bring her things—like the peach he stopped to buy at the farmers' market on his way over to Friendly's. He is saving up to buy her an ankle bracelet with both their names engraved inside. Fourteen-carat gold.

Travis dreams about Sally every night. Sally and skateboarding. Last night it was both: He dreamed the two of them were out on a road someplace all alone, and she was telling him how much she loved him, and he was kissing her and she had her arms around him, and they were doing it. Having sex. Then he was on his board again, and he did this jump he's never seen anybody pull off, not even on a video. A total midair sideways flip, landing on his back wheels. Nobody was watching but her. The only one that matters.

That's the move he's working on today as he waits for her, and he almost has it, too. He adjusts his weight and throws back his arms in a way that lifts his board and his body clear off the ground. He hopes she's watching him from the window. If she does, she will see something amazing: his skateboard nearly perpendicular to the ground, his body defying gravity, his back arched, his wheels spinning. Maybe astronauts have had this feeling. Maybe skydivers, and certain birds.

So far in his sixteen years the farthest Travis has ever gone from home was the eighth-grade trip to Boston to walk the Freedom Trail. When he came home he told everybody one trip to the city was enough for him: Too dirty. Too noisy. Too crowded. Good tar, just not enough open space to make use of it.

But since being with Sally, it's like Travis's whole world has opened up. He has to accomplish things. He wants to go to L.A., for the national exhibitions, where the pros compete. He wants to take her with him.

Nobody will know who he is when they walk in, of course. Nobody will have seen a board like his, sanded like he's done, a full quarter-inch thinner at the front edge than it is in back. "Who's the kid?" someone will ask when they call out his number. "What kind of board is that?"

"It's just some nobody from the sticks," somebody will answer. "He probably got lost on his way to the soapbox derby."

The music playing is Boyz II Men. The surface is the slickest he's ever skateboarded on. He sails out like Aladdin on his carpet. But faster. Lifts off. Lands upright. Flips again.

"Jesus," somebody says. "Did you see that?" The crowd is going nuts.

The music's blaring. People are out of their seats. A representative from AirWalks is making his way down to the sidelines to talk sponsorship.

But Travis doesn't have time for him. He has to see Sally first. He skates up to her and lifts her up onto his board, puts his arms around her, right there in the middle of the championships.

"I was so proud of you," she says. They kiss. They don't walk out of there. They fly.

This is what he is thinking about as Sally steps out the door of Friendly's, in her pink and white uniform, with the HI I'M SALLY nametag pinned over her heart. She is so beautiful. He hands her the peach.

"You nut," she says, laughing. She takes a bite. Juice drips down her chin. "Now look what you made me do."

He doesn't wipe it off. He just kisses her.

Often these days Sally has resisted going to her dad's house because that means leaving her friends. Not seeing Travis. But all this week Sally had been looking forward to going to her dad's on Friday, for Labor Day Weekend. Not that she pictured herself having some corny heart-to-heart father-daughter talk. It's just that all this stuff that's been happening with Travis wanting to have sex all the time has her confused. All those years she was in such a rush to grow up and move on to the next step. Now she guesses she's there and she wishes things could just be simple again.

She has this idea she and her dad can paint a mural on the ceiling of her old room. She's got drawings made already. Her paints are packed in her overnight bag. She'll make a big batch of oatmeal chocolate-chip cookies and they'll go to the drive-in. She wouldn't even mind it if her dad takes out his guitar and they sing all those old folk songs from the sixties.

When he picked them up at her mom's, her dad said he had something to tell them. "You know Melanie?" he said. Of course she knew Melanie. Melanie babysat for them ever since Sally was seven or eight.

"She and I have been seeing each other, kind of," he said. "I'd been meaning to tell you."

Pete was totally silent. "What do you mean seeing each other?" Sally said. "You mean she's your girlfriend? She's just a few years older than me." She felt nauseous.

"Sometimes a person's chronological age isn't the most important thing, if they're really tuned in to each other," he said. Pete was fiddling with the dials of the radio.

"She's really looking forward to seeing you guys," her dad said. "She says she's always thought you two are totally cool."

Melanie's lying in the front yard in her bikini when they pull up.

"Great earrings," she says to Sally as she approaches the car. She's skinnier than Sally these days. Last summer, when she used to come over for cookouts sometimes (and more, Sally realizes now), she and Sally sometimes shared clothes, but it would no longer be possible.

"How's summer school?" Sally asks her.

"Best thing I can say is it's over," Melanie says. "I couldn't wait to get back home and hang out with you guys." Her arm is wrapped around Sally's dad's waist as she says this. She hooks a finger in his belt loop. Sally does that with Travis. Among other things.

"I brought the new Rage Against the Machine tape," Sally tells Melanie. As long as they keep talking, everything must be normal.

"Cool," she says. "Your dad and me went to see them last week in Providence, right, Sammy? I wasn't sure they'd let an old fart that's forty-one into Lollapallooza, but they did."

Sally had wanted to go to Lollapallooza herself. But Travis had to work and she couldn't get a ride.

"What do you think?" Sally's dad says. "Melanie's only been here a couple weeks and she's already planted flowers all over the place. What was the name of these again, Mel?"

"Chrysanthemums, you idiot!" she shrieks, throwing a handful of grass at him. "Jeez, he doesn't know a thing about plants, does he? You should've seen all the weeds I had to pull out."

Sally's mom always hated chrysanthemums. There used to be peonies in this bed, and delphiniums, and roses.

Melanie runs ahead into the house. Her bikini bottom is stuck in her ass. She pulls it down and looks over her shoulder, laughing. "I hope nobody saw that!" she says.

Melanie has made chocolate-chip cookies. She has also painted hearts around the kitchen window and put a vase of daisies on the table. When Sally goes to the bathroom she finds one of Melanie's bras hanging over the shower and some bikini underpants. Her dad's bedroom smells like incense.

"Your dad told me your idea about going to the drive-in to-night," Melanie says. "I love it."

The two of them sit in the front seat, naturally—Sally's dad and Melanie. Sally's in the back with Pete.

"Don't you think your dad looks just like Keanu Reeves?" Melanie asks her. "Only better looking?"

"My dad looks like my dad!" Sally wants to scream at her. Not some movie star. Not somebody's boyfriend.

It's past midnight when they get home from the drive-in. Pete wanted to stay till the end of this really dumb movie with the guy from *Wayne's World* in it. Lying in her bed in the room next to the one her dad evidently shares with Melanie now, Sally concentrates on not listening for any sounds. She imagines them moving on the mattress like a pair of jewel thieves. She tries not to picture her dad, so she pictures Travis instead, with his hard, insistent penis and his searching tongue. She hears faint laughter and the sound of her brother's Crash Test Dummies tape. She remembers how, when she was little, her mother used to lie in this bed with her sometimes when she had a hard time getting to sleep, and the song she used to sing.

"Hush, little baby, don't say a word, Daddy's going to buy you a mockingbird. . . ."

She thinks about the night her parents told her they were separating, and how her brother had gone up to her room and knocked over her dollhouse—trashed it like a rock star. She thinks about the time she and Travis were making out in the janitor's closet at school and he was so heated up he came all over her jeans, and she had to use a roll of paper towels to clean herself off. She thinks about the time she and her dad built a model of the solar system for her fourth-grade science fair and of how, when her brother broke Jupiter the day before it was due, her dad had stayed up most of the night making a new paper-mâché planet with her.

She remembers the time, years ago, when Melanie used to come over almost every Saturday night to babysit when her parents went out. It was Melanie, in fact, who taught Sally how to make oatmeal chocolate-chip cookies. She was always their favorite babysitter.

Sally tries to picture herself kissing Mr. Edmunds, whose kids she babysits now and then, Saturday nights when Travis has an away game. Nobody would say he looks like Keanu Reeves. Dan Ackroyd, maybe.

Eventually Sally falls asleep. She wakes early—before dawn—to the sound of muffled cries and whispers in the next room. When she tells her dad at breakfast that she needs to get back home early—home meaning her mom's house—on account of a big report that's due, he doesn't argue. He seems relieved.

Sally says a prayer that when she gets home she won't see Tim's station wagon sitting out front, or his horrible kid's pink bicycle.

And she doesn't. So she runs inside, never happier to be home.

Claire is sitting up in bed reading when Sally finds her. Although Sally used to climb into bed with her mother all the time when she was little, it has been years since those days.

"Have a good weekend?" Claire asks. "How'd the mural turn out?"

"We didn't get around to it," Sally tells her. She stands in front of the mirror examining her stomach. Claire waits.

"Pete behave himself?" Claire asks.

"You know. The usual," Sally tells her—though the truth is, she has never known her brother to be so subdued. "Dad wanted him to mow the lawn, but he said he had a stomachache. Then he sat around all afternoon on the couch watching a ball game and eating Wheat Thins." She doesn't mention Melanie.

"I'm fat," Sally says. She isn't, of course.

"You nut," Claire tells her. This is their familiar routine. "You have a darling little body." Sally's sitting on the bed now. Claire puts an arm around her.

They sit that way for a minute or two, not saying anything. Claire's playing a CD of the Chieftains. "I don't know how you can stand this music," Sally tells her. "Every song sounds the same. Only my mother would listen to a group with bagpipes." In fact, she says this with a certain pride.

"It's the ullean pipes," Claire tells her. "There's a big difference."

They're silent again. Claire gets the feeling Sally wants to talk about something but doesn't know how. She puts her head on Claire's shoulder. Claire strokes her hair.

"Something going on?" she says.

"Not really. I was just remembering how we used to read in bed together."

"You could go get your driver's ed manual and climb in," Claire says.

"I really should go to bed, anyway. I didn't get much sleep last night."

Claire knows not to push. It's enough just to have Sally come to her this way and sit with her. She has been so preoccupied with Tim and Ursula, it's been weeks since she's talked with her daughter about anything more than doing the laundry or what time she needs to be picked up from Friendly's.

"I wish everything could be simple again," Sally says.

Claire knows what she means. All those years she was driving the car pool and hauling children to the beach, her marriage might not have been great, but there was an order and safety to her days. You understood when you got up what the day had in store for you. You changed the baby and put the laundry on and defrosted the chicken pieces and drove the car pool and cut the crusts off the sandwiches and looked over the math worksheets and put on the rice and cleared away the dishes and gave them their baths and read them a chapter of *Wind in the Willows* and turned out the lights, and you knew when you lay down to sleep yourself that you would do pretty much the same exact thing tomorrow. You knew nobody was going to rub your shoulders with iris-scented massage oil and whisper wonderful things in your ears, but you also knew you weren't going to say a good-bye that would hurt worse than amputation. The possibilities—for joy, but also grief —were limited. Whereas the way her life is now, Claire's like an astronaut whose tether has come loose in the middle of a space walk. No telling where she'll end up, or if she'll end up anywhere. More likely she'll inhabit a state of perpetual floating.

Sally thinks her own life is impossibly hard. "Oh, Mom," she says. She sighs deeply.

"Things are getting pretty serious between you and Travis, I guess, huh?" says Claire. She has talked to Sally about safe sex on numerous occasions, but now she's wondering if maybe she needs to bring it up again.

Sally punches the pillow and makes the same kind of frustrated, impatient sound Claire does sometimes when she's working at the sewing machine and she can't get the tension adjusted right. "When he's not around, I think about him all the time, even when I don't want to. When he's around, he acts like a jerk a lot of the time and I wish he'd just leave. Then he does and I'm thinking about him again. I wish I never even had a boyfriend. This is my last one, definitely."

Claire knows better than to laugh. She strokes her daughter's hair. There's the tiny bald spot on her scalp—no bigger than a watermelon seed—from when she was very little and she scratched a chicken pox scab. At the time Claire had wept over that. Now it seems like nothing.

"Love isn't easy is it?" she says.

"It sucks, Mom," Sally says. "You have no idea."

 FALL

To Claire, Labor Day always feels like the beginning of a new year much more than January does. The start of the new school year does it. You get a clean slate. Fresh pencils. New shoes. It's the time of year that makes her feel like starting music lessons and aerobics classes and organizing her cupboards.

So Claire has made a list for Tim, and this afternoon she has brought it over to him. On her list are the names of two good consignment clothing stores where Tim can find inexpensive but more attractive clothes for Ursula to start third grade. She has typed up the recipe for her low-calorie oatmeal bars. Also on the list is the phone number to call to get Ursula signed up for soccer, as well as the phone numbers of a few of Sally's friends who are available for babysitting. Nobody's thinking about asking Pete and Sally to do that job anymore.

Claire has also brought Tim the name of the therapist she brought Pete to that first year after they moved here when he was so angry. She has already told Tim she would of course be happy to talk with a therapist herself if it would ever be helpful. She thinks Ursula needs counseling.

She tells Tim that their library has this great system set up where you can check out framed reproductions of artworks for one month at a time. A few of those would help make his apartment a little more cheery. If he would get a bedspread for Ursula's bed, then he could teach her to make it.

"I know I seem very anal and compulsive when I talk about getting your apartment organized," she says. "But I think it's about something more than housekeeping. It's about establishing order and consistency in your daughter's life. Helping her feel things are under control here, and you're in charge."

Ursula has gone downtown this afternoon to watch a free showing of *Black Beauty* at the library. Tim was actually thinking, when he saw Claire at his door, that maybe they could go for a drive out to the woods. They could have a picnic and make love. But it's plain now, hearing her voice, that she's not in the mood for lovemaking.

"I could fix us a sandwich," he says. Claire looks over in the direction of his messy kitchen and shakes her head.

"I guess not today," she says. "I have a lot of chores to attend to."

Today, Tim knows, he was one of them.

That was the best movie I ever saw in my whole life," says Ursula when she comes in later that afternoon. Ever since Claire left, Tim has been cleaning, but he hasn't even made a dent in the mess.

"You should have seen the part where Beauty runs the race," Ursula says, reaching for a cookie and pouring herself a glass of milk, which she leaves out on the counter.

"Forget movies," Tim explodes. "Look around this place. Our life is a mess. Out of control. A disaster." This afternoon's mail brought a final disconnect notice from the phone company and a letter from the bank telling him he bounced three checks last week.

"You're a slob!" he yells at Ursula. "We live like pigs. This is hopeless."

He's holding her doll Phillip by the leg as he yells these things at her, waving him over his head.

"Stop it, Daddy," Ursula says. "You're making him dizzy."

"You're eight years old!" he says. "Can't you even throw away your Cheetos bags?"

"I'm sorry," she tells him. "You never told me you wanted me to."

"Who would ever want to come over to this dump?" he says. "It's disgusting."

Ursula knows who he is thinking about, naturally. The only one who ever visits their apartment, the only one whose opinion he cares about anymore. *The queen.* That's how Ursula thinks of her sometimes. Sometimes she is a good queen. Sometimes she is a mean queen. Sometimes she lets them visit the palace, and sometimes, when she feels like it, she visits them in their hovel. "This place is a hovel," her dad said to her this afternoon. That's how Ursula knows what it is.

Sometimes Ursula loves the queen. She wants to touch the queen's hair and watch the way her earrings jingle. She breathes in her perfume. One time the queen even squirted her perfume on Ursula's pillow. "Maybe that will take away the fish stick smell," she said. From the downstairs neighbors, Sandy and Jeff.

Other times Ursula wishes the queen was dead. She has even tried casting a spell on her. She has figured out, of course, that the purple jewel ring her dad got was for the queen, not her. She has ripped that letter the queen gave her into a million pieces. Ursula stuck the point of her scissors in the knee of the purple tights the queen gave her. She's sorry about that, actually. She never had purple tights before and now all she has is the crew socks her dad buys, but she doesn't care. The queen just wanted her to look like other little girls. Hers, for instance. And Ursula knows she never will.

Claire buys Ursula a back-to-school dress: a pinwale corduroy with a Provençal print and an Empire waist with deep pockets and piping. Not one of those shapeless fat-girl dresses, but a flattering cut for Ursula. "It's important for her to feel cute and self-confident on her first day of third grade," Claire tells Tim. So she buys this dress, even though it costs fifty-two dollars. "Now all she needs is a little pair of pumps," she tells him. She has noticed that all Ursula owns in the way of shoes are sneakers and a pair of heavy, awkward-looking loafers.

Tim takes Ursula shoe shopping. He comes home with a pair of Michael Jordan pump-style sneakers. It should be funny, only it's not to Claire. "Don't get me wrong," she says to him. "I think it's great that you teach her wrestling moves and karate kicks. Nobody's going to call me a sexist. But I also think it's important for a little girl to learn stuff that will help her fit in with other kids at school. Girls in particular. Which includes things like what sort of shoes you wear with a dress." Nobody can be crueler than a clique of third-grade girls, Claire tells him, as if he doesn't know.

So Claire explains to Tim what pumps are. She even draws him a picture. And since he has already spent more money than he should have on the Air Jordans, she suggests that he take Ursula to Fayva, where the shoes may not be the best quality, but they're cheap. It isn't that important how long these pumps last, she figures. Just so she'll have them for the first day, when all the girls are looking around and figuring out who to be friends with.

"I hate what you're telling me," Tim says. "You're telling me Ursula should just play their game. You think I should try and turn her into some kind of little doll?"

"I think right now the most important thing for Ursula is to feel she fits in," Claire says. "We can change the world tomorrow. Today, why don't we just go for making her happy?"

"And a pair of Fayva pumps is her ticket, huh?" he asks Claire. If he didn't love her so much, he would be offended. As it is he and Ursula go off to the shoe store.

When they pull up to Claire's house an hour later, Ursula is dancing. "Look at my new shoes," she says.

"Aren't they perfect?" Ursula asks Claire. "I'm going to wear them every single day."

"That's what you bought?" Claire says to Tim, who has been standing a few feet back, a little anxious looking, waiting for her verdict. *"Those?"*

Telling Mickey the shoe story over the phone, Claire actually begins to cry.

"Let me get this straight," he says. "You're crying because the guy bought his kid a crummy pair of shoes?"

"You don't understand," she says. "Tim and Ursula found the most inappropriate pair of shoes in the whole store. Pointy-toed black ankle-height boots with little heels and fake lizard-skin straps with a rhinestone. Hooker shoes. If she wears those shoes with her new school dress, the reasonable girls will have nothing to do with her. The only ones who will are the really rough crowd."

A hundred and twenty miles away, she can see Mickey shaking his head. "I don't know what you're trying to do here, Slim," he says, his voice thick with regret. "But I don't think it's working."

She tells Tim the shoes are a disaster. Her voice as she tells him this is withering, ruthless almost. She knows it, and she actually hopes he will get angry at her, but he doesn't. He tells her he's sorry, in fact. "I'm such an idiot," he says. "I can't even buy my daughter a pair of shoes. No wonder she has so much trouble at school."

"It's okay," says Claire. "I shouldn't make such a big deal of this stuff." Then they make a plan to hide the hooker shoes and tell Ursula they must have been lost. Claire says she will pick up a pair of pumps for Ursula in Brattleboro. "I know a shop that sells those little velvet Chinese slippers," she says. "Those will be perfect." She is losing her grip and she knows it, but she does it anyway.

Seteptember 15, the six-month anniversary of their meeting last March, Tim takes Claire out to dinner—not to the diner this time, but to a restaurant with linen tablecloths and *Kind of Blue* playing on the stereo and a three-page wine list. He is wearing a jacket and tie tonight—the first time she's ever seen him in one. In his pocket is a velvet box with the ring inside, amethyst, surrounded by tiny pearls. He has pawned his stereo to buy it, although he doesn't have a clue how he's going to come up with next month's rent money.

When Claire gets up from the table to say hello to someone she knows from the museum, Tim sets the velvet box down at her place. The candle on their table is flickering, so he asks the waitress for another one. He draws in his breath, smoothes the tablecloth, pours a little more wine in Claire's glass. He studies her back as she bends to say something to her acquaintance at the other table. It still surprises him the way just the sound of her voice arouses him this way.

Claire returns to the table, shaking her head. "Evidently someone at the board meeting the other night actually suggested that we hold a Power Rangers Day at the museum to boost attendance," she says. She hasn't noticed the velvet box. Tim just watches her, the woman he loves more than he ever thought possible.

"Next thing you know they'll want me out front selling French fries and Frostees," she says. She reaches for her wine.

"Claire," he says. "I want to give you something." The truth is he wants to give her everything. He just couldn't fit it all into a box.

She doesn't open it right away. They have both known for a while that they were heading toward combining their households, eventually. But there's something about seeing that velvet box in front of her that makes it more real.

"I want to marry you," he says after she's opened it. "I want to live with you. And something else. I want us to have a child."

She stares at the ring, not touching it. She hasn't said a word yet.

"I want us to be a family," he says. "I need to know you want the same things."

Claire used to assume she wanted that too. In her original vision they were all going to spend a couple of months getting used to each other. They would have dinner together two or three times a week—not so much that her kids, or his, would feel crowded in, but enough that they could begin to get used to the idea of being a family. Sally would bring Ursula up to her room and help her put together outfits with some of her old clothes. Tim and Pete would play catch in the backyard evenings, and Tim would show Pete how to place his fingers on the stitching of a baseball to throw a knuckle ball. Sometimes the four of them—not Sally maybe, unless Travis was there, in which case they could ask him to join them—would play Scattergories or Pit or Uno. She might walk them back to their house. Go upstairs with Tim and help him tuck Ursula in. Read her a chapter of *Ramona*. Kiss her good night.

When it became clear to her that her children couldn't stand Tim, Claire's thinking changed some. "I get to have a life," she reminds herself. But she also knows it will not be a good one for her if Pete and Sally are miserable and resentful. Better to go slow, give them more time to accept the situation. This is what she tells Tim as he places the ring on her finger, his own hand shaking as he does.

Claire stopped picturing a fall wedding some time ago. She no longer envisions games of Scattergories around the fireplace with their children. What she thinks now is, In a few years my children will be off on their own anyway, and the only one we'll have to deal with is Ursula. And who knows, maybe a baby, although she's not as clear as Tim is, that they could pull off that part.

Claire is thirty-nine years old. Tim too; their birthdays are just days apart. *("Poking forty with a short stick," Mickey says.)* She doesn't feel old now, but she wonders what it would feel like to be attending soccer games still at fifty.

She bends over the table and kisses Tim. She strokes his hair.

"I love you so much you have no idea," he tells her. "You don't know what it's like to feel this kind of love."

"Yes I do," she tells him as she places the ring back into the velvet box and puts it in her pocket. "And I love you, too. We just need to hold off a little longer."

Sometimes when she and Mickey were out together buying groceries or walking around the North End or heading toward Kenmore Square for a ball game, they'd pass some couple pushing a stroller. Or she'd see a man holding the hand of a pregnant woman—with his other hand resting gently on the small of her back, maybe—and Claire would experience a wave of this sad, hollow feeling, as if she were an empty pod, a dry and brittle stalk in a windy field surrounded by green, bending grasses. She knew there would be no babies for her and Mickey, knew he would never lay his hand on her pregnant belly feeling for a kick. Before he had his vasectomy, Mickey lived in horror of a pregnancy. Claire would never see his face on any child of theirs, she knew that much. Not those freckles. Not that pitcher's butt. They would never be parents together, only lovers, and as much as she loved the untouchable intimacy that came from it being just the two of them, every now and then that fact of their relationship left her with an odd feeling of pointlessness. Claire has always liked making things—meals, perennial beds, dresses, children. With Mickey, the only thing she ever made was love. They never even had a pet together. Never even a garden.

Partly she knew this feeling of hers was an old habit, a carryover from her marriage, when it had made more sense. For all the years she and Sam were together, she had found pleasure in the bounty of her own ripe fertility. In the arid territory of her marriage, she drew comfort from the knowledge that she might at any moment be pregnant—though even this diminished in the last couple of years, their lovemaking was so infrequent. There was a reason why Claire was never as exacting as she should have been about birth control. The Russian roulette she played with her sketchy combination of a too-old diaphragm, not always accompanied by spermicide, and the rhythm method allowed for a certain constant state of hopefulness in a situation that would have otherwise seemed unbearably bleak. Chance conception was her one wild card.

With Mickey there was no such prospect. So there were these moments with him when Claire felt old, used up, withered. They'd be at a movie and a baby would cry, forcing its parents to rise from their seats and hurry out of the theater, and even as she could sense Mickey's relief that it was somebody else's baby and not theirs, what she was feeling was the opposite. What was a movie compared to a small and perfect person, made by them?

But now that Claire's with Tim, and knowing how much he wants to have a child with her, this other set of images have come to her.

She and Tim are walking down a street and she is vastly pregnant. Her breasts are almost indecently swollen and her belly enormous. Her ankles have thickened and her hips have spread. Her face is full and blotchy. She has to be careful not to laugh too hard or she will lose bladder control.

The Claire in this dream has developed a fascination for brands of baby strollers. She talks with Tim, who used to be her lover and is now her husband, about when to introduce solids into their child's diet and how long to let the baby cry at night before picking her up. Her breasts, once the object of his adoration and awe, have a certain sexless utility to them now. Once the baby is born she will pop them out of her shirt at regular intervals, no longer caring much if her nipple is exposed. She wears a brassiere that resembles something her grandmother would have worn.

When they crawl into bed at night—she and Tim—they are too weary to make love. Once it would have driven him crazy to lie so close to her without being inside her. Now he is simply grateful for sleep.

. . .

It is this transformed and desexed Claire who she sees in her new and terrible fantasy, which is more depressing than the empty pod thoughts ever were.

They're walking through Harvard Square together—Tim supporting her aching back, Ursula pedaling her pink two-wheeler alongside them, in her thick glasses, with her helmet on, Pete and Sally walking a few feet ahead, pretending not to know them. They are heading someplace like a baby furnishings store, or maybe she is having her urine tested for sugar levels. Suddenly she sees Mickey.

He is striding on the opposite side of the street, in the opposite direction, with a beautiful woman. (Elegant calf muscle. Porcelain skin.) If he were simply holding her hand it wouldn't be so bad, but he is stroking her wrist and whispering something into her ear. She knows from the location of the street where they are walking which jazz club they have just emerged from. She also knows where they are going and what they will do when they get there.

Claire's knees buckle so dramatically at this point that Tim supposes she has gone into labor. "Children!" he calls out. "We have to get Mom to the hospital." Mom. That's what he has called her.

No, she says. I'm all right, really. She's standing upright again.

But it's too late. Tim's voice calling out has caught Mickey's attention. He is looking across the street with a puzzled look. I know that face, he is thinking. But from where?

There is a saxophone playing. Gerry Mulligan, she thinks. She barely remembers them all now. Which was Mulligan? Which was Stan Getz? Which was Coltrane? She sees Tim's face, full of love and concern, and Ursula's, so full of hunger and longing. She wants to run away, but she knows if she tries to run she will wet her pants. She hears the laughter of Mickey's girlfriend, and she knows he has just told her that joke about the time Miles Davis met Chet Baker in Paris. She hears cars honking and Tim's voice saying, "Hold on, honey, all you need is a cleansing breath." She hears Ursula asking for Gummi Bears and the hoarse voice of Miles, introducing "Stella by Starlight." She hears the wailing of a trumpet. And then she realizes it's not a trumpet at all. It's a baby.

Gradually their lives fall into a routine. Weeknights when the kids are home, Claire helps them with their homework and cleans up after dinner, puts in a load of laundry, writes letters up in her office, explaining to potential donors who didn't respond to her last letter why they should give money to the children's museum. Nancy may drop by for coffee, and the two of them may do yoga together. Nights when Sally stays on the phone with Travis this may mean waiting until close to midnight.

Once Pete and Sally are asleep, Claire gets into her car and goes the three blocks over to Tim's apartment, although if it's a nice night and she isn't too tired she may walk. She lets herself in the smoky hallway of his apartment building and climbs the steps as quietly as she can, so she won't wake Ursula. Tim is almost always asleep himself. Sometimes he will have drifted off in front of the TV. Other nights he'll be in his bed, naked under the covers waiting for her. She peels off her clothes and lays them in a neat pile next to the door, knowing she will need to dress quickly, in the darkness, sometime around four or five A.M. Then she climbs in beside him.

This is the best moment. Some nights just the sensation of slipping in behind him and pressing her body up against his back is enough to make her sigh. She slides her foot up his leg. Her hands, wrapped around his chest, stroke his belly. By the time she's got to his cock, it's already hard.

No matter how difficult the rest of their time together is, this part always feels simple and good. The way he responds to her, even through his sleep. His total lack of ambivalence toward her in bed. His boundless and consuming desire for her.

"You're here," he says. He always sounds surprised and grateful, even though she does this nearly every night. Not fully awake, he begins to kiss her. He finds her breasts. His hands are all over her.

She may mutter something about the evening she has spent. "Pete had a project due," she says, wrapping her fingers around the shaft of his cock. "George Washington Carver. He left it to the last minute as usual."

"Tuskegee Institute," he says, nuzzling her hair. She loves the effortless way her other life falls away from her here in this bed, but she also loves the way he embraces that part of her.

"Pete have a soccer game?" he asks her.

"Tomorrow," she tells him, cupping his balls. "Ursula?"

"What can I do?" he sighs. "My daughter is hopeless. Some kid kicked her the ball today when she was standing right in front of the goal and it was wide open. She just stood there."

"How's your proposal coming?" she asks him.

"Ursula got mad that I wouldn't play Barbies with her, and she pulled out the plug of my computer. I lost two hours' work," he says. He doesn't add that he has seventy-two dollars left in his checking account.

Claire starts to offer her opinion about how Tim should have handled Ursula in this situation, then stops. She doesn't want to think about anybody's children anymore today.

"Come here," she says. She slides under the covers.

Sometime around one or two they fall asleep. His alarm goes off at four-thirty, and though it's only Claire who has to get up, he rises with her, puts on his clothes too, although he may just sit naked in the semidarkness first, watching her dress. "I wish I could fix you a wonderful breakfast," he says. "A goat cheese omelette. Raspberries and croissants. Steamed milk for your coffee."

She slips on her shoes and runs her hand through her hair. "I'll call you later," she says. He misses her already.

Ursula rises at six. She no longer needs to wake her father. He's up already, sitting at his computer. He keeps telling her he's working on a report about estuaries and as soon as it's finished they'll have some money again and he'll take her miniature golfing, but she doesn't believe that anymore.

"Cereal or toast?" he says. "Waffle?"

She tells him she's not hungry. This is the second day in a row she has said this, but he hasn't noticed. If she got very skinny, like one of those girls in Sally's *Sassy* magazine, then he'd be sorry.

"I hate my hair," she says. She has heard Sarah McAdam say this in the girls' room at school. Although Sarah McAdam's hair is perfect. Long and straight, and golden blond. This is where her father is supposed to say, "You have beautiful hair," but he doesn't. He is looking out the window, and she knows who he is thinking about. Ursula breaks off a piece of a Snickers.

"So," he says, turning back to her. "I'll be finished with my class by four o'clock today. You want to kick around the soccer ball? We could bring Jenny."

"Would she come too?" Ursula asks him. Meaning Claire.

"I don't think so," he says. "She has to be at the museum. Besides, I was thinking it could be just the two of us."

He is such a fake. The only time he wants it to be "just the two of us" is him and her. In bed together. Making those noises.

"I know everything that happens," she says quietly. "There aren't any secrets."

He is making her school lunch, laying turkey slices on the bread.

"What do you mean, Urs?" he asks her. He doesn't look up but she knows she has him worried.

"I figured out you sold our tape player and I figured out why. That's not all I know, either."

"What are you talking about, Urs?" he says. He hopes he sounds casual.

"You know what I'm talking about," she says. She makes kissing sounds on Barbie's hard, flat plastic stomach. She begins to breathe heavily. *"Uh, uh, uh, uh,"* she fake-moans.

"If you have something to say to me, Ursula, why don't you talk to me plainly?" he tells her.

"I've told you enough," she says. "I just didn't want you to think you were fooling me."

Shedoesn't like it when you pet her that way," Ursula is telling Pete. She has ridden her bike over to their house to take Jenny for a walk and found Pete in the front yard, drinking a Dr. Pepper and scratching Jenny's belly in the sun as he reads his new issue of *Mad*. "That's not the right spot."

Pete shrugs and goes in the house. Ursula follows him in, still wearing her bike helmet.

"Also," she says, "I noticed there were some pieces of dog chow floating in her water. Jenny hates chow in her water bowl."

Pete is pouring himself a bowl of cereal as she tells him this. Who does she think she is, this twerp coming into his house telling him how to take care of her old dog he didn't want in the first place? Pete wanted a puppy.

"You miss me, don't you, Jenny?" she says. She talks to the dog in this high little baby voice of hers that gets on his nerves something wicked. "You wish you lived with me instead of these people, don't you?"

"Listen," says Pete, "why don't you just take her for a walk?"

"She's not feeling good," Ursula tells him. "I can tell her hip is hurting."

"What are you, a vet?" he says to her.

"I know everything about Jenny. I've had Jenny my whole life and you've only had her a few weeks. You think you're so great, but you don't know anything," Ursula says.

"I know you're a little brat," Pete says. He picks up his cereal and his *Mad* and heads to the computer. He turns on Wolfenstein at the loudest volume. The kid actually follows him.

"I'm going to tell my dad you said that," she says. "You're going to get in trouble."

"Jeez, I'm scared," says Pete, though the truth is, he suspects she probably could get him into trouble, on account of his mom is acting so dumb about these two. He has tried not to think about it, but none of her other boyfriends ever planted stuff in their garden or put up their storm windows.

"My dad broke a guy's nose one time," Ursula says. "My dad

knows this place on the back of a person's neck that if you touch it they're paralyzed."

"Yeah, well, I don't think your dad wants to commit child abuse," Pete tells her. "Grown-ups can get in big trouble for something like that."

"Well, I know something you don't, anyways," she says. "I know something I bet you wish you knew."

Pete has been trying to concentrate on Wolfenstein, but he has to ask. "Oh yeah?" he says.

"I know my dad and your mom are going to get married. My dad bought her a jewel ring. I saw it."

This is a sickening piece of news. Pete moves the joystick and stares at the screen, but what he wants to do is smash her fat little face under that dumb helmet she's always wearing, even now in the house.

"Yeah, right," he says. "I haven't seen any ring. Don't you think she would've told my sister and me?"

"They wanted to work out the details themselves first," she says. "Your mom was thinking I might get your room and you'd go down in the basement." She is making this part up, but it makes sense to her.

"Get out of here, twerp," he says. "My mom would never marry a jerk like your dad."

"That's what you think," she says. "That's because you haven't heard them doing the *F* word like me."

"Liar," he says. "Why don't you just shut up? Why don't you just beat it?"

"Don't you even know she comes over to our house in the middle of the night when you and your sister are asleep and takes off all her clothes and gets into my dad's bed?" she tells him. "Don't you know she stays there until it's almost time for school, and then she puts her clothes back on and goes back to your house so you won't know? You should hear the noises they make."

On the screen, Wolfenstein is slashing his sword. He has chopped off two warriors' heads now, and he is moving on a third. There is blood dripping on the bricks. A bat circles over his head. Crunch. *Got him.*

"She says, 'I love your big cock,'" says Ursula, her voice deep and low. She is practically whispering this in his ear. "She says, 'Nobody ever fucked me like that.' She has a purple bra that she left at our house one time. My dad keeps it under his pillow."

"Get out! Just get out!" he screams.

"I have to go now, girl," she tells Jenny, in the baby voice again. "Bye-bye, baby girl." A minute later he can see her riding down the street on that pink bike of hers. The last thing he sees is the top of her helmet disappearing behind a row of shrubs.

The horrible truth is, Ursula was only partly going over to their house to give Jenny a run. She was actually thinking she was going to make friends with Pete when she went over there. Her dad said maybe he'd play soccer with her if she went over there. The horrible truth is, Ursula actually admires Pete. She has watched him on the playground at school, where he is a Classroom Buddy. He is one of the most popular boys. When she told Marcy, this really popular girl that helps her reading group, that she knew Pete, Marcy said everybody in sixth grade wanted to go out with him. "Don't tell Pete," Marcy said, "but Sarah McAdam thinks he's cute and so do I." Ursula had been planning to tell Pete that. The other stuff just came out by mistake.

This happens a lot to Ursula. She makes this plan to do all these nice things, like Pollyanna. She thinks up how she's going to give Ashley a Tootsie Pop and ask if she wants to come over to her house. Sometimes she even practices these conversations at home with her dad or Jenny, back when Jenny still lived with them, and when she does it with her dad it always works out right, but when she does it at school, it's like there's this little worm that starts squiggling around in her brain. And before you know it what happens is she's telling Ashley that Derek said she had cooties and Ashley is saying, "Yeah, well, you should hear what Derek says about you," and Ursula is saying, "Well, Derek is a big pecker head," and Ashley is saying, "Now I know why nobody likes you," and Ursula is saying, "I'll tell the teacher," and she does, and then those kids get in trouble and hate her more than ever.

After the kid tells him that about his mother and Tim, Pete decides he'll find out for himself. His mother's bed is always rumpled up in the morning, but that doesn't mean anything. She could just be doing that so they'd think she'd been there. The only way to know for sure is to watch.

Ten o'clock, he calls out good night to her. She comes in his room, bends over him, kisses his cheek.

"I love you, son," she says. She's wearing perfume. Did she used to do that on school nights?

"You going to bed, too?" he asks her.

"Soon," she says. "You have a soccer game tomorrow?"

He says he does. Also he's been wanting to ask her something. "Could he please not come to my game this time?" he says. He's talking about Tim, who came to the last game and cheered louder than his own dad, who was also there, when Pete made that goal in the second half.

"Tim loves watching you play," says his mom. Why does she have to make him feel guilty all the time, like it's his job to make Tim happy?

"And Ursula admires you so much," she says. "I don't know if you realize that, but she thinks you're wonderful. She told Tim if she ever had a brother she'd want it to be somebody just like you."

She's a desperate woman. Under her perfume, he can smell it.

"I'd just rather they didn't hang around all the time, okay?" he says.

For a while there he's almost decided the kid must have been making the whole thing up. He can hear his mother downstairs, playing the record of one of those wailing country singers she loves. He hears the faucet running. He hears the dishwasher start up. The porch light clicks off. His sister is off the phone now. He can hear the Tori Amos album she always puts on to help her get to sleep. No car ignition. He looks out the window just to check, and sure enough, there's the Toyota sitting in their driveway in the same place it's been all night.

But then he catches sight of her. Not in the car, but partway down the block, under the glow of a street lamp: his mother walking in the direction of Tim's apartment.

Mickey has fallen in love. Not with one of his smooth-bellied twenty-six-year-olds this time, though. The woman is thirty-eight and divorced. She lives in Rhode Island. She has two children, one of whom is younger than Pete. Her name is Annalise.

"So what does she look like?" Claire asks him. She is trying hard to remember how the routine goes even as the room begins to spin.

"Small tits," he says. "Long legs. Incredible neck. Fixes the best margaritas I ever tasted. And can you believe it, she actually owns a Milton Nascimento CD?"

"Ethereal yet pithy," Claire says. "What about her kids? How are you going to work that part out?"

"You got me, Slim," he says. "Send them to military school, I guess. I must be losing my mind."

He volunteers nothing about the sex and Claire doesn't ask. "How's Carrottop doing?" he asks her.

"I wish Tim would take her to a therapist," she says. "Actually, I think it might be a good idea if all of us went into family therapy together."

. He sighs heavily. "You aren't pregnant, are you?" he asks her. She shivers. "No."

"So," he says, "you hear the new Crowded House album?"

Early on in their time together— *when she was fresh out of her marriage, and they were still in the phase she thinks of now as Mickey nursing her back to health—he asked her why she didn't wear perfume.*

"I just never did," she told him. "I never had any, I guess." Sam had bought her a bottle of Chanel Number 5 for Mother's Day one year, in the aftermath of the birthday when she'd burst into tears after opening his gift of a pressure cooker. As with the black garter belt he got her that other time, Sam's attempts at romantic gifts never rang true to Claire. It was as if some guy at one of his building jobs had handed him an instruction manual that said, "Garter belt, black. Perfume: Chanel Number 5."

"Well, you should," Mickey told her. Wear perfume, he meant. "It's one of life's great pleasures."

He took her to Colonial Drug in Harvard Square. "Wait till you see this place," he said as he led her in. It was the old-fashioned kind of drugstore, with Kent brushes and tortoiseshell combs and boxes of chocolates and dark wood moldings around the glass cases. One whole wall of the store was nothing but perfume testers. Next to every one was a hand-typed card describing the fragrance.

Mickey studied these cards as closely as he would if he were reading box scores. When he had half a dozen fragrances picked out, he unbuttoned the cuffs of her blouse and rolled them up enough to expose her wrists and part of each forearm. He reached for one of the little strips of paper they kept in a jar on the counter and dabbed it very lightly on her right wrist. He dipped another strip of paper into a different tester and rubbed that on her other wrist. "Oh," she said. "This one is wonderful, too."

Then the back of each hand. Then each of her forearms. He had taken out a three-by-five card, on which he wrote the name of each of the perfumes.

"I think I like this one the best," she said, pointing to number three. Ma Griffe.

"Did you think we were going to buy one just like that?" he asked her. "That's not how you do it."

They walked around Harvard Square for a couple of hours. They had a margarita at a Mexican place and shopped for used CDs at a couple of little record stores. Every ten minutes or so he'd reach for one of her arms and sniff one of their test patches. "It's not just the way the perfume smells when you first put it on," he told her. "It's what happens when you live with it. Every woman's skin is different."

• • •

They made three separate trips to Colonial Drug before they found her perfume, a scent called Il Bacio. Now, Claire sprays herself with perfume even when she knows she will be totally alone for the pure pleasure of smelling herself. Since buying that first bottle she has picked out half a dozen other scents. Il Bacio is still her favorite, but she hardly ever wears it anymore. She has learned that there is nothing—not a photograph, not a piece of music even —that summons a memory more sharply than a scent. There are times when something as simple as a blend of coffee brewing or the smell of baseball glove leather can do it to her, or a soap she realizes he used, or a certain kind of greasy sandwich that they sell outside Fenway Park.

Hearing the news about Mickey and Annalise, Claire no longer needs to throw a pot of soup. She doesn't crawl into bed. She has no braids left to cut off. If she were a drinker, this is where she would pour herself a double scotch. As it is, she climbs the stairs to her room, puts on a Lucinda Williams CD, takes out her perfume bottle, and bathes herself in Il Bacio.

W hen do we get to come over to your house again?" Ursula asks Claire when she stops by their apartment with a jar of the leek soup she's made and a pan of cornbread. This is the same question Ursula asks Claire every time she sees her and it always has the same effect. Claire can almost feel a hand constricting around her heart, a tightening in her throat. Ursula's question makes it seem to Claire as if Ursula and Tim have no life besides the one she provides them, which is a suffocating notion. And where in the normal course of things she would have pictured Ursula coming over all the time, the child's perpetual asking has the effect on Claire of wanting to withhold what she knows Ursula wants so badly. Claire despises herself for this. She feels ungenerous and inhospitable. A stern, reproachful, lecturing tone whose sound she hates comes into her voice.

"You know, Ursula," she says. "Last time you came over, all you did was ask your dad when he was going to take you home again." This is true: The only time Ursula lets up on asking to come over and play is when she gets to come over, at which point she never plays. She leans against her father, wherever he may be, and whispers to him things Claire is just as glad she doesn't hear, as well as a number she does hear. Ursula complains that Claire's kids are being mean to her. She's bored. She can never speak directly to Sally or Pete, only to her father, directing him to tell them things. He tries to get her to talk for herself, having been instructed in this by Claire, but in the end he usually gives up.

"Ursula wonders if you know that Jenny doesn't like it when pieces of dog chow get in her water bowl," Tim tells Pete, as gently as he can.

"Yeah," says Pete. "We heard already."

"Don't get me wrong, Pete," Tim will say, instantly apologetic, putting a hand on his shoulder (a terrible mistake). "I think you're doing a great job taking care of Jenny. We're both incredibly grateful to you."

"Sure," Pete says, beating a hasty retreat.

"When are we going to get to come over to your house?" Ursula asks Claire again. The first time she asked, Claire was telling Tim about a meeting she'd had with a woman who wanted to give her collection of antique teddy bears to the museum. And since one of the many things she has expressed to Tim concerning his relationship with Ursula has to do with his willingness to let her interrupt him, she kept talking as if she hadn't heard. The interrupting issue was one of Mickey's big things with Claire. *"You let your children walk all over your life,"* he used to tell her.

"You let your child walk all over your life," she tells Tim. "Which means she's walking all over mine, too."

"When do we get—" Ursula begins for the third time.

"Listen, Ursula," says Claire with a sharpness that startles her own self. "You need to know you aren't the only person in the world."

A*s if she didn't.* What Ursula knows, in fact, is that she is only just barely in the world at all. One more step and she could just fall right off the edge.

Used to be her dad would set a pitcher of apple juice next to her bed every night with a Boston Patriots cup next to it in case she got thirsty in the night. She does get thirsty, too, and though the pitcher would always be there, what she liked was for him to come and pour the juice for her, and he would, too.

"Daddy," she would call. And just like that there he'd be. Pouring.

Then Claire told her dad kids shouldn't have fruit juice in the night. The sugar sits on their teeth all night, she told him, and they get cavities. Plus apple juice has calories. Why not water?

So then he would get up and pour her the water. And then Claire said, "She's in third grade. Don't you think she can pour her own glass of water? And you shouldn't be naked like that when you come in to her, either." So now he wears a bathrobe.

"Daddy," she would call. "I need to go potty."

"When my children were her age they went by themselves in the night. If they needed to go at all, which was rare—and would be for yours too if you didn't leave that stupid pitcher next to her bed."

Like a dog he obeys. She has him by the balls. Her dad taught Ursula that expression. Now he's the one it's happened to.

So Ursula gets up by herself at night now. Here in their cold, miserable little apartment that smells of the downstairs tenants' cigarette smoke and a hundred ancient meals of fish sticks, Ursula makes her way alone down the dark hallway, past the door he now keeps not only shut but locked, to their horrible stinky bathroom that now has things like Tampax in it and a tube of something she once thought was toothpaste, only it tasted terrible, so she knows it wasn't. Now Ursula has to pull up her Garfield nightie herself as she sits her too-big butt on the chilly toilet seat, with nobody there to hand her the toilet paper, folded like a flower the way he used to.

"Here you are, miss," he used to say. *"Your rose."*

He would wipe Claire's butt, Ursula bets. He would scatter rose petals wherever she walked. He would bring her quarts of apple juice one spoonful at a time if she wanted it and brush her teeth for her. He has sold their stereo to buy jewels for her. What will he do next?

She makes her way back to her bedroom. In the old days, Jenny would have been there waiting for her, snuggled up beside her on the bed. Not now.

He has somebody snuggled up beside him, Ursula knows, although Claire is never there in the morning, and her dad never says she's been there in the night. Ursula hears her crying out in the night, though. Only it's not like when Ursula cries if she's had a bad dream. This crying is different.

Ursula tucks herself back under the covers. She holds Phillip, the anatomically correct boy doll. She doesn't like to think about his penis but she does anyways.

She just lies there that way. After a long time she can hear noises from her father's room again, and then whispering, and then Claire's feet on the steps. Finally the sun comes up.

Claire hates the woman she sees herself becoming. She hates the way she treats Ursula these days, and then she resents Ursula all over again for making her feel that way.

"Listen," she tells Ursula, "I have an idea." Her favorite church rummage sale is this Saturday. She used to bring Sally, but Sally wouldn't be caught dead shopping with her mother on a Saturday morning anymore. So why doesn't Ursula come with her? "You won't believe the buys," Claire tells her. "We can get a whole new wardrobe for a dollar."

Pulling up to Tim's apartment to pick up Ursula, Claire's feeling happy and relaxed at the thought of having a little girl to take to the St. James sale again. When she sees Ursula, in her too-tight boy's parka and her Little Mermaid pocketbook, she feels tenderness and hope.

"Have you had breakfast yet?" she says. "I was thinking we could go out for a bagel."

Buckling her seat belt next to Claire, with her purse in her lap and her hands folded on her purse, Ursula nods. "I got three quarters my dad gave me for dusting the shelves," she tells Claire. "Plus I can use the silver dollar I got from the tooth fairy if there's something really special. Maybe I'll get a present for my mom."

She discusses the baby, Keith, who lives downstairs. "I'm worried about him," she says. "I don't think Sandy and Jeff should put Snapple in his bottle. Even if it is a hundred percent natural."

Ursula is teaching Keith how to play peekaboo. She also sings to him the songs they've been learning in third grade. "I think he's very smart," she says. "Yesterday I asked him where his mommy was and he pointed to the kitchen."

"It sounds like you're a very good babysitter," Claire says.

"I'm very careful with Keith," Ursula says. "I would never let anything happen to him. If a car was coming and he was in the road, I would save him even if it meant I'd get squished."

At the Bagel Works, Claire orders a sesame seed bagel, toasted, and coffee. Ursula looks at Claire as she places her order. "I'll have mine plain, I guess," she says. "No butter."

"Are you sure?" Claire asks her. "Don't you want butter or cream cheese?" *Is this what I've done to her? Claire thinks.*

"Butter, I guess," says Ursula. Then she changes her mind. "No, cream cheese, I guess. No, butter."

"Why don't we get a little cream cheese on the side?" Claire suggests. "Just in case."

They get a table by the window. Ursula is telling her about the book she and her dad are reading now, *Charlotte's Web.* "It's so sad you can hardly bear to turn the page sometimes," she says, spreading a thick smear of cream cheese on her bagel and munching. "But you have to find out what happens next. You can't stand it one more second."

"I love to read chapter books, too," says Claire. *"I will read to you," she wants to say. "I will be good to you. I'm sorry I ever wasn't. What was I thinking of?"*

Leaving the bagel store, Ursula reaches for her hand, and Claire holds hers tight. "Do you like to skip?" Ursula asks her. So they do.

They find treasures at the St. James rummage sale. A denim Oshkosh jumper that would cost thirty-five dollars new. A Polly Flinders dress. A purple mohair sweater, just the right shade for Ursula's hair. A pleated kilt that might make Ursula look a little thick in the waist, only Claire thinks they can fix that if she wears a cardigan with it. They find one of those, too.

They assemble a pile of stuff for Ursula to try on later, because it's important, Claire explains, not to waste precious grabbing time during the first half hour of a sale like this. Ursula has included several items in the pile that wouldn't be Claire's choice—a sweatshirt with pictures of kittens on it and a pale pink shirtwaist that looks small—but Claire keeps her opinion of these items to herself. On her own, Ursula has also located a hat she wants to buy for her father, a plaid cap of the style golfers wear, and a dress for her mother.

She looks good in the jumper, as Claire knew she would. She wants to wear the mohair sweater with the kilt, tucked in, but Claire figures there will be time later for working that out.

"Show this to your mommy, honey," one of the church women wearing a sales apron says to Ursula, handing her a pair of overalls that Claire would not, in fact, have chosen. "I bet she might like to get it for you."

"She thinks you're my mom," Ursula whispers to Claire.

"If I were your mom I'd be proud," says Claire.

"You're like my mom," says Ursula.

"Really?" says Claire. She's surprised of course.

"No," says Ursula. "I don't mean you're like *my* mom. I mean you're like *a* mom. The kind of person you think a mom is going to be."

Claire brushes the hair out of Ursula's eyes.

"My mom isn't that kind of person at all," Ursula says.

W hile Ursula is out shopping with Claire, the guidance counselor from her school calls wanting to speak with Tim. Ursula's having problems socializing with her third-grade classmates, Mr. Hogue tells him. "I'd like to recommend that your daughter join a group I meet with Tuesday afternoons for children who may need some help with their social skills," he says. Tim guesses that would be all right. He tells Mr. Hogue that as soon as he gets a little money together, he plans on taking Ursula to a therapist, as Claire has suggested.

Tim hasn't told Claire the full extent of his money problems because he figures she has enough on her mind, but the truth is it's getting harder not to feel panicked about his financial situation. His course load at the community college was reduced this fall, which meant a thousand-dollar pay cut. He has received an enthusiastic response to his preliminary application for the second estuarial research grant, but the Woods Hole Foundation has informed him that they can't offer additional money until he's ready to present more detailed data, which will take months.

Meanwhile, Tim has to come up with something else. Some proofreading work for the short term, maybe, but eventually he has got to find a better job. He longs to have a child with Claire, but how can he ask her when at the moment it's all he can do taking care of the one child he's got?

Still, in spite of everything, Tim feels this abiding hopefulness that he and Claire can work things out. Sitting on the couch in his apartment now, as his daughter and the woman he loves show off their purchases from the rummage sale, he feels his heart bursting with happiness. Ursula has placed the plaid golfer's hat on his head and he's wearing a velvet smoking jacket Claire found for him, whose sleeves are too short. Ursula's dancing around in her kitten sweatshirt. "And just look at the dress we picked out for my mom," she says: pink and white gingham, with a full skirt and rickrack around the pockets.

"We'll mail it off to New Zealand tomorrow," Claire tells her. *How did Tim ever get so lucky? If nothing more good ever happens to him, he thinks, this is enough.*

It's been over a week since Claire talked with Mickey. A record, she thinks. Now that he's going down to Rhode Island all the time to see Annalise, it's been hard tracking him down. Finally Mickey calls Claire.

"So, Slim," he says. "What have you got? Tim do any more shoe shopping lately?"

She reaches for her coffee. "He's such a good man," she sighs. "He loves me so much and he's so good to me, and I treat him like shit."

"So don't," Mickey tells her. "The guy sounds like a saint if you ask me. You wouldn't catch me trying to help Pete with his math homework." As if she didn't know.

"I just wish it wasn't so complicated," she says. "When it's just the two of us, it's so good."

"Big surprise," he tells her. "Haven't you heard one thing I've been telling you these last few years?"

"Every time I try to have a conversation with him on the phone, Ursula interrupts," Claire says. "He becomes a different person when she's around."

Claire imagines where Mickey is sitting at this moment. On his porch swing with the cordless probably, sipping a margarita. In the backyard, where she planted a dwarf cherry tree. Gabe will be quietly tossing a baseball in the air and catching it. She hears Ella Fitzgerald on the stereo back in the house. The only woman, he told her once, he would leave Claire for.

"So how's Annalise?" Claire asks.

Something in Mickey's voice always changes when he's talking about a woman. A woman he's in love with that is, as opposed to somebody like Mother Teresa or Janet Reno.

"She has this way of tossing her hair," he says in that hushed tone of his, as if he were talking about Ella, and what he was saying was, "She has this way of forming a note. . . ."

"We heard Dylan at the Garden the other night," he says. "He had this great pedal steel guitar player, but old Bob himself isn't what he used to be."

"You said that the last time," she tells him. Bob Dylan has played Boston three times now since she went to hear him with Mickey—just one more way Claire measures the passage of time since she last laid eyes on this man. Mickey said the same thing then.

"Well, this time I mean it," he says. "We had great Mexican food, though. Annalise is an amazing cook."

Claire realizes she doesn't want to hear this. "I have to go," she says in a voice she knows he will recognize as very faintly hurt. "I have to take Sally driving."

"You know I'll always adore you, Slim," he tells her.

"I love you, too, Mickey," she says.

"Just don't panic over this kid stuff, okay?" Mickey says—her coach again. "Subtle recalibrations, remember. Don't lose your balance."

Claire can hear the horn honking in the driveway. Sally. And she has promised to take Pete shopping for jeans after that. Out the window she sees the helmeted figure of Ursula on her pink bicycle pedaling toward her house. Who she reminds Claire of, at this moment, is Margaret Hamilton as the witch in *The Wizard of Oz*. *"Her and her little dog, too,"* she is *cackling*. Where to run?

Back when she was married to Sam, Claire longed for the excitement and passion of an affair, of knowing she had a lover somewhere who loved her wildly. Now that she has one, it's that other thing she misses. Having a man around.

The people in her town she looks at with most envy are the

most domesticated of couples, people who would be amazed to know the time she has spent, alone in her bed, obsessing about them. Lovers she has had. It's this other thing that seems so irresistible and elusive: a man who doesn't go away. A man she doesn't have to leave. A man who would be at her side not only in bed but at her son's soccer games and in the hospital waiting room, where she has taken him to get stitches again. Someone who would have helped her clean up the terrible mess in the road outside their house the time Sally's cat got hit by a car last year. Little things other women don't even think about, like being able to move a heavy table without calling a neighbor are what she misses. Hearing the door slam followed by that old line, "Honey, I'm home." Sound of the radio broadcasting a baseball game as she plants her zinnias. A hand reaching for hers when they call Sally's name at graduation.

She knows Tim would love to be this man for her. But he is like a man who has written checks for more money than he has in his account, which, most likely, he has also done. He offers what he doesn't have to give. He promises things that aren't his to deliver.

This afternoon, though, she has such an ordinary wish. She wishes they could simply buy groceries together. Maybe they will be bringing their groceries to their two separate kitchens. Maybe he will buy peanut butter while she buys angel-hair pasta. But at least they can navigate the aisles together almost like a regular couple. So she calls him up and invites him to meet her at the A & P.

"Three-thirty at Produce?" she asks him. Sandy and Jeff can watch Ursula.

Pick three things you'd like to bring to bed with you," Claire tells Tim as they push their carts along. "And please, no whipped cream."

So he is looking. He has considered and rejected a number of fruits. Chocolate sauce. Cream pie, cocktail franks. He hesitates over the Cream of Wheat. "I love the name," he says. "That's all it is."

They don't need videos. Or *Sports Illustrated.* Caviar. Those little booklets of romantic poetry they sell at the checkout.

In the end, he chooses raisins, a disposable camera, and—though he knows there is nothing original about this—roses.

"I want to make you a bed of petals," he says. He has twenty dollars in his pocket and no food at home, and he is buying her roses.

She chooses a papaya, a feather duster, and toilet paper.

"Toilet paper?" he says.

"I want you to wrap me until you can't see an inch of my skin anymore," she says. "And then I want you to unwrap me again."

I know a secret," Sarah McAdam tells Pete. She has stopped him in the hall outside the boys' room, where he has just finished spray-painting graffiti having to do with the principal's sexual habits, so this catches him off guard. Anything Sarah McAdam says to Pete would make him nervous actually. She's the cutest girl in the sixth grade.

"I saw your mom at the supermarket," she says.

"Oh yeah?" he says. "Hot news flash."

"She was kissing some guy," Sarah says. "I never saw a mom making out before."

"You're nuts," Pete says. He knows she isn't.

"He your dad?" she asks him. "The red-haired guy?"

"Are you kidding?" Pete says. "My dad is nothing like him."

"My parents are divorced, too," she says. "You should see some of the losers my mom's brought home. You just have to hope they won't marry any of them."

"Yeah, well, my mom would never do something like that," he says, though the truth is, he is not sure of anything anymore. "If she did, I'd be out of here so fast. Back to my dad's house."

"Yeah, but he's probably got somebody really gross, too," she says.

Pete says nothing.

"Parents are totally insane," she says. "Believe me, I know."

Although Claire sleeps over at Tim's apartment fairly often when her kids are at their father's, she has never felt comfortable having him stay over at her own house when they're around.

"You know they've figured out by now that we have sex," he tells her.

Maybe that's why she can't do it so openly, she says. Ursula's young enough that she can walk into Tim's bedroom in the morning, weekends when Claire stays over, and see her father and Claire in bed together. She may even climb in between the two of them. They may even read a chapter of *A Little Princess* together. But with kids Pete and Sally's age, you know they understand what goes on in the night. If her lovemaking with Tim were less explosive maybe she'd feel differently, but as it is she knows that she either couldn't let herself go at the thought of them hearing every creak in the bed, or she would go ahead and make noise anyway, and then in the morning she would imagine them looking at her as she fixed the bagels and knowing what she'd done.

Tim thinks this is crazy. "You're making too big a deal of it," he says. "They're just kids." In fact, he says, it's a lot healthier for them to have their mother in the house with them than it is having her sneak out every night or two and be off screwing her brains out at his apartment between midnight and four A.M.

"They're going to have to get used to it sooner or later," he tells her. Claire says nothing.

But tonight, Ursula has been invited to a sleepover at the house of a girl in her class named Brianne. Pete's sleeping over at his dad's house and Sally's away at a weekend dance workshop. So Tim is sleeping over at Claire's for once.

He feels almost shy as he stands on her doorstep, he's so full of anticipation and hunger for her. They made love at his apartment last night actually. But it's different in her bed. Not just because

of the thick down comforter, the flowered sheets, the high wooden
posts at the head and footboard where he tied her wrists that time
with the silk scarves she had laid out. Not just because she keeps
a box next to her bed with three different pairs of gloves: elbow-
length white kid, black lace, red satin like a hooker. Not just
because she keeps a feather boa under one pillow that she likes to
wind around her neck sometimes, or other places on her skin or
his.

The first time Tim laid eyes on Claire's bedroom he thought it
must be her daughter's, the way she's fixed it up. There are dried
roses hanging from the ceiling and silk scarves draped over the
bed like the roof of some Moroccan tent, mirrors in unlikely places,
stuffed animals from her childhood. Her favorite dresses—twen-
ties evening gowns and velvet cloaks, silk camisoles and a bowling shirt with the name CLAIRE stitched on the back under the
team insignia JIMMY's MUFFLER—hang like crazy laundry from
the walls, in between photographs of her children and school art
projects and a shelf of bronze baby shoes that she buys at yard
sales, just because she loves babies, and she hates the thought that
any of their shoes would end up in the wrong hands.

"I want you," he says, reaching for her. So many words have
spilled out of him on this subject, sometimes he just gets tired of
the sound of his own voice telling her.

She climbs the steps. He follows her soundlessly. She closes the
door behind them. Nobody's home besides the two of them; this is
just habit. She sits on the bed like a schoolgirl, with her hands
folded in her lap and her knees touching. "I'm yours," she says.

He can't move right away. He has to just look at her awhile.
*She's a still life. She is a garden of flowers you can't bear to pick. She's
the most glorious meal anybody ever set on a table. Where to begin?*

His finger traces her eyelid. He bends to kiss her neck. He
breathes in the smell of her. He touches his lips to the hollow place
at the base of her neck that he loves so much. He feels the rise of
her breasts under his face—also her heartbeat—but he doesn't
want to move, not even to undress her.

She gets up. Claire keeps a portable boom box in her bedroom, wanting music to follow her wherever she goes—that theory of hers that life should have a soundtrack. Here in her bedroom tonight it's *Nina Simone in Paris.*

She slides one hand under his sweater and his shirt. Then the other. The sounds she makes aren't words.

"I want a little sugar in my bowl," Nina sings. Very tenderly, as if he were unwrapping a package of rare lady's slippers in the botany lab, he begins to unbutton her blouse. The thought flashes in his mind of Barbie. Her nurse's uniform that always gives him so much trouble.

The turquoise bra. He tries to remember whether this is one of the ones that fastens in the front, or the back-fastening kind. Front.

Her breasts tumble out. He still experiences a momentary shock every time he sees them again. Not only for the fullness of them, the darkness of her nipples, the smoothness of her skin. Claire has nursed two babies; hers are not the perky, upward-tilted breasts of a twenty-year-old. But even the way they droop is something he loves about Claire's breasts, as if they are bearing testimony to all the ravages of marriage and parenthood, all the ways that life takes its toll on a person. He pictures one of her babies suckling her. Pictures a baby of their own.

She has bought raspberries, though they aren't in season. She has laid them in a blue ceramic bowl next to the bed. This is Claire for you. She attends to the tiny details of lovemaking the way she attends to the details of her children's field trips and soccer games.

Naked now, stretched out on her flower garden sheets, she holds a handful of raspberries in her fingers, pressed against her nipples. She doesn't need to tell him what to do.

He is sucking the juice. Impossible to distinguish which is berry, which is breast. He is making a meal of her.

With raspberries still in his mouth he kisses her. She reaches for more. There are raspberries on her neck now, raspberries on her belly. Raspberries tumbling between her legs. His face is there, too. When he lifts his head his mouth is red and dripping.

• • •

Her husband would never have touched her that way. Times when she was bleeding, he wouldn't want to come near her. One time when she didn't know she was having her period and they were finished fucking, he caught sight of blood on his cock and actually recoiled like a man hit by sniper fire. She remembers the sound of him in the bathroom afterward. Not simply washing himself off but taking a shower.

Tim is all over her, kissing her, devouring her. By the time they fall asleep—she has no idea of the time, but it's no longer night; she hears birds—there's red everywhere.

After Ursula and Brianne finish their SpaghettiOs—which Brianne's mother serves in the can, to cut down on dishes—they get to go outside. Ursula has suggested a game where they're poor girls. Their parents left them in the woods and now they have to dig for worms for supper.

"I'm so hungry, sister. If we don't find some soon, I think I'll go into a coma," Ursula tells Brianne. She has learned about comas from "Live and Let Live," because Veronica is in one.

"What do I say?" Brianne asks her. Brianne is not very good at pretend, or anything else, actually. The good thing about her is she's not a member of the club of girls that aren't inviting Ursula to their birthday. She hasn't left snot on Ursula's seat.

"You say, 'Don't worry, sister. I just know we'll find some soon,'" says Ursula.

"Don't worry, sister," says Brianne. This is as much as she can remember.

"Wouldn't it be wonderful if somebody rich adopted us?" says Ursula. "Like Princess Diana?" She gets the feeling that Brianne doesn't know who Princess Diana is, but never mind. "Or Madonna." Brianne has to know that one, and it looks like she does. She brightens, anyway. Just a little.

They dig some more. Sure enough, Ursula has located a worm, a nice fat one. Ursula has done lots of nature things with her dad. She knows where to find crayfish and what kind of places have frog's eggs. She isn't scared of bugs, like most girls. She even has a collection she and her dad made, of animal poop. Only you don't call it poop. You call it scat.

"Here, sister. You take this one. You need it more than me. You're weaker," Ursula says to Brianne.

Brianne looks worried. She is wondering if she really has to eat the worm. She would but she is happy when Ursula whispers to her, "Just pretend."

They dig some more. "Look," says Brianne. She has uncovered something she thinks is a balloon, but Ursula knows it's not.

"Leave that," says Ursula.

A ladybug lands on her shoe. "Look," whispers Ursula. "She's magic. We get to have three wishes."

Brianne looks at her. She has never played such a hard game before.

"You go first," says Ursula.

Brianne is silent. She figures if she picks her scab, that will give her time to think. She just doesn't know what she's supposed to think about.

"What do you wish for?" says Ursula, very slowly, and a little louder than usual, as if she were talking to somebody from another country or someone very old.

"Sega Genesis?" says Brianne.

"Okay," says Ursula, sighing faintly. "My sister wishes for Sega Genesis," she tells the ladybug. "Now it's my turn."

"I wish a beautiful woman would appear, and she's driving a convertible and she has an evening dress on and she says she wants to be our mother. Her name is"—Ursula thinks for a second— "Dolly Parton."

This is a new idea for Ursula, and she likes it. She has seen Dolly Parton on TV and she thinks Dolly's beautiful. Not skinny like Vanna White, and also funnier. She has her own amusement park, called Dollywood, where she would probably let Ursula and Brianne play for free. Plus Ursula knows from a time she heard Dolly on "Oprah" that Dolly has no children of her own.

They don't get to their third wish. Brianne's mother has stuck her head out the window and now she is yelling at them.

"What do you kids think you're doing?" she yells. "Get the hell out of that street and come on in and watch TV."

Late at night—snuggled up together in Brianne's single bed, which only smells slightly of pee—they hear the fight begin. Brianne's apartment is very small and the walls are so thin that when Brianne's father throws something at the wall that backs up against Brianne's room, her kitten calendar flaps.

"Bitch!" Brianne's father yells. He is not Brianne's real father, Ursula has learned. Not from Brianne, but from Brianne's little brother, Kyle, who said, when he threw his beans at Kyle during dinner, "You aren't my real dad."

"No kidding," said the fake dad, whose name is Ernie. "You think I'd have a twerp like you for a kid?"

Kyle didn't say anything after that. A second later Ernie pitched his cigarette lighter straight at Kyle's head.

"Bingo," he said when it hit Kyle in the eye. Nobody said anything. Not even Brianne's mom.

It turns out the reason Ernie's mad now is Brianne's mother smoked all his cigarettes. "Go get me some more," he says. Not *please,* either.

"Get them yourself," she says.

"Like hell I will," he says. "You get them, bitch."

For a minute there the girls can't hear any words, except Brianne's mother saying, "Ernie. Ernie."

"You heard me," he says. "Who do you think pays the rent, anyway?"

She says she can't leave the kids. "You're shitfaced," she says.

Pressed up against Brianne, Ursula is thinking about her own dad. She thinks about his big arms and how strong they are. Even now that she weighs seventy-nine pounds, he still carries her inside without waking her when she falls asleep in the car. Her dad would never throw a cigarette lighter at the wall. Her dad doesn't even smoke.

"Stick them up your ass," Brianne's mother yells at the man who is not Brianne's real dad.

"Cunt," he says. Ursula doesn't know what this word means, but just the way he says it, she knows it can't be good.

"They always do this," says Brianne. "It only lasts a little while."

"I want to go home," says Ursula. "I want my dad."

"You can't," says Brianne. "We have to stay in bed. Ernie gets pissed if we get up."

"I don't care," says Ursula. "I have to go home now. My dad wouldn't want me to be here. I've got to call him."

"The phone doesn't work anymore," Brianne tells her. "Besides, Ernie gets wicked pissed."

Something else hits the wall, heavier than the first thing. The calendar falls on the bed. Also Brianne's My Little Pony that was on the shelf.

"We had a wish left," Ursula says. "Remember?"

Brianne is asleep again. Her eyes are shut, anyway.

I wish Dolly would come over, Ursula thinks. She knows this won't happen, but she thinks it might help if she could picture it. Dolly would bust in the apartment and grab Ernie by the belt buckle and tell him to lay off of Brianne's mother. Then she would come into Brianne's bedroom and sing them that song Ursula likes so much, "Coat of Many Colors."

Maybe if she sings to herself, Ursula thinks, it will be almost the same. She wishes she could remember how it starts, but all she can hear is the TV set.

So she just lies there, listening to that, and the sound of Brianne's breathing, and some dog that isn't Jenny, out on the street howling. As she's lying there, she realizes the bed is damp, and warm, too, and then she realizes that Brianne must have peed in her sleep. She doesn't get up, though. Who knows what Ernie would do to her then?

D*on't take this personally, Claire," Mr. Hogue, the guidance counselor at Pete's school is telling her. "I don't want you to feel Pete's problem is all that far out of the ordinary for a young person in his situation. We often see this kind of* *behavior in the children of broken homes. Not that this excuses your son's behavior. It just provides a context."*

Claire has been called in to the guidance counselor's office because a bouquet of inflated condoms was found in the boys' bathroom today along with graffiti that said, "Miss Connor sucks Mr. Bennett's dick." Mr. Bennett is the principal of Pete's school. Miss Connor is the librarian. When they inspected Pete's locker, they found the spray paint. Now he's been suspended for five days, in addition to which he will be responsible for repainting the boys' room under the supervision of Mr. Edison, the custodian.

"I don't know what to say," Claire tells Mr. Hogue. "Pete has never done anything like this before. We have our problems sometimes, but I've never known him to deface property. He's a good boy."

"I see from our records that there was a custody dispute between yourself and Pete's father," Mr. Hogue says. "Perhaps he's expressing some of his frustration at the absence of a strong male presence in the household. That can be very difficult for a boy his age, just entering adolescence."

"My son sees his father practically every weekend," Claire tells him. She will never get used to this: the way her divorce, and then what followed it, has left her in a state of endlessly defending herself, re-explaining their lives.

"And can you think of anything else that might have changed recently in your household?" he asks her. The way he asks this question, and the way he is looking at her (at her breasts, she thinks; maybe she's crazy, but that's what it seems like to Claire), she believes he knows the answer already. This is a small town. Plus Ursula attends this school, though she is seeing a different counselor in her Remedial Social Skills group.

"For several months now I have been involved in a serious relationship," she says.

"And this man you're involved with—how does Pete feel about him? Would you say their relationship is of a positive nature?"

"My son doesn't answer when Tim speaks to him," she thinks but doesn't say. "Sometimes I overhear him on the phone with his father, doing imitations of Tim. When Tim brought over pizza last night, Pete took his up to his room."

"It's okay," she says. "The usual."

"There's a group here at school for students dealing with step-parent issues," the counselor says. "Sometimes nothing can be more helpful to a kid like Pete than knowing he's not the only one."

"I don't think that would be the best idea at the moment," she tells him.

"I must tell you, Ms. Temple," Mr. Hogue tells her, "that your son's behavior has reinforced our sense that perhaps there are issues surrounding sexuality in the home which have been troubling Pete. So I have to ask you, are you comfortable that this boyfriend has in no way violated his boundaries with Pete? Or that you yourself, however inadvertently, might not have demonstrated certain behaviors that could be troubling to a young person at this highly sensitive, highly volatile stage of life?"

"I can't imagine what you mean," she says. "Pardon me. I can imagine. It's just so far from anything that's going on in our household, or anything that ever would."

"Where did he get the condoms, Ms. Temple?" he asks her. Then he sets a bag of chewing tobacco and a pair of red lace panties on top of the desk.

"I'm sorry to have to do this," he says. "But I thought you should know we found these in your son's locker, too."

The panties are hers, of course.

"We're going to have to suspend Pete from school for five days," Mr. Hogue tells her. "If I may, I'd like to suggest that you consider therapy for your son. And try to spend some quality time with him."

This is how Claire came to hit her son. She has thought about this moment many times since it happened and replayed it over in her head like an umpire's bad call. Or worse. The moment in a Preakness race when a champion filly breaks its leg, the moment in a figure skater's Olympic long program when she lands her jump wrong and crashes onto the ice and all you want to do is rewind the film and make it turn out different next time.

· · ·

It was winter. Before she'd met Tim. Before Pete had Ursula to be angry about, and Jenny, and faxes coming in at five A.M., *and wind chimes outside his window to remind him that his mother has a lover who won't leave them alone. Back when he still thought nothing could be any worse than knowing his mother and his father hated each other so much now that when he wants to show his father his Don Mattingly card, he can't just say, "Come up to my room." He has to take it out onto the porch.*

"Before you play any computer games, you've got to put your dirty clothes in the wash," she said to him. This was a Sunday night shortly after they'd come back from his father's house. These are the hardest times, second hardest being Fridays just before they go. By now she has learned not to expect a whole lot from her children on Sunday nights. Mondays she can enforce the usual rules again, but the best thing to hope for, Sundays, is for the three of them to watch a little television, have a piece of pie if she's made some, and get to bed before anybody does any terrible damage to anybody else. That winter she hadn't learned this yet.

Pete was playing Dragon Master when she said that to him about the clothes. Directly after arriving back home after his weekend with his father, Pete had walked into the house, thrown his jacket on the kitchen table, dumped his Nike bag in the middle of the living-room floor, and opened the refrigerator. His backpack and baseball glove were still in the car. Never mind that neither he nor Sally is likely to tell their mother, "Thank you for driving, Mom." What he had said to her was, "We never have anything good to eat." Then he had turned on the computer.

It's not just Pete and Sally who have a hard time Sunday nights, either. It's also Claire, who had just spent the last two hours driving the road that leads to their old house and back again. For twenty minutes she'd sat parked in the driveway of the house she used to live in, waiting for her children to come out, looking in the windows she used to look out of.

Her babies were born inside this house, on the very bed where their father now screws Melanie. Melanie's car was parked in the driveway, next to Sam's. She'd been up visiting again, evidently, and she had made them all fondue. She had played them this great U2 tape and

*lent Sally a silver miniskirt. They were the same size. "She's so cool,
Mom. It's almost like having a big sister when she's around," Sally told
Claire on the ride back from their old house. At this point Sally still
thought Melanie was just a friend of the family.*

"Pete," Claire said again. More sharply this time. "No computer
until you've put your stuff away. I'm assuming you've got your homework done."

"I'll do it in the morning," he told her. "It's just some dumb
mimeographed sheets."

"You'll do it now," she said. "I don't suppose your dad sent money
for hockey?"

*Moments like this she's like a drunk and she knows it. Knows she's
taking her children and herself to a place where nobody will have a
good time. And still she's got the pedal to the metal.*

"He said he already sent you the child-support check," said Pete.
Zap. Zap. Zap.

"Great," she said. "That should cover maybe three school lunches
and one set of rubber bands on your braces. You know what goalie
pads cost? You know what those stitches cost in the emergency room
last week, and your sister's yearbook pictures? I'm hemorrhaging
money."

"It's not my business," he said, zapping one of the hundred little
characters who seem to dance forever across the computer screen like
cockroaches. "Dad says when you start talking about money I should
just tell you it's not my business. Kids aren't supposed to think about
money."

"Easy for Mr. Good Times to say. Thank you for your insights, Mr.
Mellow. He doesn't have to think about money, either. He just leaves
it to me to come up with it all."

*She heard the voice in her head telling her to stop it. But she has
knocked the bottle over now. She couldn't keep the words from spilling
out. The Melanie part sits in her mouth like a piece of rotten fruit. But
in small ways there is this bitter bile that seeps out of her.*

"Mom," Sally was saying. "You know you're going to regret this
later. Why don't you let me fix you a cup of tea. Put on a record. Take
a bath." She was massaging her mother's shoulders.

"Just leave me alone, okay?" said Claire. "You don't know half of
what goes on."

"I don't want to," Sally said. "Even though you keep wanting to tell me."

Pete was playing Dragon Master through all of this, still ignoring her. She unplugged the computer.

"What are you doing?" he screamed at her. "I was on the third level."

"I guess that's what it takes to get your attention," she told him.

He stamped up to his room, leaving the Nike bag on the floor. Claire followed after him.

"Don't think you can get away with that kind of behavior!" she told him. "I'm in charge here."

He turned on his Tom Petty tape. Stretched out on his bed, opened a Mad.

"Look at me," she said. He turned the page.

"Look at me," she said again.

He turned another page. His jaw had this hard, clenched look she knows very well, a mouth like a hyphen. She had seen that face plenty of times before, just not—until recently—on her son.

"Look at me!" she screamed. "Don't shut me out like that. Don't push me away from you."

He didn't move.

She unplugged his tape player. He looked up then, but not to meet her eyes. He was shaking his head in that terrible way his father used to, that said, "You poor, pathetic crazy woman." This is where Sam would pick up the video camera and begin taping. "Look at yourself. If you dare."

That's when she did it. First she grabbed his shoulders and shook him. His eyes staring straight into hers had a look of defiance and contempt. His body offered no resistance.

What she wanted to say was, "Come back to me!" She wanted to tell him, "Remember who I am? Remember who you are? Remember just last spring when you hit that home run in the playoffs, with the bases loaded in the seventh? And how, after rounding third, and tagging home, you didn't even break your stride? Just kept right on running, straight into my lap? Where did that boy go?"

She wanted to wrap her arms around his wiry little body. Kiss his eyelids until he managed to wriggle free, saying, "Cut it out, Mom.

You're getting drool on my shirt." She wanted to rub her face in his
goofy, shelf-cut hair with that single wispy braid of his. My darling
boy, she wanted to say. My darling, darling boy.

Only that was not what she did. What she did was slap him across
the face. Hard, too. And the worst part was that even then he didn't
look angry or hurt or even surprised. He had that blank look.

She has never hit him again. She knows now she can't reach her son
that way. He's drifting away from her. He has this terrible anger in
him, and it's growing like a tapeworm.

Last night after she got home
from her conference with the guidance counselor, his mom told
Pete he has to send letters to Mr. Bennett and Miss Connor apolo-
gizing for the graffiti. He will also have to repaint the walls in the
boys' bathroom after school, but he can't do this for a week because
he is also suspended from school. He'll have to buy the paint,
which will cost around fifty dollars. He will have to use the money
he's been saving for the new TPX bat he's got on layaway at Ray's
Sporting Goods. The worst part is she's going to send him back to
therapy. He'd rather have her lock him in a room for a whole day,
with a pair of headphones on playing country music. Burn his
entire collection of *Mad*s. Make him eat lunch with Kiki Saunders
every day for a week and let her tell him all about her fascinating
trip to Colonial Williamsburg.

He knows kids who would run away from home at a moment
like this, but Pete thinks that's just dumb. What's the point—you
know they're going to find you in the end, and then you'll just be
in even worse trouble. That's the awful thing about being twelve
years old. You're just so totally powerless.

Did anyone ask Pete if he wanted his parents to split up? They
certainly didn't ask if he wanted his mom hanging around with a
dork like Tim, or his dad going to rock concerts with their babysitter. Here he is, a guy that's been asking for a puppy his whole
entire life, and when they finally get a dog nobody even consults
him. They end up with this hundred-year-old mutt that dribbles

pee on the floor and can't even fetch a ball. And now his mom's telling him he's got to go sit in this therapist's office that he can't stand when he should be off playing basketball, and talk about his feelings, and the longer he won't cooperate, the longer he'll have to go.

They wonder why kids like playing video games? When a guy has his hand on the joystick is probably the one time in his whole life as a kid where he actually gets to control how things turn out. That and when he turns on his boom box. Pete's mom says she can't understand the music he listens to, it's so loud and angry-sounding. *Right, Mom, he should tell her. That's the point.*

Ⅰt's thinking about the music his mom hates that gave Pete the idea, actually. Knowing he has to do something. Knowing how mad he is and how few options he has.

Next morning when he gets up, Pete puts on his baggiest shirt. Also a pair of his sister's old pants with the cuffs rolled up. He straps his backpack on his back and stuffs an old asthma inhaler belonging to his friend Benny in his pocket. If he gets caught, which he doesn't plan to, he's going to act like he's having some kind of seizure and start swallowing his tongue. Then they'd be so glad to get him out of their store they'd forget all about the shoplifting part.

His mother must be out walking with Nancy—talking about him, most likely—or she would've stopped him. Either that or she's up in her office reading faxes.

He heads for the highway leading to the mall. He pedals hard, listening to the Beasties on his Walkman to get psyched.

He parks his bike—no lock in case he has to make a quick getaway. The spaced-out girl is at the cash register. *Yes.*

He heads to the videos first, looking for Van Damme, and finds the tape he wants. He holds it up as if he's studying the names of the cast. Now he turns around so he's facing the back wall. Lifts his shirt slightly. Pushes the tape into his pants.

He heads for the pop music section, with his backpack looped over his shoulder, unzipped partway. He picks up a Nirvana tape, and Green Day while he's at it.

The hardest part is walking out the door. They have this metal detector set up, like at airports, with an alarm that goes off if you try to take something you haven't paid for. But the space cadet at the cash register is on the phone and flipping through a copy of *Rolling Stone.* When she turns her back for a second, he knows it's now or never. He tosses the backpack over the top of the detector. He's out of there.

After he's down the block, he stops to catch his breath, although he can still feel his heart beating double time. It's like the first time he jumped off the bridge at Ryan's Quarry last summer, and when he and his dad rode on that roller coaster at the Deerfield fair. He was so scared he almost wet his pants.

He has to do it again.

One of Claire's favorite times with her children when they were small was reading to them. Even when she and Sam had very little money, she always bought them books. Not paperbacks, either. She loved the thick smooth paper of a full-sized hardbacked picture book, the smell even. Their collection was vast and wonderful: Russian fairy tales with gilt-edged illustrations, every Chris Van Allsburg, every William Steig, Frances the badger, *A Chair for My Mother, Harold and the Purple Crayon, James and the Giant Peach, In the Night Kitchen.* . . .

Bedtimes at their old house, Claire used to pile Sally and Pete under the covers with her after their baths and they would have what they used to call a book festival. When they were very little, they often wanted her to read the same story over and over again. *Blueberries for Sal, Cloudy with a Chance of Meatballs, Sylvester and the Magic Pebble.* But later—on snowy days especially, if there was no school, or Sunday nights—they would pile a tall stack of picture books on the quilt and go through every one. When they begged Claire for just one more chapter of *Matilda* or *Half Magic,* she would usually say yes because the truth was, she also wanted to know what happened next. And not just that, either: She loved the feeling of her two children, one on each side, snuggled up against her with the wind howling outside and the quilt pulled up around them.

A few months after Sally and Pete had settled into their new house in Blue Hills with Claire, she had called up Sam one night to say she wanted to pick up the children's books at their old house.

"You can have some of them if you want," Sam told her. "But they aren't all yours. There's a lot of them I want to hold on to."

This was a shock. Not simply because Sam had never been a big one for reading to the children when they were little. At that moment all Claire's sense of loss and violation concerning her marriage rose from her like a great, billowing cloud so dark it covered her sky. And when the cloud finally dissipated, what was left was the image of those books.

Her children's books were, for Claire, the most tangible evidence she possessed of her hours and years as a mother. She could trace her life with her children through their pages: the way the eighteen-month-old Sally loved to stick her finger in the hole of the wedding ring when Claire held her on her lap and read *Pat the Bunny,* the way Pete placed his finger to his lips and mouthed "Shh" at that page in *Goodnight Moon* with the quiet old lady murmuring "Hush." The tune she had made up and attached to the mother's song in *Love You Forever,* and the way Pete had stopped her in the middle of singing it one night and with his eyes full of real tears said, "No more. Please. It makes me too sad."

And more. The way Sally fell in love with that phrase in *Babar* where Babar's suit is described as "a becoming shade of green" and the way, on the page where Babar brings Celeste to a pastry shop, Sally would choose the pastry she'd get, if it was her. Her gut-splitting laughter over the line in *Caleb and Kate,* where "the cart said farewell to the wheel." Her tears at the death of Old Yeller.

Claire thought about all of these things when Sam told her he was keeping half their children's books. It wasn't even so much a matter of thinking about them: She *felt* them, and how it felt was that she had to have every book, every single one.

• • •

One day when the children were on a camping trip with their father, she drove to the old house. She knew he never locked the door. Neither of them ever had.

She wasn't expecting Melanie to be there in her short shorts and the tank top she wears with no bra. Never mind, Melanie hadn't expected her, either.

Claire greeted her pleasantly enough. Then she walked into the old house and began packing up the books. She filled the boxes and the two garbage bags she had in the back of her station wagon and there were still more books left.

So she began piling books on the seat of her car. Piling them on the floor. Making piles so high she could no longer see out the rearview mirror.

Melanie stood there saying almost nothing while Claire did this. She must have known Sam wouldn't want Claire doing this. But Melanie was nineteen years old. Claire was thirty-six. What was she going to do?

"I think I gave Pete that book," she said quietly as Claire was carrying out one of the last piles. It was a Berenstain Bears paperback.

"Oh, really?" said Claire. The sweetness in her voice must have been scary as a gun. "Well, then, maybe you'd like to keep it here?" She tossed the book on a lawn chair.

"Give Sam my best," Claire said as she slammed the door of the trunk.

"I'm just house-sitting," Melanie said. "I'll be heading back to school pretty much as soon as they get back from Maine."

"Too bad," Claire said. She was drenched with sweat. Were her eyes yellow? Did her hair resemble the bride of Frankenstein's? Probably.

She climbed into the car. Heading down their old driveway, she could feel how the weight of the books had dragged down her car. Its belly scraped the dirt.

The first time Sally and Travis did it was in his car. Sally hadn't been planning on it. In fact, she had pretty much decided that she wouldn't, at least until they'd been going out a year, and maybe not then either. But when he got to the part where he always said, "I'm begging you, Sal, just let me put it in a little ways, I won't come," she was as surprised as he was when she heard herself say, "Okay."

He did come, but he had a condom on. And of course once you've done it one time, you never go back to not doing it.

It hurt actually. She knew from her friend Kim that this was likely to be the case, but since it's never that way in the movies, it surprised her how much. She thought it would be like putting in a Tampax, but it was worse.

And still she keeps doing it. Who can say why? She doesn't like sex exactly, but she likes how powerful she feels that he wants her so badly. Sally herself is pretty much the same person she always was before, but Travis is a totally changed person. It isn't just that he's calling her up so much now or the way he's always there waiting for her at her locker after fourth period, and parked out front when she gets out of ballet class, to take her home. Well, not home maybe. Not right off.

It's more than that. What has changed about Travis is the way he looks at her and the feeling it gives Sally that she could make him do anything, so long as she's having sex with him. He's an addict. Brainwashed.

They used to do all sorts of things together. They went skateboarding, for instance. They went miniature golfing, and one time they made a video of these scenes from "I Love Lucy," with him being Ricky and her being Lucy. They talked about music and their friends and their parents and school even. He told her about Mr. Sullivan, the shop teacher, who's always telling horror stories about people cutting off their fingers or getting their sleeve stuck in the planer. She told him about her father and Melanie and her mother's wimp boyfriend and his whiny daughter. They'd order pizza and hang out.

Now what they do is have sex, mostly. At first they did it in his car. She was always bumping into the gear shift or getting a charley horse from having to do it in such a weird position.

They don't have to do it in the car so much anymore, though. Not now that Sally has figured out where her mother goes at night.

So now after her mom leaves, Sally calls up Travis and tells him the coast is clear. His parents would be suspicious if they heard his car start, but he lives close enough that he can ride his skateboard over.

At first she thought it was too risky. Her mother could come back anytime, she figured. But now she knows her mother never comes back until close to sunrise. They take off their clothes and everything.

Lying there on her bed, she sometimes thinks about her mother and Tim. She doesn't want to, she just can't help it. These pictures keep popping up in her brain, of the two of them doing the stuff she and Travis do. It's hard to believe her mother would do these things, but then her mother would probably never believe the things she does, either.

At least they always use a condom, anyway. All but that one time when they'd already done it three times and he ran out. Sally is sure she must have been safe then. What could he have had left in him anyway after all that screwing? Sally isn't sure exactly how it works, but she doesn't see how a person that already came three times in one night could have any more active sperms left in their balls. Plus she figured she was due to get her period sometime soon, although it's hard to predict with Sally because she isn't very regular.

That was three weeks ago, and she hasn't got her period yet.

Claire's life by day and her life by night are so disconnected it's as if she were a double agent or a bigamist.

She sees her kids off to school, although days go by that Claire barely sees Sally, between the time she spends on the phone and the time she spends in the bathroom. Pete's suspension is over, but he no longer kisses his mother good-bye when he goes off to school mornings, and after school he always seems to be out on his bike. Tim still sends her faxes sometimes, but though his expressions of love and lust are more extravagant than ever, there is a heaviness to them now. They no longer lift her heart. *"I live in fear of not being a good enough man for you,"* he writes. *"I don't ever want to fall in love again the way I'm in love with you. It's just too draining."*

Claire lives with a different fear—the fear that she cannot be a good enough mother. She lives with the guilty dread that her own pleasure is drawn directly from the well that was meant to quench her children's thirst. If the price of her happiness is their own, she knows it's too high.

She no longer stops for coffee with Tim, and she seldom invites Ursula over anymore to bake brownies or putter around with her at the children's museum. Tim may stop in to see her at the museum and he always calls her up several times during the day, but they seldom lay eyes on each other during daylight hours anymore.

Tim is busy, too. Money's so tight he's taken another job proof-reading a computer programming manual so he can meet his rent money. After school he tries to be around for Ursula, who has made only one friend in the third grade—a girl named Brianne who hardly ever says anything and eats only dry cereal. "Where's your mom?" she asked Ursula the first time they had her over. When Ursula told her New Zealand, she said, "Where's your TV?"

He tries to make a healthy dinner every night, and they say grace now, the way Claire does. Tim gave up serving meals on TV trays after Claire told him it wasn't very cozy and familyish. But the two of them sitting in the fluorescent glow of their tiny kitchen eating macaroni is not so cozy and familyish, either. Ursula doesn't ask him so much anymore, "When do we get to go over to Claire's house?" She knows the answer is, "When her kids are away." And not always then, either. "I wonder how Jenny's doing," she says, and leaves it at that.

He has tried to make their bleak apartment a little more cheerful. That idea of Claire's about checking reproductions out of the library, for instance—he did that. He and Ursula have started some begonias from cuttings he took at Claire's house. He has found a rug at a yard sale. ("A rug is important," she says. "So you can play board games on the floor." She has a hundred rules like this, of how to make a happy home. All these years, he sees, he has been operating without the manual. No wonder he screwed up.)

Also in the interests of making his place homier, Tim has bought Ursula a beanbag chair and an easel that he found at a yard sale. Ursula has hung up a couple of her dresses on the wall in her room, the way Claire does, although the room itself is still a mess. Tim can't keep up with the laundry. The trash. The grant proposals. The bills. For three weeks in a row he has missed the recycling day, and now milk cartons spill out of the kitchen into the hall. Tim never dreamed he could feel like this much of a loser.

All those great plans he had—for taking Ursula to Family Swim Night at the Y, the two of them building a dulcimer, making a terrarium. Those have evaporated. He is lucky if, at eight o'clock, he has enough energy to give his daughter her bath and read her a chapter of *Charlotte's Web* without falling asleep in the middle, or—as often happens—discovering that though his eyes are open, the words he's speaking are total gibberish.

"Daddy," she says, poking him in the ribs. They've got to the place where Templeton the rat breaks the rotten egg and Tim has faded out again.

"Wake up, Daddy," she says gently. "This is the best part."

After he sings Ursula their song and kisses her good night, he usually turns on the television. He knows he should wash the dinner dishes, but he's too tired. Never mind grant writing and proofreading. He usually falls asleep within the first ten minutes of whatever show he's watching. Sometimes, when Claire arrives in the middle of the night, he thinks for a moment he's just dreaming. She is the one miraculous thing in his day.

This is how Claire finds him when she lets herself in sometime around midnight. If he's on the couch and not in bed she will kiss him very lightly on the cheek and tell him, "I'm here, honey." He'll wake up just enough to get up the stairs. He drops his clothes on the floor and climbs under the sheets beside her. His hands find her, if hers haven't found him first. However weary he is, just the touch of her skin is enough to rouse him. He has never known this kind of wanting before.

One night she told him she was too tired to make love. "You mind?" she said. Of course he said he understood. It was enough just to hold her. Only then, exhausted as he was, he couldn't get to sleep. He lay there all night, his body aching for her until he couldn't stand it anymore. Three A.M., three-thirty maybe, he woke her.

"Claire," he said. "I'm so sorry to do this to you, but I don't think I can stand it, having you so close to me like this and not being inside you." He felt like such a jerk.

"It's okay," she told him, not fully waking, just rolling over toward him and opening her legs to him. "I'm so sorry," he said as he entered her.

Four-thirty the alarm goes off and she gets up. "Every time I see you climb out of my bed, I want to weep," he says. "You shouldn't have to be living this way. I hate it that I'm doing this to you."

"I'm lucky I have a man I love enough to want to visit in the night," she says.

"I want to be the man you get up with in the morning, and the man you have your coffee with. In the home where we live," he says.

"Oh, well," she says, pulling up her tights. "Nothing's perfect."

He walks her down the stairs. He stands on his front step watching her go until he can't see her anymore. Then he goes inside to get Ursula up and make her school lunch and the day begins again.

It's Parents' Night in third grade and Claire has come with Tim. She has heard that Ursula's been having problems at school, so she figured it would be good to meet the teacher, and maybe some of the mothers. Maybe she'll be able to make friends with one of them and invite her daughter over to play with Ursula at her house after school on her afternoon off.

Claire and Tim are sitting at Ursula's desk together while Mrs. Kennedy makes her presentation. They are studying the pilgrims at the moment, with the plan of visiting Plimoth Plantation next month. Mrs. Kennedy is still looking for chaperones if any parents might be available. Claire has been to Plimoth Plantation twice, as a chaperone with Sally's class, and again with Pete's. In a minute she knows Mrs. Kennedy is going to mention the First Thanksgiving celebration and ask who would like to help the students make the cranberry sauce and cornmeal mush.

"Third grade is such an exciting time in your children's lives," she is saying. "Now that they've got the building blocks under their belts, they're ready to have a little fun with reading."

Nothing Claire has heard about school from Ursula suggests that she's been having fun with much of anything. "Isn't there anybody you like besides Brianne?" Claire asked her the other day.

"Yes," Ursula said. "The janitor."

"One of our most fun projects so far this year has been writing our autobiographies," says Mrs. Kennedy. "I thought that would be a good way of getting to know your children, and, of course, helping them get to know each other. You'll find their work on their desks where they left them out for you. I know they're going to be eager to hear your comments at breakfast time tomorrow. And while you're looking at your children's work folders, be sure and take a look at their dental hygiene pictures and their most recent penmanship practice sheets. The letter *G* is such a tricky one, and I think you'll agree with me, they've been doing a super job with it."

Ursula is right about this woman, Claire is thinking. She does sound like Marge Simpson.

Tim leans toward Claire. She thinks he's going to say something about penmanship. What he says is, "I know you're going to think I've lost my mind, but I have to tell you. You're ovulating right now. I can sense it. It's making me nuts."

". . . dioramas depicting the life of Squanto," Mrs. Kennedy is saying. Claire is no longer sure what Mrs. Kennedy's talking about. She feels Tim's leg pressing against her thigh. In a way nobody but Claire would notice, his breathing has also changed. She tries to concentrate on the other parents in the room. She wants to find that mother she's been looking for whose child can become a friend for Ursula. Somebody other than the very young woman, standing in the back, wearing the shirt with the words SHIT HAPPENS. She has a bruise on her arm. She's very skinny.

"So," the teacher says, "I'll just let you wander around and explore your child's world for a while."

For some reason the first mother Claire introduces herself to is under the impression that Claire is the mother of a child named Courtney. "I've been wanting to get our girls together," this other mother says. "It's so important that they spend time with the right element. These days especially." Then she bends closer to Claire. "And in this classroom, in particular, it seems there is such a rough element."

"Rough element?" Claire says. "How so?"

"There's that boy Ricky, terrorizing them on the playground with that trick where he turns his eyeball inside his head," she says. "You hadn't heard?"

Claire shakes her head.

"And that poor kid Brianne. Somebody should report her mother to Youth Services. Just look at her outfit."

Claire can only nod.

"The worst is that disturbed child. Ursula something. The one who pinches. Courtney said she stole Ashley's scrunchy the other day. She didn't even wear it. Just threw it in the trash."

Tim doesn't have to introduce himself to Mrs. Kennedy. He has spoken with her many times, not only at their conference about Ursula's problems socializing, but often when he picks her up and drops her off in the morning. Ursula has told him she no longer wants to ride the bus, so he drives her.

"I was hoping you might be seeing her warm up a little," Tim says to the teacher. "Now that everybody's getting in the groove."

"It's still early," Mrs. Kennedy says. "And of course ever since hearing the news about her mother, she's been more distracted than usual."

"News about her mother?" says Tim. "What news?"

"About her mother coming to see her from New Zealand at Thanksgiving, and taking her to Disney World," says Mrs. Kennedy. "She already explained to me that's why she'd have to miss the field trip to Plymouth."

"I don't understand," says Tim.

"And then going to Nashville to meet Dolly Parton!" she says. "We were all so impressed. I hadn't realized that your former wife is a musician, although after Ursula told us, I could see it, from how musical Ursula is.

"I think the visit will do her a world of good," Mrs. Kennedy says. "I know you do the very best you can, both you and your friend. But there are just some things nobody can give a child besides her mother. I'm sure you know what I mean."

MY LIFE
By Ursula Vine

I was born Aug. 17 1985. My mom almost dide wen I came out. Her name is Joan. Shes verry pretty. I look like my dad. His name is Tim.

I wish I dint have red hair.

My dogs name is Jenny. She duznt get to live with us any more. Jenny use to sleep on my bed. We had a speshl trick we did with newspapr.

My dad writes artacals about swamps. Sumtimes we go look for Tadpoles but not so much anymor. I have a pink bike.

Here is the most unuzl thing about me. I no what peple think even if its just in there hed. Like if they betend to like me but I know they really dont.

So you beter not say I hope Ursula drops ded. Even in your hed. Or I'll no.

Thats me!

Here is the picher of me wen I was a baby. I use to be cute. I wish I was still a baby agen, but I'm not. I way 79 lbs.

Oprah has lost weight again. Ursula was too young to remember the last time she did it, but Oprah often talks about it on her show. The yo-yo syndrome, she calls it. You go up and down. My syndrome, Ursula thinks, is just yo. Stepping on the scale yesterday at Claire's house when she was over to walk Jenny, she saw that she no longer weighs seventy-nine. She's up to eighty-three.

Ursula pours herself another bowl of cereal. Oprah's guest today is a girl about Sally's age who found out a couple of years ago that the people who had been taking care of her all these years weren't really her parents. These other people were, who lived in Florida.

It turned out there were two babies born at the same hospital and by mistake somebody switched them. The girl, Tammy, went home with the Harkins family, and the other girl, Maryanne, went home with the Kings. When it should have been the other way around.

Maryanne had this heart problem, though. After a while, when she was about Ursula's age, she died. By this point the Kings had started to wonder if Maryanne was really their daughter, but they were nice people, so they still took care of her.

But after the funeral the Kings sent Tammy's parents a note. Actually, the person who thought she was Tammy's mother had also died by this point and the dad had a girlfriend, but that's another story. In this note the Kings explained how they had the wrong daughters all these years and now they wanted Tammy back. Mr. Harkins said no.

For a while Tammy didn't want to go either. She even got a lawyer and signed this paper where she said she didn't even want to see the Kings anymore ever again. They should just leave her alone. And they did, too.

But here is the part Ursula thinks is amazing. So amazing she doesn't even notice herself pouring another bowl of cereal as they tell it.

After a while it started to bother Tammy that this person she was living with was telling her she couldn't go out with her boyfriend and she had to clean up her room all the time and not wear certain clothes, and he wasn't even her real dad. So one day she just up and left. She got on a bus to Florida, and where does she turn up? At the Kings' house. Who were so happy to see her, naturally.

"Overjoyed," Mrs. King told Oprah. "Like my heart was going to burst," she said. Just hearing this, Ursula feels like her heart is going to burst, too.

In addition to Tammy, the Kings have all these other kids that look just like her, so it turns out she's not an only child after all. She has a big brother. A couple of little sisters. A bunny. They live close to Disney World. They have an RV.

"I don't blame Bill," Tammy tells Oprah. Bill is the man that thought he was her dad. That's what she calls him now. "He just got attached to me is all. But he's not the same as my real dad. There's no substitute for blood."

Anybody can see that, just looking at them now. Mrs. King even has the same type of glasses frames as Tammy. They show Maryanne's picture on the studio monitors, and you can see she never looked anything like the Kings. So really, if you think about it, the one Mr. Harkins should be feeling sad about isn't even Tammy. It's Maryanne. She's the one that was blood to him.

"I've found my real family now," Tammy says. "And I'm never leaving them again."

Ursula sees clearly now what she needs to do: find her real family. She is not sure where they are. Maybe Florida. Maybe someplace she hasn't even learned about. This man she's living with now, this red-haired man—he may have stubby fingers like her, but she no longer believes he is blood. If she could just get on "Oprah," she believes the people she is meant to be with would see her. They would come get her and take her home with them. Everybody would hug each other. They would give her presents. Oprah would ask her to be the flower girl at her wedding to Stedman Graham. Her real mother would say, "I don't know about that, honey, we're going to be awfully busy, getting to know our little girl."

•　•　•

"I don't blame Tim," Ursula says, out loud, to Bend 'N Stretch Barbie, in the Loni Anderson voice she would use on the show. "Naturally, he got attached to me. But there's no substitute for blood."

The items Sally has set out next to the cash register at CVS include Chap Stick, bobby pins, dental floss, aspirin, conditioner, and a home pregnancy test. The idea is to have the pregnancy test blend in, so it doesn't look like such a big deal. When she picked it up off the shelf (not that anyone was looking, but if they were), she made like this was something she'd almost forgotten to pick up, maybe something her mother had asked her to get. *"Oh, and one more thing," her mom says to her. "A home pregnancy test."*

It costs $9.95. Enough for the new Tori Amos tape, or that midriff top she likes over at Russell's. Which wouldn't be the right kind of purchase right now anyway if she actually is. Pregnant. It can't be.

She has not mentioned this possibility to Travis. She doesn't talk about gross stuff like periods with him. She hasn't mentioned this to anybody, as a matter of fact. She is just going to take this dumb test home and pee in the stupid little glass tube and find out, for sure, that everything's okay. Tomorrow morning she will probably wake up with blood on her underpants and feel like a total dipshit for wasting her money this way. Still.

What cool person can she think of that's pregnant? Edie Brickell and Paul Simon had a baby a while ago. That model that's married to Rod Stewart. There must be others, but Sally can't think of them. All she can think about is the horrible-looking pregnant women she sees at the supermarket and Vanessa Jenkins in her global issues class. Her global issue is sticking out so far now she can hardly even reach her desk when Mr. Pyle gives them a pop quiz.

One thing's for sure. Once she manages to get this mess behind her, Sally is never going to let something like this happen again.

Travis can get down on his knees and beg her, but if he doesn't have a rubber, forget it. And maybe even if he does.

She makes a bargain. *Just let it say I'm okay and I'll be nice to my brother. I'll always put my dishes in the dishwasher. I'll be nice to my mother's wimp boyfriend's weird kid. I'll just practice ballet all the time and hang out with my girlfriends, and I won't do it again until I'm tons older.*

Claire has told Ursula that if nobody's home when she comes over to walk Jenny, she should just go on in the house, get Jenny's leash, and take her. So this is what she was going to do today. Only she has to go upstairs to get Jenny, because the dog likes to lie on the window seat when she's not there.

She walks into Claire's room, with its scarves and beaded gowns and flowers hanging all around. She picks up a hand mirror and holds it up, like she was a rich woman or a queen. "Which ball gown shall I wear tonight?" she says, in her Loni Anderson voice.

She unscrews the top to a perfume bottle and splashes some on herself, more than she'd bargained for. She tries on a hat that Claire keeps on one of her bedposts. She opens the jewelry box, with its rows of mysterious compartments and drawers. That's when she sees the purple jewel ring. After all the trouble her dad went to getting it for her, Claire doesn't even wear it.

Pete's room isn't nearly as interesting as Claire's—just a whole lot of baseball cards and trolls. But Sally's room is amazing.

Ursula has always wanted to see this room. Up until now she has only gotten to peek in from the hallway. It's even neater than she expected. Not neat like her dad would mean, of course— clothes off the floor; Barbies on the shelf. It's just so beautiful. Like in a Disney movie. Like a magical world.

There are Christmas lights on the ceiling. There are pictures of all Sally's friends taped on the wall, and she has so many of them. There are pictures of rock 'n' roll singers Ursula doesn't recognize and people she figures must be movie stars. There are pictures of clothes cut out of magazines and sayings cut out of newspaper headlines. There's a note to Sally from her boyfriend with hearts all over the place, and a peace sign necklace and a candle in the shape of a flamingo and a pair of ballet slippers. There's a lava lamp and a pair of purple suede boots. Ursula has to touch them, they look so soft.

Of course the best would have been if Sally had invited Ursula to come into her room when she was there, not because her mother told her to, just because she wanted. The best would be if she said, "Hey, you want to come up to my room and try on clothes? I have some things that would look really cute on you."

She puts an arm around Ursula. "I always wanted a little sister," she says. "I have this great idea for what we can do with your hair." She takes Ursula into her closet then, which is like a whole other room. A very tiny room, but the best of all.

Ursula has never seen so many different pairs of shoes. High-top sneakers and bright blue lace-up boots and gold sandals and these amazing shoes that are totally clear plastic, so whatever kind of socks you were wearing would show. Ursula picks up one of Sally's bras that's lying on the floor. It's white and lacy. Small, with a little pink rosebud in the front. Ursula doesn't think she will ever have a bra like this. Ursula wears ribbed undershirts that never come out white in the wash. Someday she knows she will need a bra (the horrible truth is, she can almost see it beginning now), but never a tiny, delicate bra like this one. She holds it up and smells it. Lavender.

Ursula slips her feet out of her rubber Little Mermaid flip-flops and puts them into a pair of green platforms. She fingers a velvet dress and a pair of fishnet stockings draped over a hook. There is this other dress she loves: purple, made out of a shiny fabric that would change color depending on where you were standing. She has never seen such a beautiful dress in her whole life.

She pulls her corduroy jumper over her head. She stands there for a moment, in her grayish undershirt and her panties. Still wearing the platforms, she steps into the purple dress. She notices a necklace she has seen Sally wearing—a silver ball on a piece of silk cord. It makes this magic jingle sound when she moves. Ursula puts it on.

"I haven't decided if I'll let him take me to the prom," she says. She makes this accent that sounds just like Julie Andrews in *The Sound of Music.* "I don't want to hurt his feelings, but I think I may love Quinton more." She got the name from Loni Anderson's son that has Burt Reynolds for a dad, only he's fighting for custody.

She is holding a pretend telephone. "No," she is saying, "I can't make it today, Roberto. I'm getting my hair done. It's such a wreck."

She emerges from the closet, out into Sally's room again. She wants to see herself in the full-length mirror. She spots the boom box and decides to turn it on. A woman with a scratchy voice is singing, "Didn't I make you feel like you were the only man?"

Imagine having all these friends. Imagine lying in this bed at night, in the red glow of the lava lamp, watching the globs of whatever it is inside slowly swirling inside the glass. Listening to rock 'n' roll music and breathing in the smell of scented candles. She would have a girl-friend sleeping over. They would tell each other secrets. "He kissed me," *the girlfriend says.* "He touched the rose on my bra."

She picks up Sally's hairbrush. She pretends it's a microphone.

"Take it," she sings in front of the mirror. "Take another little piece of my heart now, baby." She twirls the jingle necklace. She's actually dancing, and the surprising thing is she looks good.

She shakes her hair. She strokes the microphone the way she has seen them do on MTV. She makes this face singers make, as if they're having a baby. "Break it," she sings to Jenny, who is sitting there watching with her head tilted to the side in that way she has. "Break another little piece of my heart."

This is where Sally walks in, holding her CVS bag.

When *Snow White* comes to town, Claire asks Ursula if she'd like to see it with her. Ursula does.

Claire buys them the biggest size of popcorn, with butter this time. "I like to sit right near the front. How about you?" Claire asks Ursula.

"Me too," Ursula says.

"You know, this was the first movie I ever saw when I was little," Claire tells her as they settle into their seats. It's that delicious moment she has never gotten over, when you have a full box of popcorn and a whole movie still ahead of you. Just as the lights go out.

"I got so scared my mom tried to take me out of the theater, but I didn't want to go. There's this part where the stepmother turns into a witch that gave me nightmares. So if you get scared you can just close your eyes."

"I don't get scared," Ursula says. "My dad let me see *Dr. Giggles.*"

Snow White is in the courtyard singing. A bluebird lands on her shoulder. Claire puts her arm around Ursula.

"She's so pretty," Ursula whispers.

"Who's the fairest in the land?" the stepmother asks her mirror. She doesn't like the answer, of course. Who would?

"Take her into the forest and cut out her heart," the stepmother tells the woodsman.

"Remember it's only a movie," Claire tells Ursula. She can feel Ursula's shoulders tightening when the stepmother says that.

"I know," Ursula tells her. "I've seen tons of these movies on video."

"Hi ho, hi ho," the dwarfs sing. Very softly, under her breath, Ursula is humming.

Snow White finds the cottage. She cleans it up. She lies down on one of the little beds upstairs. That's where she is when the dwarfs find her.

The queen discovers she is still not the fairest. She makes the poison apple and disguises herself as an old apple seller. "Don't eat it!" Ursula calls out to the face of Snow White on the movie screen. "Don'tdon'tdon't!"

· · ·

"I knew that was going to happen," Ursula whispers to Claire. "She should have listened to the dwarfs."

"It's going to be okay," Claire tells her. But Ursula isn't scared.

"They always marry the prince in the end," Ursula says as they file out of the theater. "In real life they'd probably get a divorce."

Although she tells him she will marry him at some point, Claire has still not put Tim's ring on her finger. "Maybe we'll get married sometime around April vacation," she tells him. "Or next summer. So we won't have to deal with Christmas for a long time." She doesn't say, "So we won't ruin my children's Christmas," but that's what she means.

"It would just be such a shock for them right now if you and Ursula were to move in with us," she says. "We all need a little more time."

Tim says he could bring Ursula to her grandparents' for a few days until they got her new room set up. Claire's office.

"I get to sleep with you every night. Not just till dawn, either," he says. "I can make you breakfast. I'll make breakfast for the whole family."

"We'd have to be quieter," she says. "Pete's room is right next to mine." She doesn't say "ours." She still thinks of this as her room, her house.

If she marries Tim, she will never be able to send Ursula home anymore. Ursula will be home already.

The Bumblebees are playing the Puffballs this afternoon. Ursula is a Puffball. Claire got off work early to come watch her play.

So she and Tim are sitting together like a regular couple, if you didn't know. Claire, who knows the soccer routine well, has her coffee thermos and the stadium blanket she puts over her knees days like this when there's a nip in the air. She has also brought it today with the thought that this will allow him to place his hand on her leg, or higher.

Tim was on the bench already when she got here. Approaching him from behind, she was startled for a moment by the size of his bald spot. Mostly she knows his head from the feel of it in the dark, when her hands are in his hair. She knew his hair was thinning there. She just didn't realize how little was left.

Even though Claire doesn't have a third grader anymore herself, she knows many of these parents from the children's museum. Some have older children in Pete's class. Sally used to babysit for one of these sets of parents, now divorced. She worked on a fund-raiser with another, one of the dads.

"It must get lonely for you, on your own and all, in a town like this," he said as they were leaving the school one night, where they had been washing dishes for the Playground Committee Ice Cream Social. "Good-looking woman like you."

"I'm a lesbian!" she thought of saying.

"Not so lonely really. I've got this incredible vibrator."

"Not as lonely as it must be for your wife."

"I'm very busy with the museum," she said. "That, and all these committees."

Ursula's coach is a guy named Mike who sold Claire a washing machine a couple of years back. He must be forty, at least, but he's still in very good shape. As he jogs out onto the field in his shorts holding his clipboard, his legs look good.

"Will you take a look at the butt on that man?" her friend Cassie pointed out to her one time, during a game their sons were playing when Mike was the ref.

Mike's wife, Janet, is a very pretty woman who is always chasing one or another of their twins during games. She looks tired.

"What are you doing here?" says Theresa, another mother she knows from the Parents' Advisory Council. "You don't have any-one on the Puffballs."

"It's my friend Tim's daughter," she says, reaching for his arm. She asks him if he's met Theresa.

"Ursula's dad, right?" she says. "She took it really well about that penalty kick."

Playing goalie in the last quarter, evidently, Ursula had allowed the opposing team to sail one right past her. Some kids get upset when they let a goal in, but Ursula had just stood there.

"Truthfully," says Tim, "I don't think she pays all that much attention. She hasn't got the fine points of the game down yet."

Now Theresa's asking him something about how Ursula's candy bar sales have gone. Tim bought all the candy. Ursula was too shy to knock on doors.

"Maybe our kids could get together and play sometime," Tim says. He has heard Claire say about a hundred times by now how important that is. He's trying.

Theresa looks startled. Her son, Alex, is one of the most popular kids in third grade. Alex plays with a few of the girls, but it would be hard to imagine what he would do with somebody like Ursula. Eat her for breakfast, probably.

They settle in their seats. "You look so beautiful," Tim tells her. Every time he sees her he says this.

She kisses his cheek and puts her hand in his pocket. Mike is sending Ursula onto the field now. You couldn't exactly say she's running out to her position. Drifting, more like it.

Alex makes his foul kick. A solid clump of Puffballs surrounds the ball. Every Bumblebee but the goalie does, too. Claire had forgotten how it is in soccer for this age group. Swarm play. For Pete, who has always been a cagey, strategic player—even at this age—this was always infuriating. "It's sickening, Mom," he would say in the car on the way home from one of his games. "They play like little kids."

A thought often comes to Claire at moments like this, sitting on the bench at one or another of her children's sporting events, surrounded by all the other parents roughly her age—all of them with their eyes fixed on the field and their own particular beloved player. Who could have believed, at sixteen or seventeen, that one day they would all be sitting here—a little bald, a little heavy, in clothes no longer particularly fashionable or flattering, driving cars

no longer chosen for their power and speed but because they have
airbags? Who would have believed the things they would talk
about would be candy bar sales and whose turn it is to bring the
Gatorade Friday? Most of all, who would have bought it if you'd
told them that all the passion they once felt about things like rock
concerts and proms and getting their hands into each other's
clothes and the outcome of sporting events they themselves once
participated in would now be poured into a soccer game of eight-
and nine-year-olds, Puffballs versus Bumblebees?

"We're like salmon," Tim said to her once, in a moment of
particular frustration over his child, her children, and the impossibility of conducting their love affair in the face of all that parenthood.

"Salmon?" she said.

"Salmon swim upstream to spawn. Then die."

*Claire wonders if she is the only one sitting on this bench who ever
finds herself looking at the other parents and seeing all these roughly
forty-year-olds suddenly transformed into a bunch of her high-school
classmates. Janet—digging in her bag at the moment for a box of
animal crackers and wiping off a pacifier—is the head cheerleader.
Theresa is her friend Becky, who taught her how to roll a joint. Mike
is her old boyfriend Patrick, who she didn't go all the way with and
later wished she had.*

*What she thinks is this: We are all the same people that we were
when they were young. Claire knows she is, anyway. She still wants so
many of the same things she did when she was sixteen, too. Kisses that
last through five songs on the radio. A boy's hand on her thigh and his
voice in her ear telling her she's beautiful. His arm around her shoulders, his hand on the small of her back as they walk into a room. The
wonderful feeling—as good as sex—when he leads her into the dim
light of the dance floor and the song is "Try a Little Tenderness."*

*She knows what these men want, too. They want to play for the
NBA, or the NHL, or Cleveland or Toronto, or Boston. They want a
ninety-five-mile-an-hour fastball. They want girls who look at them
with not just affection and lust but admiration. "I can't believe that
jump shot," they say. "I worship your cock."*

Claire believes they want love, too. They want a pretty wife who cooks a big roast Sunday nights, with the kids gathered round, and two weeks every summer at a cabin on the Cape, where they go deep-sea fishing and out for lobster with only their wife, and afterward, with the children in bed and the edge taken off in the way a couple of drinks will do, they will make love, still, with less of the desperate hunger of their high-school years, no doubt, but more finesse, and their wife will have multiple orgasms and tell him she loves him more than ever.

They have discovered, by the age of forty, all the ways their own lives fall short of these things. Their wife may cook the roast, but she may no longer be pretty, the two of them may no longer touch. They may eat their meal in silence. They may get that cabin at the Cape, but what they do when they get there may be to give their children money for the arcade and then turn on the large-screen TV until they fall asleep.

Looking across the bench, Claire guesses that a few of these couples actually have a good thing going with each other. There have certainly been plenty of moments over the last five years— and all those years before, when she was married but not truly partnered—when she has watched certain of these couples as they headed off the field to their cars with an envy and longing so acute she thought she should cover her face or wear sunglasses, anyway, to conceal it. When their son is playing, her former husband often attends these games himself, and then there is this particularly grim joke in which the two of them head across the field—their son bouncing alongside whichever parent seems most in need of him that night—to their separate cars and their separate houses, their separate beds.

But even for the ones who have done better than Claire and Sam—and most of them have—this much is still true: Their own possibilities are narrowing. Not a one of these women will ever make love with Kevin Costner or—the dreamboat of their teens—Paul McCartney. Not one of the men will ever play in the NBA.

· · ·

So now they huddle on the bench, all eyes on their children, the Puffballs and the Bumblebees, in their little striped jerseys and falling-down socks. Swarming over the ball as if it were a piece of honeycomb, the last sweet thing on earth. Nobody has sustained major injury yet. There is still this hopefulness about them. You can still believe, for your children, that anything may be possible.

Mickey is losing his fastball. He has actually managed to hold on to it longer than he had any right to believe he would. Way back when Claire was with him, Mickey injured his rotator cuff. He was still a starter for his team, the Salem Hornets, then, but after every game he needed a full day of ice packs and Ben-Gay. He was saying even then that he was on his last season.

"This is my last season, Slim," he says to her now as she reaches for her coffee. "I walked three in a row in yesterday's playoff game. I'm throwing junk. Only thing I have going for me now are my wits."

Mickey's playing has always depended more on intelligence than speed, Claire points out to him. That and his ability to intimidate batters, who know he's not averse to picking one of them off now and then. "Lean over the plate and you're going to get hit," he says. The Don Drysdale approach.

"No," he says, "this is different. I used to have a good imitation of a fastball, anyway. Now I can't even fool them." Nolan Ryan knew when to get out, he says. So will he.

"So now you'll have all that additional time to get to know Annalise's kids," she says. "Maybe take them to the circus." There is a sharpness to the way Claire talks with him now. The way they talk with each other.

"Talk about inside pitches," he says. "That was mean."

"I know," she says. "I'm sorry."

"The terrible thing is," he says, "there isn't one thing I do now that I didn't do better ten years ago. I used to be a better guitar player. I've lost my lip for trumpet. I'm probably as funny as I ever was, I'm just not in the mood."

"I bet you're still just as good at one thing," she says.

"Well, sure," he says. "It's just not the same as having a fast-ball."

Sally and her mother always get their period at the same time. It's how Sally knows she's about to get hers, actually. She sees her mom's box of Tampax out in the morning, and by afternoon she knows she'll be needing it herself. "This is what I call a close mother-daughter bond," her mom joked one time. "We do *everything* together. We even get our cramps on the same day."

Only this month Sally didn't get her period, and evidently her mom didn't even notice that she was the only one taking Tampax out of the box. If her mother paid more attention, she'd also notice that Sally's been throwing up, not every morning, but many. Five o'clock, five-thirty, it comes over her—this sick, nauseating feeling first, worse than any period she ever had. Just thinking about something like pizza at a moment like this would be enough to make her throw up on the spot. As it is, she can usually hold it in just long enough to make it to the bathroom if she holds on to her belly and concentrates on something like a geometry equation or the Tori Amos poster on her wall. As soon as she gets to the toilet, though, it's all over.

Sally's been putting off taking her home pregnancy test. At this point it's pretty obvious what the results will be, but until the moment when she actually sees it on the test results she can hold on to this thin hope that maybe the whole thing's a mistake. Well it is, of course. Just a different kind.

Probably the reason her mother hasn't noticed how messed up Sally's been lately is because she's always up in her office, reading those dumb faxes her wimp boyfriend sends her. Her mom doesn't go over to his house in the night as often as she used to, but he still writes to her every day. Mornings, when Sally finally makes it downstairs for the dry toast that is all she can bear anymore, her mother will be sitting there with her coffee with a piece of folded-up fax paper sticking out of the pocket of her bathrobe. If Sally hadn't puked already, that sight would be enough to do it to her.

She tries to imagine the fax Travis would send her, if he was into sending faxes. "Love humping you, Sal." "When can I hump you again?" Or maybe for variation, "You want to hump me?"

She hasn't told him about this pregnancy mess. What's the point? It's not like they're going to get married. Not like she's even going to have it. Sally can never believe it when some girl gets knocked up at school and people ask, "Who's the father?" A father is a person that holds on to the back of your bike after he takes the training wheels off. Fathers drive you to ballet if they aren't divorced from your mom and help you with your science fair project. A father is not some person with dreadlocks and an earring, that's saving up to get a set of competition-quality skate-board wheels. Sally may be a moron that didn't know you could still get pregnant after screwing three times on the same night with a rubber if you didn't use it the fourth time, but she knows that much at least.

She wishes there was a way she could take care of this without telling her mom, but there is no way on earth Sally can come up with the two hundred and fifty dollars for the abortion, even if you didn't have to get the parental consent form signed. And not only that, she realizes. There's something else.

As ridiculous an idea as it would be to go to the Women's Health Center with Travis, she also can't imagine going there alone. Sally has plenty of friends, but it's not her friends she'd want to sit with her in the waiting room or take her home afterward.

She wants her mom, who always used to tuck her under this special quilt of her grandmother's that she saves for times when Sally or Pete is sick. When she had scarlet fever that time in fourth grade and she was out of school a week, her mom made her a tray of Jell-O and cinnamon toast every day. The first few days Sally was too sick to do anything but sleep, but after she was well enough, Claire would sit on the bed next to her and read library books. They went through the whole of *Wolves of Willoughby*

Chase that week, and *Anastasia Krupnik*. They made a paper doll of Sally and drew all her real outfits in colored pencil, along with a lot of other ones Sally wished she had. They rented the video of *Gone With the Wind* and spent one whole afternoon on the couch watching it together.

"If only he could hear her," her mother said that time after Scarlett fell down the stairs, when she was calling for Rhett. "Nobody will ever love her the way he does. She will never love anybody the way she loves him, either." They were both crying by this point.

"It's just too sad," Claire said when the movie was finally over. "What do they do with all their love in a situation like that? Where does it go?"

What Sally is wondering right now is something else. What do they do with the thing? She can't even say the word *fetus.*

Where do they put it after they take it out of you? Do they flush it down the toilet? Do they have some kind of container they put it in that they dump in some river someplace? Is this one more kind of horrible pollution that's going on that nobody tells you about?

And afterward, after your insides are cleaned out, and nobody even knows it was ever there, what happens to your brain? There is this big thing that happened to you that doesn't even show on your face. You don't have stretch marks like Sally's mom or big tits like that girl at school, Vanessa, that kept her baby. It's like the whole thing never happened—not just the baby but everything that went on between you and the boy, too. Only you know it did. And what are you supposed to do now?

Annalise and her two sons are moving in with Mickey. "You think I've spent too much time standing in front of the microwave, Slim?" he asks her. "I can't believe I'd do something like this. I just have this crazy feeling we'll be able to handle it."

Hearing Mickey talking about "we," and knowing it's somebody else who makes him plural, as she was never able to, Claire feels as though she's been stabbed.

"My goodness," she says. "That's really great."

He's saying some other things now, too. Annalise has found a job in a public-relations firm outside of Boston. One of her sons has gotten into a special program for gifted and talented students. The younger one and Gabe seem to be getting along pretty well. "We just give them a whole lot of quarters and send them off to the arcade," Mickey says. "Five bucks buys us an hour."

Claire isn't really taking this in. She is picturing Mickey's house, which she knows so well, every inch. She's picturing where Annalise's children will sleep. She guesses that the older boy, the gifted one, will go in Mickey's old study, where he keeps his autographed baseball collection and his bootleg Beatles recordings. There's a bed in there already—she knows that part well—and a picture of Mickey from back in the days when he wore bell-bottoms and a Nehru jacket and played bass in a band called Naked Truth, along with a framed check for three hundred dollars from a club date in 1969. It bounced.

They must be planning to have Gabe share his room with the younger boy, in the room with the Nolan Ryan sheets. Who knows if he even has those Nolan Ryan sheets anymore? It's probably Ken Griffey Jr. now, or maybe just stripes. Another kid—Pete, for instance—would probably run away from home at the idea of giving up half his room to the son of his father's lover. Knowing Gabe, he will probably just grin and ask the kid whether he wants the top bunk or the bottom one.

She moves mentally down the hallway of Mickey's house, past the bathroom where he bathed her once as her tears fell into the water. She moves past the window where he leaned out and called to her one time as she pulled up after her long drive. She was so happy to see his face she ran her car into the fence. She passes the chair where he leaves his trumpet out, to keep his lip in shape, and the closet where she used to keep her bathrobe. She never took it back.

She moves through the kitchen. She sees the cutting board where he chopped his jalapeños and beef jerky, a bulletin board with a clipping about the Texas Rangers game where Nolan threw his five thousandth strikeout and the baby footprint from the day Gabe was born. "You make so much mess," he'd say, sponging off the coffee that had dripped through onto the counter while she was pouring herself a cup. It was a joke between them, but she also knew he was very particular about that sort of thing. In the year that she was with him, she never saw any of his possessions change place. He likes his house just so.

Where will Annalise put her clothes? she wonders. What if one of her sons likes rap music? Will he tell her who gave him the bonsai tree and his collection of china dogs?

Claire did. Every time she came to see him she brought one: sometimes a Dalmatian, sometimes a beagle, sometimes a Boston terrier, whatever she'd spotted in a yard sale recently. Every Sunday night, in the awful final moments before leaving his house, she'd hide one for him someplace. Under his pillow first, folded inside the sports page, in his baseball glove, the bell of his trumpet, an empty spot in an egg carton inside the refrigerator. By the time she left that last time, he must've had thirty or forty.

In her mental tour of Mickey's house, Claire has reached his bedroom that he will share with Annalise now. She sees the quilt his grandmother made, Double Wedding Ring, the CD player by the bed, and the portable TV where he likes to watch the Red Sox. He has a special kind of light he can turn on just by clapping his hands; it responds to vibrations. Making love in this room sometimes, they'd make the light flash like the Citgo sign over Fenway.

"I will never love anyone again the way I love you now," he said. *"Anytime you need me, all you have to do is dial my number."*

"You still there, Slim?" Mickey is asking her. Claire has been sitting at her kitchen counter through all of this, with a cup of untouched coffee in her hand. The chips in her linoleum floor made so long ago are no longer so obvious, now that the tiles have been worn down some. She isn't about to throw a pan this time. She is very still. Tears stream down her face, but you wouldn't know it if you were on the other end of the phone, because she's barely breathing.

"You always told me you couldn't live with a woman who had children," she says when she is able to speak again. "Now it turns out you just couldn't live with me." She's gasping for breath.

"Hey," Mickey says, with the calm of a pitcher who has just thrown a couple of balls and needs to collect himself. And he will too.

"Time out," he says. "Get a grip on yourself, Slim." He speaks in the same voice he'd use with Gabe on the rare occasions when his son would misbehave at a jazz concert or in the backseat on the way to a ball game.

"All these years I believed what you told me," she says. "I thought you were going to love me forever."

"Oh, baby," he says. "What you and I had we'll never have with anyone again. But it was different with us. It was too strong a dose to drink every morning, that's all. It had to end. And when it did we had to get on with our lives."

"I know it's crazy," Claire whispers. "But I actually believed that stuff about us getting together someday when we were old."

Mickey sighs. "You've got to understand, Slim," he says. "At our stage in life it's like a game of musical chairs, where they keep taking chairs away. You don't want to be left with no place to set your butt when the music stops. Plus I'll admit it. I'm head over heels in love."

For a moment there Claire feels as if she's inside a country song. The singer is Vern Gosdin or Emmylou Harris. Her soundtrack at the moment is the saddest violin. Up on the Opry stage, a ghostly fiddler is bowing her heartstrings.

"You ready to get back out into the game now, Slim?" he asks her.

"Okay, Mickey," she tells him. Her breathing is almost steady now.

"Whew," he says, his old joker self. "For a moment there I thought you might be out for the season."

Her voice oddly flat, Claire calls to tell Tim she is just too tired to come over. He is beyond tiredness himself, in a state of weariness too numb for sleep, but when she tells him she isn't going to make love with him tonight, he's suddenly desperate and panicked. He tries to stay calm. He goes into Ursula's room to read their chapter. He spots more candy wrappers on the bed, and the clothes Claire bought her scattered on the floor.

It's her fault. She's driving Claire away. He feels guilty and disgusted with himself to be thinking this way, but right now his precious daughter seems to him like a terrible dead weight chained to his ankle. He knows he would sink with her before he'd let her drop to the bottom alone without him. But right at this second he almost hates her for pulling him under this way.

"You treat your things like nothing matters," he says, throwing an empty bottle of nail polish against the wall. "You trash our life."

"You don't love me anymore," she wails.

"You idiot," he says. "I'm not even going to talk to you when you say things like that." Claire has told him not to dignify comments like that one with a rebuttal.

"Now you're calling me names. You never do karate with me," she says. "All you ever do is talk to her on the phone and write her letters."

"Pick up your room and we can talk about karate," he says. He bends to pick up the dress Claire got her, which is scrunched up in a ball under her bed.

"Look at this," he says. "This was a good dress."

"I hate my hair," she says. "It's too long."

"We can cut your hair," he says. Claire has told him Ursula's face is too round for the short cut she wants, but he's tired, and it's her hair.

"I'm going to cut it right now," she says.

"No, Ursula," he says. "Soon as I get a little money, we'll take you to a beauty parlor. This isn't the way to do it."

"I want to cut it now," she says. She reaches for the scissors, which are plastic, with the round, dull blades of children's craft scissors. "I'm going to chop it off."

"No, Ursula," he says. "You'll be sorry."

"In the night when you're sleeping I'm going to get out my scissors and chop it off."

"Okay. Okay," he says, too weary to argue anymore. "At least let me do it, then."

•   •   •

The haircut he gives her is a terrible mistake. Without her soft
halo of strawberry-blond curls, his daughter's face is a moon. The
shearing he has given her is nothing like the wonderful boyish cut
of Claire's hair. On Claire there is something almost heartbreakingly feminine about such short hair. On Ursula what the short
cut seems to reveal is not so much skin as it is flesh. It's his neck
she has, of course. He had never realized it so clearly. His thick,
short, pink wrestler's neck. She's like a baby mouse before the fur
grows in. Pink and naked.

Ursula knows this. She studies her round, bespectacled face in
the mirror and looks as if she may cry. She chooses mad instead.

"You ruined me, Daddy," she says. Suddenly she's pounding his
chest. Pulling at his own red hair, longer than hers now. Kicking
him in the vicinity of his balls.

"It'll grow," he says to her. "You wanted this."

She's past words now. Pummeling him. Weeping. Tearing at
her head. She throws toys.

"Ursula," he says. Tim is a large person, but it takes much of
his strength to hold her.

She's in the hall now, still throwing things. He pictures shat-
tered glass. Blood.

"Daddy!" she weeps. "Daddy!"

He picks her up. He would hug her and hold her, only she
won't stop hitting. So he carries her back to her room and sets her
on the bed. "You need to calm down," he says. "I can't even talk
to you like this." He tries to head for the door—he is going to
leave her for a few minutes until they can both catch their breath
—but she has grabbed his leg. She's biting. She has actually broken
through his skin.

"Stop it, Urs," he says. He isn't yelling. He is not even angry so
much as he is just incredibly sad.

"You poop," she wails. "You peckerhead."

He grabs hold of her arm and swings her back into the room.
He reaches for the doorknob. He is going to simply close the door,
stand on the other side holding it shut if necessary. All he's trying
to do is give them time to calm down.

But as the door slams shut, he hears her scream. Her face, with its skullcap of red-blond wisps, is a mask. He has slammed the door on his child's finger.

At the emergency room they put a splint on Ursula's finger, which is sprained, not broken. Still, Tim can't stop shaking over what he's done. When they get home, he fixes her hot chocolate and reads to her from *Ramona* (who once cut her own hair, but that was funny). He sits on her bed and strokes her forehead. He sings her their song. Twice.

"Parents make terrible mistakes sometimes," he says.

"It's okay, Dad," she says. "It'll grow." She thinks he's just talking about the haircut. "You do the best you can."

Later in the night —he thinks it may be two-thirty, maybe three—Tim wakes up and reaches for Claire. When he remembers that she isn't here tonight, a panic seizes him and grips him tighter, even, than his daughter did the night before, in the places where he knows, tomorrow, there will be bruises on his skin.

He's having trouble breathing. He has to see her. He cannot go another minute without it.

He gets out of bed and puts on his jeans. He slips his feet into sneakers without lacing them. He moves into the room of his daughter, who is lying, mouth open, on her side, clutching her doll Phillip. Her breathing that he knows so well tells him she won't wake up.

He knows he's behaving like a lunatic, but he doesn't care. He goes down the steps and out the door. He goes onto the dark street, with its one wailing baby and the sizzling sound end-of-season mosquitoes make hitting someone's neon blue bug zapper. He heads down the block to her house—walking first, then breaking into a run. The Christmas lights Claire keeps up all year are lit. Otherwise it's dark.

He turns the knob slowly. She never locks the door. It's not just her heart Claire leaves out in broad daylight for anyone to take, if they had only noticed. It's her house, too.

He climbs the steps. One creaks, that he has been meaning to fix for her. Nobody stirs except Jenny, who just thumps her tail softly at the sight of him.

He moves past Sally's room, and Pete's. He steps into Claire's room, where the door is partly open. No need to keep it shut tonight.

She lies there on the flower garden sheets, in the faint pink glow of her Nautilus shell nightlight. She wears a flannel nightgown. She's hugging herself.

He touches the edge of her sheet. "One thing about me," Claire has always told him, "I'm a good sleeper." Though she always woke instantly at the first sound of a child in the night, back when hers made sounds like that, and she does now when his child cries out, she sleeps like a baby otherwise. *"Not like a baby at all, actually,"* she said. *"Babies don't sleep half as well as I do."*

He stands over her now, just watching. How long he stands there he could never tell you. He doesn't touch her. He doesn't speak. He just wanted to see her. He bends over her to feel her breath on his face. Then he goes home.

Usually Ursula only wakes in the middle of the night if she needs to go pee, but she doesn't need to pee and she wakes up anyway. The first thing she does is feel her head and remember her hair is gone. The next thing she does is reach for Phillip. She wants her dad, but she's not allowed to go into his bedroom in the middle of the night in case she might be there. Claire.

Then it comes to her that her dad isn't in their apartment now anyways. She can feel it. He has gone over to Claire's house. Ursula's alone.

She lies there shivering. After a very long time she hears her dad's footsteps on the stairs, and a long, heavy sigh. Wherever he went to—and she thinks she knows—he has returned. Tonight he only left her for a few minutes. But there's no telling when the day will come that he will leave and just never come back.

It's morning now, their children off at school, and Tim has come to have coffee with Claire before work. He's surprised when he walks in by how loud she has the music turned up. "If you needed me I would come to you," an unfamiliar voice is singing. "I'd swim the seas to ease your pain." Something about the way Claire is just sitting there, still in her bathrobe though it's past nine o'clock, worries Tim. Or would, if he didn't already have so much on his mind. It took all he had just getting Ursula to school this morning, she was so upset about her hair.

"I can't believe you still haven't gotten her to a therapist," Claire says sharply when she sees the bruises on his wrist. He isn't ignoring her when he remains silent. There is just nothing he can say.

"Did you ever call the number I gave you about Parent Effectiveness Training?" she asks him. "Did you even buy a garbage can for your kitchen so those cereal boxes aren't spilling out all over the place all the time?" Even as she raises this last question she knows how ridiculous it is talking with him about garbage cans at the moment.

"I won't stop loving you," she says, still not looking at him. "But it could be that I simply can't be with you. Your daughter wants to destroy us, and if you let her, she will."

She has more to say, too. About Ursula pinching kids at school. About Ursula going into Sally's closet and trying on her underwear. About something she found in her dollhouse: the mother's head broken off and set inside the toilet. She knows it was Ursula that did it. Who else?

Cassie, the mother of Pete's friend Jared, called her this morning to say that Ursula has been spreading a rumor around school. She has been telling kids that Pete and Sarah McAdam had sex in the boys' bathroom. Ursula says she knows this because her father is going to marry Pete's mother. "Is that true?" Cassie had asked Claire. The marrying part, she meant. She knows the part about Pete couldn't be, although Jared had come home saying that all the kids were talking about it.

"I hadn't even discussed the idea of getting married with my own kids," Claire says to Tim. "And now Ursula's spread it all over the school."

"I'm sorry," he says, so softly Claire can barely hear him. "She's just a kid."

"When will you stop making excuses for your child?" Claire yells. "She's an incredibly destructive kid."

"Please," Tim says, holding up his hands as if to ward off blows. "Please stop. I can't bear to hear any more right now."

"I thought we could be a family," Claire says. "Instead I feel I'm losing the family I had."

"No more now, please," he says. "All I wanted was to love you." He's backing out the door.

"You have a few things to learn about how to care for a person you love," says Claire. "I feel like you've dumped this toxic garbage all over our lives." She's still pelting him with more words as he stumbles, hunched and beaten, down her walk and crawls into his car.

This was hardly the first time that Claire told Tim Ursula is screwed up. It has become her major theme with him. That and the messiness of their apartment. He has just never gotten angry before. But suddenly it explodes out of him like a fist. When he was younger he got into fights a lot at school, and with Joan he would sometimes feel a rage so terrible he actually put his hand through a window one time. But he has never felt this kind of fury toward Claire. A fury almost as powerful as his love for her. There is a connection in fact. His rage has something to do with the terrible sinking sense he has that he's losing her, and that there is nothing he can do about it. He hates Claire for the thoughts he knows she has about leaving him. He hates her for not loving his daughter. He hates her for the way she has almost made him stop loving his daughter himself.

He would never stop loving Ursula. But lately he has had these dreams that she goes away. Her mother takes her. And how he feels isn't bereft and heartbroken as he would have been once, just at the thought of losing his child. When he thinks about her going away, his chief feeling is relief. *Now I can have Claire.* His love for her is sickening.

"I have this perpetual sense of how I disappoint you," he writes in his fax, which scrolls through her machine an hour later, just as she is finally gathering up her folders and heading out to the museum.

You don't need to tell me any more than you already have how inadequate and fucked up I am. You don't need to list all the ways I fall short of your ideal of a man and a parent, all the ways my child fails to match the image in your mind's eye of the eight-year-old girl of your dreams. And I know that in three hours and a trip to Kmart you could transform my living room, and that in ten therapy sessions and a few weeks of low-calorie meals you'd have Ursula whipped into shape too. I know you would do a better job than I can about every single aspect of my poor, miserable, failed life. Except for one area. You do not do a better job of loving me than I do of loving you.

Do you understand—did you ever bother to try?—that completing this grant proposal is the only thing that offers me the remotest possibility of financial stability? Do you even know who I am or what I do, or what it might be I give my daughter besides a tidy living room? I can dress Ursula up, down, or in between. Get her hair screwed up or fixed up. Buy her sandals or pumps or Converse high-tops or fucking army boots. Get her therapists, and therapists for the therapists. I could come up with a little grant of a grand or two from some foundation and a cute little storage room full of matching furniture and rugs and the board games to play on them and turn this dump of mine into a dollhouse, and if I did I guess maybe you could love me. Accept me, anyway. But that is not the man I am, not the man you said you loved.

I never claimed to be the wonder parent you are—the

Miracle Dad to your Miracle Mom, Ward Cleaver to your Martha Stewart. It seems to me that I presented myself as a confused parent. So you tell me to go to the parents' garage in the form of some therapist's office for the old behavioral over-haul. And I will go there. But I am running out of money, in case you hadn't noticed, and the only way I could avoid having the phone service disconnected that allows me to send you my testimonials of undying love was to let a few things slide for a little while and do my work. You just don't have the patience or the constancy to wait.

There is a jugular-ripping quality to your criticism of me that I decided this morning I don't need and can't bear to hear anymore. Even as I backed out your door this morning, you kept laying barbs on me, from this incredibly cold spot in the Antarctica of your heart. For the first time since meeting you, I could imagine what it must have been like to be your former husband. I sympathized with him.

So once again it seems you have found another human being with a dick who has set out to methodically disappoint you. How could it be that so many men require this of you? An entire half of the species set out to prove they are utterly stupid, lazy, or incompetent.

I will not wait my turn in the deli line to disappoint you in love yet again. Somebody else can take my place. I am not going to live one more day in the land of belittlement—a mutt and his mongrel child who have somehow wandered into your thoroughbred world.

Ah yes, it's beautiful all right, where you live, in Twinkle Town. You have let me visit you there, on your amazing eighteen-hole course of interesting obstacles, novelty pleasures, your exquisitely groomed putting green. But woe to a lover who steps off the artificial turf and enters the trenches sur-rounding your compound.

You love the impossible, and come to despise the attainable. The only man you believe in reveals himself every day in your life in the form of two or three chips missing from your kitchen floor tiles and a ridiculously high phone bill. You will live forever with the illusion that only he could have given you what you need, if he had only been willing to give it to you.

   I love you more than I ever knew was possible, but I know now I am not the man you're looking for, if such a man exists. Good-bye.

Ten minutes after getting his fax, Claire is on Tim's doorstep, her face a mask of grief. She can't speak. She falls into his arms and he takes her. "My life is a shambles," he says as they undress amid the piles of laundry and reprints from *Environmental Digest,* the bodies of half-dressed Barbies and Ursula's lone Ken. "I know," she says. "Mine too."

She's tired of talking about this and all the other things that go wrong in people's lives, theirs in particular. She's weary of having to think about what to do all the time. She's exhausted by choices. So what Claire does next is not so much a choice she makes as it is a choice she prefers not to think about. She chooses to let their bodies take over from their brains for once. In the mutual exhaustion of their cease-fire, Claire feels this wild, drunken recklessness come over her, though she is stone sober as always.

Other times, fantasizing about a baby with him, it has been when things were so good and they were so hopeful. At this particular moment she's like a gambler wiped out of all but her last ten chips, and she guesses he's the same. So there on his bed, with his cock exploding semen into her and her diaphragm back home in the drawer of her bedside table, they empty their pockets.

Even though Claire says now that she will marry him and that she wants to set a date even, Tim has never felt such anxiety about her as he does now. In the last couple of days he has seen something in her that never used to be there and it frightens him. There is this numb quality about her. "Sometimes when I talk to you or touch you," he says to her, "I feel like I'm sending radio signals into space."

She doesn't answer.

Not that she's physically withdrawn. In fact, Claire has never made love so ferociously before. Always before it has been Tim who was crawling all over her and couldn't get enough. The day she came to him after he sent her his terrible angry fax, Claire was like a person who hasn't been touched in a year, a person eating her last meal. She scratched his skin. She pounded his back. She kissed him so hard the next day his lips were swollen.

It's a thrilling thing to see her this way, but it also leaves Tim with a heavy sense of foreboding. There is a burn-it-up quality about her these days. Even about her failure to practice birth control, which she told him about afterward. This was what he wanted, of course. Only something feels wrong. "We might as well," she said. "Sometimes there's nothing to do when you're standing on the edge of a cliff but to jump."

He can't say when it happened, but Tim's life has gotten out of his control. The Estuarine Research Institute sent him a letter last week telling him they can't pay him the first installment for his mussel study until the first of the year, when new federal funds become available. He has managed to pay his phone bill by hocking his VCR and his camera, but he doesn't know how he'll manage to come up with next month's rent in the next five days, and his landlord has already told him no more extensions. Tim has had to cancel the appointment he made with the therapist Claire was so eager for him to see with his daughter, even though he knows she needs to talk to someone badly. When Ursula heard he sold the VCR she threw one of her shoes at him and called him a fuckhead. He has to send her to her room so often now the plywood of her door has actually split in one place from Ursula's kicking. "You hate me," she screamed at him this morning. "You wish I wasn't even born."

Tim dreams about a life without her. Lying in his bed waiting for one of Claire's visits, he imagines what it would have been like for the two of them if they'd met ten years ago, or twenty, before either of them had incurred the scars of so many old injuries or acquired the baggage of ex-husbands, ex-wives, angry children, and the guilt that comes from trying to undo their pain.

For just a moment Tim allows himself the fantasy that he is

Travis and Claire is Sally. He is seventeen years old, riding up to her house on a skateboard, with no care greater than successfully executing a jump over the curb. She comes running out the door to meet him. "Let's take off someplace," she says to him, laughing. Who knows where they're going or when they'll be back? Maybe never.

In his real life of course, the best Tim can do is steal little scraps of time with the woman he loves: a furtive kiss in the supermarket parking lot, a couple of hours' desperate, clutching lovemaking sometime between midnight and dawn. A phone conversation interrupted by the call of his child. A fax she must rip off the machine quickly, before her children see.

This weekend, though, Tim has arranged to go away with Claire for a night in the mountains. He can't afford it, but he'll take her out to dinner. They won't talk about their children. It will be just the two of them.

Claire's pregnant. She doesn't even need to take the test. Even though it's been years, she remembers the feeling well. She knows enough about fetal development to understand that what is going on in her is not actually the movement of an organism that is, at this point, no bigger than a pen mark. Still, there's this fluttering in her, like a very small trapped bird. Even when it makes her clutch her stomach and run for the toilet, she has always loved this feeling. *A baby,* she says. She's had enough of words on fax paper and discussions with Nancy about self-actualization. Enough therapy sessions and calculations about how old everybody will be when. There's no debating the existence of a real, flesh-and-blood baby.

"I don't see why we can't just throw them all together and let an omelette of a family happen," Tim said to her. "It won't be the way you'd want it to happen or the way I would. It would settle somewhere, that's all. And we'd deal with that."

Okay, she thinks. We'll do it.

Claire and Tim leave Ursula with Sandy and Jeff. Claire's children are staying at their house with Nancy, who has agreed to sleep over for the night.

They drive north to the White Mountains. They find a motel with individual cabins—fireplace, TV, kitchenette, $37.50 a night—on the banks of the Pemigewasset River. From the bed they can hear the water running over the rocks. Claire will tell him her news here. They'll have thirty-six hours in which the only child mentioned will be theirs.

He has brought massage oil and wine, which Claire won't drink now, though she hasn't told him why.

"You know what I want to do?" she says. "Watch the World Series naked, eating lobster." Tonight is the seventh game, Philadelphia versus Toronto at the Skydome. Mickey is in Toronto, in fact. Annalise managed to get tickets from her cousin, who works in the Blue Jays' press office.

"No wonder you're in love," Claire said when he told her.

"There are other reasons," he said.

They hike on Mount Jefferson until early afternoon, when the rain begins, then go back to the room. "The strangest thing happened to me out there," he tells her. He had wandered off for a moment to look at a rock formation. Rounding a bend in the trail to catch up with her again, he had spotted this woman. I never saw somebody so beautiful, he was thinking. How could he think such a thing, he asked himself, when he was in love with Claire? But there you have it. He did.

"Only then I realized it was you," he says. "I swear, there was this moment when I saw you with your hair drenched and your hands in your pockets, looking out across the ridge, and I didn't think, There's this woman I know so well and love so much. I just thought, There's this stranger and she's grabbed my heart. Day after day I keep falling in love with you all over again."

. . .

Tim and Claire have found a restaurant in Lincoln that advertises one-pound lobster dinners for $9.95. They go in and explain to the hostess that they want a couple to go.

"I'm sorry," she says. "We don't do takeout. This is a sit-down restaurant."

"But couldn't we just buy them and carry the food out?" he asks her. "We don't need the butter and rolls. Just the lobsters would be fine."

She tells him no. "This isn't that kind of place," she says.

Claire steps in now. "Well, suppose we had sat down to eat and we didn't finish our meal," she says. "You'd wrap the leftovers up and let us take them home, right?"

"That would be different," the hostess says.

"Oh, come on," Tim says again. He has a fire laid in the fireplace. The game starts in an hour.

"Those are the rules," she says.

So they sit down and order. Tim has a beer while they're waiting. Claire orders juice. At the table next to them is a woman Claire can tell is a single parent with her three young children. She has dressed up for this dinner and she is trying to have a real conversation with her kids—the oldest two, anyway. They're playing with the sugar.

"How do you think they did that special effect where the guy's arm melted like that?" she says. None of the children responds.

"I've seen that movie," Claire could tell her. Also the movie that is this woman's life. More Saturday nights than she can count she has found herself putting on a dress and spending more money than she had any business spending, just to go out into the world of grown-ups and have dinner at a place like this, even though it was with her children.

"So what do you think," says Tim, "are they going to name Paul Molitor the Most Valuable Player?"

This is just their game. She has already rated the entire Phillies roster according to which ones she would soonest have sex with. Mitch Williams being dead last.

"I like Molitor well enough," she says. "But I have to go with Cito Gaston. Or Jimmy Key."

"Interesting choice," he says. "Especially since he was traded to the Yankees two years ago."

Their lobsters arrive. They crack the claws to make it easier later back at the Rocky Knoll Cabins. He takes a bite. She does the same. Then Claire grabs her stomach dramatically and doubles over. Tim calls the waitress.

"I'm terribly sorry," he says in a hillbilly accent. "But as you can see, the little lady here is fixing to toss her cookies. It's that durned morning sickness again. So if you wouldn't mind just wrapping up our lobsters . . ."

The waitress looks at Claire suspiciously.

"Unless, of course, you'd rather have her stick around and throw up all over your restaurant," he says, standing up dramatically and speaking loud enough that everyone in the place can hear him. "We've got a pregnant woman here, for God's sake!"

The waitress goes for the hostess. Claire picks up her coat and heads for the door. She is in the car waiting for him, laughing so hard she has tears in her eyes, when he comes out a minute later carrying their two foil-wrapped lobsters, along with corn and cole slaw, rolls, salad, and a little plastic container of drawn butter.

"You were right, you know," she tells him.

"What are you talking about?" he says.

"I am. Pregnant."

He actually kisses her feet.

They watch the game on the floor in front of the fireplace wearing nothing but their plastic bibs. She loves the animal feeling of digging into the soft pink lobster meat with her fingers, the butter dripping over her skin. He licks it off. Every once in a while one of them will comment on a play. At one point Claire imagines she sees Mickey in the crowd as the camera pans the box seats, but it happens so quickly she can't be certain. The woman next to him was very beautiful, that's for sure. Which would fit.

Sometime around the fourth inning they move onto the bed. *"A baby,"* he says, *stroking her belly, her breasts. "I can't believe we're going to have a baby."*

He feeds her Ben & Jerry's chocolate ice cream, which is more like soup now. John Kruk doubles to right field and Claire climbs on top of Tim.

She decides she hates the Phillies, who seem to spend all their time on the bench chewing tobacco and spitting. "Imagine kissing a man who chews tobacco," she says.

Sometime around the seventh inning she drifts off to sleep. This is the first symptom of pregnancy to hit her strongly. She is so tired all the time.

His hands on her hair, just gently stroking her, wake Claire just in time to see Joe Carter round the bases on that last, glorious home run of his. Mickey will love this, she thinks. He is out there somewhere, explaining to Annalise what pitch Williams should have thrown that might have left Carter swatting air. *"You never want to give a guy like Carter a high fastball at a moment like that in the game,"* he will be saying. *"Big mistake."*

"I want to see you with your belly out to here," Tim says.

"Kind of a Mitch Williams look, huh?" she says. But he can't joke anymore. There are tears in his eyes.

"I want to rub your back. I want to rub your feet. I want to take care of you in a way you've never been taken care of before. I have so much love for you," he says. "I don't know where to put it all."

Driving home from the mountains, Tim keeps saying the same thing over and over: "We're pregnant."

"Let's get this straight," Claire says. *"I'm* pregnant. You just helped get me this way, okay?" There's a sharpness to her voice as she says this. She doesn't say it, but Mickey used to make fun of men who talked about pregnancy as if it were a shared condition.

"Next thing you know, they'll say they're breast-feeding. Then

they'll be going through the change of life," he said. She wishes Mickey didn't interrupt her life all the time this way with his observations but that's what happens. "Go away, Mickey," she wants to call out.

"Do you think we can have a home birth?" Tim asks her. She knows he has always been sad that he never got to witness Ursula's birth because of the emergency cesarean.

"I don't know, Tim," she says, strangely embarrassed. "I'm pretty old for that kind of thing."

"I wouldn't want to do anything that would endanger our baby," he says. "I was just thinking how great it would be if we could have it right there on our bed." *Our bed.*

"And then Ursula could be right there, too, to bond," he says. "And Sally and Pete, naturally."

Is it just the pregnancy, or why is Claire feeling queasy?

"You know what I was thinking?" he said. "I know you'll want to breast-feed, but it would be so great if we got a breast pump to pump your milk, so I could feed the baby right from the beginning."

Back when she was pregnant with Pete and Sally, Claire was always trying to interest Sam in feeling their kicks, but now when Tim puts his hand on her belly, she lifts it like a wet fish and sets it back in his own lap.

"If you don't mind, I'd rather you didn't touch me there at the moment," she says. *What a bitch. And the worst part is, he apologizes.*

Now he's talking about demand feedings versus a schedule. What does she think about having the baby in the bed with them for the first six months or so? Just until she's old enough to go in with Ursula?

Or *he.* "Imagine," he says. "It never even occurred to me we could have a son."

"I want to take him camping," Tim says. "We'll start out just sleeping in the yard under the stars. I'll take him down to the pond and show him all the different kinds of peepers. We'll collect frogs' eggs and mushroom spores and animal scat."

"What would you think about the idea of disconnecting the television?" he asks her. "I hate what it's doing to Ursula." Now, there's an idea that would do wonders for his relationship with Pete.

He's talking about Waldorf education and Suzuki violin. He doesn't want to be one of those Little League fathers who are always screaming out instructions to their kids on the field. "Stop me if you ever hear me doing that, promise?" he says. "I want to build you the most beautiful rocking chair in the world. I want to knit you a shawl to cover yourself while you feed our child. You will be a madonna to me."

There's a call on Claire's answering machine from Sergeant Wallace of the Blue Hills Police. Jenny has been hit by a car. Because nobody was home when it happened, the Animal Protection Society has taken care of it. She was so badly injured the only humane thing to do was have her put to sleep.

Tim will be picking up Ursula right about now at the neighbors'. Sally is out somewhere, with Travis no doubt. Mickey has also called to say could you believe Carter's home run? What was Williams thinking of, giving him that pitch?

She is just standing there taking this in when the phone rings again. Tim. "I just had to tell you again," he says, "that was the best day of my life."

She gives him the news about Jenny.

Ursula knows how it happened. Jenny missed them so badly—Ursula and her dad, her real family. She had gone looking for them. She was crossing Elm Street, one block down from their apartment, when the car hit her. She was on her way home. She probably had her tongue hanging out the way she does when she's excited. Her ears were flopped back from running. I'm free at last, she was probably thinking. I finally got out of there.

Pete was the worst, the way he kept playing that horrible loud music all the time. How was Jenny supposed to sleep? They never did tricks with her. They didn't talk to her. One time when Ursula was over she had heard Sally say, "That dog is on my bed again. Will somebody please come take it away?"

Now she should be happy. Jenny's body was taken to the Animal Protection Society, where Ursula and her dad picked her up Sunday night after they got the news. If she and her dad had been just a few hours later, Jenny would already have been cremated. They got there just in time. But not really.

Ursula didn't go into the room with her dad, but she was waiting when he came out. He had Jenny in his arms, wrapped in her special blanket, which he and Ursula had brought. Her face was covered, but one of her paws was drooped down from underneath the blanket. Pete and Sally evidently never clipped her nails.

Her eyes were closed, and it looked like there was actually a tear in the corner of one of them, although Ursula knew it was really just that goo she got sometimes. Somewhere inside there must be blood oozing out of her, but on the outside she looked fine. Ursula herself knows how that can be. To look at Ursula at that particular moment, for instance, you would never have guessed all the things that were oozing out inside her.

They drive to a place her dad knew from his research work, way out in the woods. There's moss in this place and ferns and a nice smell Jenny would like. If Jenny was here—not just this dog body, but the real Jenny—she would want to dig. Also chew sticks.

They have brought her chew bone. Also her collar. Her dad has also brought a shovel. After he sets Jenny on the moss, still wrapped in her blanket, he begins to dig.

There should be a song, Ursula thinks. She thinks about the songs they've been learning at school. "Buffalo Gals." "Eating Goober Peas." The theme song from "Gilligan's Island" that Mrs. Kennedy taught them during recess one time when it was too rainy to go out. None of them is right.

She sings that song "I Will Always Love You." "If I should stay, I would only be in your way," she sings. "But I will always love you."

"Remember how she used to chew on your Pound Puppy?" her dad says. "Remember that time we left a box of eggs on the counter and she ate all twelve of them? Shells and all."

"Remember how she liked to run into swamps and eat frogs?" Ursula says. "And sometimes when she came out of the water there would still be a frog's leg hanging out of her mouth. And then she'd burp and it would be frog breath?"

"When you were born," her dad says, "we worried she might be jealous. But she just lay there next to your little sleeper bed guarding you. Sometimes she'd lick your face."

"Her farts were the worst, weren't they, Dad?" Ursula says. They are laughing now. Also crying.

"Especially that time we gave her the garbanzos."

"How old was she, Dad? In dog years?"

"She was ninety-eight, Urs. She had a good life."

"All except the end."

"You were always so good to her."

"But in the end she must have wondered where I went. She must have wondered why we'd leave her like that."

"I don't believe dogs think like that," he says. "She knew you would always love her."

"She was my sister," Ursula says. "The only sister I had. I'm an only child now."

Claire and Sally are parallel parking. "One-half car length beyond your space, sharp turn in the direction you want your rear end to go, angle back, right your front end, pull up straight," Claire recites. This is Sally's fourth attempt at this particular parking space.

"Shit," says Sally. "I give up. They hardly ever put parallel parking on the test, anyway."

"Let's just drive around the rotary again a couple more times," Claire says. Sally turns sixteen and takes her test in a few weeks.

"If I don't pass, I'll die," she says to Claire.

Claire can dimly remember a time when getting her license seemed like the most important thing in the world. In the end, she supposes, many things that once seemed so important to a person fade away. It's just impossible to imagine at the time you're going through them.

Four years ago, for instance, she would never have imagined herself spending her life with any man other than Mickey. And now look at her—pregnant, and planning to marry Tim. Sitting on her front porch with him last night, she felt so peaceful. At the time he was just telling Claire about bringing the salmon back to the Connecticut River. His department at the college has a grant from the state to build a couple of salmon ladders in Bellow's Falls. He had this look of such pure joy on his face, delivering this news, that she had leaned over and kissed him. "I want to make you proud of me," he said. "I want to be the best husband to you. The best father to our baby."

This is a good man, Claire told herself. Don't let him go.

A couple of years ago, in the middle of the custody hearings, Claire would have supposed she could never again look at her ex-husband Sam without wanting to spit, she hated him with such passion. These days she is like Mount St. Helen's, back where she comes from, in Oregon. The entire top of the mountain blew off when the volcano erupted. The trees burned down. The animals died. The molten lava destroyed every living thing for miles around. But now there is this new green growth sprouting up. *Forgiveness.*

"You don't have to blow so hard all the time," Mickey told her. "Just blow."

With Sally, too, Claire is recognizing that there is no longer any way to control what she does with her life. Her getting a license is only the beginning. No matter how old her daughter is, Claire will never stop worrying about Sally or stop being her mother, and she will never stop trying to guide her as wisely as she can. But she is also realizing lately that even as she embarks on this late-life pregnancy of hers, a particular phase of her mothering of this particular child is drawing to an end. Like the paper boats she used to make with her children every spring that they launched into the brook behind their old house, her daughter's little craft will soon go bobbing out of sight. Then all Claire will be able to do is hope she stays afloat, or that when she takes on water, as she surely will, she'll bail hard and swim if necessary.

"I was just thinking, driving around the traffic circle with you, how long it's been since you and I had a chance to talk," Claire tells Sally from her unaccustomed spot in the passenger seat.

"We talk, Mom," says Sally. "You should see how it is in some kids' families. It's lots worse. Travis's family eats their dinner in front of 'Lifestyles of the Rich and Famous' every night."

"Well, to me it seems as if we're out of touch," Claire says. "And now here you are about to get your license. You'll be gone even more now."

"You'll still see me, Mom. It's not like I'm moving out or anything."

"You may not be going anywhere," says Claire. "But your life is changing. Mine too."

"Can you believe what he did there?" says Sally. "Guy changed lanes without even putting his blinker on."

"You haven't told me much about what's going on with you and Travis, but I figure it must be pretty serious by this point," Claire tells her. "I hope you'd always feel you could talk to me about that."

Sally is concentrating hard on the road. She checks the rearview mirror and adjusts it slightly. Claire is suddenly struck by her daughter's extraordinary beauty. She is not quite sixteen yet, but for a second Claire catches a glimpse of what she will look like as a woman. A heartbreaker.

"I trust you to make good decisions for yourself," says Claire. "I just hope you make your choices based on what feels right for you. Not anybody else. I didn't always do that myself at your age. I was so eager to please everybody."

"It's okay, Mom," says Sally. "I'm fine." *Just pregnant, probably.*

"And the other thing is, if the moment comes where you and your boyfriend become sexually active—whatever boyfriend it might be at that point—and it's something you want to do and you feel you're ready, it's so important that you protect yourself. I know you hear that all the time at school, but sometimes in the heat of the moment, people don't always behave so sensibly." *Claire should know.*

"Mom," says Sally. "I know this stuff." This would be the perfect moment to tell her mother that as a matter of fact, there isn't much point anymore in having this conversation because the very thing her mom's so afraid of has happened already.

She might just tell her, too. For a second there she thinks with longing of what it would be like to lay her head on her mother's shoulder and cry her eyes out the way she used to when she was younger.

"I wouldn't want you to ever think because I've got a boyfriend myself these days that I don't care about what's going on in your life," says Claire. "Nothing matters more to me that that."

Sally is silent. Just driving.

"I know you and your brother aren't crazy about Tim and Ursula," she says.

"What you do is your business," says Sally. "I don't have to love the guy. Or his kid." *Here's a whole new thing to dislike about Tim and his kid, Sally thinks: The way the two of them keep popping up right in the middle of something that's going on in her family, taking up everybody's energy. She was actually having a decent conversation with her mother just now. She might even have pulled the car over and collapsed in her mother's arms and told her that she's scared out of her mind, too scared even to take the home pregnancy test that has been sitting in her closet for almost two weeks. But now it's like those two red-headed idiots in their bike helmets just hopped in the backseat of the car to join the conversation.*

"I was wondering how it would be for you if Tim and I, you know, made it more official," her mother is saying. She'll save the baby part for another day.

"What do you mean, Mom?" Sally says. She stares at the road.

"We've been thinking we might move in together before long. Get married." She wishes Sally would say something, but she just grips the wheel and stares straight ahead. She's supposed to concentrate when she's driving, but this is different.

"Do what you want, Mom," says Sally in a flat voice. "I'll be gone in a couple of years, anyway."

"There's lots of wonderful things about him if you'd give him a chance," Claire is saying. "Ursula too . . ."

"It doesn't matter," says Sally. "I'll be going to college soon, anyway."

Pete's in luck: The spacey blond cashier is at the register at Coconuts.

"New Elvis Costello tape come in yet?" he asks her.

"Nah, I don't think so," she tells him. "It's not supposed to come out till next week."

"I didn't mean that Elvis Costello tape," Pete says. "I meant the other one. The one before that. The one where he sings country."

"Jeez, I never heard of that one," she says. "Take a look in the *C*'s."

"Would you mind checking it for me?" Pete asks her. "I have this problem with my vision today. Pinkeye."

She looks at him a little oddly, the way his sister does when he tells her he didn't touch her Rollerblades. But she goes to check.

"I was thinking it could be in the *E*'s, too," he says. "At some places they put them there."

"We keep him in the *C*'s," she says. Never mind. He takes out a Baggie with a dog turd inside. He sets it on the carpet. This is part of the plan Pete thought up to distract her later.

The younger guy Pete was expecting to see in the stereo equipment section must be off today. It's this real geezer-ish person. Even better.

"My grandfather sent me money for my birthday," he tells him. "I was thinking I might get a portable disc player."

"They're in the case," the guy says. "We've got Aiwa, Panasonic, and Sony. All pretty much the same unit, only the Sony runs an additional twenty bucks, and in my opnion all you're getting for your money is the name. There's not much to see."

"I'd just like to take a look at them up close," Pete tells him. "I got pinkeye."

The geezer hestitates a moment, then sets the three disc players on the counter in front of him. When Pete asks to see the headphones, he takes those out, too.

"The most recent Elvis Costello we have is this one," the blond cashier calls out to him. "I never heard of any country album. You've gotta be thinking of someone else."

"No, it's him, all right. My friend saw it here the other day." Now he leans over closer to the geezer. "Would you mind checking for me?" he asks. "Sometimes I'm not sure about her."

Amazingly enough, the guy doesn't argue with this. He heads over to the C section. Pete slides the Discman into his backpack. Like clockwork.

This is where Pete is supposed to step in the dog turd and act upset. He is walking over to the turd when he sees her. The kid from hell. *Ursula.* She is wearing her bicycle helmet and those thick glasses as usual, and she is looking in the video section with that geek father of hers. He's wearing a helmet, too, if you can believe it.

"We're looking for the temporary tattoos," he's saying to the blond cashier. "For Halloween."

Pete wishes they weren't here, but there's no turning back now. He slides into the dog turd and falls flat on his face. It's even more dramatic than he'd intended.

"Shit," he says. "I can't believe you have dog turds in here."

"It's Pete with poop all over himself," Ursula says in that deep, husky voice of hers that sounds like some porn star or a phone sex person.

Tim is rushing over to him now, taking a handkerchief out of his pocket. "Here, son, let me help you," he says.

Son. Give me a break.

"These were new shoes," Pete is saying, though nobody seems to be listening but Tim. "My mom will kill me."

"No she won't, Pete," Tim says. "She'll understand it wasn't your fault."

"You don't get it, Daddy," Ursula is saying, louder. "He put that piece of poop on the floor in the first place. He did it on purpose. He put something in his backpack, too."

Ursula stands over him like a toadstool, with that blank-eyed pink face of hers. He wishes his eyeballs could shoot out laser beams. He would like to smear dog poop all over her. Instead he bursts out crying. The gray-haired man is coming over to him now. Also the blond cashier. A crowd has formed.

"You'd better open up that backpack for me, my boy," the gray-haired man says.

"You want me to call the authorities, Mr. Ellis?" the girl says.

"You better believe it," the gray-haired man says. "Just because he's a kid doesn't mean we can afford to let him off easily. We're looking at a serious juvenile offender here. Maybe he can set an example that will discourage some of his buddies."

The most sickening part of all is that at this point Tim actually puts an arm around Pete and whispers to him, "Don't worry, Pete. I'll help you."

Right. With any more help from him and that daughter of his, Pete might as well go jump off a bridge.

They have actually locked Pete in a cell like a criminal. It's police policy with juvenile offenders like him, the sergeant explains to Claire, to treat these kids like any other offender. "Give them a taste of what they've got to look forward to if they keep up this way of life," he told her. "Scares some sense into them sometimes."

"Kid have a father?" he asks her. *No, I'm the virgin mother, she thinks of saying.*

"We're divorced," she says. "I called him. He'll be over, too." Before she's even got all the words out, Seargant Donohue is nodding as if he assumes he knows the whole story. *Broken home. Troubled child. No consistent male role model. Weak, ineffective, defeated single mom. Kid's sure to be a mama's boy or a hood.* She's on trial again.

"Pete never did anything like this before," she says. Never mind the incident at school with the graffiti, though they will probably find out about that one now, too. "He's a really good boy. There must have been some unusual circumstance."

"This guy who was there when the arrest occurred—the one with the little girl?" he says. "He tells us he's your fiancé?"

"Tim was there?" she says. This is news to Claire.

"Oh, sure," says the sergeant. "It was his kid that alerted the store manager to the problem. Then you probably don't know that your son assaulted her."

"Assaulted?" says Claire.

"Punched the little girl in the stomach, as I understand it," says the sergeant. "The father could have chosen to press charges, but he didn't. The whole thing will be in the police report. The little girl is talking to the social worker right now, as a matter of fact. We don't want to release her until we're confident she hasn't experienced a traumatizing level of harassment."

Social worker. Harassment. Press charges. Police report. No.

"My son has had a difficult relationship with Tim's daughter," says Claire. "But it's not entirely his fault. Sometimes Ursula has a way of manipulating a situation to make herself look like the victim."

Claire's experience of the last five minutes has taught her something: In a true crisis, she will always defend her child above all others. If it means abandoning Ursula or Tim she will. In a burning building the ones she'd rescue first would be her own children.

Sergeant Donohue has led her into the squad room now. There is Ursula, wearing several of the items the two of them bought at the St. James thrift shop (orange turtleneck, purple flowered shorts with red tights), sitting at a desk across from another officer, her hands folded in her lap. Her voice is deep, hushed, serious.

"I bet Pete didn't really mean to punch me," she is saying. "Even though he did tell me one time he was going to kill me. It was probably just a accident."

"Has he ever assaulted you in the past, Ursula?" the officer asks her.

"Well, not exactly," she says, taking a slow sip of her milkshake. "Unless you count pinching. But he did make my dog die."

Only now does Claire catch sight of Tim, standing a few feet behind Ursula listening to what she says. *"Stop her!" Claire wants to scream. You know it isn't like that.* He isn't saying anything.

"Sweetheart," he says, catching sight of her. "It's all going to be all right. We'll iron this out. Pete just needs a little help right now. Same thing you're always reminding me about Ursula. You and I both know he's not a bad kid."

She looks at him as if he were a stranger. For a moment she understands precisely the way Pete must have felt when he punched Ursula, because that's what she feels like doing to Tim.

Claire expected Sam to make this all her fault but he didn't. He just said he wishes he'd understood sooner what was going on with Pete. Clearly their son has been going through some hard times. He must be terribly unhappy to do something like this.

"I didn't tell you, but he called me last week to say he'd like to stay with me for a while," Sam tells her. "I told him to tough it out. I figured you'd just get mad."

"Maybe it would be a good thing," she tells him. She feels incredibly tired all of a sudden, and not just because of the pregnancy.

"I'm on a big framing job right now," he says. "But as long as he doesn't mind lots of spaghetti for dinner, he's welcome to bunk in with me."

Claire doesn't want to talk about it right now. She just wants to get Pete out of here. But she isn't fighting him, either. "Can we see our son now?" she asks the sergeant. Tim just stands there watching her go. Her and Sam.

I felt it was only fair to warn you," Vivian is saying. "Everybody wanted to know why you weren't at last night's board meeting naturally, and it turned out Marjorie Saunders's daughter was over at Coconuts when this alleged incident or whatever took place yesterday. So there was no keeping Pete's arrest from the board at that point. You know what Marjorie's like. Then, of course, Doug Weintraub wanted to know what this could mean for the museum's credibility with donors, that our director's son was involved in events of this nature. I said, 'This makes no difference whatsoever as far as I'm concerned, Doug. I'm behind Claire a thousand percent. Two thousand.' But you know the board. Doug's word always shakes everybody up, probably because he's an attorney. So the question was raised whether you'd be able to provide the kind of leadership we need at this point in time."

"What are you trying to tell me here, Vivian?" says Claire "Am I fired?"

"Heavens, no, what would give you that idea?" says Vivian. "I just thought you might want to be particularly careful about the way you conduct yourself at the moment."

Right. No disreputable-looking teenage boyfriends up in my daughter's room then, I suppose? No hostile ex-husbands. No questionable graffiti in the sixth-grade boys' bathroom. No out-of-wedlock pregnancy. No middle-of-the-night visits to my lover's apartment. No dirty faxes, definitely.

"Don't get me wrong," says Vivian. "The board all agrees you're doing a super job, especially when we consider the kind of pressure you're working under at the moment. Some people just wondered if maybe, given all that, you might want to take a leave of absence or something of that nature."

And what would I do for money? Claire thinks. "Thanks, Vivian," she says. "But I'm just fine."

"Well, that's terrific. That's what I told them, too. And if you need the name of a good counselor for your son, just let me know. Not that either of my boys ever got into this kind of scrape, knock wood. But I know a gal whose son got into a little trouble a while back dealing cocaine. She took him to this woman over in Brattleboro who straightened him right out. Like a charm."

"Thanks, Vivian," says Claire. "I'll keep that in mind."

Sally Jessy Raphael's guest this morning is a girl who divorced her parents. Her mother locked her in a dog carrier, she said. Her father sexually abused her from the age of seven. "He used to come into my room after David Letterman," she said. "He said it got rid of his headaches."

Ursula pours herself a bowl of cereal. Her dad is out someplace having a job interview. They are almost out of money again. This supermarket job, if he gets it, will only be for a little while, until his grant comes through. Sandy will take care of her nights.

"So how did you go about it?" Sally Jessy asks her.

"You have to file formal charges, of course," the girl says. She's only a few years older than Ursula.

"I talked to my counselor at school," she says. "She helped me get the ball rolling."

"And how is it for you now?" Sally Jessy asks her. "Do you miss your parents?"

"Well," says the girl, "I got to see them on a talk show last week. The actress that's playing my mom in the movie is much nicer than my real mom. She was in that 'Movie of the Week' about the grandmother that murdered the kid."

"Do you feel you have been permanently traumatized by these experiences?" a woman in the audience asks.

"Not really," says the girl. "My counselor said the important thing is to get it out. The worst thing is holding it in all the time."

The home pregnancy test has been sitting in the back of Sally's closet for two weeks now. There just doesn't seem to be any point in Sally's taking it anymore, her symptoms are so obvious. Not just the nauseous feeling in the morning, either. She's also tired all the time. Her chest has actually begun filling out and she's too bloated to snap the top of her jeans comfortably, so now she mostly wears her overalls. In ballet class last week Madame LaFehr actually told her she should think about cutting down on her calorie intake.

The other day in driver's ed, when Mr. Wayne showed them this really grisly movie about teenage drunk drivers, Sally had to run out of the room or she would have thrown up right there. She knew from experience, because a couple days before, when she and Travis stopped at a joke shop to try on Halloween masks, Travis showed her this one really gory mask of a face covered with eyeballs, and that's exactly what happened. After Sally ran out of the store, Travis went back inside and cleaned up the mess, and didn't even say a thing about it to her afterward. He bought her a Coke to get the bad taste out of her mouth.

Sally told Travis it's all because she's so upset about her family.

First her dad turns out to be shacking up with Melanie, then her brother gets arrested. Now there's this horrible news about her mother marrying the dork boyfriend, which means the Kid from Hell will move in with them. As if living with their farting dog wasn't bad enough, now she's got to share her house with a creepy eight-year-old who sneaks into her room and tries on her clothes and talks to herself all the time. Not to mention the father, who acts like a dog himself, the way he follows her mom around all the time. When he looks at her sometimes, he practically drools.

A girl named Bobbi that used to be in Sally's gym class told her one time last year about this special Chinese tea you can drink that makes you get your period, absolutely no matter what. Finally yesterday Sally got up her courage and asked Bobbi if she could have some. "Not for me or anything," she said. "Just somebody I know."

So this morning when she got to school, Bobbi was waiting at her locker for her with a plastic Baggie full of these crumbly brown leaves. "Brew it in boiling water and let it sit twenty minutes," she told Sally. "Drink five pots a day."

This is Sally's third. She's sitting on the floor of her closet, letting it steep. It's so disgusting it has to work. She'll either get her period or else she'll just die of the taste.

She is just taking her first horrible gulp of the stuff when Travis appears in the doorway. "Listen," he says. He has his hat on backward and his skateboard under his arm, as usual, and he is holding a bunch of carnations. "I know what's going on," he says, "and I want you to know I love you."

Because he's a first-time offender, Pete was given a suspended sentence for his shoplifting conviction. The judge has sentenced him to a hundred hours of community service at the soup kitchen and six months of counseling wih the Blue Hills juvenile officer. He will pay back the money he owes Coconuts at the rate of twenty dollars a week—all the money he earns from his paper route. He's not complaining about any of this. Pete's style is to be cool and tough. Announcing to his

friends the story of his arrest and sentencing, Pete adopts a gang-
ster accent. "Just remember, kids," he says, chewing on an imagi-
nary cigar. "Crime doesn't pay." Only his mother would know
how mortified he is.

At the moment, for instance, he is silent and nearly unreachable,
but Claire has learned to let him be. After a week and a half of
living at his father's house, Pete has returned home without discussion or explanation. Because he's grounded, except for the paper
route and times when he goes out to perform his community
service, he spends most of his time up in his room listening to
music and sorting through baseball cards or out in the yard, throwing pitches at the trampoline. It wouldn't surprise Claire if what
her son pictures in the center of the strike zone is the face of
Ursula, or Tim, but he doesn't talk about either of them. Whatever
it is he's picturing when he pitches, it's working. Now that baseball
season's long past, he's throwing strikes again.

But today Pete has something else going on. Every October he
constructs a Halloween scene in the front yard of their house. One
year it was a sea of white hands made from inflated hospital gloves
scrabbling up through the dirt as if they were trying to get out of
their coffins. Another year he made a ghostly figure from bed-
sheets draped over a stepladder, holding in his outstretched ghost-
arms a bowl filled with cold spaghetti strands and Ping-Pong balls
painted to resemble eyeballs. He set an old doll of Sally's with
matted hair and the eyeballs missing in a chair lit by a single blue
lightbulb. He got an old rusty bicycle at the dump and wired a
life-sized plastic skeleton on the seat, its bony fingers clutching the
handlebars, pedaling through a rat-infested graveyard. Every year
children come from all over town to see what Pete has built, in
such numbers that Claire always has to stock up on three times
the usual amount of Halloween candy for trick or treaters.

Looking out the window sometimes while her son works—
painstakingly arranging rubber snakes and rewiring his increasingly complex lighting systems—Claire sees the same intent,
focused concentration she remembers in Sam the time he plastered
their bedroom at the old house in preparation for Sally's birth, and
another time, when he built a grape arbor for her birthday. Today
it almost takes her breath away, seeing in the face of her well-loved

son the face of the man she has worked so hard to let go of over the years. It has taken her a long time to get to the point where she can once again allow herself to remember the things about her children's father that she loved. Today, oddly enough, she does.

At the kitchen window, Claire studies Pete's handsome profile and his muscular, widening back as he clambers with the grace of a cat burglar along the edge of their roof wiring a string of papier-mâché bats to the porch. She sees Sam the way he was the day she met him.

She'd bundled herself up in layers of sweaters and taken her skates out onto a lake in Ann Arbor on the coldest morning of that Michigan winter, thinking she'd be the only person at their school who'd get up that early on a Sunday morning to take advantage of the black ice. She was out in the middle of the lake working on the most elementary figures—a three-turn, waltz jump, backward crossover. She executed them clumsily at best.

Suddenly there he was, slashing across the ice so swiftly his blades left a spray of fine white powder as he flew past her. He moved with such effortless beauty he actually took her breath away. It was always what she loved about Sam, she realizes. Never the way he was to her, but simply, the way he was.

Like his father, too, her darling, precious son is more often than not elusive as a moth, as beautiful and untouchable as a deer in the forest. She catches him on the run now and then—with the kisses she insists he give her on his way to school or a ball game; the talks they manage every now and then, when she's sitting on the edge of his bed at night and he's too tired to fight it. He's toughest when he's most hurt, she knows, and most accessible and tender when he's most secure and happy.

Except for two hours he spent mopping floors at the soup kitchen this afternoon, Pete has spent the entire day working on his Halloween scene. He's still out there working as the last of the daylight disappears. Finally, at six-thirty, Claire steps outside to call him in to dinner. She actually gasps when she stands back and sees what he has built in their front yard.

The scene he has constructed this year is unlike any Pete has ever made—not so much grisly or comical this time as it is hauntingly beautiful.

He has constructed an entire forest in front of the house, made from actual birch branches he dragged in from the landfill, strung with a cobwebby tangle of thread and filmy shreds of torn fabric and unraveled panty hose that drip down like Spanish moss. In among the branches he has strung not only bats but tiny white fairy-like ghosts made from pocket handkerchiefs. He has set up a fan on the front porch that blows them in such a way that they appear to be dancing. Dangling from the largest of the birch branches is the figure of a man hanging from a noose. The dead man is made of old clothes stuffed with straw, but instead of the usual rubber mask or Magic-Markered pillowcase for his face, Pete has given the man a head molded from chicken wire wrapped with bandages. His expression is as agonized as anything Edvard Munch ever painted. The head droops to one side and the legs hang down limply, but Pete must have inserted stiff wire poles into the arms—Claire's tomato stakes, maybe. They reach out toward her so beseechingly, Claire actually shivers.

"This is a work of art, Pete," she says. She puts an arm around his stiff, bony shoulders.

"Wait a second," he says, kicking straw over the extension cord. He bends to push a button on his tape recorder, which is propped up to one side, under the porch.

It's that organ adagio by Albinoni. The piece of music Claire sometimes listens to late at night when she always supposed her son was sleeping. She thinks it's the loneliest-sounding piece of music she's ever heard.

U p in Ursula's room, Ursula and Brianne are working on their costumes. Brianne's mother has bought her a costume: one of those sets they sell at Woolworth's for $4.99—a polyester tunic that says BARBIE FOREVER on the front and a stiff plastic mask with red lips and a blond flip hairdo and holes for your eyes. But Ursula has told her this costume is really dumb, and Brianne isn't arguing. She is used to things about herself being dumb. She knows Ursula is lots smarter than she is, and whatever Ursula tells her must be so.

Ursula says they can make Brianne look like a real Barbie doll.

She happens to have a very fancy purple bra Brianne can put on. Ursula has safety-pinned the back to fit Brianne's skinny chest and stuffed socks in the front. Now she is applying lipstick to Brianne's lips. Not real lipstick, unfortunately. Claire never leaves that over at her dad's house. Ursula has to use a red Magic Marker on Brianne's lips.

Brianne is thinking it might get cold, trick or treating in nothing but this purple bra and the black stretch pants Ursula has told her to put on, but she doesn't say anything.

"If you get cold, you can put this on," Ursula tells her. She hands Brianne a long pink feathery thing she found in Claire's bedroom. Also some white-lace leather gloves. She wishes they had some high heels for Brianne, but Claire didn't have any, or Sally either.

"What are you going to be?" Brianne says. Ursula says it's a surprise.

Trick or treating isn't for five more days, but Ursula wanted Brianne to come over after school today so they could get everything all set up. She has a secret plan.

She takes out a cigar box she has been keeping in her jammy drawer. "Think about a person you don't like," she says to Brianne. "Now you got to get something that belongs to them and bring it to me. You think you could handle that?"

Brianne nods. She wishes they could just do the candy part. That's her favorite. But even though she isn't very smart, she has a person in mind.

Kid or no kid," Tim's landlord has told him. "If you don't come up with the rent you owe me by the thirtieth, I'm putting you out on the street like a goddamn pumpkin." So Tim's been working practically nonstop for two days now, proofreading a computer programming manual. If he finishes tomorrow and Express Mails it to New York, he could conceivably have a check by Friday. Otherwise God knows what he'll do. Stick up a 7-Eleven, maybe.

Tim's just so grateful to be getting some uninterrupted time at his desk for a change that he hasn't been paying a lot of attention to what Ursula and Brianne have been up to. As soon as they were finished with their hamburgers—Ursula finished, anyway; Brianne never eats anything—they hurried back into Ursula's room, where he has heard them whispering and giggling all evening. He should send Brianne home, he knows. It's a school night, and Ursula should be taking her bath. But he's so glad his daughter has a friend, and glad that he's finally getting some work done, he's decided to let them play for a while longer.

He's just about to go check on them when they appear at his desk. They are wrapped in sheets and wearing makeup. Ursula has on the black fright wig she insisted he buy for her at Woolworth's, that used up one of his last ten-dollar bills. She wants fifty cents to run to the convenience store at the end of the block for a Snickers, a trip he now lets her make on her own. "It's not for me," she tells him, knowing his new policy on candy bars. "It's for Brianne. She's hungry on account of she didn't eat dinner."

He hands the girls a couple of quarters.

"Be back in ten minutes, no more," he tells them.

Just as Travis comes whizzing up to Sally's house on his skateboard, a pair of small figures tear across the street directly in front of his path. He's so startled, he almost crashes into them, but he does a one-eighty instead and they hustle off like mice. They have a sheet or something over their heads, so all he can make out is their shadow. He doesn't pay much attention, truthfully—to the sheet people, or the Halloween stuff Pete has evidently set up in the front yard. All he can think about is Sally.

He leans his skateboard against the porch steps and rings the bell. Through the front window he spots Sally coming down the stairs sucking on a Popsicle. She's the most beautiful thing he's ever seen.

"What are you doing here?" she says. "I told you I didn't want to see you."

"I wanted to show you something," he says. Somewhere in the

yard he hears noises, like a small animal rustling in the bushes. He's so excited he doesn't even turn around to look.

"What now?" she says. Sally's period is now six weeks late.

He pulls his shirt off, though it's a chilly night.

"Yeah, yeah, I know. Great bod. Fantastic muscles. Now get lost, would you? I already told you I don't want to see you. This isn't your problem."

"Will you look?" he says. He steps into the light. He stands there motionless, bare chested and shivering. He holds out his long, sinewy arm.

Now she sees it: Just at the place where his bicep meets his tricep, Travis has got himself a tattoo. It's a heart with doves flying out one side and a rose at the other. In the center is Sally's name.

Huddled under a Raggedy Ann and Andy bedsheet, Ursula and Brianne scurry down the street clutching the magic box. They have to be quick on account of Ursula's dad told them to be back in ten minutes. Brianne doesn't have a bedtime but it's way past Ursula's. Plus it's cold out, and dark.

Some big kid on a skateboard nearly smashes into them as they cross the road, but he swerves and misses them. "It's here," Ursula tells Brianne. Claire's house.

Only Claire's house has never looked like this before. There's a forest of strange, spindly trees growing in front that never used to be there, and all these little white creatures flying around among the branches. It's a still night, but just in this spot, with its weird blue light and ghostly forest, a strong wind blows. Ursula can't tell where it's coming from, but there's music like you'd hear at somebody's funeral.

"I'm scared," says Brianne. "I want to go home now."

"Don't be dumb," Ursula tells her. She happens to know from personal experience that Brianne's house is just as scary anyway. She takes out the box and the plastic shovel her dad bought her so she'd play with kids at the beach.

"There's a guy hanging up in those trees," Brianne tells her. Ursula says it's just pretend, but she isn't so sure herself. She thinks of Jenny buried in the woods under that patch of moss. "Come on," she says, leading Brianne into the backyard. "We don't have much time."

When they're done, they wrap the sheet around themselves again and run all the way to Brianne's apartment house. Even from outside, Ursula can hear Brianne's stepfather, Ernie, yelling at Brianne's mother and Brianne's brother crying. When Ursula gets back home, her dad has a hot bath waiting and a plate set out with an oatmeal cookie and a glass of milk.

What did you go and do that for?" Sally says to Travis when she is finally able to stop laughing. "That's the dumbest thing I ever heard of."

He doesn't know what to say. He has no words for how he feels about her. If there is a reason for why he got her name tattooed on his arm, in fact, that's it. He couldn't think of a single other way to tell Sally he will love her forever. The thought of her is seared into his brain like he's been branded. He's like one of those rats they train to run through the maze in biology lab. Open the door and all he knows to do is run for her. There is no move he can make on his skateboard, even, that is big enough, fast enough, dangerous enough, amazing enough for this feeling. In art class, when Miss Blanchette told about this painter that cut off his ear and sent it to a woman he was in love with, Travis could understand how a guy could do something like that. Only he didn't want to do anything that would gross Sally out. He wanted to do something beautiful. Something that would make her know he doesn't just want to get laid. Although he does want to get laid. But more than that, he wants to be with her always. He wants to marry her and be a father to their kid. This isn't some dumb crush.

"Didn't you ever think what it will be like having my name tattooed on your arm, someday after we've broken up and you're going out with somebody else?" she says to him now. "Or were you planning to only have girlfriends named Sally for the rest of your life?"

What is she talking about? He is planning to only have one girlfriend his whole life. He is planning on it being her. Even though she tells him to go home now. Even though she has called him an idiot and told him she's having an abortion. Even though she has slammed the door in his face and walked into the house, leaving him standing on the front porch with his shirt off and tears streaming down his face in the chilly October evening. Tonight he can't ride his skateboard home, even. He leaves it on the porch and walks all the way home.

Sally's up in her room again. Claire has tried to talk to her, but she said she just wanted to fix herself a pot of tea and go to sleep and Claire didn't push it. She's about to call Tim and tell him she's too tired to come over when the doorbell rings. It must be ten-thirty, quarter to eleven.

A woman stands on the front porch in the blue light of Pete's Halloween display. She's wearing a white fur jacket over blue jeans that are too big. Claire can see she could be beautiful if she weren't so thin. Her hair is a wild auburn mane with dark roots showing. Even at a distance of a couple of feet Claire can smell that she's been drinking. She's holding some kind of a package and a set of car keys whose key ring Claire recognizes as the insignia of the Texas Rangers.

"Your address was in the book," she says. Drunk, for sure. "I drove from Boston."

Claire realizes she knows this face, although the woman has changed from how she looked in the only photograph she saw of her. On Mickey's wall.

"You know who I am?" she says.

"Bev?" Claire says. She's surprised the name comes to her; she hasn't thought about this woman for years, but now she remembers Mickey's stories about her.

Bev was an old girlfriend. The one right before Claire, in fact.

A nurse. Claire remembers now she took it hard when Mickey told her he couldn't see her anymore. In the first month or two after Claire started visiting Mickey, he used to tell Claire he had the feeling Bev was driving past his house at odd hours. There were a lot of phone hang-ups, too. Mickey didn't like Claire picking up the phone at his house in case it was Gabe calling, he said. But she remembers Mickey standing there saying, "That's you, isn't it, Bev? If you have something to say to me, that's one thing, but you can't just call me up this way anymore." Finally he changed his number.

One day Gabe got a package with no return address: an autographed picture of Nolan Ryan inscribed with his name. "Bev always had a way of getting into a locker room," Mickey said. "Only woman I ever met who was crazier about baseball than me. Only woman I know who could calculate a batting average."

Mickey adored her, as he adored them all. He had told Claire that. "She had the most amazing green eyes," he said. Looking at them now, Claire can see this is true. "And the most perfect ribs." That would be harder to determine.

Now she is extending her hand to Claire. "I know you may not believe this," she says, "but I feel very close to you." She floats past Claire into the hallway. Claire follows as if she is the guest.

"I heard all about you, naturally," she says. "Mickey had a real thing about you. I have to hand it to you that the kid part didn't stop him."

Claire thinks about running away. The woman is in her house, there's no changing that. But she could leave, herself. Only she is frozen.

"He used to tell me there was something so wholesome about you. And of course your tits didn't hurt, either."

"Mickey and I—" Claire begins. *They what? What can she say? Where would she begin?*

"Oh, I know, believe me," says Bev, laughing. *"Mickey and I, too."*

"I think you should have a cup of coffee," Claire says. "You shouldn't be driving like this. You need to go to a motel."

"I wouldn't be so worried about some other person if I were you," she says. "You have enough troubles."

Claire tries to think what Mickey would say right now if he were here. Mickey or maybe Miles. Or Yogi Berra.

"Did you know he continued to come see me all through that year you were visiting on weekends?" Bev says. "Wednesdays, usually. He probably told you that was his basketball night, right?"

She is lifting something out of the box she has been holding this whole time. It's a tape recorder. Battery-operated, evidently, because now she turns it on. She has set the tape up carefully in advance so his voice is right there at the precise moment she pushes the button.

"Of course she's cute," he is saying. That soft Alabama voice she'd know anywhere. "Nice enough body, too, for a breeder. But she'll never be you, baby. I never had a lover like you and I never will. Just like I know you'll never have a lover like me now, will you, baby?"

"So why do you keep seeing her?" a woman's voice asks him. Bev.

"Hey, baby, we've been through this. You want babies and I'm not going to give them to you. You've got to get on with your life. I'm just weaning myself gradually, that's all. You think it's easy giving you up?" Claire can actually hear an album she knows well playing in the background. Ella singing "Smoke Gets in Your Eyes."

"Claire's fresh out of the stable," he says. "Neglected housewife syndrome. I'm just her transition person. We go to a few ball games. I made her a tape. She actually had me singing this cornball country number with her. What a hoot."

"But you." He sighs deeply. "You're a whole different thing. You're my drug. I'll never get enough of you. You're my true love. Love of my life."

She snaps the machine off. Claire has slid to the floor. From a place deep in her belly comes a sound that doesn't seem recognizable. It's a low moan first, then a wail—sounds that could have been made by an animal, wounded but not killed and left by the side of the road.

"Did he tell you I got pregnant by him one time?" Bev asks her. Although she's clearly drunk, she speaks with surprising clarity.

"I actually believed we might have the baby, too," she says. "Love is blind, right? He went with me for the abortion, naturally. That's Mickey for you. Massaged my feet all that afternoon. When we got home he wrapped me in blankets, played me great music, fixed me a margarita. The works. A week later he called to say he'd met you. I didn't hear from him for a while after that. He changed his number. But after two, three months he called me up, said he had to see me. That's when the Wednesday nights started."

Her tone of voice changes suddenly. "How many children is it you have again?" she asks. "Two or three?"

"Two," says Claire.

"You're lucky," says Bev. "Even if it did, you know, mess you up."

"Mess me up?" Claire says.

"Mickey told me he figured a pair of hooters like yours would be hitting your belt buckle before the next Democrat got elected," she says. "I think that's how he put it. And then there was the other matter."

Claire doesn't even ask. She knows whatever it is, Bev is about to tell her.

"The reason he raised the issue was, I work for a plastic surgeon. And he wanted to know if I thought somebody like him could help you. 'No way a woman can birth a batch of babies and keep a nice tight nookie,' he said. Or words to that effect."

Finally Claire is able to speak. "You have to leave now," she says. "I hope you won't try and drive all the way back to Boston tonight." She stands at the open door.

"I'll be fine," Bev says. "It was you I was worried about. That's the whole reason I drove all this way to talk to you. You see, I finally started running my personals ad again after all these years of being so hung up on Mickey. The old biological clock, you know? I haven't talked to Mickey in two, two and a half years, mind you. And what should I get in the mail the other day but an envelope addressed to my PO box, written in that familiar handwriting. It was that letter he sends out when he's answering somebody's ad, where this woman friend of his tells what a great guy he is. 'Dear friend, and blah blah blah.' I knew you must have written it, naturally. I may not be a fucking Girl Scout leader, but I just didn't want to see you taking as long to figure him out as I did."

Claire opens the door. Out on the front porch Travis has evidently left his skateboard lying directly in front of the steps. Bev picks it up and hands it to Claire. "Kids these days," she says. "What can you do?" She takes a couple of steps toward her car, then turns around one more time and studies Claire up and down slowly.

"Let me guess," she says. "I bet he called you Slim."

Mr. Hogue, the school guidance counselor, wants to speak to Tim. Tim says he was meaning to give Mr. Hogue a call himself. He's been wanting to know how Ursula's been doing in the social skills group. It's been a few weeks since they've spoken.

"I think we need to speak in person, Mr. Shepherd," Mr. Hogue says. "Your daughter has raised some questions in our sessions which need serious evaluation."

Ursula has told the school guidance counselor her father abused her. She told him her sprained finger came from the time he threw her in her room and slammed the door on her finger. She told him her father called her a fucking idiot. She told him he locks her up in her room all the time. She said he told her she's trashing his life and he wishes she was dead. She didn't want to tell on him, but she heard on "Sally Jessy Raphael" that it isn't healthy holding stuff in.

When the social worker from the Department of Youth Services was called in, Ursula told them some other things too. Her father smashes her toys. He makes her get up out of bed in the middle of the night and hang up her clothes. He killed their dog. She said her mother is always trying to call her, but he takes the phone off the hook. One night he picked up his scissors and cut off her hair. "And now look at me," she said.

"My daddy doesn't say no to drugs," she said. "In the night he acts crazy."

Sitting here in the guidance counselor's office (the principal is here, also Miss Post, the social worker, and Ursula's teacher, Mrs. Kennedy), Tim holds out his hands to them. Because they didn't have enough chairs to go around, his is child-sized. He feels ridiculous, clumsy, out of place. "This is insane," he says.

"You understand, Mr. Shepherd," the social worker is saying, "we have a legal obligation to investigate charges of such a serious nature. We have had to report this to the DYS. I have met with your daughter several times now. We weren't at liberty to inform you until we'd gone through the proper channels."

"I don't take drugs," he says. He didn't do the other things either, of course. This just seems like the most concrete place to begin.

"You can ask Claire Temple about me. You know Claire. She's on the Parents' Advisory Board here." *A mom, he's thinking. Someone they will respect and trust.*

"Actually," says Mr. Bennett, the principal, "your daughter has raised questions about Mrs. Temple also. She says Mrs. Temple has been leaving her children in the night and coming over to your house. Ursula has made some very serious allegations as to the possibility that your daughter has been allowed to witness inappropriate sexual conduct between Mrs. Temple and yourself. All of which may well explain the difficulties Mrs. Temple's own child has been experiencing lately."

"What are you talking about?" Tim asks.

"We have a report of an incident involving a washing machine," Miss Post says. "Something about handcuffs."

Tim can no longer speak. He is sitting there with his head in his hands. He can only shake his head. *No no no no.*

"We will have to conduct a home visit. A series of them, actually. And you understand we have had to notify the child's mother in—" Miss Post looks at her file.

"New Zealand," says Tim.

"Correct," she says. He has this silly feeling that he has finally given the right answer. The first time in this whole meeting.

"She said she was flying over. I understand she'll be arriving tonight."

Joan stands in the doorway of Tim's apartment carrying a suitcase and some kind of object made of feathers and mud that has the unmistakable image of what Joan would insist on calling a vulva in the center. She is wearing black and her hair has been buzz-cut so you can see what her skull will look like someday when she's dead. She's very thin. Her skin is like milk with the fat content gone.

"I want to see my daughter," she says. Ursula is up in her room, where she has been crying. "I didn't mean to get you in trouble, Daddy," she said to him when he told her what happened. "I didn't know it was going to turn out like this." He could have been angry, but what Tim felt most strongly at that moment was something else. The need to hold and comfort her. "It's going to be all right," he said. "I'll make it better." Though he can't imagine how.

"She hasn't seen you in almost two years, Joan," he says now. "This isn't the way to do it. We need to talk privately. You need to go find a motel and come back after she's gone to bed."

"You really think I'm going to leave her with you? Knowing what I know?"

"I've been taking care of her for nine years, Joan," he tells her. "I don't think a few hours will kill her."

"I'm seeing her now," Joan says. She has stepped into his hallway. On the wall is the Maxfield Parrish print he checked out from the library of a house on a hill, glowing softly in the dying light of a spring day. The smell of macaroni and cheese—Ursula's favorite—comes from the kitchen. A vase of freesia sits on the table. He bought them for Claire. Thinking about their baby.

"Is it dinner soon, Daddy?" Ursula calls down to him.

"Stay in your room, Urs," he calls to her. But then she's there in the hallway. She sees her mother. For a moment she stands totally motionless.

"She got so big," says Joan. "Her hair." She is also just standing there, still holding the mud and feather object.

"I brought you this," she says to Ursula. "It's an artwork I made. It's a female goddess icon. You can hang it over your bed to give you power."

"Mommy," Ursula says. Her voice is barely audible. She doesn't move.

"You got so big," Joan says again. She puts the icon down and walks toward her daughter. A little stiffly, she hugs her.

Then Ursula is crying. "I knew you'd come," she is saying. "I knew you wouldn't forget me. I told them at school you were coming. They didn't believe me but I was right."

"I was just so busy with my work," says Joan. "I thought about you a lot though. I've been keeping a journal for you. With all my thoughts and feelings."

Tim stands there watching this. He puts a hand very gently on Ursula's shoulder. Otherwise he says nothing.

"I know some terrible things have happened," says Joan. "But now I'm here we'll take care of all that. You don't need to be scared anymore."

"Jenny died," Ursula tells her. Tim can tell that Joan is having a hard time remembering who that is.

"I'm in *Up, Up and Away* now in reading," she says. "I'm on the Puffballs. We almost won last time. All we needed was two more points."

"The social worker says your father did some bad things," says Joan. "We're going to talk it all out. I'm going to take care of everything now."

"For God's sake, Joan," Tim says. "You know what she told them wasn't true. She'll tell you that herself. She was trying to stir things up."

"This is so typical," she says. "The rapist blames his victim."

"What are you talking about?" he says. "I didn't do anything to her."

Joan has got down on her knees now. Ursula is sitting on Joan's lap, a little awkwardly since she is so big and Joan's so small. Ursula is talking baby talk.

"I have a Bend 'N Stretch Barbie now," she says. "Also Stacie, and Aerobics Barbie, and Pretty Pal Skipper. I'm going to be a witch for Halloween."

"Just look at this place," says Joan. "Candy wrappers on the floor. If I had any idea I would have done something long ago."

Tim has finally cleaned up his apartment for the home visit of the social worker. He has bought a bookshelf and throw pillows. He has put all his estuary notes into the plastic filing crates Claire was always urging him to buy. He has put leftovers into Tupperware and set out the vase of freesia Claire has yet to pick up on their kitchen table. Tim hasn't seen her in days. They are like two people who have fallen overboard, caught up in their separate swirling eddies of current and pulled in different directions, too busy simply keeping their heads above water to search for each other.

Ursula has even tidied her room nicely for once. Tim hasn't explained to her everything that's been going on, but he could tell when she came back from dinner with her mother that first night that Ursula understands plenty. For the last two days Joan has been staying with Ursula out at the Days Inn on the highway. She and Ursula eat room service and swim in the pool.

"My mom says girls need to be with their mothers at a certain age because certain things happen to their bodies that men don't understand," Ursula told him. "Blood starts dripping out their tinkler. And pretty soon it's going to happen to me.

"I told my mom it was really just an accident when you slammed the door on my finger," she says. "But she said there's no such thing as accidents. Everything is meant to be."

Joan took Ursula clothes shopping yesterday. She bought her a black velvet dress and a prism. "Whenever you see a rainbow I want you to think of me," Joan told her.

"My mom says there's tons of baby lambs in New Zealand,"

Ursula says. "Her and Elliott have this place they go where you get cookies in the shape of stars."

"You are not going to New Zealand," Tim says. "Not now, anyway."

"I told my mom that," says Ursula. "I told her I have to stick around and play soccer with the Puffballs."

"And what did she say then?" Tim asks.

" 'We'll see.' "

T he new social worker's name is Ed. "I don't want you to feel like I'm judging you or anything," he says as he shakes Tim's hand.

"Although you are," says Tim. He leads Ed inside the apartment. He has sprayed room deodorizer, but you can still tell that Sandy and Jeff must have had fish sticks again yesterday.

"All we try to do is look out for the interests of the child," he says."As a parent you can understand that."

"Right," says Tim. He is thinking about Brianne's fake father, over on Leverett Street, throwing the cigarette lighter at his fake son. Why isn't Ed over there?

"I understand you're an environmental nut," says Ed.

"Not a nut," says Tim. "Just environmental."

"Right-o. Thank goodness we have people like you looking out for the rainforest and everything," he says. "And that hole in the ozone layer. That's what's got me sweating bullets."

"My dad and me go bike riding all the time," Ursula tells him. "He gets me tadpoles and crayfish and cocoons."

"That sounds like a lot of fun," says Ed.

"One time my dad made me this jar of fireflies for my room," she tells him. "We let them out after a while, though, so they wouldn't die."

"Maybe you'd like to show me your room, Ursula," Ed says to her. "Maybe we could talk privately for a little bit."

"You wouldn't believe how nice my dad is," Ursula says. "He reads me *Charlotte's Web* every single night. He made pumpkin cupcakes for my whole class. He makes the best macaroni and cheese."

"On the issue of the sexual allegations," Ed is saying to Tim. Ursula is watching television now. *("Usually we just watch educational," Ursula has told him. "Never the violent stuff.")*

"Your daughter asserted in her earlier statement to the guidance counselor that you and Mrs. Temple engaged in sexual acts while she was present," he says.

"She was asleep," Tim says. "The door was always closed. It wasn't any different from what any other couple does in the night. None of us would have children if we didn't have sex now and then, right?" He has tried to bring a little lightness into this conversation, but his remark falls flat. He doesn't even amuse his own self.

"Your daughter seems to know a great deal about the nature of these sexual encounters, for a child who was sleeping," Ed says. "She gave us very specific— I might even say graphic—descriptions of certain sounds she heard, certain language. It's a little hard to imagine how an eight-year-old child would know to make up a line like—excuse my language, Tim—'Never stop fucking me, baby.' "

Tim is beyond embarrassment. "Maybe she heard something one time," Tim says. "You know the sort of things people say when they're making love. Any one of us could sound pretty stupid if you put a tape recorder under the mattress." From the look on Ed's face, he guesses this might not be true for Ed and his wife.

"What you say in the privacy of your bedroom may be your business, Tim," says Ed. "The issue here is the traumatizing effect on an impressionable child. In particular what concerns us is an episode involving Mrs. Temple being tied to the washing machine while you performed an act I can only surmise to have been anal intercourse."

"It wasn't even Claire," says Tim. "It was somebody else. A long time ago. Ursula and I talked about it afterwards. It was all right." The more he says, the deeper he gets.

"And then there are the allegations of substance abuse on the part of yourself and Mrs. Temple," Ed is saying. "I understand Mrs. Temple comes from an alcoholic family. Also that she has been evaluated by a guardian ad litem in the past for instances of possible instability and abuse in her parenting."

Suddenly Tim feels so weary it's hard even keeping his eyes open. It's becoming increasingly difficult for him to remember how it was that he ever thought things could be all right. He knows he used to have such large hopes for his life with Claire. He knows he used to believe that Ursula would love and accept Claire, and Claire's children would accept Ursula, and he and Claire could sleep in the same bed together every night and that they would all be a happy family one day. How could he have been such a fool? The whole thing is so clearly a disaster. Tim's life looks to him now like the closet in his bedroom, where he threw all the unsorted laundry and papers and toys and game pieces and shoes he didn't have time to put away this morning, before the social worker's visit. *Rubble.*

The thought of Claire's pregnancy comes to him now. He realizes with shock that it has been a whole day since he has thought about this thing he wanted more than any other. Their dream drifts away from him like Moses in his bulrush basket, floating down the Nile and disappearing from sight. Tim wants to dive in and swim after him. But the water is thick as mud. Tim is so tangled in the reeds, he can't move.

In the Village Room of the children's museum Claire is arranging the little wooden houses on the banks of a felt lake. She sets a boat by the edge of the lake and a tiny wooden duck beside it. She places a little wooden family in the boat. *Mother, father, sister, brother.* This is the way the families come when she orders them for the museum. Sometimes there's a baby, too.

Even during times less difficult than the one she's going through at the moment, Claire has always enjoyed these moments in the museum when the place is empty or nearly empty and she is setting up the toys. Lining up the buildings along the roadways and linking the pieces of wooden Brio track, Claire gets a small good sense of being in control. *Here's the church. Here's the school. Here's the store. Here's the hospital. Here's the playground.*

Claire is so absorbed in doing this that she doesn't notice the woman come into the room. She simply looks up and sees a small, dark figure with dark maroon lipstick and the palest skin she has ever seen. Paler than Ursula's, even—almost transparent. Her hair is cut very close, like a bathing cap. She wears a pair of work boots heavy as a marine sergeant's. She's carrying a very large shoulder bag.

At first Claire is surprised to see a woman like this at the children's museum. Maybe she's an artist come to offer her services as an exhibit designer. She doesn't look like anybody's mother.

Except Ursula's. Tim has told her that Joan's in town, come to investigate for herself Ursula's charges of child abuse. Now Claire recognizes her from the picture Ursula keeps in her treasure box.

"I'm Joan Vine," she says. Her last name is the same as Ursula's on her birth certificate.

She doesn't offer her hand. Claire can see the nails are bitten past the quick. "I know who you are."

"Claire Temple," Claire says anyway.

"I've heard about you from my daughter," says Joan. "I decided I'd give you a chance to speak for yourself."

Claire says maybe Joan would like to come into her office.

"Actually I'd rather not do this in your space," Joan tells her. She moves in the direction of the Mineral Room. She sits, lotus position, against a piece of sandstone. She takes a notebook from her shoulder bag.

"I hope you don't mind if I take a few notes," she says.

"I don't think we should view this as an interrogation," says Claire. "I'd rather just talk woman to woman. One thing we have in common is concern for Ursula."

"Really?" says Joan. "You have some odd ways of showing it."

"You have a very gifted and sensitive daughter, Joan," says Claire. "I understand you'll always be her mother and nobody can take your place. I wouldn't try. But I care about Ursula a lot."

"My daughter and I have a very special relationship," Joan says.

"Just because I'm not always physically present in her space doesn't mean we aren't totally on the same wavelength. She and I are bonded in ways you couldn't understand."

Wavelengths may be fine for you. Claire wants to yell. *But where was your aura at Ursula's soccer games? I guess you were so damned tuned in you didn't have to call her up Sunday nights? You figured she'd just know you were in her space?*

"I guess you know I have two children myself," Claire says.

"Yes, I heard," says Joan. "I gather from my conversation with your former husband that you've had problems parenting in the past."

Pyrite. Sandstone. Mica. Rose quartz. Focus on the minerals now, Claire tells herself. Become stone.

"You called Sam?" Claire says. "Then he must have told you that I was granted primary custody of our children. I'm a good mother to my children. I have tried to be good for your child too."

"It sounds to me as if you've forgotten who Ursula's mother is," says Joan. "You didn't give birth to her. You don't know the pain I went through. You have no idea how I feel."

Up until now Claire has sat almost motionless listening to this woman. Now she rises and takes several steps toward her. Claire looks down at her with more puzzlement than rage. She takes in the sight of Joan: her perfectly plucked brows, her exquisite black dress, the heavy silver choker wound, snakelike, around her thin neck, the row of gold studs lining her right earlobe. Claire shakes her head.

"Actually," she says, "I do have some idea of what it's like to give birth. What I can't imagine is what it's like to be a mother who lets the eighth anniversary of her daughter's birth pass—not to mention a couple hundred days before that—without even a phone call. It's true I have no idea what it must feel like to be you. But I wonder, do you have any idea what it feels like to be Ursula?"

For a second it almost looks as though Joan might cry, but she clears her throat and fingers her choker instead. "I suppose this museum is governed by a board of trustees?" she says.

Claire nods, barely hearing her. Her heart is still pounding.

"I have to assume this board isn't aware of your record of child abuse or my daughter's current charges of sexual misconduct," Joan says. "I think perhaps those are the people I should be speaking with." She's gone.

The woman's a nut," Nancy says. The two of them are sitting in Claire's kitchen. Nancy has fixed them a pot of tea from the bag of tea leaves Sally has left out. "Jesus, where did you get this stuff?" she says, spitting a mouthful into the sink. "It tastes horrible."

"Joan may be a nut," Claire says, "but she's going to speak to the museum board about me. I could lose my job over this."

"And you actually think they'll take this woman seriously?" Nancy says. "Look who we're dealing with here: a woman who takes up with some guy a couple months after her kid's born, and has her husband babysit while she's off making sculptures of pussies and fucking. She lives in New Zealand, for Christ's sake. She hasn't seen her kid in two years. Who taught Ursula how to make corn-husk dolls? Who took her to *Snow White*? Where was Mrs. Clitoris then?"

"You know what Vivian's like," says Claire. "If she takes it into her head that the board should get rid of me, she'll terminate my contract tomorrow and bring in some computer expert who'll put the whole museum on the Internet and replace the teddy bear collection with monitors."

"Hello?" says Nancy. "Remember who I'm talking to here? Claire Temple, Blue Hills's answer to Betty Crocker. The only person I know who actually told me with a straight face one time that she thought babies' dirty diapers smelled good. So long as they were breast-fed, if memory serves me right. Sound familiar?"

"You don't know everything," Claire tells her. "You don't know how people can make you sound if they want to. You say you're going to cut off your braids and they make you out to be suicidal. You lose your temper and slap your son and you're a child abuser."

"Don't turn yourself into a victim," says Nancy. "You can't lose sight of who you are. You may have to fight for that job of yours."

But Claire has been under siege for so long from so many different directions, she's no longer sure what's real. Maybe she really is an unfit mother. Maybe she has done something terrible to Ursula.

Sometimes Claire finds herself looking at Ursula, bent over her coloring book, humming that "Gilligan's Island" theme song, and she thinks, Yes, this is good after all. She's just a little girl, for goodness sake. I'm the grown-up here. I can love this child.

But then there are times when she'll hear Ursula pounding at the door, wanting to bake or play in Claire's dollhouse, or simply wanting, and just the sight of her round, hungry, perpetually disappointed face pressed up against the screen door makes Claire want to run in the opposite direction.

And something worse, too: Sometimes she looks for Ursula to fail. She wants to show her up in front of her father. "See," she wants to say to him. "My children are better than yours. I have done a better job of raising them." She is ashamed and sickened, but sometimes she even thinks she wants Tim to choose her over his daughter. Knowing this, Claire's not even sure anymore that Joan doesn't have a point, mounting whatever kind of crusade against Claire she has planned. She used to know as clearly as her own name that if she was nothing else in life, she was a good mother. Now she isn't even sure what a good mother is. All she knows is her son may be going to live with his father and her daughter says she doesn't care what her mother does; she'll be going off to college in a couple years, anyway. What kind of a lunatic is Claire that now she's going to have another child?

Only she isn't. She wakes to find her nightgown covered with blood and a cramping in her stomach as if there's a hand wringing her insides out. She heads to the bathroom, bent over like an old woman. She sits down on the toilet, and when she gets up there's something that looks like a blood clot floating in the water. She reaches her hand down and scoops it up. Nothing much to see: a little filmy tissue, a web of red. Somewhere in there she knows there was the beginnings of what might have become a baby, but what can she do—bury it in the garden, in a box like the one Ursula gave her that time?

She stands there for a moment holding it in her palm. She says a prayer. Then she places it back in the toilet and flushes. The water swirls like the curl of a wave, creating a hollow place in the middle that's totally still. There's a sucking noise, and then the water's still again. It's gone.

Later she will realize there is a certain horrible comedy to this moment:

"Tell us when it was that you came to understand the meaning of life, Ms. Temple," the voice asks her. Does it belong to the judge they called the Marital Master back in domestic court perhaps? Is it the voice of Vivian, at a board meeting, or Sergeant Donohue of the Blue Hills Police? Unclear. Only her answer is.

"Well," says Claire, "I'd have to say the truth was revealed to me when I was standing over the toilet bowl, watching my two-week-old fetus disappear down into my sewer pipes. Suddenly it was as if the mist lifted from over the water and I saw my life before me."

It is right at this moment that Claire realizes she will never become Ursula's stepmother. She will never marry Tim. She knows she will never shed another tear over Mickey or waste another breath complaining to Sam about child support or soccer cleats. Her son may go stay with his father for a month, or three months, or even six, but she knows he'll be back. Her daughter may be getting her driver's license, and she has almost certainly been having sex with her boyfriend, but she's not done needing her mother. She may never have needed her mother more, in fact.

Claire's family doesn't look like the one in her dollhouse (boy in police custody; mother eating lobster naked with her boyfriend, on the verge of losing her job for sexual misconduct charges). But they are a family, all right. They are even, in their twisted, dysfunctional, damaged, beat-up way, a reasonably happy one.

Even though it's usually Claire who calls Mickey—and in the four days that have passed since the night of Bev's visit she hasn't—Claire knew that Mickey was going to call her eventually. This morning he does.

"Okay, Slim," he says. "Who died?"

"Everybody's fine here, Mickey," says Claire. Her voice is flat. She doesn't reach for coffee this time. He will know from the sound of her that something's wrong.

"Let's see," he says. "I know for a fact I didn't give you the clap. I'm not taking you to court to win custody of your kids, because I'd rather play for the Chicago Cubs, if you must know the truth. I haven't told you lately that you always sing almost a half-step flat, and I am not about to tell you *The Bridges of Madison County* was the most moving reading experience I ever had. I give up. What did I do?"

"I don't really feel like talking to you this morning, Mickey," she says. "I'm pretty busy. Halloween and all."

"That bad, huh, Slim?" he says. "Okay. Have it your way. Call me when you feel like it."

She feels like it many times. But she never does. Ever again. And the interesting thing is, neither does he. It's over as simply as that.

The board of directors of the Blue Hills Children's Museum has called a special meeting today. Normally Claire would be present for such a meeting, but because the issue at hand is certain allegations made against her by Ursula's mother, Joan Vine, Vivian has explained that she will have to be excluded from the discussion. "You know we all love you to death," Vivian told her when she called this morning to explain the situation. "But in an organization of this nature, with people entrusting their children to us, we just can't be too careful about the type of individual we have on staff. I know I don't have to explain to you why the least sign of impropriety could open such a can of worms."

So Claire has the day off, and since it's Halloween, she has spent the afternoon carving jack-o'-lanterns with Pete and Sally to keep her mind off other things. Like what she will do for money if she loses her job at the museum, for instance. And how she is going to tell Tim she can't see him anymore.

It's five o'clock now, and she still hasn't got a call from Vivian. The pumpkins sit along the front porch railing, candles flickering. The birch branches and the ghostly scarecrow figure hanging from the noose cast long, eery shadows on the sidewalk as the last of daylight disappears. That organ music is playing again and the portable fan has been turned on. "I have to hand it to you, Pete," Sally tells her brother—actually putting an arm around his shoulders. "This is the most amazing scene you ever built. The trick-or-treaters are going to go nuts."

Because she has been feeling sick and crampy all day—the aftereffects of the miscarriage, combined with her terrible anxiety about her job—Claire didn't have time to put a costume together. So she has dressed up in her Pioneer Woman outfit to pass out the candy. She adjusts her mop cap and checks her face in the mirror just as the first trick-or-treater arrives. A Power Ranger.

He scoops up a handful of candy corn and Hershey kisses. He's followed by Pippi Longstocking, the Little Mermaid, and two more Power Rangers. Next comes a young couple with two very young children. The youngest one, a toddler, wears a home-sewn pumpkin suit whose pattern Claire noticed in *Redbook* this month. The older one, who looks to be around four years old, wears an even more elaborate home-sewn outfit. She's a bunch of grapes.

Claire remembers the days when she sewed outfits like that. The year Pete was three she worked for a full week making him a dragon suit. Just before they went trick-or-treating, Pete burst into tears and said the fabric felt scratchy. At the last minute she dressed him in a pair of sweatpants and a sweatshirt and Sam's old number from the Boston Marathon pinned to the front.

All the crazy, pointless efforts people make, Claire thinks. Trying to make life perfect for their children. Who are we kidding?

These days, of course, Pete would die before he'd let her go trick-or-treating with him and his friends. He and Jared are hoboes this year, in costumes they threw together themselves in ten minutes. Who knows where Sally is?

So many trick-or-treaters are stopping by, Claire doesn't even try to close the door and sit down in between knocks. She just stands on the front porch with her bowlful of candy as they parade past. The little ones with parents hanging back proudly on the sidewalk, so eager to shield and protect. The older ones, whose parents have long since recognized the impossibility of keeping the ghosts at bay and checking every apple for razor blades.

A trio of figures approaches—two short, one tall. The larger figure stands in the shadows of Pete's display while the two smaller ones mount the steps of Claire's porch, their hands outstretched. One is dressed like a hooker, Claire thinks, although when she asks the girl who she's supposed to be, the child says Barbie. She's wearing a pink feather boa just like one Claire has up in her bedroom somewhere.

The other child is a witch. She wears a black wig and her face is covered with green makeup. Only when she says "Trick or treat" does Claire realize it's Ursula. The figure in the shadows is Tim, of course. He hasn't said anything.

"My goodness," Claire says. "I didn't even recognize you."

"Heh, heh, heh, my little pretty," says Ursula.

Tim approaches her now. "You look beautiful," he whispers. She kisses his cheek.

"How do you feel?" he asks her. She called to tell him about the miscarriage. The one time they have spoken in days.

"I'm okay," she says. "I'll stop by later after the trick-or-treaters go home."

"I love you," he says softly. His tone as he tells her this no longer holds out hopefulness or joy.

"I know," she says. Another band of trick-or-treaters is mounting the steps. The witch scoops a handful of candy corn into her bag and disappears down the street.

At nine-thirty Vivian finally calls her. "I have to be totally frank with you," she says. "It was a tough meeting. That woman shared some pretty damaging allegations with us, and a number of members of the board took the position that we couldn't risk the exposure, keeping you on. But enough of us went to bat for you that the board voted to keep you on in a probationary status. So long as no further allegations arise, naturally."

Claire knows she should be grateful and penitent. But all she can do at the moment is say something about needing to hand out some more trick-or-treat candy.

Midnight now, her children finally in bed and the candles burned down, Claire heads to Tim's apartment. She makes her way down the street littered with smashed pumpkins and trailing rolls of toilet paper, knowing this will be the last time.

He's waiting for her in the living room of his sad, fishy-smelling apartment house. In the light of a single naked bulb, his face looks different to her than before. He has the face of a ruined man. A man she will leave, has left already. A man whose heart she will break.

"I'm so sorry," she tells him. They are both past tears.

"How did I manage to screw things up so badly?" he says. "I only wanted to love you."

Claire puts her arms around Tim and presses herself against his big, solid body. For the first time since she has known Tim, his cock is not hard for her. It's as if Tim has withdrawn permission from his own body to want her anymore.

"I think Ursula and I should leave this town," he says. She knew this was coming. "I know you don't want to see me anymore, and without you I can't bear to stay."

Her finger strokes his hand. She touches his hair. The gestures of a mother, not a lover.

"Can you come to bed with me?" she asks him.

He can never say no to her. He watches Claire undress the way

Ursula would watch the unveiling of the most perfect doll anybody could ever give her, only it isn't being given to her, actually. Only shown. She unfastens her bra and lets her breasts tumble down over his face. *Rapunzel, Rapunzel, let down your long hair.*

He raises his head from the pillow to meet her nipple—first one, then the other, with the same wild, desperate foraging of an infant left without milk for longer than Claire would ever leave any infant of hers.

"Will you ever know how much I loved you?" he says.

He speaks in the past tense, she knows, not because he has stopped loving her. He speaks in the past tense as if he were a dead man. If dead men could speak.

Ursula wakes even earlier than usual this morning, so early that her father is still sleeping. Alone.

She finds a sweatshirt and sweatpants in the pile on her floor, also her Little Mermaid backpack. Into it she packs Phillip, a set of smell markers, her Bend 'N Stretch Barbie, Jenny's collar, her Halloween candy, and the shell her mother gave her that time. She fastens on her bicycle helmet and tiptoes down the stairs. She lifts the kickstand of her two-wheeler and settles onto the seat. She doesn't know where she's going, except that it will be away from here. She pedals fast as the wind.

Sally isn't pregnant after all. Not anymore, anyway. She checks the color key on the back of the home pregnancy test she finally administered and rereads the directions twice to be sure she's read them right. White circle: no pregnancy. She's free. Within half an hour of taking the test she has begun to bleed.

She would call somebody up and tell them, but the only one who ever knew in the first place was Travis and he's been acting so weird he'd probably be disappointed. She has to do something though. She wants to dance. She wants to run. Most of all she just wants to get out of here.

Just at this moment Travis sails up on his skateboard. Last time he saw her, when he showed her his tattoo, she was in such a terrible mood, but seeing him now, with his arms outstretched and his hair flying and all four wheels in midair, she can't help but be moved by him. She grabs his shoulders in both her hands and whirls around in a circle with him. "Let's drive someplace," she says.

They take her mother's car and head for Wilson's Dam, out behind the old reservoir. Sally drives. He has brought her the new Dead Milkmen tape. He is just so happy Sally isn't mad at him anymore. He feels sad about the baby. But mainly he just has to touch her again.

Sally is so grateful she isn't pregnant, nothing else matters. I won't ask for anything ever again, she is thinking. I'm so lucky.

"Hey, why don't you keep both hands on the wheel and let me take the wrapper off?" Travis tells her, reaching for the tape. "You know how much shit you'd get in if somebody caught you driving with no adult in the car and no license? Me too."

He removes the wrapper from the tape and sticks it in the cassette player. He puts his hand up inside the front of Sally's short shorts. He begins to nuzzle against her neck.

"Hey," says Sally. "Not now, okay?" She hasn't figured out how to tell Travis yet but she isn't going to do it with him anymore.

"Man, you don't know how bad I missed you," he says. "All morning when I was bagging groceries, all I could think of was what I'd do if you wouldn't see me anymore. I'd go crazy. I don't know what you did to me. I still got a brain and a liver and intestines and stuff, but it's like my dick rules. And you rule my dick."

"I've been thinking about the sex part, too, Travis," Sally tells him. "I mean, I like you so much and we have all these great times and everything. But I've been thinking I shouldn't have rushed the other so quick. I want to take it slower."

"I will, I promise," he says. He figures she's talking about this foreplay stuff Adam was telling him about. "I've been a jerk. I'm always so fucking anxious to get it off, I sometimes forget how it is for you."

"I wasn't talking about that," says Sally. "I meant sex in general. Slowing down."

"Not doing it anymore?" he says. "You gotta be kidding. I'd die."

"Either that or you could just find somebody else and get laid by her," says Sally. "There's probably lots that would be happy to do it with you." She hopes she sounds a little sad but the truth is it would be a relief. She thinks about doing things like lying on the hammock and reading Agatha Christie mysteries. Sewing. Dancing. Going for bike rides with her friends. Why was she in such a hurry to get on to the next step?

"I thought we'd be together always," Travis says to her. "I didn't picture us ever breaking up."

"Are you still onto that marriage weirdness?" says Sally. Now she isn't even sorry at all anymore. She's almost mad, that he could be so dumb. "Jesus, I'm not even sixteen years old."

"You don't know how much I love you, Sally," Travis tells her. "I want to be with you forever."

"We just screwed a few times is all," she says. "No big deal."

"It was to me," he says. "It is to me."

"Listen," she says. "I think maybe I'd better just go home now. I'm not in the mood to go to the dam with you at the moment and you probably aren't, either." She begins to pull a U-turn on the narrow dirt road that leads up to the dam.

Travis grabs her arm. "Don't go," he says. The car swerves back out across the road. Sally turns the wheel again, points it toward home.

"Sally," he cries. "I want to show you how I feel about you. It's like my whole self is exploding." He reaches for the wheel again, but she fights him off this time. The car jerks to the left. Sally sees a VW bug heading in their direction. "Travis," she yells. "Stop it!" Their car is pointed straight for the bug.

"Jesus!" Travis screams. Sally swerves wildly to avoid the other car. She means to hit the brake, but her foot slams down on the accelerator instead. They careen over the guardrail of the bridge and into the water.

Claire is already at the hospital when Sam arrives, straight from his building job. For once, seeing him, she doesn't think about slammed doors or dinners poured down the garbage disposal or lawyers' bills and child support. She actually forgets for a second who he is to her now except for what she can't ever forget, that he is the father of their daughter, who lies on a table somewhere on the other side of the double doors at the far end of this room, where she has been for over an hour now without anybody saying what's going on.

She puts her arms around him; he doesn't resist. "It took an hour just to get the two of them out of the car once they pulled them out of the water. There was an inch or so of airspace or they would have drowned," she tells him. "Sally was driving, God knows why."

Sam can't speak. "What—" he begins.

"Her arm is broken. Also a couple of ribs," Claire tells him. The easy part. "They're still checking her for internal injuries."

Even now, in the terrible fluorescent light of the waiting room, Claire can't help thinking what an astonishingly handsome man he is, this familiar and elusive stranger who is her children's father. In all the years she's known him—half her lifetime, practically— she has never before seen him weep. They weep together, actually: wild, heaving sobs in each other's arms. She pounds her hands against his back. He buries his head against her breasts. Crazily, the words come to her now that she said to him last time he picked the children up: *"How many times do I have to ask you to please wait on the porch?"* If he laid his head against her her lap she wouldn't push him away.

As abruptly as they fall against each other, they break apart.

"When are they going to know something?" he asks.

She shakes her head. They don't explain the rules here, you just wait for somebody in a green tunic to call your name. Two hours ago Claire had certain other hopes and dreams, though she's at a loss to say what they might have been. Her universe now is the waiting area outside the emergency room. All she wants out of life now is a doctor to come and tell her Sally will be okay.

One emerges, with a couple Claire realizes must be Travis's parents. She's suddenly ashamed that she'd forgotten about him. One look at Eleanor Goforth and she knows it can't be good. Her husband—Don? Dave?—looks blank and stricken.

She would go up to them, only they have nothing to offer each other right now, except the mutual wish that their children had never laid eyes on each other. The doctor is writing down something for them on a piece of paper. Another woman has joined them—not a doctor; not dressed like one, anyway. She has an arm around Eleanor's shoulder and a hand on Dave's arm. It is Dave. She leads them into an elevator.

"Any word on Sally yet?" Claire asks the doctor. He says the broken arm has been set and it looks like there weren't any serious internal injuries. "You and your husband can go in to see her in just a few moments," he says.

"How about Travis?" Claire asks him.

"He's lucky he's alive, the way he hit the windshield. Another half-inch and we'd be looking at a broken neck," he says. Claire feels her body relax slightly.

"As it is, he's got two broken legs, multiple fractures," he tells them. "The fracture to the left leg is relatively simple. The problem is, the boy has a compound fracture to his right femur and a smashed kneecap. It's too early to tell yet if we can save the kneecap, but we're definitely looking at severe limitation to motion in the right hip and knee, combined with the possibility of sciatic nerve injury and severe chronic pain, long-term. He'll be in traction twelve to sixteen weeks. After that we'll know better what we're going to be dealing with."

Who knows how long Claire stands there then? At some point Tim comes rushing into the emergency room, dragging Ursula behind him. He lurches toward Claire and throws his arms around her so tightly he knocks the wind out of her, then pulls back. He's like some prisoner in the visiting room of a jail, looking at her through the glass but forbidden to touch her.

"We heard about the accident," he says. "Is she going to be all right?"

He doesn't add that he heard the news at the police station, where he had gone to pick up Ursula, who was found late this afternoon pedaling her bicycle down the highway five miles outside of town.

"Is there anything I can do?" Tim asks.

Later she will change this view, but what Claire feels at that moment is that there is nothing any of them can do, there is simply no way anything will be all right ever again. Looking into the face of this man who would give her anything he had, only he has nothing to give her, Claire can only say, "Please go home. I need you to leave me alone."

Because he's in traction they have set up a television on the ceiling for Travis. He's watching a snowboarding video at the moment. At least that's what's on. Hard to say whether he's actually watching.

Flat on his back with his hair fanned out against the sheet, Travis looks like an angel to Claire. His hair forms a halo around his face, which is extremely pale. His cheeks have the soft blond fuzz of somebody who has not yet shaved long enough or often enough that the hair has turned to stubble. He wears a white tunic onto which somebody has pinned a button that reads SHIT HAPPENS. A troll holding a skateboard is propped on the table next to his bed, along with a ceramic jack-o'-lantern full of jelly beans and several vases full of lowers and a Mylar helium balloon that reads "When Life Hands You Lemons, Make Lemonade." The balloon must have been here awhile. It has begun to droop.

When Claire suggested that they go visit Travis, Sally said she couldn't handle it. Travis's mother, Eleanor, has called every day since Sally got home from the hospital a week ago asking her to please come. Her son is so depressed, maybe Sally could lift his spirits. After ten hours of surgery, the orthopedic surgeon was able to piece together Travis's kneecap and femur with the aid of a considerable amount of hardware, but it's doubtful whether he'll ever walk without a cane. No more skateboarding, that's for sure.

Hearing this, Claire called Nancy, who used to be a physical therapist. "Let me put it this way," Nancy told her. "The femur is one big bastard of a bone to break. Only thing worse would be to mess up your kneecap."

"But he's so young and strong," Claire said. "And he's in such good shape."

"That'll help, all right," she said. "But I can tell you the kid isn't going to win any dance contests. It's Tiny Tim Time."

So here they are finally: Sally in her cast and Claire carrying a plate of the peanut-butter-chip cookies Travis always liked so much. She wanted to get him a tape, too, but when she asked Sally for a suggestion, Sally said, "Give it up, would you, Mom?"

"Hey, Travis," Claire says to him. She figures it would make him uncomfortable if she kissed him, so she just pats his shoulder. "We've missed you. Pete wanted me to say hi."

"Hi to him, too," says Travis, who is making an effort, Claire realizes, to cover a bedpan that lies beside him on the bed. "Hey, Sally."

"Hi, Travis," she says. "You look better than I expected."

"Yeah, well, you must have expected something pretty disgusting, then," he says.

"No, really," she says. "I like your hair like that." They must have shampooed it for him here. The dreadlocks have been replaced by fluffy curls, like baby hair almost.

"You still going to be able to get your license?" Travis asks her.

"It doesn't matter," Sally tells him. "I don't care about that."

"I guess you know the deal, huh?" Travis says to her. "They had to put me back together with a bunch of steel rods and screws. I'm a cripple. Not to mention I'll never pass through another metal detector without setting off alarms, huh?"

"It's amazing the things they come up with in medical science now," says Claire. "Synthetic hips, artificial joints . . . I remember when you'd hear a person had something like leukemia and you'd know they were dead for sure. Now they've got a fantastic cure rate. Not that you've got some terminal illness or anything. And you're so young. . . ." Her voice fades out.

"Right," he says.

Over by the window, in a spot Travis can't see because he's unable to turn his head, Sally has covered her face with her hands.

"I just wanted to say I'm sorry," she tells him. He lies there like a fallen soldier. More like an arrow actually, shot into space, that misfired and landed in the dirt. That straight.

"It wasn't your fault really," Travis says. "I was being an ass-hole. That'll show me, huh? Now I'm screwed. Next thing you know I'll take up knitting and start listening to Tori Amos."

This is where Claire walks out of the room. If he says anything else she doesn't hear it.

Tim calls. "I know you have enough on your mind," he says, "but I thought you should know. Joan wants to take Ursula back to New Zealand with her. Ursula says she wants to go."

In the old days Claire would have had a hundred opinions to offer about this. She would tell him not to be such a victim. She would tell him you don't let a nine-year-old decide what's best for her life any more than you consult a toddler on whether or not she feels like wearing her seat belt. Time was Claire would have typed up a list of phone numbers for Tim. Told him the names of lawyers and guardians ad litem to avoid (hers, for instance). She would have told him to have Galen write a letter about the laundry room incident. She would have slid her hands under his shirt and down the front of his jeans and then she would have begun to stroke his cock, which would already have been hard by the time her hands got there.

Now all Claire can say is "I hope things will work out for her there. I hope they work out for all of you."

• • •

The morning before Ursula leaves for Christchurch Claire takes her out for a bagel. Ordering for the two of them, she says, "Two toasted sesame. Cream cheese on both." They sit by the window.

"My team gave me a soccer ball with everybody's name on it," Ursula says.

"They're going to miss you," says Claire. "Luckily the season was almost over, though."

"My mom says we're going to get me a bunk bed in New Zealand," Ursula says. Also a puppy.

Claire says that's good. Once she might have said something about having friends for sleepovers, once Ursula has the bunk bed, but now she leaves it. Not her problem.

"Guess what?" says Ursula. "When we were packing up my stuff, we found my black shoes. The ones with the rhinestones."

"That's good," says Claire. "So you'll have them for your new school."

"My dad's going to pack up all my Barbies and mail them to me," she says. "But not my bike. It's too big. So I get a new one. With streamers."

"You can bring your helmet, though," Claire says. "I always thought it was great the way you wore your helmet without your dad having to get after you about it."

"A person can get brain damage," Ursula says. That wise, sensible, matronly side of her. Claire pictures her as a mother suddenly, and thinks she will probably be a very tender one.

"Keith is going to miss me a lot," Ursula says.

"No kidding. That baby could be howling, and the minute he'd see you he stopped. How do you do that, anyway?"

"I'm magic," says Ursula.

They chew on their bagels. Claire takes a sip of her coffee. "I know you and I had some difficult times," she says to Ursula. "It must be very hard to be a kid when their parents are divorced. Seeing them having some boyfriend or girlfriend."

"It's okay," says Ursula.

"I want you to know I think you're a good person. I never met anybody like you." Claire chooses her words carefully with Ursula, because she has come to believe that it's true what Ursula says. She may not be magic, but she knows what a person is thinking. She can tell when you lie. If Claire said, "I loved being with you" or "I wish you were staying," Ursula would never believe it.

"It wasn't your fault," Claire says. No further explanation necessary.

"They're making this new kind of Barbie," Ursula says. "She has a little tape recorder inside and she says all these dumb things like 'I hate math' and 'I hope Ken asks me to the dance.' "

"I wouldn't want one of those, would you?" Claire says. "The best part of Barbie is getting to make her say anything you want."

Ursula nods.

Claire has brought Ursula two of the dolls from her dollhouse that Ursula particularly liked. The baby and the grandfather. She has wrapped them in a hankie.

"It's good Grampa's going to New Zealand," Ursula says. "He was really getting on Grandma's nerves, you know. He just refused to hold in his farts."

Claire needs to see Tim one more time. But the day after Ursula leaves, a personal injury lawyer calls her to say he's representing Eleanor and Dave Goforth in a suit charging negligent entrustment resulting in grievous injury. Because of the age of their son and the extent of his injuries, the Goforths are seeking half a million dollars in damage.

So she has to attend a meeting with the lawyer provided by her insurance company, who informs her that because her daughter was not operating the car with a valid driver's license, Claire may not be covered. She and Sally also have to appear before the juvenile officer of the Blue Hills police force, which has charged Sally with unlawful operation of a motor vehicle. There's a call from her divorce attorney, who has chosen this moment to remind Claire that she still owes him eight thousand dollars, and if she doesn't begin making regular payments, he'll have to exercise his lien on her property. And she has to get some kind of car to get around.

Sometime in the middle of it all, Claire pulls up to a stoplight and sees that the person at the wheel of the car next to hers is Tim. His Subaru is piled high with boxes—Ursula's stuff, probably, that he's sending to New Zealand.

It startles Claire how old Tim looks, hunched over the steering wheel waiting for the light to change. Probably because she's driving an unfamiliar vehicle, he doesn't notice Claire for almost a minute—longer maybe—and then he does, and for a split second his face brightens as if he's forgotten everything that's happened to them and all he's experiencing is this pure, visceral memory of her. But as swiftly as his face is overtaken with pleasure, it falls, and a terrible look of weariness and defeat comes over him. The light changes to green. He lifts his hands in a gesture that says, "What now? Empty. Nothing here." They both drive away, opposite directions.

The next week things are quieter. The insurance companies are meeting. Sally's getting more X rays. Pete continues to be scarily good; there is simply no room for him to be anything else. Claire and Nancy actually do yoga one night, but all she can think as she twists herself into the eagle posture is, What if I had smashed my kneecap? What if Pete or Sally did?

Out of nowhere comes word that a retired dairy farmer who died earlier this year has left a hundred and fifty thousand dollars to the children's museum to create an exhibit about cows. They're going to have to build a whole new wing onto the museum just to accommodate the milking machines. "You never told me you had this up your sleeve," Vivian says to Claire. "I've got to hand it to you."

Every morning Claire thinks, I'll call Tim today, but she doesn't. He doesn't call her, either. Except for communications from the insurance company lawyer, the fax phone on her third floor is silent.

The morning of her fortieth birthday—a Sunday—Claire wakes very early and goes for a walk. She ends up on his street.

Tim will know it's her birthday of course. There was a time when they had talked about how they would mark it—a night in a motel maybe, a trip to Bar Harbor. He never told her, but back in the summer when he was doing fieldwork, he had actually written to the U.S. Botanical Society to register a particular variety of lichen he found up north that he believed had never been identified before. He wanted to give it Claire's name. It was going to be a birthday surprise.

The sun is still low against the horizon when Claire rounds the corner to the spot where his apartment house comes into view. Same trip she made so often all fall, but in the opposite direction. Amazingly, though it is not yet seven, and cold enough that a person can see his breath, Tim is sitting on the front step with a coffee cup and a pad of paper. He sets down his pen as she approaches.

"Happy birthday," he says. His own was just a few days ago. "So now I guess we can say we're poking fifty with a long stick."

"How's Ursula doing?" she says.

"Okay, I guess," he tells her. "Joan won't put her on when I call. She says Ursula needs space. I got a letter last week, though. She's changing her name to Ariel. How's Sally?"

"Fine," Claire tells him. Why start in?

"Guess what?" he says. "My grant finally came through. Not the Estuarial Institute, but this other foundation I applied to almost a year ago. I got enough to hire a research assistant and everything. Wouldn't you know, just when I've thrown in the towel." He has given notice on his apartment. He's leaving town as soon as the semester ends next month.

"I have to tell you something," she says. "Last night when I went to get your ring out of my drawer to give back to you, I couldn't find it. I don't know what happened to it. I don't want to start suspecting one of Pete's or Sally's friends, but I'm positive I left it there. I turned my whole room upside down looking."

He pictures her bedroom. Roses and scarves everywhere. Antique gloves flung in all directions. Dresses in a heap on the floor. Raspberries.

"Never mind," he says. "I have no use for it."

"If I find it, I'll send it to you. Just be sure you let me know where you end up."

"I have to figure that out myself first," he says. He actually smiles.

She puts a hand on his cheek. "You were the best man I've known," she says. "You loved me the best."

"I know," he says. "That's not always enough, is it?"

"Sometimes it's possible to try too hard," she says. "Like when you overbeat whipped cream and it turns to butter."

"The whipped cream stage was great, anyway," he says. "I wouldn't have missed it."

He rips a sheet of paper from the top of the pad he has set down beside him on the steps. He folds it slowly and places it inside an envelope that he has also laid on the steps. He licks the envelope and seals it. Then he hands it to her.

"I wanted to say good-bye," he says. "I was going to leave this in your mailbox. It didn't seem right to fax it."

She puts the envelope in her pocket. "I have to go," she says. "My kids will be getting up. You know the routine."

From inside the house they can hear a baby's cry. His downstairs neighbors' son probably. He wraps his arms around Claire and holds her for a long time. Then she walks home.

C*laire, Claire, Claire, Claire, Claire," he has written. Her name covers the top of the page. Fifteen, maybe twenty times, he has written it.*

> *I recognized the night I met you that I could be scorched by my love for you. And I am. There's not much left of me but ash.*
>
> *Even now, though, my heart expands when I think of you. I love you so much that life without you seems like no life at all. I guess I loved you so much that somewhere along the way I lost sight of my own self. Somehow I will have to get that person back.*
>
> *It's almost funny: Each of our marriages taught us the awful loneliness that comes from an insufficiency of love. Who would have believed an equal devastation might result from too much? I will love again one day, though at the moment*

it's still impossible to imagine. But I will never give myself over to love this way again.

I can't regret our strange, sad, impossible time together. However great and glaring my flaws, in the harsh light of your endless and unforgiving scrutiny, I wouldn't want you to ever suppose a lack of passion for you was among them. I will want you forever, and I have to say you were the absolute best woman I have ever known.

You know, for as long as I can remember, I've wept every time I have heard Lou Gehrig's farewell speech to the Yankees. This morning watching the sun rise, in the clutch of so much loss and hurt, I know what it meant when a dying Gehrig said he considered himself the luckiest man on the face of the earth. Because even as this love I have for you is just about killing me, that's how I feel about having had you in my life. You brought forth a capacity for love in me I never knew I had. For seven months you were with me with my every breath. You are with me still.

To hurt you is to hurt me. To lose you is to lose a part of myself. It's going to take a long time figuring out how to live my life without you.

 WINTER

The counselor she takes Sally to after the accident has warned Claire that her daughter will most likely feel the need to punish herself, and she's right. For weeks after she comes home from the hospital, Sally barely eats. When her friends call, she tells her mother and Pete to say she can't come to the phone. After a while hardly anybody calls anymore except Travis, and his calls are the hardest of all.

"When are you going to get it?" she hears Sally saying to him into the phone one night. Her voice is scarily cold, almost withering. "I'm a jerk, okay? I wish it was me that got their legs wrecked, but it wasn't. Every time I hear your voice I just feel like an even bigger asshole. So I don't want to hear from you anymore, understand?"

He does understand evidently. He hasn't called since. In the end, after Claire's insurance company absolved itself of liability in the Goforths' lawsuit on the grounds of an exclusion of unauthorized use of a vehicle by a minor, the Goforths were successful in recovering damages in the amount of two hundred thousand dollars from their own insurance company—on top of medical costs. "You're incredibly lucky," several people have told Claire. They're right, naturally. Claire knows she's also lucky that the children's museum board voted to renew her contract for another year.

Above all, of course, she is just so incredibly lucky that her own child is all right. Physically, anyway.

Sally is legally prohibited from driving until her eighteenth birthday now. She is also on probation for operating a motor vehicle without a license, reckless endangerment, and a couple of other charges Claire forgets. It will be a very long time if ever before her daughter will sit behind the wheel of a car again.

Even taking rides from her friends seems too much for Sally at the moment. "I guess I'll let my mother drive me," Claire heard her say the other day when one of the few girls who still drops by pulled up in front of the house to see if Sally needed a ride to the SATs. She sits in the passenger seat beside Claire now, the way she did when she was little. Buckled, always, with her notebooks in her lap. Claire didn't realize until after the accident how seldom Sally had ridden with her in recent years. Now with her reluctance to ride the school bus, and her trips to physical therapy, and therapy, and her dad's house, Sally is a more frequent passenger in Claire's station wagon than her brother, even. She doesn't complain when Claire plays her country music station, either.

In fact, she never complains about anything, never shows much emotion, period. She has this impassive look just about all the time now that makes Claire want to scream, "Where are you?" She did once, in fact. Sally didn't answer.

Sally's birthday arrives—the date she had circled with red Magic Marker back in January. "I GET MY DRIVER'S LICENSE TODAY!" she had written on her calendar.

Claire makes Sally a cake and lights sixteen candles for her. "Make a wish," says Pete, and then they all fall silent, knowing what her wish must be, and how impossible. Pete's present to her is an incense burner in the shape of a teepee. Claire gives her a locket shaped like a heart and a J. Crew sweater. "Thanks a lot, Mom," she says flatly. "These are great." She goes back up to her room and closes the door.

Sally comes straight home after school these days, as she never used to. At first while her cast is on she can't go to ballet class, but even afterward, when Madame LaFehr suggests that she start working at the barre again, Sally stays away. Where, at first, she had got very thin after the accident, now she seems to live on yogurt and M & M's. Her face is looking puffy and her waist has thickened in a way that the old Sally would never have tolerated. She has taken to watching afternoon talk shows.

One morning, carrying out the trash, Claire finds Sally's toe shoes stuffed into the bottom of her wastebasket. She starts to retrieve them, then thinks better of it. Claire can still remember the feeling of standing in front of her bathroom mirror that day long ago, holding up the nail scissors as she cut off her long braids in a moment of perfectly exquisite misery. Sometimes, she knows, a person has to give up something she loves to make her own particular bargain for peace. There is no short cut through pain. She buries the toe shoes back in the trash.

By midwinter, long after her arm is healed, Sally's still spending every afternoon lying on her bed listening to Tori Amos and Cowboy Junkies, or watching the parade of miserable stories on "Oprah" and "Ricki Lake" and "Jerry Springer." Finally Claire can't stand it anymore, seeing her daughter living this way. One afternoon in early February she leaves work early. She climbs the steps to Sally's room and knocks at the door. She waits a moment, then walks in.

"Come on downstairs," she says. "Do you realize we haven't made a single Valentine yet?"

When Sally was little, she and Claire would work for weeks, making a card for every member of her class. Pete never had the patience, but Claire and Sally would spend hours making them. They kept their Valentine supplies spread over the dining-room table for weeks: glitter and doilies and red construction paper; seed catalogs for cutting out pictures of flowers; glue sticks, sequins, stickers, buttons. In recent years their Valentines have shifted from a seven-year-old's idea of prettiness to a fifteen-year-old's notion of cool—with clippings from the *National Enquirer* and ads for acne medicine from Sally's old copies of *Seventeen*. Last February Sally made Travis a card using a collage of pamphlets some fundamentalist Christian group had left in their mailbox promoting chastity and Bible reading as the answer to the AIDS crisis. Claire made Sally a wooden box that year, with plastic charms and candy message hearts glued all around the sides and a picture of the two of them, mother and daughter, stuck on the top, with johnny-jump-ups she'd pressed the summer before urethaned around the edges. "For my darling daughter," she wrote on the front. "Nothing has ever brought me more joy than you and your brother."

Even now she would say that. Never more joy. Or more pain, either.

So now they sit at the dining-room table making Valentines again. Surprisingly enough, Sally didn't fight the suggestion. She isn't making a joke card, either, from the looks of it.

For Pete, Claire makes a Valentine featuring her son's face glued on a baseball card of Mike Piazza and the words "Most Valuable Player" written in gold glitter across the top. For Sally this year Claire can think of no words or pictures sufficient to say what she wants.

All those years she spent sewing doll clothes and baking elaborate birthday cakes, searching for lost toys and driving through blizzards to pick up some friend of Sally's for a sleepover—all so her precious firstborn child should be spared pain. She might as well have been some character in a fairy tale trying to rid the kingdom of every poisoned apple, every spinning wheel. That's how impossible it is, she knows now, for a parent to protect or rescue her child.

She starts to make Sally a mirror encrusted with sequins, then sets it aside. She draws a picture of her daughter in the middle of a flower garden, her daughter dancing, then rips them up. She copies out a poem she has always loved, that Anne Sexton wrote for her daughter Linda. "O Little Girl, My String Bean, My Lovely Woman." Also no good. Beautiful as the poem is, the woman who wrote it ultimately killed herself, leaving two motherless daughters. What's the message in that one, Claire would like to know.

In the end, she gives Sally the simplest Valentine. A plain red heart—nothing more. Sally has made a gorgeous Valentine herself, with lace and ribbons and fake jewels, but she puts it away.

"What are you doing?" Claire asks her. "That's one of the most beautiful Valentines you ever made."

"The dumb thing is," she says, "I don't have anyone to give this to."

"You will," Claire tells her. "It won't always be like this. I promise. Even though right now, I know, it feels like your heart is broken forever."

Sally looks up at her suddenly, and at first Claire thinks she's going to make some angry, cynical remark of the sort she has gotten so good at lately. Only she doesn't. What happens is, Sally's eyes, which have looked blank and hollow for three and a half months, slowly fill with tears. First just a couple, then a downpour. She falls into Claire's arms and lays her head against Claire's shoulders, weeping so desperately and long that when Pete walks in from basketball practice and the two of them finally look up, they realize they're sitting in total darkness.

"Jeez, what's been going on here, anyway?" he says, surveying the wild mess of sequins, glitter, and weeping women.

"We're going to be all right," Claire says. For the first time in ages she knows that's true.

 SPRING

After a long hard winter the snow finally begins to melt. Claire goes out to clear the leaves off her flower beds. The ground is hard and covered with ice crystals, so she decides to soften the soil a little to make it easier for the shoots of her daffodils and crocuses to push through.

Her trowel hits something hard deep in the dirt. At first she thinks it's a rock, but when she starts to dig it up, she sees it's actually a cigar box tied with dental floss. Something Pete buried long ago in a game of pirates maybe. She opens it.

Inside is a collection of objects tucked into a tangle of twigs and straw like the contents of an Easter basket or the nest of a magpie. There's a cheap metal cigarette lighter and a dog's rabies tag. There's a shell and a Brownie pin and a baseball card Claire recognizes as Pete's treasured Electric Diamond Frank Thomas Tribute card that he was looking for months ago. There are a couple of baby teeth and pieces of fingernail with the last remnants of red polish still showing. There's a tampon and an old agate marble that looks as if it came from the children's museum. A dried rose that must have been picked from the collection on Claire's ceiling. A crude drawing of a naked man and a naked woman, with the penis and breasts exaggerated. There's a Barbie head with all the hair cut off short as Ken's, and a horrible smile drawn on in ballpoint pen. There's a feather and a dried animal turd and the blue ribbon off of Pete's bear that he keeps hidden under his pillow. Claire thought she was the only one who knew that. There's a tiny doll, no bigger than a ten-week-old fetus, made out of corn husks, with a tiny red heart sticker on its chest and a needle pierced through the center.

There's one more object in the box, but this one is wrapped in many layers of toilet paper, which Claire unwinds.

Inside is the amethyst and pearl ring.

The year the space shuttle *Challenger* was launched with Christa McAuliffe inside Pete was five years old. Young as he was, something about that mission had captivated him for weeks before the countdown, maybe because there was a mother on board who had children about his age. Pete and his family had attended a parade in New Hampshire the fall before in which Christa and her kids had ridden in an open convertible and Pete got her autograph. Her picture hung on his bedroom wall after that, and on the day of the launch he went off to school wearing the spacesuit they'd ordered from the Air and Space Museum for a Christmas present. The whole school had gathered in the auditorium to watch the launch together. Three hundred children had counted down in unison and watched as the *Challenger* lifted off. When it exploded, nobody realized what had happened at first, so they had cheered, thinking this was just an additional blast of rocket fuel propelling Christa higher into space. It took a few seconds before everyone began to realize that something had gone wrong.

When Claire heard what happened, she rushed right down to Pete's school to get him, knowing he'd take the news hard. She ran to his classroom, where the teacher had hurriedly distributed mimeographed dot-to-dot pictures of Valentine hearts. If you hadn't known Pete, you might have thought he was okay, bent over his dot-to-dot, but Claire knew better.

It was weeks before he slept through the night again. "I dreamed you fell into a giant hole and we couldn't get you out," he would tell his mother. "I dreamed I came home after school and everyone was gone. I couldn't find you anyplace."

He kept thinking their appliances were going to blow up. He made her unplug the toaster every time she was finished using it. Also the washing machine and the dryer. He thought if you counted backward bad things would happen.

Gradually he got better. He started watching TV again and he didn't run in and check on her every twenty minutes when he was playing in the yard. But one thing that didn't go away was his wondering about the explosion itself. He had heard that fragments of the spacecraft showed up on beaches all over Florida, and he knew NASA was gathering them up and piecing them together. What Pete wanted to know was what happened to the people in the spacecraft? Where did they end up? Where did they go?

Claire had wondered this same thing, and she never did come up with a satisfactory answer for him. She thought it might be more comforting to think of the astronauts and Christa up in space somewhere as some kind of glittering celestial dust, reflecting the light of the stars. Pete didn't want to think of them landing on beaches in pieces, that was for sure. Or vaporized completely.

"They're inside everybody who remembers them," she told him. "Inside you. Inside me. Inside their families. Every time we remember them, it means they're not completely gone."

Memory is a funny thing, Claire thinks. So long as you have it, you never totally lose hold of a person. And they never quite release you.

When memory fades—and it does—things that used to be almost unbearably sad to you become tolerable. Life no longer seems so heartbreakingly poignant. But the price of being freed from painful memory runs high. It's a little like what Nancy told Claire back when her doctor put her on Valium. "I don't feel so depressed anymore," she said. "But then, I don't feel so much, period."

Who would have believed Claire would ever find herself at a Red Sox game without glancing even once at the seats near third base where Mickey always sits? Who would have believed she could invite a man over for dinner, as she did last Saturday—a casual date, nothing serious—and that when he spotted her Johnny Hartman and John Coltrane CD, she'd say, "Here, let me play it for you. Wait till you hear the way he sings 'My One and Only You' "? No big deal.

Who would have believed the day would come when Claire could run into her daughter's old boyfriend, Travis, inching slowly past the Bagel Works in a wheelchair—Travis, the same boy who just last September used to sail up to their house on his magic carpet of a skateboard with the grace of a dancer or a magician? Last fall he seemed so bitter and angry she thought he'd never get out of that bed and turn off those snowboarding videos. When Claire saw him on the street yesterday he told her he was going to a rehab center in Burlington where they thought they'd have him using a cane by summer. "Say hi to Sally for me, okay?" he said.

Once Claire would have told you it could never happen that when she'd attend her son's baseball game on a Saturday and run into their former babysitter Melanie, she'd actually wave to the young woman from across the field. Melanie is her children's stepmother now, nine months pregnant with Sam's child.

"You might want to get new bumpers for that old crib in the attic if that's the one you're going to be using," Claire tells her. "The bars aren't spaced as close together as they should be." She has even given Sam and Melanie the box of the kids' old baby clothes she had been holding on to all these years thinking she might need them herself. She won't.

She hands Melanie Pete's overnight bag. He's going to his father's house for the weekend. "He's going to try to convince you he doesn't have any homework," she tells Melanie. "But he'd better get started on his Famous American report or he'll be in trouble later."

"I'm psyched to give him a hand," Melanie says pleasantly,

looking over the mimeographed sheet sticking out of his bag. "Buckminster Fuller was so cool."

"If I don't see you before you go into labor, good luck," Claire says. "They tell you the pain is terrible and maybe it is, but you know something? Once it's over you won't even remember."

It still astonishes Claire sometimes that a woman who loves the touch of a man as much as she does should find herself sleeping alone every night. As the years have passed in which her life has continued in this unattached way, it's the sleeping together part more than the sex she misses most. Sex she can find. Passion even. It's not an impossible task finding an agreeable man to kiss her wildly in the middle of the night. The rarest thing would be waking up with a man beside her in bed and having coffee together in her ratty bathrobe with her glasses on instead of contact lenses and no makeup. The rarest thing would be a night in which she slept in the arms of a man. Just slept with him.

When her children were small and she was still living with her husband and sleeping with him in their chilly bed, she used to get up in the middle of the night sometimes and wander through their house. Often she would go into her children's rooms and lie down beside them, curl herself around their hot little bodies as they slept, just listening to their breath. Her children have always been sound sleepers; they never woke when she did this, although they might shift in their sleep, adjusting themselves to her presence in the bed. If she wrapped her arms around Pete he might let out a small sigh. One time after a particularly terrible fight with Sam, when she climbed in with her daughter, Sally had spoken in her sleep. "The dolphins are coming," she said.

These days Claire stays in her own bed, with its canopy of printed scarves from Florida and California and Niagara Falls draped overhead and her piles of feather pillows and the garden of upside-down dried roses shooting out from the ceiling like a storm of arrows. She still keeps a CD player beside the bed and listens to music as she drifts into sleep: Joni Mitchell's *Blue,* Steve Earle singing "My Old Friend the Blues," Mark Knopfler's movie soundtracks, with that heartbreaking guitar of his, the melancholy trumpet and vocals of the beautiful and doomed Chet Baker. "There's someone I'm longing to see," he sings. "I hope that she turns out to be someone to watch over me."

Claire takes various men to bed with her, but only in her mind. Lying there with no light but the faint glow of her Nautilus shell and the music playing faintly, she runs through her list and chooses one. Sometimes it's a lover she has known. More often it's not. She may choose her son's basketball coach one night and the man behind the fish counter at the supermarket some other time. If she's seen one of their movies recently she may choose Tommy Lee Jones or Sean Connery. She went to bed with Dwight Yoakam once. Another time it was Andre Dawson, her favorite player on the Red Sox, before he got traded to the Marlins.

One man she never takes out and makes love with this way is Tim. Another one is Mickey. Another is Sam.

She is not crazy. She's just getting by, is all, and this is one of the ways she has learned to do it. Now his hand is running through my hair, she thinks, and then she follows his touch as his fingers make their way down her neck and spine. Making love this way, with an invisible lover, it takes a lot of concentration not to lose your place. It's like a game she sometimes plays with Pete when a song they both know very well comes on the radio and she turns off the volume for thirty seconds or so, but she and Pete keep singing. The idea is to discover, when you turn the volume up again, that you're at just the right point in the song still. They are so good at this with certain songs (R.E.M., for instance, singing "Everybody Hurts"), Claire has joked to Pete that they might as well sell his boom box and all his CDs. "We can just imagine the whole album now," she says. "Kind of a virtual-reality thing."

In the virtual reality of her solitary lovemaking, Claire's lover holds her very tightly, one step away from hurting her. She wraps her legs around his neck, digs her heels into his back, holds his face between her hands, breathes the air directly from his mouth. She presses her palms against his chest. She moves her pelvis as if she were dancing. She may also run her hands along her own belly and over her breasts, imagining that the fingers she feels are someone else's. "I want to fill you up," he says to her. "I want to drink you."

Alone in her bed, she may even whisper the things she would say to him. Or maybe it's not words at all she utters but animal sounds, a bird's song. She runs her fingers up and down the shaft of his cock. Sometimes he enters her from above, sometimes she's on top, impaled on him. Or he may be pressing against her back, with his arms wrapped around the front of her, cupping her breasts. She hugs her pillow as he thrusts into her, until the moment when she imagines his body reaching that impossible tension followed by explosive release.

The bed will be damp now. She's drenched in sweat. The only measure she has of time is that Chet Baker is singing a different ballad now: "It's Always You" or maybe "Let's Get Lost." "Isn't it Romantic?"

It's not, of course. She's just acting out a little play, the same way Sally used to—and then Ursula—with Barbie and Ken. Different scenes but the same idea. You imagine a world and you make yourself a character inside it, and who's to say it's any less real than all the little plays everybody's actually performing around you? Who's to say a real flesh-and-blood man between her sheets would be any more present for her in the end than the ones summoned from her imagination?

One good thing about these men Claire conjures up: They never break your heart. And you never break theirs either.

 FALL

Labor Day. Sally's off visiting colleges, but Claire has driven to the old house to pick up Pete from his weekend with his father. She opens up the back of her station wagon to make room for his bags. Six and a half years her son has been going back and forth between his parents' houses and he still transports his stuff in brown paper bags.

Claire's in the process of attaching the rack for their bikes when Melanie comes out. "He's almost set," she says. "But you've got to come inside and see this."

Claire walks into her old kitchen. "This way," says Melanie, and she leads Claire into the downstairs bedroom. Pete is sitting in a rocking chair that Claire once used to nurse her children. Melanie and Sam's baby, Seth, lies against Pete's stomach, drinking from a bottle. Claire studies the tiny clenched fists, the folded-over ears, the round, smooth head so new you can still see a pulse, barely below the surface of the skin at the soft spot. "He's almost finished," Pete whispers. "You wouldn't believe how this little guy chows down."

The bottle is empty. Seth begins to fuss, arching his back and sputtering. Claire is surprised to see that instead of handing the baby over to Melanie as she would have supposed her son might do at a moment like this, he just lifts Seth onto his shoulder and rubs his back gently. He's singing a song she recognizes from the most recent Green Day CD.

"Pete's great with Seth," Melanie says. "He's really going to miss his big brother."

Shortly after Claire had moved out of this house she went back one time when the children were at school to pick up the last of her things. Sam must have come home early from work that day. He was still wearing his painter's pants and the T-shirt they bought years before on a family trip to Luray Caverns with a picture of a rock formation on the front that looked like a fried egg. Sam and Claire were still trying to be friends at this point, so he was helping her carry boxes out.

When the last of the boxes had been packed in her car, they walked back into the house. She needed a glass of water.

He ran the water to make it cold. They had an artesian well. Claire has never tasted water so good.

"Thanks," she said, setting her glass down. They just stood there for a moment. And then he put his arms around her more tenderly than she could remember. She put her arms around him then too and for a long time they simply held each other.

He kissed her. There was no playfulness and you couldn't call it passionate either, although there was a hunger to the kiss that Claire has seldom experienced—even with Mickey, even with Tim. Not a hunger borne of any hopefulness; they had no future together and they knew it. Just a bone-crushing sadness. A grief and regret so enormous you couldn't see it in a person without wanting to comfort him. Even if, as was the case, there resided in you at that moment a grief and regret equally crushing. A sorrow beyond words.

Then without speaking they walked into their old bedroom.

They were the only two people in the world that day who could understand all the thousands of things that contributed to the dizzying sadness of this moment. They had stopped at a VFW hall on their first date and danced the polka and an old man named Heinz had bought Sam a shot of whiskey and told him, "There's nothing better in life, son, than the love of a good woman." He raised his glass with the prayer that they'd be dancing the polka on their fiftieth anniversary. Downed his drink in a single gulp.

As she walked home through the streets of Ann Arbor with Sam that night, something possessed Claire to say to him, "Show me a trick." Why she asked him that she still doesn't know. It's not a question she asked any other man, before or since.

"All right," he said. There in the middle of the street he stood on his right leg and held the other, bent in front him, with his right hand. Then he jumped, lifting his right leg off the ground and through the hoop his other leg and arm had formed, and he landed solidly on the other side. Sometimes Claire actually thinks that was the moment she decided to marry him. *I married a man because he jumped with such amazing grace,* she thinks.

The first time she cooked him dinner she made potato chips from scratch. Twelve of them. He painted their names on the mailbox at the end of their road: Mr. and Mrs. Sam Temple. For their first anniversary he gave her a card with a rose on the front and the words "To My Treasured Wife."

He was the only other person who had been there that night they lay in each other's arms and he whispered, "I want to have a baby with you," and she whispered back, "Me too." She can still see him walking through the rooms of their old house in the middle of the night while Sally screamed inconsolably, singing her "You Picked a Fine Time to Leave Me, Lucille."

She remembered the day they were so broke they couldn't buy diapers, and she was crying, and he had taken out his paintbrush and made a stack of thousand-dollar bills that he showered over her head like confetti. He knew, if he remembered, what her body looked like before babies. She had seen him catch a fly ball in deep center field, in midair, to make the third out of his softball league's championship game.

And though they had also witnessed each other's worse moments—more of those, no doubt—this much was true: They had been young together, and they were the containers of each other's youth. They were as ridiculous a pair of life partners as Sonny and Cher, standing at their twin microphones in their striped bell-bottoms and love beads, singing "I Got You Babe." They had made each other promises before either one of them had a clue as to how impossible it would be to keep them. They were poorly suited for each other. They were foolish and unwise and naive and selfish and blind—two people whose single greatest common bond was the sense of loss and old hurt each of them carried into their marriage like a dowry. Still, they had spent their biggest hopes on each other, and they would never be so extravagant again.

And they were also the parents of each other's children. Claire has only to look into the face of her son and see his father. Sam must do the same with their daughter. How can you look at your child without finding in him some piece of his other parent? How can you not love that piece?

He led her over to their bed that day. The mattress had been stripped. Maybe it was about their marriage being over. Maybe Sam was just preparing to wash the sheets. They removed their clothes wordlessly and without touching—each of them attending to their own buttons and zippers, untying their shoes, peeling off their socks, laying them down on either side of the bed like the elements of a religious ritual from a church neither one of them ever attended. He got in on his side. She got in on hers.

There on the very mattress where their babies were born—the stains of her blood still visible—they made love for the last time. It didn't last particularly long. It wasn't particularly great, although she knows she wept and she thinks he may have too.

Afterward they both dressed without saying anything. She had another glass of water. Then she drove away.

After all these years, all those hours on the telephone, and all that missing him, Claire sees Mickey again. Not really Mickey, actually. She sees Mickey's son, Gabe, who has evidently come to the Boston Science Museum, as Pete has today, on a school field trip. Claire is a chaperone.

It has been five years now since she saw Gabe—he was not yet nine then; he's got to be fourteen now, and he must have grown six inches—but she recognizes him instantly. Because it's Mickey's face he has. Shyer, rounder, same freckles, more hair, a butt that shows the promise that he may become a pitcher after all. He's horsing around in front of that slice of a giant redwood that's displayed in the museum lobby, with little red light bulbs placed at various concentric rings within the wood indicating the age and growth of this particular tree. The year Christopher Columbus landed. The year of the Black Plague. The year Christ was born.

Gabe doesn't see Claire and wouldn't recognize her if he did, she knows. Many women have come and gone in his father's life since Claire left it. "You keep getting girlfriends with *C* names," Gabe told Mickey once, a year or so after she'd left, referring to the arrival on the scene of a woman named Cynthia, close on the heels of a Carolyn. That was, she guesses, Gabe's last acknowledgment of her place in his life or his father's.

So Claire just stands there for a while watching this boy who is, within a couple of months, the age of her own son, although he is fairer-skinned, more knowledgeable about jazz certainly, and less well acquainted with the inside of a principal's office and a police station.

I read him the chapter about forcing bases, she thinks. We made Christmas cookies one time.

"You don't have to do that stuff around here," Mickey had said to her almost sharply when he came home from his game and found the two of them in his kitchen, taking the last of the cookies out of the oven and cleaning up the sprinkles. "That's not who you are to me."

"But maybe it's who I am to him," she said.

In fact, Claire always had a particular tenderness for Gabe. Maybe it was even love. Claire believes there was also a time when Gabe had a feeling that was something like love for her. Not the love a son has for his mother. Unlike Ursula—that other child who, if their paths cross five years from now, will not recognize her— Gabe has always had a very present mother on the scene. Whatever that woman's story is, Claire will never know it now.

There was this wonderful aspect to the time Claire spent with Gabe that came specifically from the fact that she was not his mother. She didn't have to provide birthday parties and rides to after-school activities, didn't have to pick up after his friends, didn't have to make every sorrow in his life go away, wasn't solely or even majorly responsible for the quality of his days. She didn't suffer when he stepped up to the plate and struck out. She could just lie there on Gabe's bedroom floor with him, quizzing him on baseball statistics. Or lie there on Mickey's couch doing absolutely nothing at all with him but being there. There has never been another child in her life about whom she felt that way.

Somewhere inside Gabe's gangly body, Claire suspects, there may be a dim memory of her. She supposes if she went up to him now and introduced herself—"I'm your father's old friend Claire" —a flicker of recognition might cross his face. He would know, at least, that what he used to feel about her, when he felt something, was good. *Good but gone.*

Her own son approaches her now—a heartbreakingly handsome young man who will soon be taller than Claire. "Can I have some money for the gift shop, Mom?" he asks her. "They've got these neat hologram postcards. I wanted to send one to Dad."

She hands him a five-dollar bill. "I swear," she says, "sometimes I get the feeling I'm hemorrhaging money." But she's smiling when she says it this time, and he is, too, when he answers her.

"Right, Mom," he says. "We've heard. And I'm going to empty the dishwasher every morning for the next twenty jillion years, remember? And take care of you in your old age." One of the many things she loves about her son is the way, even now, he's not ashamed to kiss her when his friends are around. Then he disappears again, naturally. He has asked Sally McAdam if she wants to sit with him at the planetarium show. She does.

· · ·

"Where does the love go?" she wants to call out, right there in the middle of the Boston Science Museum. There is a question for some expert. Only which floor would she go to find her answer? Physics? Biology? Electricity? Or maybe the planetarium?

She knows there is a thing that happens in your body when you love somebody and you see them. Or you stop seeing them. Or you want to see them but you can't. Or you see them again after a long time of not seeing them, and realize that it was there all the time, like a dormant virus, just waiting to take hold of you again. Your eyes may fill with tears. You shiver. Your stomach may turn over.

You have a hard time catching your breath, and when you are again able to make a sound, the sound that comes out of you is different.

Claire also knows that sooner or later that will change. It may take a long time, and like the scar under her chin or her stretch marks, it may not disappear completely, but it fades, and when it does, that feeling—or maybe it's the absence of feeling, like the eventual absence of pain following the amputation of a limb, like the absence of a fetus after a D and C, like the space in your closet you get because the person who always used to mess it up has moved out, that is saddest of all.

"I will love you forever," the man says to the woman. "No matter what happens, no matter where our lives may lead, this will never change. This is real as rock. I will never stop loving you. Nobody will ever love you again the way I love you now. I will never love anybody again the way I love you now."

Only he will, of course. He will not love her forever—not the way he does when he speaks these words, anyway. They are real when he says them, but they disappear, like the bones of a hummingbird in a cigar box. Like a fern that turns into petrified rock. Like an extinct species of bird. Like Nolan Ryan's fastball. Like the last note played on a single guitar string at the most wonderful concert you ever attended, and the last flickering flame from the lighter of the last cheering fan in the dark stadium afterward. Like a continent that drifts out to sea, creating a whole new geography, a whole new globe. Like a star that exploded, leaving only an aurora borealis.

And what do you do then, after the love is gone? When you go to a ball game and run into a person you used to love so much the thought of passing a single day without hearing the sound of that soft Alabama voice of his was unimaginable? What do you do when a big red-haired man passes you on the street, with his red-haired daughter, and you know for a few months there you thought you were going to live with this man for the rest of your life, for a few weeks his sperm and your egg were actually lodged in your uterus on the way to becoming a person who would probably have had red hair? What do you do when you find yourself sitting on the bench at a soccer game beside a man who once held his hand against the small of your back as the two of you skated on black ice under a full moon over Lake Michigan, once showered you with hand-painted thousand-dollar bills, once held his cupped hands between your legs, waiting as you screamed to catch the baby whose head was even then ripping your skin apart as she burst out into the world? What do you say to this man you once married, and once divorced, who has also ripped you deeper, harder, and drawn more blood than childbirth ever did?

You say, "How've you been? Nice day for a game, huh?" You say, "What do you think, will those Red Sox ever get an outfield?" You may kiss the red-haired man on his cheek perhaps, and ask the red-haired daughter what grade she's in now. You may duck into a café and have a cup of coffee together. You say to the man on the soccer bench, "He looks like you when he runs." Then you get back into your car and head out onto the road again.

AUTHOR'S NOTE

Given the choice, I would have been a musician, not a writer. But I play music when I write, and the choices I make about the music I listen to as I write have a lot to do with the work I go on to produce. I create a soundtrack for myself when I'm sitting at my keyboard, and the story comes out of that soundtrack. In the case of this novel, the soundtrack consisted of a lot of my favorite songs about love. They're pop songs, jazz, folk, Celtic—with a heavy emphasis on country, not because my novel was set in the South, but because the themes of my story are the stuff of country songs. I wanted a reader to feel, after reading this, a little like how I feel, after listening to Loretta Lynn or Patty Loveless or Patsy Cline or George Jones or Vern Gosdin. The best way I knew to get in the mood was to play their music as I wrote.

I put a lot of music into my fiction, because my characters also listen to a lot of music. The lyrics of the songs they play serve as a way of expressing—first to themselves, then to the people they're with—what they long for and what breaks their hearts. I know it's true for me, and I think it's true for a lot of other people, that many of my ideas about love were formed as a result of listening to a range of songs, from Cole Porter to Lucinda Williams to Paul Simon. Partly as a homage to the artists who wrote and performed these songs, but also out of a belief that introducing readers to the

music I love will enhance the experience of reading my work, I
wanted to make that soundtrack I created for myself available to
the readers of my work—although, of course, each of us also needs
to create our own soundtrack, at times, featuring the songs that
reverberate for us in particular.

But on the chance that you might want to know what's featured
on my playlist, I've put together a list of the songs I was listening
to when I was writing *Where Love Goes*. In no particular order,
here they are:

Patsy Cline—"I Fall to Pieces"
Joao Gilberto/Stan Getz—"Para Machucar Meu
    Coracao" (the whole album, actually)
The Waterboys—"How Long Will I Love You?"
Traveling Wilburys—"End of the Line"
Suzy Bogguss and Chet Atkins—"I Still Miss
    Someone"
Loudon Wainwright—"So Many Songs"
Peter Gabriel—"Mercy Street" (and every other song
    on *So*)
Townes Van Zandt—"If I Needed You"
Ella Fitzgerald/Louis Armstrong—"They Can't Take
    That Away from Me" (and a heap of other Ella
    Fitzgerald recordings)
Jennifer Warnes/Leonard Cohen—"Joan of Arc"
Van Morrison—"I'm Carrying a Torch for You" (and
    a few dozen other Van Morrison songs)
George Jones—"He Stopped Loving Her Today" (and
    just about anything else George Jones ever sang)
Marc Cohn—"True Companion"
Timbuk 3—"Wheel of Fortune"
Zachary Richard—"Big River"
Bobbie Cryner—"Too Many Tears Too Late"
Lyle Lovett—"If I Were the Man You Wanted"
Randy Newman—"Falling in Love"

Roberta Flack—"First Time Ever I Saw Your Face"
Dougie McLean—"Ae Fond Kiss"
Dolly Parton—"I Will Always Love You" (and a lot of
    the old Dolly and Porter Wagoner duets)
Maura O'Connell—"Blue Train"
Dwight Yoakam—"Ain't that Lonely Yet"
Paul Simon—"Hearts and Bones"
Nancy Griffith and Arlo Guthrie—"Tecumseh Valley"
Crowded House—"Fall at Your Feet"
Mary Chapin Carpenter—"Something of a Dreamer"
Otis Redding—"I've Been Loving You Too Long"
Johnny Hartman and John Coltrane—"My One and
    Only Love"
Alison Krauss—"I've Got that Old Feeling"
John Gorka—"Bigtime Lonesome"
Greg Brown—"Spring Wind"
Dave Mallett—"Red, Red Rose"
Mary Black—"Past the Point of Rescue"
Steve Earle—"Goodbye"
Tom Waits—"Whistle Down the Wind"
Kieran Kane—"I Keep Coming to You"
The Mavericks—"Neon Moon"
Joni Mitchell—"Amelia" (also the entire *Blue* album)
Silly Sisters—"Somewhere Along the Way"
Patty Loveless—"Here I Am"
Vern Gosdin—"Time Stood Still"
Chet Baker—"Someone to Watch Over Me"
Cheryl Wheeler—"Almost"
Nina Simone—"I Want a Little Sugar in My Bowl"
Steeleye Span—"Dawn of the Day"
Vince Gill—"We Won't Dance"
The Roches—"Expecting Your Love"
Travis Tritt—"Foolish Pride"
Kate and Anna McGarrigle—"Heartbeats
    Accelerating"

Bruce Cockburn—"Someone I Used to Love"
Lucinda Williams—"Passionate Kisses"

Joyce Maynard has produced a not-for-profit CD sound-track for her novel, featuring nineteen songs about love, including some songs and artists featured on the playlist above, as well as others not listed on these pages. To get one, send $6.98 postage and handling for each CD to *Where Love Goes,* P.O. Box 1135, Keene, NH 03431. Call 1-800-501-9919 to charge your order.

ABOUT THE AUTHOR

Joyce Maynard was a freshman at Yale when she published her memorable *New York Times* cover story, *An Eighteen Year Old Looks Back at Life.* She has been a reporter and "Hers" columnist for the *New York Times,* a frequent contributor to National Public Radio's "All Things Considered," a monthly columnist for *Parenting,* and has written for numerous national magazines, as well as the author of the novel *Baby Love.* For eight years her weekly column "Domestic Affairs" was published in newspapers nationwide. Her most recent novel, *To Die For,* is now a movie produced by Columbia Pictures. Maynard edits and publishes the *Domestic Affairs Newsletter,* devoted to personal storytelling, from her home in Keene, New Hampshire, where she lives with her three children.